SURROUNDED!

Something moved beyond the line of trees, a flicker of white passing through shadows.

Startled, Jessica squeezed the .38's trigger. The bullet hit something alive. There was a cry of pain, followed by the heavy thump of a body hitting the ground. Another sound behind her spun her around, but this time her finger froze on the trigger as she saw a man step into the clearing.

A man, but not a normal man.

Too big and with a face like something out of a nightmare. Jessica could only stare at him.

The sound of snapping twigs came again.

More nightmares stepped into the clearing.

Jessica's knees began to shake. The gun felt heavier in her hands now. She began to move backward, but heard another sound of snapping twigs behind her. She stopped. A hopeless thought streaked through her consciousness. *I'm surrounded.* She gave a moment's consideration to putting the .38's barrel in her mouth and pulling the trigger. Suicide was certainly a better option than whatever these monstrosities had in mind for her. . . .

Other *Leisure* books by Bryan Smith:

SOULTAKER
QUEEN OF BLOOD
THE FREAKSHOW
DEATHBRINGER
HOUSE OF BLOOD

DEPRAVED

BRYAN SMITH

LEISURE BOOKS NEW YORK CITY

This one is for Keith Ashley and Matthew Shannon Turbeville.
Two of my oldest friends and readers of the original Depraved.
How's it feel to finally see that title in print, guys?

A LEISURE BOOK®

October 2009

Published by

Dorchester Publishing Co., Inc.
200 Madison Avenue
New York, NY 10016

ISBN 10: 0-8439-6292-5
ISBN 13: 978-0-8439-6292-5
E-ISBN: 978-1-4285-0745-6

The name "Leisure Books" and the stylized "L" with design are
trademarks of Dorchester Publishing Co., Inc.

Printed in the United States of America.

10 9 8 7 6 5 4 3 2 1

Visit us online at www.dorchesterpub.com.

ACKNOWLEDGMENTS

Once upon a time (the early 90s, to be somewhat more precise) I wrote a horror novel called *Depraved*. The book in your hands is not that *Depraved*. Over a period of several years a number of people read that old novel. This note is purely for the benefit of those in that select group, to clear up any confusion. Again, this book is not the story you read. This book is an all new story utilizing an old title that just felt right. I think you'll agree it's apt.

As usual, I want to first and foremost thank my wife, Rachael. Thanks for sharing your life with me. I also want to thank my brothers Jeff and Eric, my mother Cherie Smith, Dorothy C. May, Jay and Helene Wise, Keith Ashley, Shannon Turbeville, Kent Gowran, Mark Hickerson, Tod Clark, Edward Lee, Brian Keene, Derek Tatum, David Wilbanks, Scott Bradley (the James Caan of horror list compilers), GAK, David G. Barnett, Brittany Crass and Alan Hudson, Don D'Auria and everyone else at Dorchester, Paul Goblirsch, Elizabeth Rowell, Paul Legerski, Nick Cato, Paul "noigeloverlord" Synuria, Mark "Dezm" Sylva, Fred and Stephania Grimm, Ben and Tracey Eller from worldofstrange.com, Joe Howe, John Horner Jacobs, Steven Shrewsbury, Maurice Broaddus, Eddie "EvylEd" Coulter, John Everson, Rhonda Wilson, the whole Hypericon gang, all the regulars at my Keenedom board and on MySpace, and all of you out there who keep buying the books. Really, I can't thank any of you enough. Your support is much appreciated. Now who wants to buy me a beer?

DEPRAVED

CHAPTER ONE

She'd been driving for hours by the time she finally found what felt like the right place. Hours in the heat of mid-summer in a car with no air-conditioning. The car was a relic. She could feel the springs through the worn-down-to-almost-nothing upholstery. A cracked cylinder casing made the engine very loud. A scruffy struggling musician named Hoke had wanted two thousand dollars for the red 1963 Ford Falcon Futura. A sometimes-employed session musician, Hoke had once upon a time played drums on a Top 40 country single. But he was broke. *Hoke is broke,* he'd said. It'd almost seemed funny at the time. But Nashville was full of guys like Hoke. Country slackers betting everything on a long-shot dream of hitting big in the music biz, forever fluttering around the edges of that elusive "break." A great many of them wound up selling or hocking everything they owned to stay off the streets. She'd dated more than a few such dreamers. More than one had broken her heart, until she'd become hardened against the type. Which explained why Hoke's cut-rate charm and easy grin had failed to move her. In younger days, she would have been all over him. Would maybe have dragged him into the Falcon's backseat as an extra way of consummating the deal.

But that, as they say, was then, and this was—

THUMP! THUMP! THUMP!

The banging sound from the trunk again.

And then a muffled cry.

Christ.

"Shut the fuck up, Hoke!"

The cry came again, a voice turned hoarse and ragged from hours of intermittent screaming and pleading.

The Falcon's radio was factory original. AM dial only. She'd thought she might look into ways of modernizing the sound system, while retaining the authentic original look. An XM or Sirius radio setup wired up under the dash, maybe. She'd read about such things. Would have been cool. But obviously that couldn't happen now. She would have to ditch the car. She snapped on the radio and found a static-garbled gospel station. She left it there, knowing the antiquated radio would have difficulty locking on any signal out here in the sticks. The singer sounded vaguely like Al Green, so this was fine with her. She turned the volume up and the sound swallowed Hoke's cries.

She glanced again at the gas-station map spread across the passenger seat and decided this was indeed the place. Old Fork Road ran parallel to the long-deserted town of Dandridge. In less than a mile from her current location it would branch off into a numbered rural route and wind deeper into the wilderness. She tapped her thumbs on the Falcon's big red steering wheel and watched for the fork in the road. The car's odometer was stuck at 62,536 miles, so tracking distance was a matter of guesswork. The road narrowed as it snaked and twisted. The tall trees to either side of the road shadowed the Falcon's interior and provided welcome relief from the heat. But then an edgy feeling took root within her. She was sure she'd gone more than a mile on Old Fork by now. So where was the fucking fork in the goddamn fucking road?

She looked at the map again and almost missed it as she

clumsily steered the Falcon around a sharp curve in the road. She let out a screech and slammed the brake pedal to the floor. The Falcon's tires squealed on the cracked and faded asphalt, and she heard a louder thump from the trunk over the gospel music. The sudden jolting stop had probably not been fun for Hoke.

Good, she thought.

Fuck him.

An abrupt welling of tears stung her eyes.

"Why did you have to do it, you bastard?"

The sound of her own voice shamed her. The tears shamed her, as well. Not because she blamed herself in any way for what had happened. Fuck no. And not because she wasn't entitled to feel the pain that was ripping at her soul. She just didn't want Hoke to hear evidence of her misery, or to have even the merest shred of satisfaction over how thoroughly he'd wrecked her emotionally. She fought to keep her hand still as she reached for the gearshift and put the Falcon in reverse. She sniffled and blinked back more tears as she backed up and put the car on Rural Route 42.

She'd never seen it coming.

Maybe because she was too trusting. Or maybe because he just didn't seem like the type to take advantage of a woman. Too good-looking and too self-possessed. Something in his grin and the crinkle of his eyes told her this was a man who would never have trouble getting laid. Women of a certain type would flock to him. Buy him drinks in bars, instead of the usual other way around. And fall easily into bed with him. Certainly he would never need to force himself on a woman. These weren't things she thought consciously as she negotiated the deal for the Falcon with him. They were just things most women would know on an instinctive level.

So she'd felt no trepidation when he'd invited her into

his ramshackle east Nashville house for a drink after they'd agreed to terms. The air-conditioned cool of the house felt nice after thirty-plus minutes of inspecting the Falcon in Hoke's driveway. She accepted the bottle of Yazoo Dos Perros from him gratefully and closed her eyes after one delicious swallow, feeling a deep weariness in her bones as a result of too little sleep the night before. A long night of barhopping had taken a serious toll, and she looked forward to getting home with her new car so she could crawl into bed and catch up on her rest.

But thoughts of rest were vanquished the moment she felt Hoke's hand on her waist.

Her eyes snapped open and she looked up at his grinning face. "What are you doing?"

His pale blue eyes twinkled. "Let's have some fun, honey."

He pushed himself against her and his other hand slid around her slim waist, settled at the small of her back, his callused fingers slipping beneath her black T-shirt to probe at her firm flesh. She cursed him and tried to push him away, but he slammed her against the edge of the kitchen counter and thrust his crotch at her. Terror gripped her as she felt his erection spring against her. She tried to twist away from him, but he held her fast and laughed at her. She raised the bottle of Dos Perros, but he swatted it away from her, and it shattered on the tiled kitchen floor.

"You're being stupid," she told him, thinking maybe she could reason with him. "You can't do anything to me. You'd never get away with it."

He licked his lips and looked at her breasts, which looked ripe beneath the stretched-tight fabric of the V-necked T-shirt. "Oh, yeah? How ya figure?"

"My roommate knows where I am, for one thing."

He lifted his gaze and looked her in the eye then.

"Outside you told me you lived alone. Get your story straight, sweetheart."

Shit.

He reached for the button of her sexy designer jeans. She screamed and clawed at his eyes. He swatted her hands away, but not before one nail bit into skin and etched a bloody groove across his cheek. He yelped in pain and drove a fist into her stomach. The blow blasted the air from her lungs and sent her reeling to the floor. Then he was on top of her, and there were more blows from his hard fists. His face changed during the assault. The easy grin was gone, replaced by an almost feverish look of hatred and desperation. *Why,* she wondered, the word repeating in her head over and over. . . .

WHYWHYWHYWHYWHYWHYWHYOHGOD-WHY

But there would be no answer to that question.

He got her clothes off and did what he wanted with her. When he was done, he left her there, nude on the kitchen floor, spilled beer soaking the tips of the long blonde hair spread around her head like a fan. She should have grabbed her clothes and run then. It would have been the logical thing to do. But she wasn't thinking in a logical manner by that point. She'd barely been thinking on a conscious level at all. She stayed there on the floor while he wandered in and out of the kitchen, whistling an old Hank Williams song, sounding as if he didn't have a care in the world. Then he disappeared for a while. When he came back, he was fully dressed again. The familiar grin was back in place as he stood over her, but there was a coldness in his eyes now. A deadness. How could she not have seen it before? Surely she would have seen it, if she'd just looked deep enough. But no. This asshole had the air of a man well schooled in the art of obscuring the truth about himself.

The grin became a sneer. "Get your clothes on and get out. I'm keeping the car."

His words broke the mental paralysis gripping her. She got shakily to her feet and retrieved her clothes from the floor, some of which were soaked with beer. She put them on, retrieved her purse from the kitchen counter, and walked out of the house without a word. She walked down to the bus stop and waited for the bus that would take her home. She exited the bus at her usual stop and went into her apartment just long enough to change clothes and fetch the .38 her army-captain daddy had given her for her eighteenth birthday. Then she left and caught a bus back to Hoke's place.

She didn't show him the gun at first.

Just looked at him when he opened the door and said, "I want it again."

And he laughed and said, "Had a feeling you were the type. Come on in, honey."

Once the door was shut behind her, she brought out the gun and said, "We're going for a ride in my Falcon."

So now here she was, driving a stolen car down a back road in the middle of nowhere with a man she planned to murder stowed in the trunk.

Yes, it had been quite a fucking day so far.

Chapter Two

"Get out."

The Falcon's rust-flecked trunk lid stood open. Hoke blinked against the abrupt intrusion of bright sunlight and stared up at her. He was in a fetal position, his knees tucked up against his chest. He looked ragged. His hair was soaked with sweat. His flesh glistened where the sun hit it. The trunk was big, typical of cars of the precompact era, but it was crowded with many years' worth of accrued junk. An old battery, two pairs of jumper cables, a filthy and rotting old blanket, empty bottles and beer cans, a stack of moldy newspapers, a rusted tire jack, a folded tent, and more. It could not have been a comfortable ride for the fucking rapist.

She suppressed a smile and kept her voice hard as she said again, "Get out."

Hoke blinked hard one more time and focused on the .38's looming barrel. He stared at it for a long, silent moment. His throat moved as he swallowed with difficulty. Then he looked at her, and she wanted to scream at the absence of terror in his blue eyes. "Come on, sugar. You ain't gonna kill me."

Fury seized her. She reached past him and grabbed the tire jack. A fluttery hand moved to intercept her, but she was too fast. She swatted Hoke's hand away, shifted the .38 to her left hand, and hoisted the tire jack in her right. The old jack was caked with rust, but it was a solid hunk of iron. She shifted her grip on it and swung it down. Hoke had time to utter one weak cry of alarm. Then there was a meaty thunk as the jack smashed against his knee. The weak cry became a howl of agony. She lifted the jack again, adjusted her aim, and delivered one more blow, this one a harder strike to his right hip. He howled again, and then he was blubbering, begging her not to hit him again.

She tossed the jack to the ground and aimed the .38 at the space between his watery blue eyes. He looked at her again and his jaw quivered. This time she allowed herself a small smile. There was the terror she'd hoped to see before. She thumbed back the .38's hammer, and a thin sound somewhere between a whimper and a moan escaped his trembling lips.

"Get out. I won't tell you again."

Hoke's chest hitched as he visibly struggled to respond. His mouth opened. His teeth chattered. "Y-yeah. O-okay. P-p-please . . ."

He gripped the edge of the trunk with a shaking hand and began to haul himself out. She kept the gun leveled at his chest as she moved back a few steps, staying alert for any indication of a sudden lunge in her direction. But he made no such attempt, was clearly incapable of it at the moment. His knees creaked audibly as he set his feet on the ground and stood upright. His gaze stayed on her a moment longer. Then he frowned as he began to perceive his surroundings. His head swiveled as he surveyed the little clearing in the woods.

He looked at her again and said, "Where in tarnation are we, little girl?"

She bit her lip and gripped the .38 harder. Another tiny ounce of pressure on the trigger would send a slug ripping through his heart. And she wasn't ready to do that. Not yet. She eased her finger off the trigger and said, "My name is Jessica. Not honey. Not sugar. Not sweetheart. You won't call me any of those things again. Got that?"

He just stared at her. His eyes were flat, unreadable. Then he licked his lips and shrugged. "Sure thing, Jess. Hell, didn't mean to offend you none."

Her eyes narrowed to slits. "Sort of a funny comment from a fucking rapist."

An odd thing happened.

He laughed.

And that damnable grin was back. His eyes flickered with genuine amusement. "Aw, come on, girl. I didn't rape you."

She wanted to scream at him then. Wanted to shoot him in the kneecaps and listen to him cry and scream as he writhed in agony on the dusty country ground. But she kept her tone even as she said, "What?"

His resurgent grin didn't falter. "You heard me, baby. Hell, you were givin' off signals like nobody's business while you was checkin' out my ride. Bending over in them sexy jeans when you looked at the engine, liftin' that sweet ass of yours in the air. Even wiggled it a little. Same deal when you checked out the interior. Posin' like a fuckin' Penthouse Pet all over my car. And there was the way you looked at me when you thought I wasn't lookin'. With them bedroom eyes. Like you wanted to fuck my poor little brains out right then and there. Shit." He chuckled. "I was just givin' you what you wanted." Another chuckle. "And you know it."

She looked at him. Really studied him. He was maybe thirty. Maybe as old as thirty-five. Shaggy hair a darkish shade of blond. Skin bronzed from years of wallowing in summer sun. Attired in khaki cargo pants and a Grateful Dead T-shirt. Puka-shell necklace around his throat. Designer sandals on his feet. This was the man she meant to kill. The scumbag sociopath who'd raped her. A goddamn goofball. Looking at him, it was hard to take him seriously. A memory surfaced. Herself prone on his kitchen floor. The smell of spilled beer thick in her nostrils. The strange look of hate on his face as he grunted above her.

"Get on your knees."

His grin died then, and he squinted at her. "What?"

"You heard me."

He was silent for a moment. Then he said, "What if I don't?"

"Then I shoot you where you stand."

He locked eyes with her. "Hell you will."

She shifted her aim slightly, almost imperceptibly, and squeezed the .38's trigger. The gun's report was massively loud in the otherwise-empty clearing. The slug punched a hole through the Falcon's open trunk lid. Hoke fell screaming to his knees. He looked up at her through eyes streaming with sudden tears, hands clasped before him in an almost prayerful pose.

"Please . . ." He was blubbering again now. "P-p-please . . . I didn't mean you no harm. You got to believe me. Please . . ."

Jessica moved a step closer, aimed the .38's barrel at the space between his eyes again. "Say you're sorry."

His face was a study in confusion for a moment, then his head bobbed repeatedly, nodding several times in a vigorous gesture of assent. "Yeah. Jesus. Shit. I'm sorry, girl. Oh, fuck, I am so fucking sorry. Please don't kill me. Please . . ."

Jessica's face remained expressionless as she said, "I accept your apology."

Hoke abruptly ceased his blubbering. He frowned at her. "You do?"

"Yes." The barest of smiles glazed the corners of her mouth. "But unlike God, I am not merciful. I'm going to kill you now, Hoke."

"What?" The word was a thunderous exclamation of disbelief. The man's features twisted in an expression that evoked feelings of betrayal, as if she'd just breached the terms of some unspoken covenant formed between them in these last moments. On some level, he'd really believed she would spare him in exchange for a simple apology. "But you can't do that. You can't. It's . . . it's . . . *wrong!*"

She thumbed back the .38's hammer again. "Say goodbye, Hoke."

"You can't do this." He changed tactics now, attempted to reason with her rather than plead for his life. "You can't get away with it. People will look for me. The cops will come after you."

Her smile broadened some. "Oh, but they won't. I never gave you my full name. None of your friends know me or even saw me. I didn't tell anybody about you. I found you on craigslist and called from a public phone. There's nothing to connect you and me, Hoke. Face it, I'm gonna get away with this. You're going to rot out here in the middle of nowhere, and I'll go on with my life."

He spluttered. "But . . . but . . . the car! The Falcon! They—"

"I'll have to ditch the car, of course. After I get back to Nashville and wipe it down."

Fresh tears spilled down his cheeks. His chest heaved. He continued to plead at her with his eyes, but he didn't say anything. He was out of arguments. Maybe out of hope. She looked at his legs, watched for a coiling of calf muscles indicating a last-ditch lunge for the gun. But his whole body remained slack, frozen in a posture of defeat. He bowed his head, a penitent awaiting the final deadly blessing of the bullet.

The .38's barrel was aimed at the crown of his skull now.

This is it, she thought.

Do it.

She drew in a deep breath.

Held it a moment.

And began to apply pressure to the trigger.

The snapping of a twig jerked her gaze away from Hoke. Her head snapped to the left and then to the right. She saw nothing. She backed carefully away from Hoke and turned in a slow circle to survey the edges of the clearing. Still nothing.

The sound came again. Louder this time. Definitely

the snapping of a twig. Someone or something moving around out there. Animal or human. Some deep-down instinct told her the latter. It was something to do with a perceived deliberateness in the movements.

"Who's out there?" Her voice emerged thin and reedy, projecting fear and confusion rather than the strength she'd wanted to show. "Come on out and show yourself!"

Hoke was checking out the edges of the clearing, too. His expression had changed. It didn't exactly project hope now, but some of the terror had drained from his features. "You heard the lady!" he shouted in a hoarse voice. "The bitch means to kill me. Do something, goddammit!"

Jessica continued to spin in a slow circle. A chill went up her spine. She still didn't see anything, but she experienced that creepy, precognitive awareness one feels when being surreptitiously observed by unseen eyes. Dammit. There shouldn't be anyone out here. The area around Dandridge was supposed to be deserted for miles. The woods here bordered neighboring town Hopkins Bend, but she'd been sure no one from there would wander this close to the blighted ghost town. No one with any sense ever wanted to go near Dandridge, where, if you believed the government's story, terrorists had exploded a dirty bomb years earlier.

After several more silent moments elapsed, she allowed herself the hope that she'd only imagined an unseen human presence. It was understandable, of course. Her nerves were on edge. And despite her resolve, she was frightened out of her wits. She wasn't a killer by nature. This was admittedly an extreme thing she was doing. She meant to see it through, but that didn't mean she was unaffected by the prospect of taking a human life. It would haunt her the rest of her life, despite the righteousness of her position. Little things like auditory hallucinations and other faulty perceptions were to be expected, given the circumstances.

Something moved beyond the line of trees, a flicker of white passing through shadows.

Startled, Jessica squeezed the .38's trigger. The bullet hit something alive. There was a cry of pain, followed by the heavy thump of a body hitting the ground. Another sound behind her spun her around, but this time her finger froze on the trigger as she saw a man step into the clearing.

A man, but not a normal man.

Too big, and with a face like something out of a nightmare.

Jessica could only stare at him.

Hoke let out a low whistle and said, "I think I done shit my shorts, sugar."

The sound of snapping twigs came again.

More nightmares stepped into the clearing.

Jessica's knees began to shake. The gun felt heavier in her hands now. She began to move backward, but heard another sound of snapping twigs behind her. She stopped moving. A hopeless thought streaked through her consciousness. *I'm surrounded.* She gave a moment's consideration to putting the .38's barrel in her mouth and pulling the trigger. Suicide was certainly a better option than whatever these monstrosities had in mind for her.

The first one through the trees moved a step closer to her. He wore only faded and tattered overalls over a body roughly the size of a houseboat. Something vaguely like an elephant's trunk dominated the center of his jowly face, where a nose should have been. One eye socket was much larger than the other. A bulbous red eye protruded from it. The trunk twitched in her direction. Jessica's stomach churned. A big double-barreled shotgun was propped on the man's shoulder. He grinned at her, showing her a mouth full of rotting teeth.

He began to lift the shotgun off his shoulder.

No time to think.

Jessica glanced left, glanced right.

Saw the only possible way to go.

And took off running.

The shotgun boomed behind her.

CHAPTER THREE

"We're gonna have to stop here."

Pete Miller slowed the VW Jetta and cranked the steering wheel slowly to the right, easing into the gravel-strewn parking lot. He pulled to a stop next to a gas pump that looked like a relic from another age. It had spinning rotary numbers rather than the digital displays he was used to seeing. There was no slot for a credit or debit card.

"Welcome to 1970." He made a sound of annoyance. "Guess I'll have to go inside."

Megan Phillips looked up from the paperback novel she'd been reading—a lurid-looking thing called *City Infernal*—and squinted at him from the passenger seat. "Inside? Why?"

Pete rolled his eyes and hooked a thumb at the antique gas pump. "Because apparently we passed through some kind of time warp a few miles back. Fuck. I hope these rednecks take credit cards."

"Don't you have any cash?"

He shrugged. "Didn't think I'd need any for a while."

"Maybe you should hit up their ATM while you're in there."

Pete showed her a deadpan expression. "Oh. Yeah. Right. And while I'm at it, I'll grab us each a chilled latte and a copy of the *New York Times*."

Megan wasn't looking at him anymore. Her attention had returned to the apparently fascinating book. He watched her lick her lips and turn a page. She scrunched down in her seat and brought the book closer to her face. She said, "Sounds good, honey."

Pete looked at her. He loved her. He really did. Or maybe it was just lust mixed up with a serious case of like. But that was splitting hairs. He was genuinely fond of her, both for her lithe, supple little body and her fun personality. They'd been dating for seven mostly drama-free months, which was some kind of record in his experience. They had yet to have that first big fight, which he'd found normally occurred somewhere within the first two to three months of a relationship. The girl was beyond easygoing. She had achieved a state of mellowness so rarefied, it was almost Zen-like. The disagreements they did have were minor and were usually resolved in a matter of minutes. Pete liked to remind himself of this in moments like these. Yes, she could be a bit slow on the uptake, but otherwise she was fucking perfect.

He leaned over for a kiss and said, "Be back in a snap, baby."

She lifted her face for the kiss and smiled after he planted an enthusiastic one on her soft, bee-stung lips. "Hurry back."

He grinned. "You know it."

He got out of the car, threw the door shut, and started walking toward the little general store. He knew it was a general store thanks to the sign in the window to the left of the front door. It read, in carefully printed black block lettering against a white background, Hopkins Bend General Store.

A bell rang as he pushed through the door into the store's musty interior. Two men playing cards at a rickety wooden table glanced up as he came in. They regarded him with hollow, unreadable expressions for an uncomfortable moment. One of the men spat on the floor. What the hell? Was that some kind of colorfully rustic judgment of his character? Hard to tell. Not that he cared what these rubes thought. He was just passing through on his way to another grand adventure in his young, prosperous life. They, on the other hand, would spend the remainder of their dreary days rotting away in this nothing little Podunk town. You sort of had to feel sorry for the poor, ignorant sons of bitches. He shoved his sunglasses up over his forehead and flashed them his best winning smile before moving farther into the store.

Another man sat behind a counter at the far end of the store. An enormously fat man, wearing a faded and sweat-stained red T-shirt that looked ready to give beneath the strain of his vastly protruding belly and redwood-sized biceps. He had a jowly, florid face. A fat lower lip pooched out as he slowly flipped through the pages of a magazine. He wore a weathered cap with a slogan emblazoned above the bill: American by birth, Southern by the grace of God.

Pete thought, *Bubba the Hutt.*

He then made a mental note to keep the observation to himself.

The store itself consisted of two aisles stocked with food and household items, as well as a cooler stocked with only the cheapest American beer. A scan of the selection indicated even Budweiser would be thought a luxury in these parts. Another cooler next to the counter was stocked with little cardboard bait tubs. He considered buying one to gross out Megan, then recognized the impulse as pure insanity. But perhaps he could pick up some other memento of their backwoods detour. Something they could chuckle over years later as they regaled their children with tales of their adventures en route to the big outdoor music festival in Tennessee.

Whoa. Wait.

Children?

Where had that thought come from? At twenty-three, he was still too young to be thinking such things. Hell, he was still practically a kid himself. He figured he had another five to ten years before he could seriously start to think about settling down. Megan was fun for now. And how. He liked her to pieces. But she wasn't wife material. She was someone to have fun with while he was young. A girl he would recall with a sort of sweet nostalgia in later years, but without regret for the loss. His eventual wife would have to be someone smarter and more down-to-earth. Someone . . . not fun. His brow creased as he thought these things. His mind had gone around a dark corner without his even realizing it, and he wasn't happy about it.

As an antidote, he thought of Megan naked and laughing as he licked whipped cream off her breasts at that motel in Kentucky the night before.

He grinned.

Mission accomplished.

The dark thoughts banished, he stepped up to the counter and cleared his throat.

The big redneck didn't look at him. "What ya want?"

The man's thick drawl was barely intelligible and added to his growing distaste for the man. He looked and sounded like something dredged up from the bottom of a swamp. Pete's conscience spoke up then, telling him that there was more than one kind of prejudice. The people in Hopkins Bend lived a different kind of life from the one he knew in Minnesota, where he and Megan lived on the outskirts of the Twin Cities. But different didn't necessarily equate with bad. Or wrong.

It was just . . . different.

But knowing this mattered very little. The man unsettled him. The store unsettled him. The scowling card players unsettled him. This was alien territory. He didn't belong here. He knew it, and the other men in the store knew it. He suddenly wanted nothing more than to be gone from this place. He considered leaving then and there. But the Jetta was very low on fuel, and he wasn't sure how far away the next gas station was.

Just get it done, he thought. *Get it done and get the hell on out.*

The man looked up from his magazine. There was a disturbing flatness in his dark eyes. "Well, boy?"

Pete cleared his throat again. "I, uh . . . need to fill up at your pump out there."

The man's jaw muscles moved almost imperceptibly. He was chewing something. Gum or a wad of tobacco. Pete figured the odds favored the latter. "Pump's broke."

Pete frowned. "Oh. Well. Okay, then. Um . . . could you maybe tell me how far to the next gas station?"

The corners of the man's mouth dimpled and lifted slightly, forming the ugliest smile Pete Miller had ever seen. A smile to make nuns and young mothers wake up screaming in the middle of the night. "Don't matter none."

"Is that—" Pete's frown deepened. "I'm sorry . . . what did you say?"

The big man reached beneath the counter, groped for something, found it, and stood up. Pete gulped at the sight of the pump-action shotgun and felt his knees turn to jelly as the man aimed it at his stomach. He raised his hands before him and began to back away from the counter. He kept moving until the men from the card table intercepted him, each seizing an elbow and wrestling him to the dirty floor.

Pete thrashed with all his might against the men holding him down. He saw the man with the shotgun emerge from behind the counter and walk past them to the front door. The wooden floor groaned beneath his heavy tread. Pete's mind reeled. Thoughts for his own safety were temporarily forgotten. He couldn't let these bastards get to Megan. The very thought made him want to scream. It was funny, the kind of things a man could suddenly know in the midst of intense crisis. He would throw his life down for Megan, do anything he could to save her. He loved her. Oh, Jesus, how he loved her.

He screamed, and one of the men clamped a sweaty palm over his mouth. Pete bit down on the fleshy curve of the man's thumb and wrenched his head backward as the man's hand came away from his mouth. The big man was at the front door now. Pete expected to see him step through it and return in a few moments with a shrieking Megan.

But that didn't happen.

Instead, he flipped the sign on the door around to read CLOSED. Then he pulled a shade down over the door and moved to the windows, where he did the same.

Then he locked the door.

And Pete realized something.

He'd never told these men he had a traveling companion. And, if his guess was correct, a cursory glance outside would show an apparently empty VW Jetta parked at the pump. Because Megan would be scrunched way down in her seat, absorbed in the story she was reading and utterly oblivious to what was happening inside the store.

For the moment, she was safe.

But that wouldn't last forever. He had to think of a way out of this fucked-up situation before these animals caught wind of Megan's presence. But what could he do? He began to hyperventilate as his mind scrambled for elusive answers. Then he heard the plod of the big man's booted feet coming back across the wooden floor. A moment later, one of those feet pressed heavily into the small of his back.

The man cleared his throat phlegmatically.

And spat.

Pete winced as moisture splashed against the back of his neck.

His voice emerged as a whine. *"Why are you doing this?"*

A rumbling sound emerged from the big man's chest. It might have been an asthmatic laugh. And then he said, "Say good night, bitch."

And that was all Pete Miller knew for a while.

The stock of the shotgun crashed against the crown of his skull.

CHAPTER FOUR

They lived in a ramshackle cabin out in the woods, same as most of the rest of their kin. The wilderness surrounding Hopkins Bend was dotted with similar cabins, many of them more than a hundred years old. A few were even said to date to the time of the War of Northern Aggression, or earlier. Some of the oldest structures had rotted down to almost nothing. Abigail Maynard was thankful the roof of their own cabin sagged only slightly. No one would ever mistake the Maynard domicile for some goddamn

Beverly Hills mansion, but it was sturdier than most. And the Maynard clan was relatively prosperous by local standards. There was always plenty of food on the table and jugs of homemade whiskey to drink.

A young, towheaded Maynard boy came running through the open front door of the cabin as Abby rocked restlessly in her chair and stared at the dark, cracked screen of a television that hadn't worked in almost ten years. The boy, a skinny little runt of about twelve, ran past her, shouting, "Grandma! Grandma!"

The boy's voice grew fainter as he slammed through two more doors en route to the kitchen. The boy was Daniel. Abigail tried to remember whether he was one of the several birthed by her older sister, Ruth. Ruth had been dead a bit more than a year, the victim of some mysterious wasting disease. That had been a sad goddamn thing, her passing, but at least big sis had done her part in continuing the family line. Abby thought a moment, striving to keep the various bloodlines straight. Ruth had given them Daniel, John, Andy, Wilma, Angelina, Michael, and . . . let's see . . . oh, yes, and Jack and Carl, the twins.

Eight young ones, courtesy of the much-missed Ruth Maynard.

Laura Maynard, Abby's five-years-younger sister, had already popped out two additional brats, with a third on the way.

And her brothers had impregnated their various wives and mistresses multiple times.

Abby was odd girl out.

She had never been with child, though it wasn't from lack of trying. She'd coupled with numerous local men on many occasions. Even Big Joe, a cousin twice removed, had failed to successfully plant a seed in her apparently barren womb, and he'd impregnated each of her sisters at least once. Abby's lack of success in this area shamed her. She hadn't contributed properly to the welfare of the clan. The menfolk did the hunting and providing, and the women were responsible for everything else. It was her duty to bear children. If Abby couldn't squeeze out at least one squalling little bastard, what good was she?

Her failure in this department had been weighing on her more heavily of late. She was getting older, having just celebrated her twentieth birthday the week before. Most of the women she knew, including her sisters, had given birth for the first time by no later than fifteen. Time was passing, and she was in danger of turning into a pathetic spinster. A lot of the local men were still hot to fuck her, but lately it'd come to seem barely worth the effort. To take her mind off it, she stared at the broken television and tried to imagine what TV shows would be like ten years since the last time she'd seen one. She would often dream up shows in her mind, conceiving fleshed-out characters and concepts in various scenarios similar to the cop shows and soap operas she remembered. These would become very vivid in her head, and it was easy for her to mentally project the imaginary shows onto the broken screen. Easy, but frustrating. She sometimes wished she could write her ideas down in a book to make them more permanent. But she couldn't read or write very well.

She became aware of how tightly she was gripping the arms of the rocking chair and forced her muscles to relax. She drew in a calming breath, held it a long moment, then slowly expelled it. She then forced herself to rise from the chair and leave the room. She went the way Daniel had gone, toward the kitchen. She caught the scent of a stew simmering on the wood-burning stove before she reached the kitchen and felt a mild pang of hunger.

Her mother looked up from the big pot as Abby came into the kitchen. "There ya is. What you been up to, girl?"

Abby couldn't meet her mother's gaze. "Just sittin'."

Carol Maynard harrumphed. "Just wastin' away, ya mean."

The words were like a dagger to Abby's heart. Ma never missed an opportunity to remind her of her failures as a woman. And she couldn't raise her voice in argument, or the big bull of a woman would beat her half to death with whatever was handy. She knew this from painful experience, so she didn't say a thing in reply.

Carol made another sound of disapproval as she continued to stir the big pot. "You could be out lookin' for the right man, but all you ever do is sit and rock in that chair. What good are ya, girl?"

"None, I guess."

"You sassin' me?"

"No, ma'am."

"See you don't."

"Yes, ma'am."

Abby looked at Daniel, her little nephew. The boy was hunched over a bowl of stew at the kitchen table. He leered at her between sips from his spoon. "My mama used to say you should have your dried-up pussy sewn shut, for all the good it does."

Carol came away from the stove in a blur of motion. The boy's grin froze on his face an instant before she knocked him to the floor. The boy cried out as his spoon went skittering across the kitchen floor. Carol grabbed him by the back of his shirt and yanked him to his feet. "Don't you disrespect your elders, boy. Apologize to your aunt." When the boy hesitated, she swatted the back of his head and said, "NOW!"

The boy winced and spoke meekly. "I'm sorry, Aunt Abby."

Abby's voice was just as soft as she replied, "It's okay."

"The hell it is." Carol swatted the boy one more time and said, "Now get on out of here. And don't come back until you can act right."

Abby sighed. "Ma, that wasn't—"

Carol shook her head and went back to the pot, dismissing her by turning her back. "Shut up, girl. The boy was wrong to talk out of turn that way, but he was right." Her voice was hard, devoid of even the tiniest detectable shred of compassion. "Why don't you make yourself useful, and go check on the holiday catch?"

Tears formed in Abby's eyes. She quickly turned away from her mother. "Yes, ma'am."

She went to a closed door in the far-right corner of the kitchen and opened it. The door opened to a small pantry. There were shelves of canned goods and jars. She walked past these and opened another door. Beyond the second door was a set of rickety stairs leading down to the dank earthen cellar. Down here were more shelves stocked with cans and jars. A number of large jugs were set on the ground against the far wall. These were filled with the Maynards' reserve of special 'shine. The cellar's interior was illuminated by two oil-burning lanterns.

The dinner was chained to an overhead rafter.

Abby approached the holiday prize and eyed it up and down.

She poked its smooth, flat belly with an index finger. "You still look a mite skinny. This rate, there won't be enough of you to go around." She made a clucking sound. "Too bad your fat little friend got took by the Colliers, or we'd have a helluva feast. Now tell me the truth—if I try to feed ya, you're just gonna spit it out again, ain't ya?"

The dinner nodded and uttered a muffled curse.

Abby smirked. "Not even if I was to stick your pretty

feet in a big pot of scalding water? That worked last time, didn't it?"

The dinner whimpered and looked at her through eyes shiny with fresh tears. She thought of the incident upstairs and felt a new surge of self-hatred. She balled a hand into a fist and drove it into the dinner's flat belly, causing it to scream behind its gag and flail away from her. But there was only so far it could go. Abby moved a step closer and drilled another blow into its stomach. She listened to it sob and felt a tiny portion of her frustration drain away. She knew the feeling was only temporary, but any relief at all was a blessing these days. So she kept at it, slamming her fist into its midsection until it ceased resisting and hung slack from the chain.

Abby watched it turn slightly in the flickering lantern light.

The dinner had long, tapered legs, a slim waist, and large, plump breasts. It had a nice face, too, with big brown eyes, a small, straight nose, and pouting lips. Its firm, creamy flesh glistened with sweat in the lantern light.

Abby placed a hand on its hip and caressed it. The dinner stared at her. Her hand moved from its hip, glided over its round ass, cupped its pert breasts, traced a slow, curving trail down its concave belly, and dipped between its legs.

The dinner arched its back and moaned softly.

Abby smiled. "You like that?"

The dinner looked at her and said something Abby couldn't make out because of the gag. Abby tugged the gag away and said, "What'd you say?"

It heaved a big breath and looked her right in the eye. There was a surprising hardness in that gaze. A clear determination. This one's spirit hadn't been broken yet, which was kind of amazing. Usually they were gibbering idiots by this point, stripped of their sanity through torture and recognition of the hopelessness of their situation. "I said, if that's the way you like it, I can show you some things that'll rock your fucking world."

Abby chuckled. "I just have to let you down, right? Maybe sneak you out of here?"

The dinner's hard expression didn't change. "Yes."

"Do you think I'm stupid?"

"No. I—"

Abby punched it in the stomach again, harder than before, throwing every last ounce of frustration and self-hatred into the blow. It blasted the air from the dinner's lungs and left it gasping for breath. Abby put the gag back in place and hurried out of the cellar. She delivered a brief report to Carol Maynard—a stone lie about forcing several spoonfuls of gruel down the dinner's throat—before returning to the sitting room and her rocking chair.

She rocked and stared at the broken television screen.

Her mind conjured new images for the empty screen, but these weren't the usual cop-show and soap-opera scenarios. These featured certain acts involving herself and the outsider woman chained to a rafter in the Maynards' cellar.

She gritted her teeth and rocked.

CHAPTER FIVE

Jessica Sloan ran for her life. She dashed past the still-kneeling Hoke and the Falcon and plunged through the line of trees at the far end of the clearing. Taking her chances out here in the woods was likely tantamount to suicide, but it was the only even remotely viable option available to her. She heard a second boom of the shotgun and ignored it. There was a chance the big gun would cut her down in her tracks, but a backward glance would doom her just as surely. There was only time for forward motion, for flight.

She thought longingly of the Falcon for a brief moment, ached to feel the thrust of the roaring old V-8 engine carrying her swiftly from this place. But they would have taken her easily if she'd made a play for the car. She pictured it in her head. The convertible's top was down. She could have leaped over the closed door. But then she would've had to get the key out of her pocket, put it in the ignition, start the engine, slap the car into gear, execute a three-point turn, and slam the gas pedal to the floor. The grotesquely deformed men had been no more than ten feet from her on both sides. There just wouldn't have been time.

Damn it.

A low-hanging branch hit her in the forehead and shattered as she charged onward through the woods. She trampled thick undergrowth and was thankful she was wearing sneakers rather than the heavy, high-heeled boots she'd worn on her first visit to Hoke's house. She moved between the trees in a random zigzag pattern, darting a hundred feet to her right, ten or twenty more straight ahead, another thirty or forty to the right again, and so on. Her gaze was shifting all the time, rapidly scanning the area immediately ahead of her for impediments, and she managed to avoid numerous rocks and vines with astonishing nimbleness and an almost balletic grace. All that time spent training in the gym and running her daily miles was paying off in ways she never would have imagined. A less well-conditioned woman wouldn't have stood a chance. She was further aided by the gentle downhill slope of the land in this direction, which allowed her to set a pace she was certain the big, lumbering men behind her couldn't possibly match.

She heard the gentle trickle of water before she slipped through a thicker line of trees and saw the little stream winding through the woods. The stream was no more than three or four feet across. The water would come up to no higher than her knees. She could leap it easily or wade through within the space of a heartbeat or two. But the crystal-clear flow of water stopped her in her tracks. She stood panting at the edge of the stream for a moment and risked her first backward glance. There was no one behind her. She listened for sounds of pursuit and heard nothing. That didn't necessarily mean anything. The men lived in these woods. They might not be able to match her speed, but they would be skilled at the art of stealthy tracking. It would behoove her not to linger long at the stream. If she stayed still long enough, they would eventually catch up to her. And if that happened, she doubted she'd be able to get away again.

She didn't feel winded yet—the half mile or so she'd come was nowhere near the limits of her usual endurance levels—but this could be her last chance for a cool drink of water for some time. It would be smart to take advantage of it.

Quickly, though.

She dropped to her knees at the edge of the stream and set the .38 on the rocky ground. She pulled her long hair back and tied it in a loose knot. She knelt closer to the stream, dipped her cupped hands into the cool, amazingly clean water, lifted them, and drank. The water tasted wonderful. She dipped her hands into the stream again and again, slurping water down with abandon for several moments. Then she shook excess moisture from her hands and sat panting. She felt refreshed and more than ready to resume her flight from the hideously deformed men. But now that she'd allowed herself this brief pause, some disturbing thoughts and questions began to catch up to her.

What *were* those things?

They were men, but not normal men. They looked like . . . mutants. Like a generation of feral mountain men who'd grown up in the aftermath of an all-out nuclear war. She thought of the area she was in and searched her memory. Were there any nuclear power plants operating in these parts? Say there was one somewhere nearby. Was it possible there had been a Chernobyl-style accident, only on a smaller scale? The government might have hushed something like that up, same way the Russians did with the Chernobyl meltdown. Another thing to consider was the dirty bomb supposedly detonated by terrorists in nearby Dandridge. But no, that was too recent an event to account for the kind of deformities she'd seen, which must have occurred in the womb. Another, more outrageous possibility occurred to her. Perhaps they weren't human at all. Maybe they were demons or aliens. But she dismissed this notion as obviously ludicrous.

Aliens in overalls wielding shotguns. Unlikely, to say the least. Which brought her back to the more logical culprit being some long-standing environmental contaminant.

Oh, shit.

She glanced down at the stream, thought of the water she'd drunk, and felt her stomach twist. *Oh, shit.* She tried to stay calm. This was no time to give in to panic. So . . . assume the water was tainted. So what? On a rational level, she knew she hadn't consumed anywhere near enough to ignite a tumor or some other awful illness. The mutants were the way they were thanks to generations of exposure to whatever had fucked up their gene pool. The water wasn't going to kill her.

She began to relax, felt her breathing start to even out again.

But then a resurgent thread of anxiety began to wind through her.

Yes, the water wasn't going to kill her.

But the mutants might.

She groped for the .38, felt her hand close over the handle, and began to stand up. Then she froze in a half-standing, half-kneeling position and scanned the line of trees on the opposite side of the stream. She didn't see anything other than trees, but she was sure she'd heard something. Her head swiveled slowly left and right. Then she saw it, a little flicker of movement behind the thick base of one of the tallest and oldest trees. She surged to her feet and pivoted in that direction, swinging the gun toward the big tree.

She thumbed back the .38's hammer.

The ratcheting of deadly metal was ominously loud in the otherwise-silent woods. The sound would scare anyone. Good. She relished the opportunity to make someone other than herself afraid. Keeping the gun aimed at the tree, she quickly waded through the stream and came up dripping water from her shoes and jeans on the opposite side. She made no attempt at a quiet approach as she walked toward the tree, and the tactic soon produced the desired result.

A bare-chested young boy in a straw hat and jeans stepped away from the tree and began moving backward. He was scrawny and had a wiry build. Early teens, at best. But an exact age was hard to surmise, thanks to his deformed face. His lower jaw was slightly elongated. He had just one eye. The other eye wasn't missing. It'd never been there in the first place. There was no second socket where the other should have been. His nose was too big and curved upward. Thick, throbbing veins pulsed at its sides.

Like the men back at the clearing, he looked like something from a nightmare.

Only this time the nightmare was afraid of *her*.

The boy's chest was heaving. He was shaking all over. And he was trying not to cry. Jessica's revulsion gave way to simple human compassion. She eased the .38's hammer down, pointed the barrel upward, and moved a step closer to him, causing him to flinch.

"Easy, kid," she said, striving to keep her tone even and nonthreatening. "I'm not going to hurt you, okay? I just need a little help, that's all."

Maybe she could reason with him. Perhaps persuade him to guide her out of the woods. After all, he wouldn't know his older cousins or whatever were chasing her. If he could help her find her way back to Old Fork Road, she would at least stand a reasonable chance of making her way back to some semblance of civilization.

But the boy let out a high whine as she came another step closer.

Then he turned and bolted.

"Shit!"

Jessica shoved the .38 into her waistband and took off after him. She overtook him with ease, throwing an arm around his waist and driving him to the ground. She flipped him over and straddled him to keep in place. He let out a wail of anguish, and Jessica began to panic again. He was making too much noise. The bigger ones would hear him and get a fix on her location. Innocent boy or not, the little fuck was putting her life in jeopardy with all this commotion. She knew what would happen if those men managed to get their hands on her. Rape and mutilation. *Damned if I'm gonna let that happen.* She scanned the ground around her and spotted a solid hunk of rock that would fit easily in her hand. She grabbed it and lifted it high over her head.

The sound of a round being slotted into a rifle chamber stopped her.

A man's voice said, "Wouldn't do that if I were you."

Jessica looked over her shoulder and saw a man in overalls and a flannel shirt. A John Deere cap sat atop his head. He was aiming a hunting rifle at her head.

She dropped the rock. "I didn't want to hurt him. I swear. I just had to stop him from making that noise. There are some fucked-up-looking people after me."

This man wasn't like her pursuers, at least not at first glance. He sported no obvious deformities. He looked like a normal hunter. Then he said, "Fucked-up-looking, huh? I reckon you're talking about the Kinchers. That boy's one of 'em. They all look like that."

Jessica frowned. "You know them?"

"We all know each other 'round here, darlin'."

"What's wrong with them? Why do they look like that?"

The man moved a few steps closer to her, carefully keeping the rifle's barrel aimed at the back of her head. "Ain't none of your concern. You're gonna need to come with me, girl. Once you're back at my place, the Kinchers'll have no claim on ya."

"No!" the boy exclaimed. "She's for us!"

Jessica glanced down at him.

He was grinning now, no longer afraid.

She thought about what the man had said. And she thought about the boy's comment. It all added up to a world of shit for Jessica Sloan. The Kinchers wouldn't have a claim on her, but this man would, and she had a funny feeling he wouldn't treat her any better than the mutants.

Jessica let the hand that had been gripping the rock settle over the butt of her .38. "My daddy always told me to never trust strangers. I should have listened to him better in the first place, or I wouldn't be in this fucking mess today."

She yanked the .38 from her waistband, and rolled away from the Kincher boy. The crack of the rifle resounded in the woods, but she kept rolling and the round missed. She quickly sized up a shot while the man slotted another round into the chamber.

She squeezed the trigger.

The bullet caught the man in the throat and flung him backward.

The Kincher boy got up and started to run.

Jessica got to her knees, sized up another shot, and squeezed the trigger again. This round took the boy square in the middle of his bare back, and he fell instantly dead to the forest floor. She felt a small pang of regret for killing the kid, but was comforted by the knowledge that she'd had no choice. She went over to the fallen hunter and retrieved his rifle. She searched the pockets of his overalls and found a folded Buck knife, as well as some extra shells for the rifle. She put the knife and extra bullets in her pockets, tucked the .38 back in her waistband, and stood up, rifle in hand.

She paused a moment, listened.

She heard something, a soft crunch of undergrowth.

Maybe it was a deer.

And maybe not.

She turned and started running again.

Running for her life.

CHAPTER SIX

The chapter was over. Anxious to know what happened next, Megan Phillips flipped to the next page and continued reading. She read several more pages and reached the end of yet another chapter. The book was really good. She didn't read a lot of horror novels. This one had been an impulse purchase at a yard sale in Kentucky they'd stopped off on the way to Tennessee. There'd been a meager selection of maybe twenty books available, most of them best-selling thrillers that all seemed interchangeable, nothing that really grabbed her attention. But the back-cover copy for *City Infernal* had intrigued her, so she'd bought it, figuring if it sucked she was only out a buck, so what the hell?

It did not suck.

In fact, she'd been riveted to the story from page one, to the point of almost completely ignoring Pete over the last couple hours. She paused in the middle of the first paragraph of yet another new chapter and lowered the book to glance at the dashboard clock.

The time was four thirty-five, late afternoon transitioning toward early evening. It was the middle of summer, so the sun would be up for a few more hours yet. They'd hoped to make Chattanooga before nightfall, a goal that was still just within reach, but they needed to get moving soon.

Megan frowned.

She'd been so engrossed in her book, she'd failed to note what time it'd been when Pete went into the store. But it seemed to her she'd read quite a bit since his departure. She flipped through the book and judged it at around fifty-plus pages. She set the book on the dash and sat up straighter in her seat to peer at the store. Right away she saw the "closed" sign hanging in the door. Well, that was troubling. She scanned the gravel parking lot and spotted only one other car, some beat-up black sedan from the seventies or eighties.

She got out of the car and stood there for a moment, a hand on the door as she appraised the situation. The road was devoid of traffic. She heard no subtle hiss of distant tires traveling this same lonely stretch of country road. The musical twittering of a bird was the only discernible sound at all. Leaving the door open, she stepped away from the car and moved toward the store. As she neared it, she saw that a blind had been drawn down the length of the door. The window blinds were also closed. She tried the door's handle and found it locked.

"Shit!"

She turned away from the door and kicked the ground in frustration, sending several pebbles skittering across the dusty lot. She stood with her hands on her hips and scanned the surrounding area again. The emptiness and silence were eerie. She began to feel paranoid. She could almost believe she was the last person alive on earth, the lone survivor of some mysterious apocalypse that had occurred while she'd been reading. Or maybe the fucking Rapture had finally happened, sweeping up all the pure souls and leaving behind only sinners like herself. But that made no sense. If the Rapture had happened, she felt certain Pete would still be here with her. He was a sinner, too. In fact, they'd done quite a bit of fun sinning together.

She liked sinning with Pete.

In fact, she just plain liked Pete, the man, a lot.

It was this thought that made her spin back toward the door and try the handle again. It still wouldn't budge. She shook it harder, and the door rattled in its frame. She then banged on the door with the base of a fist. "Hey! Anyone in there? Open up!"

She banged her fist against the door several more times, then stepped back and waited, hoping—praying—she would hear approaching footsteps from the other side.

Nothing happened. No one came.

She moved to the closest window and tried to see around the edge of the blind. The store's interior was dark, but thanks to the sun she was able to make out a single aisle and a shadow-shrouded counter at the far end of the store. She couldn't make out much beyond that, but the darkness told the story—there was no one in the store. She started to really panic now. It was clear something very wrong was happening. She held in a whine, worked hard to make herself calm down. She wouldn't have a hope of finding or helping Pete if she gave in to hysterics.

She tried to think.

The way she saw it, she had two options. She could fetch her cell phone from the car and dial information for the local sheriff's number. Or . . .

Fuck it.

She walked to the end of the building and began to move carefully along its garbage-strewn left side. Here there were overflowing plastic garbage barrels, stacks of old tires, and assorted bits of automotive detritus. As she picked her way through the landscape of junk, she began to hear sounds from the rear of the building. At the corner, she crouched behind a stack of tires and saw a thin, gaunt-looking man in a flannel shirt and jeans standing with his arms folded at the back of an old van. The van's rear doors stood open. The man seemed impatient, as if he was waiting for someone else. He stood slouched to one side, tapping a foot and scowling at the back of the store. She watched him unfold his arms and insert an index finger in a nostril. She wanted to approach this man to ask him if he'd seen Pete, but some instinct held her back. Even from this distance, the man projected a creepy, ingrained malice.

The man straightened as a door at the back of the store banged open. And in a moment Megan was dismayed to have her instincts proven correct. Two men—one thin and haggard like the first man she'd seen, the other hugely fat—emerged from the back of a store. They carried an unconscious Pete between them, the toes of his shoes dragging through the gravel as they approached the van. Megan sucked back a helpless whimper and pressed herself closer to the wall, praying they wouldn't spot her.

Oh, poor Pete.

The first man she'd seen said, "About goddamn time."

The other thin man snickered as they reached the van. "Would've been a lot sooner, but you know Gil, had to have his fun with the boy first."

The first man sneered at the fat man. "Ya old pervert."

Megan's heart sank.

Anger like nothing she'd ever known possessed her. A molten, murderous rage. She wished she had a gun. She would run out there right now and kill them all. She had always been a pacifist. And she hated guns. But now . . .

Yes.

She could kill them all.

Without blinking a fucking eye.

But knowing this did her no good at all. Did Pete no good. She would have to use her mind to figure a way out of this nightmare for both of them. She watched the men toss Pete into the van's dark interior as dispassionately as other men might heave a rug. After a moment more of additional conversation, two of the men got in the van. The engine started. The third man started moving toward the store.

Toward her.

Megan's breath caught in her throat.

Oh, shit! Oh, Jesus!

She scooted backward, felt her back strike a trash barrel, making it wobble. She turned and straightened it. Then she got to her feet and ran. She stumbled once. Then a second time. But somehow, through some miracle, she remained upright as she threaded her way through the junk at the store's side. Terror and desperation pumped adrenaline into her bloodstream, and she was able to move faster as she reached the front of the store.

She spotted the Jetta.

It was close.

The approaching rumble of the van told her there'd be no time to get in the car and make a run for it. She'd have to come back for it after the van was gone. The road next to the store was still empty of traffic. She crossed it and plunged through the line of trees beyond. There, she crouched behind one of the larger trees and watched the store. The van appeared and rolled across the gravel to the edge of the parking lot. After a moment's hesitation, the driver pulled the vehicle onto the paved road, turned to the right, and accelerated.

She watched the van disappear and thought, *Oh, Pete. I'm coming for you, baby. I swear.*

Just as she was about to step out from behind the tree, she saw the third man appear. This was the first one she'd seen. A gaunt man with hard, pitiless eyes. She moved back behind the tree and watched him approach the Jetta. He moved to the passenger's side of the vehicle, pausing a moment to frown at the open door.

He turned away from the car and scanned the line of trees beyond the road.

Megan's heart slammed.

She slid down the tree and hugged its base to keep from falling onto her back. She was certain he would sense her location, that he would cross the road to collect her any moment now. Then they would take her to wherever the other men had taken Pete.

Oh, God.

But the man just shrugged and threw the door shut. Then he moved to the other side of the Jetta and got in the car. Megan remembered that Pete had left the keys dangling in the ignition. Tears stung her eyes as she watched the man start Pete's car and drive it away from the closed-up general store, following the path of the departed van.

Then it was gone, her only obvious means of escape from this redneck hellhole.

She let go of the tree and sat with her legs folded beneath her on the forest floor.

She cried. Her body shook with the force of her sobs.

And she thought, *Oh, Pete. What am I going to do? Oh, God. Please help me. . . .*

CHAPTER SEVEN

The snuffling, squealing sounds of pigs woke him up. Hoke's eyes fluttered open. A round, pink creature on four stubby legs waddled by him. Another, larger pig followed close on its heels.

Hoke groaned.

He ached all over.

The ground beneath him was wet and mushy and strewn with hay. He groaned again as he summoned the strength to roll onto his back. Above him was an arched wooden roof. Sunlight blazed through the wide gaps between the slanted lengths of age-stained lumber. He sat up and took a look around. He was in some decrepit old barn. Maybe a dozen pigs of varying sizes wandered aimlessly about its interior. He saw stacks of hay against one wall and various pieces of farm equipment against another. There were two horse stalls, but they were empty. Damn the luck. Hoke had never been on a horse in his life, but he'd seen his fair share of cowboy movies. How hard could riding a horse be? Just jump on, kick the four-legged fuck's hindquarters, holler YEE-HAW! and ride like the fucking wind, right?

But horse or no horse, he meant to get the hell out of this backwoods cesspool. Like right now. None of the monster men who'd taken him seemed to be around. So no time like the present. The big barn door stood wide open. All he had to do was walk out and keep on walking.

That goal in mind, he hauled himself up and started walking toward the door.

And came to an immediate halt as one of his abductors walked into view. Hoke gulped. It was the first one he'd glimpsed back in that clearing, back again to scare the ever-loving crap out of him. The mammoth dude with the big red eye and the trunk nose. *Fuck. Look at the guy.* He didn't look like he could be real, like he had to be a hallucination, some flashing nightmare thing glimpsed during the very worst moments of a monumentally bad acid trip. A really, really, seriously, like, incredibly fucking-bad acid trip.

Like, the worst acid trip ever in the entire history of tripping on acid.

Times ten. Times a hundred.

Hell.

Times the highest possible number known to man or God.

But Hoke was stone-cold sober and knew the thing was no hallucination. The fucker was real all right, large as life and ugly as sin. He felt a strange awkwardness as he met the thing's livid gaze. How did one interact with a genuine monster on a social level? Hoke had no idea, other than to bluff his way through. He forced a smile and said, "Hey, dude."

The creature bared its teeth and hissed at him. It tilted its chin upward, opened its mouth, and said something that might have made sense to one of the other monster men. Some kind of hillbilly gibberish interspersed with the odd recognizable snippet of English.

Hoke nodded. "Uh-huh. Right. Listen, I've got a gig tonight. A little showcase thing at the Bluebird Cafe. You've heard of that, right? It's world famous. There any chance one of you guys could give me a ride back to Nashvegas? I'm good for the gas, no problem."

"Yash hippen okra chinka dork!"

Or something like that.

Hoke cringed. He held up his hands in a placating gesture and moved back a step. "Right. Okay. You're busy. I understand. Maybe check with your buddies and get back to me about it."

The man raised the shotgun and pointed it at Hoke's head. Hoke kept his hands up and retreated a few more steps. He was plenty scared, but he was also more than a little annoyed. There was altogether too much of this pointing-guns-at-his-head business going on today. First that snooty bitch. Now this ugly motherfucker. A guy could get a complex. What had he done to deserve this kind of treatment?

The deformed man strode into the barn, shoved the shotgun in Hoke's direction, and roared at him. "YASH HIPPEN NO WAY CHINKA SHAH!"

Hoke cupped his hands around his mouth. "HEY, LOOK! I CAN YELL, TOO! GUESS WHAT, UGLY? I DON'T UNDERSTAND A SINGLE FUCKIN' THING YOU'RE SAYIN'!"

"You got a death wish, son?"

Hoke spun about and gaped at the vaguely defined form of a tall, slim man standing in shadows at the rear of the barn. The inadvisability of turning his back on a shotgun-wielding mutant redneck in close quarters occurred to him a moment too late. He glanced over his shoulder and was relieved to see that the monster man was still standing just inside the open barn door. He decided to risk focusing his full attention on the mystery man.

He squinted, tried to see the guy a little better. The man was wearing jeans and dusty cowpoke boots, but the shadows made it impossible to make out anything else. "Who the fuck are you, and where the blue hell did you come from all of a sudden?"

The man struck a match and applied the flickering flame to the end of a cigarette. The light cast by the match failed to illuminate the man's features. He drew deeply on the cigarette and exhaled a cloud of smoke. "Me?" he said at last. "I'm Garner. And I've always been here, boy."

A tickle of dread started at the base of Hoke's spine. He took an unconscious step backward. He wasn't sure why, but he was suddenly more afraid of the shadow man than he was of the monster with the gun. A primal unease settled deep in his gut. Every nerve ending tingled with the need to be a thousand miles away from Garner. But he couldn't just run. The monster would intercept him with ease. Maybe unload both barrels of that shotgun on him, cut his sorry ass in half.

Hell, maybe that'd be for the fucking best at this point.

Garner chuckled. "Jebediah won't kill you for running. Not without my say-so. But you would most certainly regret the attempt anyway."

Hoke was unable to restrain the whimper that came then. "What do you want with me? What the hell's up with this godforsaken place and these fucking monsters?"

Garner dragged on his cigarette again. "I have a very specific purpose in mind for you, son. But we'll talk about that later this evening. These monsters, as you call them, are the Kinchers, the living descendants of Isaac and Gladys Kincher."

Hoke scowled. "The fuck is that supposed to mean to me?"

Garner laughed. "Why, just everything, son. You see, the Kincher clan was involved with a dispute with my own people long, long ago. They raped and killed my closest kin. It was left to me to exact revenge. And that I did."

Despite his fear, Hoke was curious. "But . . . how? And how long ago was this?"

Another draw on the cigarette. The tiny red ember danced in the shadows. "The answer to your second question is 1872. And I did it by laying a curse on their bloodline. It was me who turned the Kinchers into monsters, son."

Hoke brayed laughter.

"I sense doubt."

"Oh, no. Totally believe you, dude." Hoke wiped tears from his eyes. "Seriously, you really had me going until you got into the curse business. And what's up with trying to make me believe you've been around since eighteenwhatever? You must think I'm—"

The man called Garner stepped out of the strange, clinging shadows.

Hoke took one look at him and started to wobble.

He said, "Aw . . . fuck me . . ."

And then he fainted.

CHAPTER EIGHT

Ma was gone. She left for a while every evening for a spell, often to look for a man to bed. She was old and built like one of those big trucks, the eighteen-wheel kind she'd seen the couple times she'd been out to one of the big highways. Thick and sturdy, and liable to belch a blast of noxious steam if you got in her way. And yet there remained a number of local men more than willing to fuck her. It had a little to do with her position in the community, but Abby didn't kid herself. She'd heard the stories. Ma was a monster in the sack. The younger boys hereabouts spent their days ogling skinnier, fresher-faced girls, but many of them privately speculated in hushed, awed voices about what it might be like to be schooled in the ways of the flesh by Grandma Maynard.

Abby rocked and stared at the broken television. Her fingers curled tight around the arms of the rocker as she fantasized about heaving a brick through the cracked screen. It was a new notion, one simultaneously frightening and invested with a potential sense of liberation. She wasn't sure why she felt that way, really. Chucking a brick through the blank screen wouldn't change a damn thing, other than breaking the cursed thing's hypnotic hold over her. She would still be here. Would still be a prisoner of her frustrations and feelings of failure. She would still sit here and rock, her already quietly desperate existence rendered an even duller shade of gray by the demolition of the thing that gave her dreams shape and form, that framed the yearnings of her imagination.

Ma would be gone for a while.

Maybe for a long while.

Thinking about it, Abby abruptly ceased rocking.

Yes.

The miserable old cunt was horny. More than usual. She'd been too busy for her evening excursions these last few days, spending endless hours cooking and cleaning, preparing everything just so for the big weekend feast. Ma was always ornery, but she'd been especially edgy today. Quicker with a backhand than usual—and much more ready to sting you with that poison tongue. But she'd finished the last of her major preparations this afternoon, and she'd soon departed with an uncharacteristic big smile on her face and a jug of whiskey in her hand.

Abby smiled.

Hell.

Ma might be gone all night.

She thought of the holiday dinner hanging on its chain in the cellar and felt a strange tingle of excitement. Strange, yes, but not a mystery. She knew what the tingle was. It was something she wasn't supposed to feel. Not if she meant to stay right with the Lord. She glanced at the weathered old Bible propped on the little table to her left. She couldn't read it, of course. Couldn't read anything. But her daddy used to read it to her in halting, awkward tones when she was little. After he died, she slept with the old book for a time. But she took little comfort from it and soon discontinued the habit. She wondered what Pa would think if he could know some of her more shameful thoughts.

You know, she thought.

She well remembered the feel of his broad, thick hand tanning her bony backside when she was a child. If anything, Luke Maynard had been even more willing to mete out punishment than Ma, which meant he was just about as fearsome as the devil himself.

But he's gone. Gone forever.

And so, she reminded herself, was Ma. And, at least for a short time, Abby was free to do whatever she desired.

She rose from the rocking chair. Went to the kitchen. To the pantry. To the door beyond, and down the stairs to the cellar. The dinner raised its head as she approached and stared at her. She looked the same as always. Defiant, but weary. Every time she looked in the dinner's eyes there was just a touch more of that weariness. Abby recognized the signs. This one was stronger than most, maybe was the strongest ever in her experience, but its fighting spirit was beginning to ebb. Soon it would resign itself to the inevitable.

Abby tugged its gag away from its mouth.

It heaved its usual big breath and glared at her. "What do you want? Come to beat me again?"

Abby's heart was beating too fast. "If I help you escape, will you take me with you?"

The dinner's unswerving gaze projected open disbelief. "You're toying with me again, aren't you?"

Abby shook her head. "No, ma'am."

The dinner coughed. "Okay. What's the catch? There is one, right?"

Abby nodded.

"Of course." The dinner grimaced, glanced up at the manacles biting into its slim wrists. Then it looked at Abby and said, "Well . . . spell it out."

Abby told it what she wanted.

The guarantee she needed.

A meager enough list of demands, she thought, considering the dinner's only other option.

The dinner was silent for a long moment. It stared at the damp, earthen floor and thought about what it'd been told. After maybe a full minute, it raised its head and said, "You can't just let me go now? While they're away?"

Abby shook her head. "Tomorrow night, the night before the holiday feast. That's the right time."

The dinner made a sound of immense frustration. "But that makes no sense. We can be far away by the time they even realize we're gone."

Abby shrugged. "There are things you don't understand yet. You'll just have to trust me. Tomorrow night is perfect. I promise you."

The dinner rolled its eyes. "Okay. Whatever. But you have to do something for me, too."

"Oh?"

The dinner laughed. "Convince me. Make me believe you're not just"—another, more pointed glance at its manacled wrists—"yanking my chain."

Abby smiled. "Okay."

She retrieved an old wicker chair from a dark corner of the cellar, set it in front of the dinner, and sat down.

Then she began to talk.

She spoke without interruption for a long time.

An hour or longer.

Telling the dinner all about her life.

CHAPTER NINE

She couldn't stop thinking about her Prada bag. It was the real deal, not one of those knockoffs like the one she'd bought from a street vendor in Tijuana years ago. The fake had looked almost good enough to pass for the genuine article, but it began to fall apart after a few months. An end of the strap came loose first, which she reattached with messily applied epoxy. Not exactly a hip look. She could have replaced it with a cheaper, more eye-pleasing bag, but she clung to the cheap and battered Tijuana souvenir with a stubborn tenacity that earned endless withering comments from her friends. Then, less than a month ago, her mother took her out to dinner for her birthday. At some point between the end of their meal and the arrival of dessert, Jessica excused herself to go to the bathroom. When she returned, a little gift bag stuffed with brightly colored tissue paper sat in the middle of the table.

She hadn't known what to expect. Some sort of necklace, maybe. Something silver. Cynthia Sloan knew her daughter preferred silvery jewelry to gold and had gone that route for more than one previous birthday. So

the expensive, genuine Prada bag had come as something
of a surprise. More of a gasp-inducing shock, actually.
Jessica wasn't one to squeal and gush over gifts, even
really nice ones, but she made an exception this time. It
was a leather runway bag from the new fall collection.
Cost? Who knew. Some ungodly amount. And then
there was the card, with its longish, heartfelt note from
her mother expressing deep love for her daughter, along
with the wish that she'd been better able to express that
love over the years. She should have known something
big was up then, but she was too distracted by the check
enclosed with the card. A check written in the amount
of five thousand dollars—two grand of which she'd
planned to hand over to Hoke today for the Falcon. The
last time her mother had given her money had been for
her eighteenth birthday, and that had been a hundred
bucks. Big money to her at the time. She should have
questioned the unusual extravagance, but she'd been too
overwhelmed, too touched by the affection expressed in
her mother's note.

A week later, the day after Jessica finally deposited
the check in her bank account, Cynthia Sloan shocked
the whole family by killing herself, doing the job via a
combination of pills and a deeply slashed wrist. No one
knew why she'd done it. There'd been no fatal medical
diagnosis. She hadn't been having an affair. Her loving
husband of thirty years had always treated her with great
tenderness and care. The surviving Sloans had talked
about it endlessly in the ensuing weeks, hashing out
theory after theory, each more unlikely than the last, and
had come up with nothing.

She was just gone, that's all.

Gone, and never coming back.

Tears spilled from Jessica's eyes as the memories assailed
her. She nearly stumbled over a vine as she swiped at the

moisture with the back of a wrist. Spying a big rock ten yards to her left, she decided to take a break. Some time had passed since the last time she'd heard anything remotely like the sound of a pursuer. She could stop for a minute, long enough to get herself together, at least. She unslung the rifle, sat on the rock, and propped the weapon between her legs. She wiped the tears away and tried to make herself focus on the problem at hand.

Goddammit, she had to get that bag back.

And not just for sentimental reasons. Her wallet was in the bag, along with her driver's license, social security card, and multiple credit cards. All but one of the credit cards was maxed out, though. And she wasn't too worried about the possibility of identity theft. Somehow she doubted the ability of the mutant rednecks to do much damage in that regard. Shit, she doubted they could spell their own names. No, there was just one thing the bag contained that she really needed right now.

Her fucking cell phone.

Her ticket out of this nightmare, if she could just get her hands on it. But that would mean going back to the car. Back to where she'd first glimpsed the men the hunter had called the Kinchers. Those monsters. Just the thought of it made her shudder. A deliberate march back in that direction would be pure madness. She thought of the Kinchers some more and for the first time wondered what had become of Hoke. He wouldn't have been able to take off running like she had, not after the hours spent in that cramped and filthy trunk. So they had either killed him or taken him somewhere. Either way, his current situation was even more dire than her own. The thought brought a small, trembling smile to her face. She hoped the Kinchers were running a redneck train on him even now, cornholing him endlessly with enormous, mutated cocks, making him scream and mewl like a baby as the ceaseless pressure ruptured his rectum. This made her think of what Hoke had done to her earlier in the day and the smile disappeared.

Jessica glanced upward, narrowing her eyes against the glint of sunlight visible through the canopy of tree leaves. She had at least a couple hours of daylight left. And if she hoped to make any progress toward getting out of the woods before nightfall, she would need to get moving again.

She stood up and slung the rifle strap over her shoulder again. She turned in a slow circle and realized she was no longer sure what direction she'd been heading in before she stopped. Frustration assailed her again. She wasn't a wilderness person. Nor did she have any survival skills, despite her father's oft-repeated advice over the years that she needed to prepare herself for a coming global catastrophe. She loved her dad, but the career military man bought into certain strains of right-wing paranoia a touch too enthusiastically for her taste. He honestly believed some form of apocalypse was right around the corner. Pure nonsense, of course, but now she wished she'd taken him up on his frequent offers to teach her basic survival skills. They sure as shit would come in handy right about now.

The hell with it, she thought.

She stopped turning, picked a direction, and started walking. She still didn't know where she was going, but had a vague sense the direction was still carrying her away from the clearing from which she'd fled. A vague sense wasn't much to go on, but it was better than nothing at all.

She walked maybe fifteen more minutes before the thickness of the forest began to recede. The trees were less densely bunched. The undergrowth wasn't so profuse, and there were almost no bushes. A few minutes later her breath caught in her throat as she glimpsed the dark outline of a smallish structure visible through the line of trees just ahead of her. She walked ten more yards and stood behind a tall tree at the edge of another clearing, this one a good bit larger than the one where she'd meant to execute Hoke. A decrepit shack sat in the approximate center of the clearing. She had come upon the cabin from the side, but from this vantage point she could see a lone man sitting in a wicker chair on the cabin's sagging porch. A pickup truck that looked like it could be from the 1950s was parked in front of the cabin. Though the truck was ancient, it didn't quite have the look of a long-unused relic.

Please let it run.

There was no one else in the clearing. No one visible, at least. Could be there was someone in the shack. A woman preparing an evening dinner, maybe. Or there could be someone sitting in another chair on the opposite side of the long porch. But these considerations couldn't deter Jessica.

This was her chance.

And maybe the only one she would get.

She unslung the rifle and slid a finger through the trigger guard. Staying behind the line of trees, she moved twenty yards to her right until the man disappeared from sight. She didn't want him to see her until she was right on top of him. Until the barrel of the rifle was in his fucking face.

He would have no choice but to turn over the keys to the truck. There would then be the matter of whether to kill him or subdue him until she was gone, but she wouldn't think about that until the time came.

She took a deep breath.

Gripped the rifle a little tighter.

And stepped into the clearing.

•

CHAPTER TEN

Megan Phillips emerged from the line of trees, skipped over the shallow ditch, and stood with her hands on her hips in the middle of the two-lane road.

She thought, *What now?*

For the next several moments, the raw, blinding terror that had driven her into the woods went dormant as she considered her next move. She was even able to set aside her desperate concern for Pete during this brief time. These feelings hadn't deserted her. Not at all. They were just . . . on hold. It was sort of blissful, in a strange, bittersweet way. It was a fragile feeling, one she knew would shatter with the merest wrong nudge, but she meant to savor it while she was able.

She stared at the locked-up general store on the other side of the street. Maybe she should break a window, get inside the store. There would be a phone somewhere in there, surely, and she could use it to dial the local sheriff's office or 911. Would they have the 911 system in this ultra-rural shithole? She'd always taken the system's seemingly ubiquitous nature for granted. But she'd never lived in an area where the general population density wasn't in the millions. And most of the places she'd visited on vacation were much more developed than this . . . town? Did it even qualify as a town? She wasn't sure. A glance in either direction showed only more woods and winding stretches of gray asphalt. The general store was the only building in sight. Say she did manage to get inside the store and find a phone—how long would it take the local authorities to drag their asses out here? The return of one or more of the men who'd taken Pete ahead of the arrival of the law was certainly well within the realm of possibility.

And what then?

They'd grab her, too.

And that would be that, the end for her and Pete. They'd be raped and murdered. Then tossed in some pit and doused in lime. Or they'd be kept for a time as sex slaves. Maybe for years. Why not? Who would ever find them out here? No one who cared about them knew where they were.

Okay, so the hell with the breaking-and-entering idea. The whole notion had been absurd from the start anyway. Sweet little Megan Phillips, former cheerleader turned neohippy, chucking a rock or brick through the window of a store?

As if.

Megan turned to the right and stared at the empty road. This was the way the rednecks had gone. The way Pete had gone. He was out there somewhere, maybe still unconscious, maybe awake now and suffering God only knew what manner of indignity or violation. Some of the desperate, gnawing terror began to creep back in then. New tears bloomed in her eyes.

"Oh, Pete . . ."

She started walking. She had no way of knowing where they'd taken him, of course. It could be anywhere. But she couldn't just keep standing there. Walking was at least doing something. And maybe she'd get lucky, spot some kind of clue, or spy a likely destination for the kidnappers. It made no logical sense. She wasn't a detective. And she wasn't psychic. She couldn't see through walls or read

minds. But it was better than nothing, better than just
waiting around for something to happen.

At first she walked straight down the middle of the
road, the soles of her shoes scuffing the faded yellow line.
She moved to the shoulder when it occurred to her this
would be a good way to get mowed down by a speeding
driver coming blind around a bend. And getting turned
into road pizza wouldn't do Pete a damned bit of good.

She walked and walked. Ten minutes passed. Fifteen.
And still there'd been no hint of civilization. No other
cars or trucks had come along. She recalled that sense
of eerie aloneness she'd experienced after getting out of
the Jetta in the general-store parking lot, as if she were
the lone survivor of some unknown apocalyptic event.
The feeling returned now, more intense than before.
She glanced over her shoulder. The general store had
disappeared from view. It was just her and this stretch of
gray road winding through a thick wilderness.

The summer sun was hot on her skin. Sweat beaded
on her brow. She pulled up her hair and arranged it in a
loose knot at the back of her head. She was glad for the
thin, breathable fabric of the skimpy halter she'd worn,
but wished she'd put on shorts this morning instead of
the tight jeans that felt so constricting now. She mopped
sweat from her brow with the back of a hand and wiped
the moisture on the jeans. She wished for a knife or a
pair of scissors. She could duck into the woods and strip
out of the jeans to cut off the legs, turn them into shorts.
What a relief that would be. Then she thought of other
things she might do with a knife or scissors and her
thoughts darkened. She imagined slitting the throat of the
fat man with a knife. Pictured herself plunging the scissor
blades into his eyes. She could almost taste his blood,
almost hear his screams. The violent fantasies triggered a
reflexive sense of repulsion, but this was short-lived. She

summoned the images again, and this time they stoked
her anger and added fuel to her determination to find
and free Pete.

She kept walking.

In a few minutes she noted the sun glinting off something some twenty yards ahead. She couldn't immediately
discern what it was. Her curiosity piqued, she quickened
her step and soon paused to pick up the object.

Frowning, she turned it over in her hands. "Huh.
Weird."

It was a piece of a woman's wallet, made of lime green
leather, with a removable section that included sleeves
for credit cards and a clear plastic frame for a driver's
license. The wallet contained a platinum Visa card and a
license for a woman named Michelle Runyon. Michelle
was pretty, with long, glossy, dark hair, pouting lips, and
cheekbones a *Vogue* model would kill for. She was from
Philadelphia. The ID gave her height as five feet seven
and her weight as one twenty. She had brown eyes, and
her date of birth was 7-11-1983.

Two years older than me.

Megan stared at the picture of the beautiful young
woman and felt a fresh sense of dread as she wondered
what had become of Michelle. She looked back the way
she'd come. Maybe Michelle had stopped at the Hopkins
Bend General Store. And maybe those horrible men just
hadn't been able to stop themselves. After all, how often
would anyone who looked like Michelle show up here?
So maybe they'd taken her. And maybe she'd chucked her
wallet out the window of their dirty old van as they'd
taken her to the same place they'd just taken Pete. An
act of desperation. Maybe someone who could help her
would find it someday? And if she couldn't be helped,
maybe her body could be found and given a proper burial.
Megan shuddered as she thought about it. The theory

felt right to her on a primal level. She was convinced it was close to what had happened.

She examined the wallet a little more closely. It was coated in dust, but did not appear to have endured the ravages of time and weather. Her thumb traced the edge of Michelle's delicate jawline.

"I'll find you if I can, Michelle. You and Pete."

As she stared at the woman's lovely image, something disturbing began to flutter around the edges of her consciousness. She frowned, struggling to get a hold on whatever it was. And then she had it. Her eyes widened. She looked at Michelle's image and thought of her own driver's license.

Soon the men who'd taken Pete would find her purse in the Jetta and see her license photo.

They would realize Pete had not been traveling alone.

They would be coming back this way.

Soon.

And *fast*.

The sound of an approaching car made her jump. She scanned the road ahead and didn't see anything. The noise grew louder and she realized it was coming from behind her. She turned and her heart leaped with joy at the sight of the slowing law vehicle.

She sniffled. "Oh, thank God."

She shoved Michelle's ID and wallet into her rear pocket as the car pulled up alongside her. The emblem on the door identified the vehicle as belonging to the Hopkins Bend Sheriff's Department. A door opened on the other side of the car. A man in a tan uniform stepped out and stared across the roof at her. He was stocky and just shy of six feet. Glasses with reflective lenses covered his eyes. A brown hat sat atop his head. He had a thick, salt-and-pepper mustache. A toothpick jutted from a corner of his mouth.

He spat the toothpick out and said, "Trouble, miss?"

Megan opened her mouth to tell the man about what had happened to Pete, but a rush of emotion surged within her and she choked on the first word. Until that moment, she hadn't realized the extent to which she'd been holding everything in. Hot tears cascaded down her cheeks as she struggled to speak.

The man came around the car and took her into his arms. She fell against him and sobbed into his jacket. He patted her back and said, "There, there. It's gonna be okay. You get it out."

Megan regained some semblance of control. She scolded herself. Right now Pete needed help, not tears. She broke the man's embrace and moved back a step. She swiped at her eyes and said, "I'm okay."

He folded his arms and stared at her. "Start from the beginning." He smiled. "When you're ready."

Megan heaved a big breath, psyched herself up, and told him everything she could remember about the incident at the general store. The man lifted a hand and stroked his chin as she talked.

When she was finished, he nodded and said, "You're talkin' about the Preston boys."

Megan shrugged. "I don't know their names. Just what they did. You sound like you know them. Any idea where they might have taken Pete?"

The man unfolded his arms and grinned. "Well, ma'am. Here's the thing. The Preston boys have a first-rate reputation in these parts. I don't for a minute believe they'd do what you're sayin' they done."

Megan gaped at him. "Wh-what?"

"Matter of fact, it sounds kinda like crazy talk to me. Are you on drugs?"

Megan made a sound of disbelief. "Oh ... my ... God. Are you serious?"

The man's expression turned hard. "Dead serious." He placed a hand on the butt of his holstered pistol. "I'm gonna need you to turn around and brace your hands against the roof of the vehicle while I pat you down."

Megan took an instinctive, unconscious step backward. "You can't—"

The man yanked his pistol from the holster and aimed it at her in a rigid, two-handed stance. His voice lashed out at her. "DON'T MAKE ME SAY IT AGAIN! TURN AROUND AND BRACE YOUR HANDS AGAINST THE ROOF OF THE VEHICLE! NOW!"

Shaking, Megan did as she was told. Tears filled her eyes again.

What else could she do?

Oh, God. Please help me.

The man stepped into position behind her and knelt. His rough hands patted their way up the length of one leg and then up the other. He then stood and slipped a hand between her legs. His fingers flexed and pushed hard against her. She sniffled. More tears came. He pushed his crotch against her upthrust ass and she felt his bulging erection. Megan's whole body shook. She couldn't believe this was happening. This man was an agent of the law. He was supposed to be helping her. Instead he was . . . *assaulting* her. The man's fingers pushed more insistently against her vagina a time or two before slipping away to roam over the front of her body. His hands cupped each of her breasts in turn, squeezing them roughly.

Then he abruptly pushed away from her.

His fingers plucked something from her pocket.

Megan gulped.

The wallet.

Before she could even begin to contemplate what he would make of that, he was wrenching her hands up behind her back and slapping on handcuffs.

He leaned into her again, whispered in her ear. "I've got you now, bitch. Got you good. That woman's been missing for weeks. I'm arresting you for suspicion of kidnapping and murder."

Megan opened her mouth to protest, but he shut her up with a swat to the back of the head. He opened the back of the cruiser and shoved her inside. After he threw the door shut, he lit up a cigarette and took his time about getting back behind the wheel.

When he was in the car again, he turned in his seat and grinned at her. "Don't you worry none about those federal and state charges, little lady." He chuckled. "Out here, we believe the local law knows best."

He laughed again and blew cigarette smoke at her through the security screen. Then he settled himself behind the wheel, put the car in gear, and did a three-point turn in the middle of the road.

Megan fell sideways on the seat, felt the warm leather press against her wet cheek as still more tears came.

The car drove back in the direction from which it had come.

Toward the sheriff's office, maybe.

Away from Pete.

Megan closed her eyes and wondered if this nightmare would ever end.

CHAPTER ELEVEN

Pete Miller was having a nightmare. Something to do with zombies chasing him through a cemetery at night. And there was someone running ahead of him. A girl. She had a kind of goth or punk look. And she was topless. It was like a scene straight out of a Z-grade horror flick on late-night cable. But the weird thing was how very real it felt. He could almost smell the stink of the rotting corpses struggling to catch up with him. And he even knew the girl's name. Melinda. She was hot as hell, but she was a stone-cold crazy bitch. The tone of the dream shifted subtly. He realized he was one of the zombies. Melinda had killed him. And now he was chasing her, burning with a primal need to rip flesh from her body with his teeth.

The van bounced through a pothole, and Pete woke up.

The vivid nightmare images stayed with him for a few moments, temporarily blotting out bleak reality. He felt he could slip back into that world for real, with just a little concentration. It was a very odd and unsettling sensation. Then he became aware of the loud rumbling of the old van's engine. Someone was sitting on his back, keeping him pinned to the floor. Couldn't be the fat man, or he wouldn't be able to breathe. This had to be one of the scrawny card players.

His eyes widened.

It all came back, every horrible moment of it. The shotgun aimed at his belly. The card players wrestling him to the floor. The heavy boot on his back. The painful crash of the shotgun's stock against the back of his head. And then the blackness. Flashing images and sensations as he slipped in and out of consciousness, usually only for a few grim seconds at a time. No longer in the store proper, but in a back room stuffed with crates and boxes. His body bent over one of the crates. His pants hauled down. The fat man on top of him. Grunting. Shoving. Cursing. The other man laughing. The blackness mercifully taking him away again. And now here, fully awake again in the back of a smelly old van, being taken God only knew where. The stark truth of it all hit him with brutal force. These men were going to kill him. They were going to do some unspeakably ugly things to him, probably, and then they were going to fucking kill him.

He suddenly longed for a return to the world of the zombie nightmare.

Or, no. Not there.

Where he really wanted to be was in the Jetta with Megan, riding fast away from this place. He wanted to go back in time and decide against taking the detour that would take them through Hopkins Bend. The detour would only have saved them an hour, and what was the hurry anyway? He liked spending time with Megan. Liked being alone with her. It was always better when it was just the two of them, with no one else around. She made him feel good about himself. Being in her presence made the world feel like a more interesting place. Vital and vibrant. Full of possibility, with a new adventure or fun revelation always just around the corner. The world was a duller place when she wasn't around. A grimmer place.

Oh, Megan.

He couldn't bear the idea that he'd seen her for the

last time. Or heard her sweet voice for the last time. Kissed her for the last time. The notion filled him with a bottomless despair. But a more pragmatic part of him hoped it was so anyway. This part of him knew the only way he'd ever see her again would be if these monsters returned to the general store to grab her, too. And that idea tore at his heart, made him feel as if an abyss had opened within his soul.

He was helpless to stop the sob that lurched out of his throat.

The man sitting on his back shifted and said, "I think the boy's wakin' up, Gil."

Pete didn't recognize the voice. Had to be one of the card players.

He twisted his head and looked up at the man. "Where are you taking me?"

The man's thin, wormy lips stretched and curled, revealing teeth stained dark yellow by decades of smoking, some of them black with untreated cavities. He held a length of rusted pipe in his hands. Pete assumed the man would rap the back of his head with it if he caused trouble. "Ain't none of your concern."

"I beg to differ."

The man's lips stretched even thinner as he snickered. "Oh, you're gonna be beggin', boy. That's for damn sure."

Someone else laughed. Something in the timbre of the sound sent a cold finger of dread down Pete's spine.

The fat man.

Gil, this one had called him.

The laugh came from the front of the van. Pete couldn't see the asshole, but he assumed the fat fucking pig of a rapist was driving. So where was the third man?

Gil made that phlegmy, throat-clearing sound Pete recalled from the general store. "We're almost there."

The van slowed and made a left turn. Gil tapped the gas pedal and the van picked up speed again, but now the vehicle jounced and shuddered in a more pronounced way. Something about the sound of the tires was different, too. Pete decided they were on a dirt road now. Great. Even deeper into the sticks. Even if Megan did manage to get away and alert the authorities, his body was never going to be found.

The van lurched to a stop.

Pete heard Gil wrench the gearshift and twist the key back in the ignition. The engine shut off, and for a moment all he heard was a twitter of birds through the van's open windows. It was an almost peaceful moment, in a strange way. Then the van lurched again as Gil opened the door and shifted his great weight out from behind the steering wheel. A moment later the van's rear doors came open, and bright sunlight made his eyes blink faster.

Pete turned his head again and looked at Gil. The big man moved closer, and his bulk nearly blotted out the sun. The pump-action shotgun was in his hands again. "Let's get this bitch out, Carl."

Carl stood up and knelt to grab a handful of Pete's sweat-soaked shirt. "Up and at 'em, faggot."

Faggot.

Huh.

Kind of a strange choice of epithet, given what had been done to him at the general store. "Fuck you."

The pipe struck the back of Pete's head hard enough to elicit a pained yelp. But even as he cried out, Pete realized the man had pulled the blow, striking him just hard enough to hurt and prod him forward without knocking him out again. He didn't bother talking back again, knowing harder, angrier blows would follow. So he got shakily to his feet and allowed himself to be

manhandled out of the van. Pete stood blinking in the
sunlight, a hand held at his brow. Gil kept the shotgun
trained on him as Carl let go of him long enough to shut
the van's doors. Then an end of the pipe jabbed against
the small of his back.

"This way, boy."

Pete sighed.

And did as he was told.

What else could he do?

They walked around the van, and Pete saw a sprawling,
ranch-style house. Surrounded by wilderness, it was the
only house in sight. So much for screaming for help or
hoping for an eventual rescue thanks to the prying eyes
of a nosy neighbor. The pipe jabbed his back again, and
the three of them walked toward the house. The front
door opened, and an old woman with a warty, fairy-
tale-witch face stepped out. She wore a dirty apron over
cutoff shorts and a bra. Her legs bore traceries of varicose
veins, and her heavily tattooed skin looked like rawhide.

"Check it out, Ma." Carl jabbed him with the pipe yet
again. "Got us another outsider for the holiday feast."

Ma eyed Pete up and down, her gaze lingering on his
crotch long enough to make him uncomfortable. Then
she snorted and said, "Put it out back with the other."

Pete frowned.

It?

The old hag disappeared back inside the house, but not
before Pete got an eyeful of the faded tattoo that covered
her back—an image of a large-breasted, nude woman
astride a Harley Davidson motorcycle.

Pete shivered.

Jesus, these are some fucked-up fucking strange-ass people.

For the first time, he wished they'd just killed him at
the start.

Another jab with the pipe got him moving again. They

went around to the back of the house, and Pete saw a row of interlinked chain-link cages. Most functioned as dog pens. The dogs growled as they approached. Pete saw Dobermans, a Rottweiler, a pit bull, a German shepherd mix, and various other mutts. They all regarded him with wary, threatening expressions. These weren't pets. They were vicious killing machines, no doubt kept and trained for blood sport. Pete had read news stories about such things.

Oh, my God, he thought. *They mean to feed me to these fucking animals.*

But Pete knew this was wrong when they reached the last pen. Another human being, naked and dirty, sat curled in a corner of the pen. A woman. Her arms were wrapped around her knees as she rocked and whimpered. She looked up at them as they approached, met Pete's anxious gaze for a moment, then looked away.

Carl fished keys from his pocket, unlocked the padlock on the pen, and grinned at Pete. "Get in, boy."

Pete just stared at the woman.

She had a slender body and looked as if she might be pretty, but it was hard to tell because her hair was matted and she was covered in grime.

Pete's whole body shook. "No. Please. No. No."

He was whining now. Couldn't help it.

He heard a whiff of air, and then Carl's pipe cracked against the back of a knee. Pete cried out and pitched forward, fell to his hands and knees. Gil stepped forward and kicked him hard in the ass with one of his heavy boots.

Pete was in the cage now.

He looked up at the woman.

She rocked faster, pressing her face between her knees.

The gate slammed shut behind him. He heard the click of the lock.

He closed his eyes, felt the rough dirt against his cheek.

Gil said, "We'll be back to check on you later, boy. Don't have too much fun while we're gone, ya hear?"

Carl cackled and then they were gone.

Pete thought of Megan.

Run, he thought.

Please.

Run and don't look back.

CHAPTER TWELVE

The look on the man's face when she came out and pointed the rifle's barrel straight between his eyes was strangely satisfying. She'd spent so much of the day as a victim, running and fearing for her life. The deadly encounter with the hunter and the Kincher boy was an anomaly, a quick and dirty minitriumph in the midst of a greater struggle, over almost as soon as it had begun. Now she was the hunter, the terrorizer, and dammit, it felt good. It also felt primitive and uncivilized, this reveling in the shock and terror playing across the face of a human being, and maybe later, if she survived, she'd look back and feel bad about this.

But right now?

Fuck, yeah.

Jessica and the man in the rocking chair stared at each other. His jaw hung slack. His eyes were wide with dumb disbelief, the dull orbs reflecting incomprehension as well as abject fear. A corncob pipe dangled from one corner of his mouth. He had a thick beard and a mop of bushy

dark hair. His clothes looked homemade. His appearance
might have made her laugh, had the circumstances been
a tad less dire.

Christ, he looks motherfucking Amish!

"You're not fucking Amish, are you?"

The man's expression shifted subtly. He was still afraid,
still wary, but a bit of the blind terror drained away. He
removed the corncob pipe from his mouth and held it
delicately between a thumb and forefinger. "No, ma'am.
Ain't no Amish in these parts."

Jessica breathed a relieved sigh. "Good. I didn't want to
have to shoot some peace-loving Amish dude. Not sure I
could live with that."

The man's gaze shifted from her eyes to the rifle and
back again. "Yes, ma'am. I can see how that'd be the case."

Jessica scowled. "Don't be a smart-ass. I'm still aiming
a loaded weapon at your face, and you better believe I
won't hesitate to put a big fucking hole between your
eyes if you do anything to make me jumpy."

The man flinched. It was a small thing, barely
noticeable. But she was glad to see it. Couldn't let him
get too comfortable, or allow herself to be lulled into
thinking she was safe. She wasn't safe. And this guy was
still the enemy.

He swallowed a lump in his throat and sat very still as
he looked her in the eye again. "Yes, ma'am."

Jessica shot quick glances to her left and right. They were
still alone here, so far as she could tell. Still, it wouldn't do
to tarry long here. She moved up onto the porch, careful
to keep out of leaping distance from the man's rocking
chair. She walked backward toward the far end of the
porch, listening to the loud creak of the wooden planks
beneath her feet. She stopped at a window and peered
inside. She saw a sparsely furnished room she guessed
accounted for maybe half the little cabin's living space.

There was a sofa, a table, and some chairs. A thick, black-covered book with red-tinted pages sat in the center of the table. A Bible, most likely.

The room was unoccupied.

Jessica breathed another relieved sigh and moved a few steps closer to the man, though she still kept a prudent distance. She looked out at the clearing, scanned the entire visible perimeter, and saw that her initial guess had been correct. They were alone. But probably not for long.

She made her face go hard when she looked at the man again. "I'm not here to fuck around. I'm gonna ask you a couple quick questions and I want immediate, no-bullshit answers. Got it?"

The man nodded, didn't say anything.

"What's your name?"

"Ben."

"Anyone else here, Ben?"

"Not just now. Wife's gone into town. Errands. Reckon she'll be gone a few hours."

Jessica nodded. "Good. That's real good to hear, Ben. I really don't want to kill more innocent people than absolutely necessary. And if you cooperate, I won't even have to kill you."

Did his jaw tremble slightly at the statement?

She thought so.

And here was that strange, primal satisfaction again. Maybe she was a monster at heart. Like Hoke.

No.

Not like Hoke.

Never like Hoke. That animal. That fucking animal.

Jessica tightened her grip on the rifle.

Ben's voice sounded strained as he said, "I . . . I certainly don't want to die."

"And I certainly don't want to have to kill you." Her voice sounded strange to her ears. Strained, in a different way, with tight, razor-wire tension. "But I will, Hoke. I fucking will, if you piss me off."

Ben frowned. "Hoke?"

Fuck.

For a moment, she trembled on the edge of a meltdown. In that moment, surrender was possible. Defeat seemed inevitable. She'd been able to put aside thoughts of the rape for much of her desperate flight. But in that moment it all came back. In vivid, Sensurround memory. Hoke's musk, that unwashed-man smell. The feel of his skin against her own as he thrust against her. The sweat beading on his brow. The way his mouth twisted, his handsome face becoming ugly.

She gave her head a hard shake and glared at Ben. "Never mind. I want the keys to that truck, Ben. Right now."

Ben's shoulders sagged. "I'll give you the keys, ma'am, but they won't do you no good."

"Bullshit."

Ben held up his hands, palms turned upward. "God's honest truth. Truck don't run."

The words were a sharp knife slammed through the center of Jessica's heart. She bit her lip to hold back a whimper. She fought hard to keep herself together. It wasn't time to give up yet. He could be bluffing. "We'll just have to see about that, Ben. Where are those keys?"

He nodded at the cabin's closed front door. "Inside, hangin' on a hook in the kitchen."

Jessica moved back a step, made a gesture with the rifle. "Stand up. We're going inside. I'll follow with the rifle at your back. Any sudden moves, and I'll put a round through your spine. Leave you paralyzed on the fucking floor. And you better believe I can do it. My daddy's a hard-core military man. Taught me everything he knew about shooting, and that's a lot."

This was mostly bluster based on half truths. Her father had given her a gun, had even taught her the basics of shooting. He hadn't, however, taught her any Special Forces stunt-shooting shit. But she figured what she'd said sounded badass enough to pull the wool over this simple hick's eyes.

Ben got shakily to his feet, looking even more frightened now than he had in those first moments. "I ain't no kind of threat to you, ma'am. I promise."

Jessica made the gesture with the rifle again. "Get moving. Keep your hands where I can see them when we're inside."

Ben nodded and wiped moisture from his mouth with the back of a shaking hand. He opened the cabin's front door and stepped inside. Jessica followed him into the cabin, keeping the rifle's barrel aimed at the small of his back. She kicked the door shut behind her. She'd at least want the warning of the creaky door opening should someone else show up unannounced. Ben walked past the table and past the weathered-looking sofa, keeping his hands up as he headed toward a closed door in the room's far-right corner.

"That the kitchen through there, Ben?"

He paused at the door, nodded. "Yes, ma'am."

"Go slow."

Another nod. "Yes'm."

He reached for the knob, turned it slowly, and pushed the door open. Then he raised his hands again and stepped through into the kitchen.

Jessica paused outside the door and watched him walk into the middle of the room, which looked to be about half the size of the sitting room. She saw a wood-burning stove and another table. Some cabinets and another door that led outside.

"Stop right there."

Ben stopped, kept his hands held up.

Jessica stepped into the kitchen. She'd just moved past the door when she sensed the quick movement to her right. Someone had hidden behind the door as Ben opened it. She began to turn, but something heavy struck a glancing blow off the crown of her skull and sent her tumbling to the floor. Her vision blurred and pain lanced up her shoulder as her side crashed against the wooden planks. She rolled onto her back in a panic, fighting to clear her head even as someone snatched the rifle from her hands. She squeezed her eyes shut, hard, and when she opened them again, she saw two men standing above her. Ben, and a younger man who might have been his brother or cousin, the similarity was so striking.

Ben was holding the rifle.

The other man held a heavy black cooking pot.

They weren't looking at her.

Probably thought she was down for the count.

Idiots.

Ben propped the rifle over his shoulder. "Took your goddamn time 'bout comin' to the rescue."

The other man shrugged. "Hell, Ben. Didn't know there was trouble till I heard the lady jawin' in the sittin' room." He glanced at Jessica. She kept her eyes at half-mast, feigning semiconsciousness. "She's an outsider."

Ben laughed. "And here it is, the holiday feast comin' up. It's our lucky day."

Feast?

What were these redneck assholes babbling about?

Hell, did it matter?

She brought her knees up to her chest and then shot her legs out, striking at the other man, who stood closest to her. Her feet smashed against one of his knees, eliciting a high yelp of surprised pain. The man dropped the pot and fell back through the open doorway. Jessica stayed in

motion, sweeping Ben's legs out from under him before
he could get the rifle aimed at her. The rifle flew from his
hands, struck the floor with a clatter. Jessica kept moving.
A hot shot of adrenaline hit her veins with a cocainelike
kick as she just kept on moving, sweeping up the rifle as
she surged to her feet.

The man in the sitting room was starting to stand up.

Jessica aimed and fired.

The round took him in the temple. Blood and brains
splashed the sitting-room table.

Almost calm now, Jessica stared down at Ben. He was
shaking. He held his hands up, palms up. Beseeching
her.

She sneered. "You lied."

She reversed her grip on the rifle and knelt to smash
the stock against his face. She heard a crackle of cartilage
as his nose gave way. The crunch of his teeth as the rifle
came down again. His mouth filled with blood. The rifle
came down yet again.

Again.

Again.

Jessica stood up after he'd stopped breathing. She
looked at the man in the sitting room. She looked at Ben.
And she shook her head. "How many of you fuckers am
I gonna have to kill today?"

She found the key ring on the hook Ben had
described.

He hadn't lied about everything.

She took a quick look around, thought for a flashing
instant about searching the place.

No.

No time to fuck around.

She went out to the truck.

CHAPTER THIRTEEN

Abby wasn't the sort to let her conscience bother her too awful much most times. Her first concern in all things was always herself. There were times when it was necessary to appear selfless, especially when it came to family matters, and so she was frequently forced to perform and behave in ways that went against her secret beliefs and desires. In earlier years, this hadn't been much of a problem. She'd been so certain her life would unfold in a particular manner. Get knocked up soon after hitting her childbearing years. Have a baby. Get knocked up again. Repeat until she was too old and fat to do it anymore. Until, she thought with the usual pang, she'd become a new incarnation of her mother, a matriarch, head of the Maynard clan and heir to a legacy of truly storied proportions.

Abby grimaced.

Yeah. Queen Shit of Shit City.

It seemed so shabby a thing to have coveted now, but once upon a time she'd actually looked forward to assuming her mother's role in the community. The Maynard name still meant something, even so many years after the arrest and subsequent electric-chair death of Evan Maynard, whose Prohibition-era trafficking of illegal hooch had netted the family a sizable fortune. Much of that money was still around, hidden in secret caches all over Hopkins Bend and the surrounding area.

Including Dandridge, where no one went anymore. The location of some of those caches went to the grave with Evan, who'd personally executed seven men he'd suspected were federal-government informants.

Abby, however, knew the location of at least one of the caches. She thought of the money she'd seen and experienced the usual little shiver of greed mixed with a sense of creeping dread. She'd counted it once. More than fifty thousand dollars in tightly curled wads of very old currency. She'd discovered the jug by accident two or three summers back, happening across the sealed Mason jar while poking around in the cellar's darkest corners during one of Ma's absences. It'd been so tempting to take the money and run from Hopkins Bend. But fear and doubt kept her from acting on the impulse. The money was so old. And it was a bright, shiny new world out there. Things were done differently out there now. Those ancient bills would draw attention, maybe cause her all manner of unexpected difficulty.

So she'd stayed put.

And now here she was, taking a stroll through the woods in an effort to clear her head of mental clutter so she could think straight. To consider whether she was truly ready to betray her family in the most profound way possible. But the question of whether she could do this wasn't what was nagging at her conscience.

No. Hell, no.

Instead, she felt bad about having lied to the dinner. She'd told it she would help it escape. And maybe she would. But maybe not. She'd conveyed a certainty she didn't feel. She hadn't made a final decision about what to do. But it didn't need to know that yet.

Michelle, she thought.

Her name is Michelle Runyon.

A woman. A human being with a God-given name.

Not a *thing*.

So strange to think that way. Abby had participated in every holiday feast for as long as she could remember. She'd always done her part, without hesitation and without squeamishness. And why not? It was just the way things were in Hopkins Bend. The way they'd always been. Growing up immersed in the traditions, you learned to think of the outsiders as nonhuman. As disposable. And, yes, as things. It wasn't too hard to pinpoint exactly when her thinking in this regard had begun to change. She guessed it had started last summer, with that boy, one of the Maynards' three contributions to that year's feast. The others had been his parents. The deaths of the adults failed to move her. But the boy was different. The Maynards had never taken one so young. He had only been twelve. She knew this because the boy's mother had screamed the words over and over in the last moments before Carol Maynard slit her throat: *He's only twelve! He's only twelve!*

But Ma was unmoved.

She slit the boy's belly open with a large carving knife as he bucked in his chains and unleashed the high, shrill scream that haunted Abby's nightmares for months.

So, yes.

It had probably started then.

Abby shivered and shunted the uncomfortable memories aside as her thoughts returned to the matter of Michelle Runyon. It wasn't hard to figure why she was entertaining thoughts of escaping Hopkins Bend with the woman. She was beautiful and fiercely intelligent. She projected an amazing strength, even gagged and chained to the rafter. Had this quality been absent, Abby might well have resigned herself to nothing more than deriving some small pleasure from molesting the woman. She'd always gotten a kick out of that. Doing things to them when they were powerless to stop her. She'd reveled in the way the warm human flesh trembled beneath her touch. But with Michelle it was different. She wanted something more. A special kind of intimacy. A wrong kind, by the local standards. And so now she wondered what Michelle thought of her.

Abby snorted.

She kicked a rock and sent it skidding into a bush.

You know what she thinks.

And she guessed that was true enough. She didn't doubt that Michelle saw her as a monster. After all, she'd experienced the brunt of Abby's always-boiling inner rage on more than one occasion. She could only hope her long, soul-baring recitation of the facts of her life could begin to turn the woman's opinion of her around. She remembered how some of the hardness had drained from Michelle's face as she'd listened to her story. And maybe it was just wishful thinking, but she felt she'd detected a glint of something like pity in her eyes toward the end. She didn't doubt the woman now felt at least some sympathy for Abby, knowing the things she'd endured in her life. What she didn't know was whether that sympathy would translate into a true willingness to help her transition into a new kind of life somewhere else. Michelle had pledged to do this. But it could be the woman was lying. Someone in her position might say anything, promise anything, to get out of that position.

She'd been walking for a while, long enough for the sun to have begun its long descent toward the horizon. She glanced up through the trees. It was still bright out. Would still be bright for another hour or two. She stopped and turned around, standing still for a moment. She looked at the trees around her. Scanned the undergrowth. It would all look the same to an outsider, an unchanging landscape of typical Southern wilderness.

But Abby knew these woods intimately. She could tell her approximate location and distance from home with nothing more than a glance at a familiar grouping of trees. Right now she reckoned she'd come almost a mile from the main Maynard cabin. As she stood there, she heard a distant crack of a rifle. It did not concern her. The hunters in this area were skilled and careful. She considered heading in the direction of the gunshot to see who was doing the shooting. It had to be one of the Crawford men, coming from that way. Could even be Mitch Crawford. She'd fucked Mitch a time or two. Maybe he'd be up for some action now. That could be just what she needed. A good, aggressive outdoor fuck. It would clear her mind, maybe be the thing to give her the courage to run or get these crazy ideas out of her head once and for all.

She took a few steps in that direction and stopped.

She'd heard something

She stood stock-still. Held her breath. Strained her ears. The sound came again. A grunt. An animalistic sound. But human. And now there was something else. A whimper. Something in the timbre of the latter suggested the source was female. She stood still for a few more moments, listening, knowing she was hearing the sounds of rutting. She turned her head to the left and saw a large thicket. The sounds were coming from the other side of the bushes. She stepped out of her sandals and moved slowly, carefully, in that direction. She reached the thicket, and then, lifting the hem of her white cotton dress, she dropped to her hands and knees, then down to her belly, and began to crawl into the thicket. She slithered between the thin and brittle branches, moving over leaves and rocks as smoothly as a snake. When she reached the other side of the thicket, she stopped, rose to her hands and knees again, and peered through branches and an obscuring cover of leaves at the couple fucking on the forest floor. Doing the very thing she'd been thinking of doing with Mitch Crawford. She became aware again of an aching, itchy horniness that had taken root within her earlier in the day and had only intensified in the hours since.

A large, muscular man with a broad, powerful back lay astride a nude woman. They were turned away from her, the man's feet pointing toward the thicket. The woman's shapely sun-browned legs were spread wide and reaching for the sky. The woman writhed, and her fingers dug into the man's shoulders as he thrust against her. Abby's breath grew short as she watched the man's taut, naked buttocks ride up and down. Her nipples hardened against the fabric of her dress. She reached beneath the hem of her dress and slipped a finger between her legs, felt the already-abundant moisture there. She touched her clit and bit down on a moan of her own. And a crazy thought entered her head—maybe the couple wouldn't mind another partner joining in? But before she could act on the impulse, she heard the woman cry out.

"Yes! Yes!"

Abby's breath caught in her throat.

She knew that voice.

It was Laura, her younger sister.

She jerked her hand away from her clit and just managed to choke back a sudden surge of nausea. The disgust she felt wasn't only because she'd become aroused while watching her baby sister fuck. That was some of it, yes, but the much larger factor was the realization of who she was fucking. She'd known there was something . . . not quite right about the man from the moment she'd spotted the couple. Though he was obviously young, there wasn't a hair on his head. However, she'd only been mildly curious about this until the moment he'd arched his back high and wrenched his head far to the side in a moment of apparently extraordinary ecstasy.

Abby's stomach lurched again.

Dear God!

It was one of the Kincher men. One of the younger ones. He had a very prominent forehead, a nose that looked made of putty, and one large eye. At least half of the latest generation of adult Kinchers had been born with just one. His body was otherwise a work of art. Hard and thick with muscle. Sculpted and perfect. But the large head and facial deformities ruined the appeal of the body. Or at least it did for Abby. Laura seemed to have a differing opinion. As Abby struggled to keep her gorge down, Laura's ecstatic cries became unintelligible, gibbering squeals. She grabbed the man's buttocks, urged him to thrust harder still, a command he obliged with enthusiasm.

Abby couldn't take it anymore.

She slithered back through the thicket, emerged standing to swipe dirt and leaves from her dress. But the disturbing tableau wouldn't leave her mind. She kept seeing her sister's legs twisting in the air. Kept seeing her slender fingers digging into the Kincher man's back. And worst of all was the memory of the man's face, twisted in an expression she guessed was ecstasy, but that somehow only made him look more horrible. Like more of an abomination.

The Garner Blight.

The phrase, as well as its relevance to the coming holiday feast, sent a chill through her as she found her sandals and slipped them on. It was something she didn't allow herself to think about much. Few ever spoke his name aloud, except during holiday season. He was the real power in these parts. Even Evan Maynard had bowed to him, and had supplied the required summer offerings every year.

Garner.

Her stomach twisted again.

She tried to shove the name out of her mind, fearing he would come to her if she consciously thought it too many times. It was said he would. Abby didn't know whether she believed it, but she did know she did not wish to find out.

Think of something else! her mind screamed at her.

She did.

She thought of her finger on her clit as she watched Laura fuck the Kincher man.

She gagged.

Dropped to her knees and pitched forward as the sickness came lurching out of her. Sweat broke over her brow, and her teeth chattered between spasms. She was so sick she never heard the sound of approaching feet, didn't realize anyone was there until she saw their shadows.

She turned and looked up at them.

Laura's leering smile was one of the ugliest things she'd ever seen. "Hi, sister. Been watching us? Enjoy the fucking show?"

They were still nude.

The Kincher man's cock was still erect, wet and dripping. Abby stared at it with a helpless fascination. She shook her head. "N-no. I was . . . I was . . ."

Laura snorted. "Oh, I know what you were doing. Guess I don't blame ya none. Wanted to see how to do it right, maybe learn somethin'. Ain't that right?"

Abby started to stand up. "I'm going home."

Laura shook her head. "Not yet." She dug an elbow into the Kincher man's ribs. "Get her."

Abby turned to run.

But the man was too fast. Was on her after just a few strides. Then he was riding her down to the ground. Flipping her over. Lifting her dress and sliding between her legs, his hardness instantly finding that still-wet place.

Then plunging in.

Abby screamed.

She screamed and screamed.

And between the screams, she could hear her sister's mocking laughter.

Abby closed her eyes, held on, and waited for it to end.

CHAPTER FOURTEEN

Turned out there was more to Hopkins Bend than the general store and endless acres of lush wilderness. A drive of less than ten minutes took them out of the woods and into a developed area that was at least vaguely recognizable as something resembling civilization. They passed houses and double-wide trailers, passed a business that rented heavy construction equipment, and then entered an area that was clearly the town's main drag. In fact, the street's name was Main Street. Megan sat up and scanned both sides of the street, looking for something, anything, to give her some small shred of hope. She saw a hardware store and a small grocery store. A pawnshop and the office of an insurance agent. A used-car dealership's parking lot drew her attention. She saw the usual array of affordable compacts. Newish Saturns and Hyundais. Accords and Subarus. All to be expected. But it was the shiny late-model foreign number that made her gaze linger. It was all sleek lines and dramatic curves. She thought it might be some model of Ferrari or Lamborghini. But that was ridiculous. Surely no one in Hopkins Bend could afford a six-figure luxury sports car.

Unless . . .

The sheriff's deputy chuckled. "I see you checkin' out that Lambo. Kind of a funny coo-inky-dink."

"What do you mean?"

Another chuckle. "That ID you found? The Lambo belongs to her. Or did, until the Maynards got hold of her."

Megan frowned. "Isn't that risky? Selling vehicles belonging to known missing persons?"

"Nah." The deputy glanced at her reflection in the rearview mirror. "Sam Brown, man who owns the place, only sells to locals. The place doubles as a chop shop. He's got an understanding with the county clerk, gets fresh tags and registrations for every outsider's car. Pretty sweet setup he's got there, actually. If the Preston boys have your ride, it's gonna end up there, too."

"So you people have every possible angle covered."

"You know it, honey."

A sense of weary resignation settled over Megan as the deputy eased the cruiser to a stop at the street's only traffic light. There was no way out of her predicament. No hope of escape or liberation. What was happening to her wasn't an anomaly. In Hopkins Bend, outsiders were fair game. They were prey. It was embedded in the culture here, probably had been for generations.

"I guess you're going to kill me."

"Ain't decided on that yet, girl. Hell, there's all kinds of possibilities for a cute little thing like you."

A shiver went through Megan at his words. The implications were obvious and troubling. She knew she was going to be raped. Repeatedly. And perhaps by multiple individuals. That was a horrible enough thing to contemplate. But rape wouldn't be the end of it. She

imagined months or even years confined in a Hopkins
Bend jail cell, an unofficial prisoner and slave of the local
law. And all the while her family would never know what
had become of her. The thought of the pain her mom
and dad would go through made her eyes water.

"You people are animals."

The deputy glanced at the rearview mirror again.
"Now, honey, you know that's out of line. I'm shocked
to hear that kind of insensitivity from a big-city gal like
you." The deputy grinned. "Aren't you people all into
being politically correct? Don't you know it's wrong to
judge other cultures?"

Megan grunted. "If by some miracle I get out of this
backward backwoods pit of hell, I believe I'm going to
be readjusting my thinking on a lot of issues."

The deputy laughed, didn't say anything.

The light turned green.

The cruiser moved through the intersection at a lazy
pace and pulled into the parking lot of a small, official-
looking building two blocks farther down the street.
There was a flagpole flying the flags of the Confederate
States of America and the state of Tennessee. Megan
didn't bother making a comment. It made total sense that
a place like Hopkins Bend had chosen to simply ignore
the outcome of the Civil War. At this point, she would
be shocked if the locals didn't still keep black people as
slaves. The small parking lot was about half-full, with two
more Sheriff's Department cruisers facing the street at
opposing angles and one civilian car, a Jetta that was a
few years older than the one owned by Pete.

Formerly owned by Pete.

The deputy pulled the cruiser into a space just to the
left of the building's front entrance. As the deputy parked
and shut the engine off, the door opened and an elderly,
gray-haired woman in a blue dress stepped outside. She

smiled and waved at the deputy as he stepped out of the cruiser. Then she came across the sidewalk and peered through a rear window at Megan.

"Oh, my. She's just darling."

The deputy smiled. "Ain't she just?"

The driver's-side door stood open. Megan heard them clear as a bell. It stood to reason the old woman would be able to hear her, too.

She drew in a deep breath.

This was probably going to be pointless.

But what the hell.

The effort would cost her nothing, and she had nothing to lose.

"Please help me. This man has arrested me illegally. He's probably going to kill me. Or rape me. Or both."

The old woman's smile broadened. "Such a lovely face. So fresh. And such a clear complexion. Where did you find her, Hal?"

"Out on Old Fork Road."

The corners of the old woman's mouth drew down to convey disappointment. "Oh, darn. I was out that way earlier. Wish I had gotten to her first. I would so love to sit on that sweet face."

The old woman licked her lips.

Megan's stomach churned.

Oh, Christ . . .

Everyone here was just demented, even the sweet-looking little old ladies.

Hal laughed. "Maybe we can work something out. I'm keeping my options open with this one."

The old woman smirked. "I bet she'd cost me a pretty penny."

"You know it, Martha."

The old woman and Hal turned away from her then and engaged in a bit of small talk. Inquiries about the health of relatives and bland comments on the weather. At last they said their good-byes, and the old woman got into the Jetta and drove away.

Then Hal opened the back door and hauled her out of the cruiser. He kept a hand on one of her cuffed wrists and steered her toward the building's front entrance. He leaned close against her, and his breath was warm against her ear as they pushed through the door into the building.

"Welcome to your new home, sweetheart."

Megan was taken aback at how quaintly rustic the building was. Two small holding cells faced an open work area containing two metal desks and three tall filing cabinets. A ceiling fan spun lazily overhead. There were no computers in sight. An office was visible through an open door. She saw a man's booted feet propped on a wooden desk. She heard a man's voice emanating from the office and had the impression she was hearing one end of a phone conversation. Something about a holiday feast coming up this weekend. Strange. There were no major national holidays happening this weekend. Had to be some local thing. And she guessed the man in the office was the sheriff. She doubted there'd be any help from him.

Hal unlocked one of the cells and pushed her inside. He followed her in to remove the handcuffs. Then he turned her around and eyed her up and down, taking his time with it, gaze lingering at the swell of her hips and the thrust of her breasts. He licked his lips and grabbed his crotch, made an adjustment.

"Take your clothes off, bitch."

Megan's whole body trembled. Tears spilled down her cheeks. She'd known this was coming, but now that the moment was actually here, it was more than she could bear.

"Please . . . don't do this. . . ." She backed away from him, moving until she felt her legs touch the metal frame of the small cot set against the back wall. "I'm begging you. Please . . ."

Hal grinned. "Oh, good. You're begging already. I always get off on that." He gripped his zipper tab and began to slide it down. "I told you to take your clothes off. It's gonna go a lot harder for you if you make me say it again."

Megan's fingers fumbled with the snap of her jeans. She had to do as he said. She knew he was right. He would make it worse for her. Worse than she could imagine. She forced her fingers to be still and at last was able to pop open the snap.

"Hold on now." This was a new voice, male, deeper than Hal's, rumbling with authority. "What's happening here?"

The other man stepped into the cell, moved past Hal to get a better look at Megan. He did a quick appraisal and uttered a low whistle. "Lord, look at her."

Hal nodded. "Yeah. I'd like to do a bit more than look, boss, if you get my drift."

This man was the sheriff. Megan knew it without having to be told, but it was confirmed a moment later when he introduced himself as Sheriff Rich DeMars. DeMars was tall and stocky, maybe an inch or two over six feet, with a big gut that was out of proportion to the rest of him. A big beer drinker, she guessed. A string tie was knotted at the collar of his starched white shirt. A large, shiny badge was pinned to the shirt's pocket. A Stetson hat sat atop his head. Basically, he looked like every northern person's ultimate nightmare image of a small-town Southern sheriff. The only thing missing to complete the picture was a fat, smoldering stogie dangling from a corner of his mouth. Didn't all corrupt good old boys smoke cigars? She knew it was a notion gleaned from a lifetime of watching old TV shows and bad movies and therefore unconnected to anything like reality. She also knew these were some pretty inane things to be thinking in a situation as dire as this one. But she couldn't help it. Her sanity was a fragile thing now, her thoughts careening from delirious absurdities to the bleakest moments of despair and back again.

DeMars shot Hal a smirk. "Maybe later, boy. And maybe not. I'm thinking we could get top dollar for this little number at the Sin Den."

Megan swallowed hard, found her voice. "What is the Sin Den?"

DeMars smiled at her. "Strip joint. Local family owns it. Big place way out in the woods. You could do a lot worse than be a dancer-whore for the Prestons."

Megan's knees went weak. She dropped onto the cot and stared up at the sheriff, her eyes beseeching him. Pleading. "Please . . . I don't want to be a . . . whore."

DeMars chuckled. "I reckon you don't." He looked her over again, smirking the whole time, his eyes alight with greed and lust. "But, honey, it ain't up to you."

The big man steered a disappointed-looking Hal out of the cell. "Come on, ol' buddy. I got a call to make. And don't look so hangdog." He chuckled again. "Hell, maybe I'll let you have a go at her before we haul her out to the titty bar."

Hal's grin returned as he stared at her through the cell's bars. "I like the sound of that. Can't wait to bust my nut in that hot little cooze."

Megan's stomach twisted again.

She turned down on her side and stretched out across the cot, feeling its springs dig into her hip. She closed her eyes and tried to will the world away. She was tired. So very tired. Physically tired from the long car ride

and the walk down that lonely country road. Weary
from worrying about Pete. And sick unto death of being
appraised and discussed by the people of Hopkins Bend
as if she were nothing more than a piece of meat.

The cell door clanged shut.

Megan didn't hear it.

She had already slipped into the world of dreams.

Things were no better there.

CHAPTER FIFTEEN

Hoke Mitchell awoke with a scream on his lips. The
scream felt like a coiled and rusty chain being ripped
from his lungs in one long, savage yank. The force of the
primal terror driving the thunderous exhalation from his
lungs strained every muscle in his body, set every nerve
ending afire. He lurched into a sitting position as the
scream died, breathing hard, sweat pouring from his brow
and into his eyes. The terror generated by the screaming
nightmare still held him firmly in its grip. Even so,
he needed barely more than a second to realize that
something odd and unexpected had occurred during his
time behind the veil of sleep.

The pigs were gone.

The barn was quiet.

And every article of clothing had been stripped from
his body. He stood up and took a look around. No sign of
the clothes. His heart sped up as a singularly disquieting
idea gripped him. He slapped a hand behind him, probed
at his asshole with a finger, and breathed a sigh of relief. It
did not feel violated. He would not have been surprised

to find evidence to the contrary. Still, it was strange. Why had they taken his fucking clothes? Perhaps they assumed basic modesty would render him less likely to flee. Which only proved how little these backward sons of bitches knew about Hoke fucking Mitchell.

Modesty was not one of his virtues.

Hoke started toward the barn door, which still stood wide open, letting in the bright sunlight. The intensity of the light had dimmed a tiny bit. He reckoned nightfall would be here within an hour or so. His best bet was to get into the woods and hide until then, then maybe see about making it back to civilization under cover of darkness.

He reached the barn door and came to a dead stop.

Hoke stared.

Hoke said, "Gulp."

Well, here was the answer to the mystery of the missing pigs. The little pink bastards were arrayed in a loose-knit group outside the barn door. They were not snuffling around and cavorting in the usual manner of your usual carefree pigs. The eyes of each animal turned to regard him with expressions that conveyed equal measures of malice and warning. The identical expressions of the animals hinted at a weird kind of group intelligence. A hive-mind kind of vibe. Each eye followed him as he stepped out of the barn, tracking him with the keen and deadly patience of a combat sniper. Hoke was no animal-behavior expert, but he was pretty sure this was not the sort of thing pigs would normally do. Or *ever*, really. The scrutiny of the animals was deeply unsettling, but he wasn't about to let that stop him.

Shit, man. They're just piggies.

He stepped forward, intending to thread his way through the animals. There really weren't that many of them. He should be beyond them and streaking toward the woods within seconds. He adjusted his thinking on the matter when one of the smaller animals came scuttling forward and nipped at his instep.

"Ouch! You little motherfucker!"

He hopped a time or two, grimacing at the pain, then kicked out at the animal as it came back into range. His wounded foot connected with its hard little belly and the little guy crashed into a couple of his buddies and knocked them down. He recognized he was still in a desperate situation. Probably a life-and-death kind of deal. But for a moment it didn't matter, as he was unable to hold in a burst of maniacal laughter.

"Pig bowling!"

But the moment of mirth was short-lived. The little pig regained its footing and came toward him again. Slower than before. Dark eyes pulsing with hate. This time its buddies came with him. Two of the larger animals hovered near the little guy in an almost touching gesture of protectiveness. The big ones snorted and bared their teeth. The way their snouts crinkled when they did this creeped him right the fuck out. The aura of menace the animals projected was incredible.

They looked . . . evil.

"This is some bullshit right here. Look, fellas. I ain't about to be bullied by a pack of satanic fucking pigs. Y'all done fucked with the wrong motherfucking drummer."

He took a step toward them again.

Bared his own teeth and growled.

He raised a fist to convey a willingness to kick some serious pig ass, fully expecting the squat little animals to recognize his natural physical superiority and get the hell out of the way. But the pigs did not back down. One of the larger ones squealed and charged him, the others following immediately in its wake.

Hoke let out a shrill scream.

Turned.

Ran.

And sought shelter in the first likely looking place he saw, one of the empty horse stalls at the other end of the barn. He ran into the stall, threw the door shut, and whimpered with relief as he heard the metal latch click home. Some of the pigs thumped against the wooden stall door, making it rattle in its frame.

The door stayed shut.

Hoke dropped to the hay-strewn ground. He crossed his legs and hugged himself, shaking as hard as he had in the first moments after waking from that terrible dream. The one in which . . . in which . . .

Hoke stopped shaking.

His throat constricted, and his heart skipped a beat.

And he breathed the name: "Garner."

A voice spoke behind him, a throaty whisper barely audible above the squealing of the pigs. "Right here, son."

Hoke knew there'd been no one else in the stall a moment ago.

But there could be no denying it—Garner was here anyway.

And he . . . he was . . .

Hoke shivered and stared at the ground.

Garner chuckled. "You and me have some things to talk about, son. So don't you go passing out on me again."

Hoke heard the soft crunch of straw as the man's booted feet moved toward him. His helpless shaking increased. Being this close to that thing made him want to leap out of his own skin. A glint of light off something to his left drew his attention. He squinted and leaned toward it. The object was partially covered in the straw. What he could see of it was smooth and gray, with a kind of curve to it that was suggestive of . . .

Hoke leaned to his left, brushed the obscuring straw away.

He froze.

An age-polished human skull leered at him. There was a hole at the crown. Maybe a bullet hole. But the way the edges of the hole were so splintered suggested something else. The strike of a pickax, perhaps? Garner was standing right behind him now. The skin at the back of Hoke's neck drew tight. His hands curled into hard fists. He gritted his teeth and tried not to scream again.

"Leave me alone." Barely able to breathe, he pushed the words through his teeth. "Please . . ."

He stared at the skull, tried to imagine how it might feel to have the heavy blade of a pickax slammed into your head.

"Turn around, son. We'll talk now."

Hoke gave his head a single emphatic shake. "No. I don't want to. Please. I don't want to see you. You can't make me."

Garner laughed softly.

He said, "Oh, but I can."

And then he did.

CHAPTER SIXTEEN

A cautious peek through the cabin's front door verified that her luck was still holding out. No one had come running to investigate the sound of the gunshots. Someone was watching over her. Or maybe not. On second thought, it wasn't as miraculous as it seemed on first blush. A rifle's report would not be a remarkable or unsettling sound in any rural, wooded environment. Still, she knew she couldn't afford to drag her heels. Someone would be along soon enough.

She took a deep breath.

Stepped outside.

Exhaled.

And eyed the old truck, which was parked maybe ten yards away, roughly parallel to the porch, its front end pointed toward a narrow gap in the trees surrounding the clearing. The truck looked as if it might have been a deep shade of red once upon a time. Back during the Eisenhower administration, perhaps. But all the rust made it hard to tell. Its metal skin was pockmarked with holes. The rust had eaten clean through the old sheet metal in many places.

A flutter of anxiety tickled her stomach as she stepped off the porch and hurried toward the truck. Maybe Ben had told her the truth about it. *No.* She couldn't accept that. It would start, by God. It *would*. She would fucking *will* its old engine to turn over, if necessary. The heap was her ticket home, was maybe her only viable means of deliverance from this rural hell.

Keeping the rifle raised, she circled the truck for a quick closer inspection. The tires were all bald or balding, with barely any detectable tread left on most of them, but none of them were flat. She wouldn't waste time checking the engine. It would either start or not.

Time to find out.

A groan of tired metal assailed her ears as she pulled open the driver's-side door. She set the rifle on the seat and climbed inside. Once she was ensconced behind the big steering wheel, she gripped the wiggly door handle and yanked the door shut. It closed with a resounding metallic thunk that was louder than expected and made her jump. The worn and ratty bench seat was too high, and her feet dangled inches above the pedals.

"Shit."

She reached under the seat and found the adjuster bar. It seemed hopelessly stuck at first, but after a few frantic yanks she was able to lower the seat closer to the pedals. The steering wheel was now a little higher than she'd like it to be, but what the hell, at least she'd be able to drive without scrunching down like some kid playing grown-up behind the wheel of her parents' car.

Another deep breath.

And now for the moment of truth.

She looked at the old key, rubbed her thumb across the raised Ford emblem, and breathed a quick prayer to the automotive gods. On an impulse she raised it to her lips and kissed it. Then she inserted it in the ignition slot, muttered one last beseeching prayer, and turned the key.

The engine sputtered. Once. And another time.

It didn't turn over.

Jessica's left hand gripped the steering wheel hard as she turned the key again. The engine sputtered again. And stopped again. She felt something like panic stirring inside her, an unwanted intruder tapping on her psyche's brittle back door. But she wouldn't let it in. No, not yet. She was sure the engine's gasps had been livelier last time.

She turned the key back and paused a moment. She stared at the truck's scratched and dented dash, imagined for a moment that she was addressing a sentient creature. "Come on, you old bitch. Give it up for Mama."

She turned the key again.

The engine sputtered.

Sputtered and caught, filling the clearing with the throaty rumble of old-time Detroit-manufactured muscle. Jessica let out a whoop and clapped her hands together. Long-ingrained instinct made her reach for the seat belt. Her fingers brushed age-grimed seat leather. There was no seat belt. Or if there was one, it was buried somewhere deep in the crease between the seat back and the bench. No time to dig for the fucking thing. No time for anything but acceleration.

She reached for the wheel-mounted gearshift, wrenched it over to the appropriate position. "Fuck it. We're riding hell-for-leather."

Hell-for-leather.

A laugh surprised her.

It was a thing her father used to say. She'd never been sure what it was supposed to mean. But the phrase seemed somehow right for the situation.

She pressed the gas pedal down and steered the old Ford toward the gap in the trees. A moment later, she was on a very narrow, rutted dirt road. She didn't know what she'd do if another car or truck approached from the other direction. The road was just barely wide enough to accommodate a single vehicle, a fact emphasized now by the scrape of low-hanging tree branches against the truck's metal hide. The possibility of someone blocking her path out of this nightmare country unnerved her for a moment.

A very brief moment.

Because she knew damn well what she would do.

She saw it in her head. *Another car, some other old jalopy, comes around a bend in the winding road. Stops. She watches the other guy get out. She makes a quick assessment. He's local. No one local can be trusted. She throws the door open, yanks the .38 from her waistband, and shoots the other guy dead, no questions asked. Then. No time to fuck around. Grabs the rifle and takes the other guy's car. She keeps moving. Never stops. Never looks back. Getting home again by any means necessary.*

More nervous laughter.

Christ, I'm turning into the fucking Terminator.

She'd killed at least four people today. Maybe five. She

remembered the first shot she'd fired into the woods in those last moments before the Kinchers showed themselves. Remembered that flicker of movement and that thump like a falling body. *Probably five.* Either way, it was a hell of a body count for a woman who'd never fired a weapon in anger (or fear) prior to today. And there was something else to consider. Something nearly as disturbing as the actual fact of the killings themselves. She would never have guessed herself capable of such ruthlessness, of such near savagery. An image of Ben's smashed-in face made her grimace.

Just don't think about it, she told herself. *There'll be time for thinking and probably lots of fucking therapy later. Maybe.*

Right now, she should only concern herself with staying focused and getting free.

Some of the tension gripping her slipped away as the road began to perceptibly widen. She steered the Ford around another curve and felt even more relief. Just up ahead, maybe thirty yards farther along, the narrow road intersected with a significantly wider, paved road. Jessica began to feel something like triumph as she rolled up to the paved road.

Then the other car came streaking by.

Jessica gasped and jammed the Ford's brake pedal to the floor. The old truck rocked and skidded to a halt on the dirt road. At the same time, she heard the gritty growl of the other car's tires squealing on blacktop. She looked to her left and saw that the other car had fishtailed to a stop.

Its driver's-side door flew open.

A man came charging out of it.

He had something in his hands. A pump-action shotgun. She looked at his car. Those flashing lights above the roof. She looked at his face. Those eyes unreadable behind reflective lenses. His face grim, jaw set.

So close.

Less than twenty yards away.

He would be able to see her now. Would know she was an outsider.

Jessica seized the Ford's steering wheel and cranked it hard to the right even as she stomped on the gas pedal. The truck lurched onto the paved road and shot forward. A second or so later, the rear window exploded in a hail of shattered glass. The boom of the shotgun was an afterthought in her ringing ears.

Jessica screamed.

The wheel spun out of her hands.

She grabbed it again and cranked it hard to the right, missing a chase-ending crash by a millisecond. She glanced at the rearview mirror and saw that the cop was no longer shooting at her. He was running in the other direction. He would be back behind the wheel of his cruiser shortly. In another moment he would be after her. And he would catch her, she had no doubt. This old heap would be no match for a modern law-enforcement vehicle.

This time panic didn't just tap at her psyche's back door.

It bulled in, flash-frying her nerves in an instant as she fought to regain the edge that had taken her this far. Another glance at the rearview mirror showed her the cruiser was after her now. Its siren came on, piercing her ears like a drill.

Stop, she thought.

Stop and get out.

Grab the rifle and start shooting.

And why not? What would one more count of murder or attempted murder mean at this point? She looked at the rifle. Thought about it some more. Chewed her lower lip. Fretted. And she just didn't quite have the nerve.

This wasn't the same thing as tangling with backwoods rednecks. She was actually running from the law. A trill of mad laughter escaped her lips. If only her dead mother could see her now. Her little girl. Fugitive and stone-cold killer.

Her eyes misted.

Oh, Mom.

I miss you so fucking much. But maybe we'll be seeing each other sooner than expected.

Another glance at the rearview mirror revealed an unsettling truth. The cruiser was right on her ass now. Not that it mattered. She had no intention of giving up or going down easy. It was just about blaze-of-glory time. Despair gripped her at the sight of more flashing lights dead ahead. Two more cruisers parked at angles, blocking the way out.

What the fuck?

No fucking way the local law could have organized a roadblock for her that fast. It was intended for someone else. Or had been. Didn't matter. It was her roadblock now. And there was no denying she had damn near reached the end of the road. Her luck had finally run out.

But she didn't slow down.

There were other cops or deputies on the opposite sides of the vehicles. Various weapons were aimed in her direction.

Jessica crossed herself.

She pulled the .38 from her waistband.

Waited another heartbeat, just long enough to make out a face.

Then she put her gun hand through the open window.

Aimed. And fired.

CHAPTER SEVENTEEN

The Kincher boy shot his seed deep inside her, bucking away at her with a pure animal frenzy that exceeded anything in Abby's experience. The force of his pelvis thrusting against her, mashing her hard into the ground, caused excruciating pain. The pain was exacerbated by the sharp rock wedged into the small of her back. Each powerful thrust was accompanied by a corresponding stabbing sensation. Her blood leaked onto the ground. The boy's frenzy increased as he came, his loud grunts giving way to a horrible, mangled scream, a sound that seemed to Abby like the shrieking of a demon. Then, spent, he thrust against her a few final times, slower, shaking and sighing as he grinned at her, the awful, distorted curl of his elongated mouth a promise of nightmares to come.

The boy climbed off her and staggered over to a tree stump, where he sat and continued to grin as he worked to catch his breath.

Laura stood over her. Arms crossed beneath her bare breasts. A smirk on her face. "You done got the shit fucked right out of you." She laughed and the smirk deepened, curling in a way that was almost as ugly as the Kincher boy's satiated grin. "Shoulda heard yourself screamin', girl. Bet you came ten times."

Abby glared at her. "Wasn't screamin' 'cause I liked it."

Laura snorted. "Uh-huh. You keep on tellin' yourself lies. It's what you're good at."

Abby looked at her sister, struggled to contain the rage boiling inside her. She had never exactly loved Laura, but she was family, and she'd felt something like affection for her. But now that was gone, replaced by a black hate she felt deep in her heart. She sensed it wasn't a fleeting thing. This hate was permanent. And she knew there was only way to keep it from eating her alive.

"I'm gonna kill you."

Laura flinched.

She looked into Abby's eyes, saw the burning hatred there, and for a moment looked genuinely afraid. Then she shook herself and the smirk returned. "Hell you are. You might wanna kill me, you miserable old bitch, but you ain't got the balls."

She dropped to her knees, wrapped a hand around Abby's throat. "But I could kill you, you useless cunt." Laura's face went hard, made her look far older than her seventeen years. She tightened her grip on Abby's throat, making her gag. "I could kill you now, and nobody would care. Nobody would miss you for a second, and you fucking know it. You're a waste of air. A failure."

Abby grabbed Laura's wrist, tried to twist her hand away from her throat.

Laura just dug her fingers deeper into the tender flesh. "That the best you can do, girl? I could really do it, ya know. Just keep squeezin' till you're gone. And you wouldn't be able to stop me. Know why?"

Abby whimpered.

Laura leaned closer, leering at her now. "I'll tell you why. It's because you're weak. You're weak, and I'm strong. And that's why I'm gonna have everything you were supposed to get. And when I'm in charge, things are gonna change. Ma tolerates you, just lets you sit around the house and mope. I ain't gonna have that, sister baby. No sir. You're gonna have to pull your weight or pay the price."

She leaned closer still, her lips almost grazing Abby's mouth. Her voice dropped to a register so low it was nearly inaudible.

But Abby heard it.

And what Laura said was "If I was in your shoes, I'd maybe think about leavin'. For good."

Laura let go of her throat and Abby sat up, gasping for breath.

Laura stood and left without another word, the Kincher boy trailing after her.

Abby touched the tender, bruised flesh of her throat and thought about what Laura had said. She would take her sister's advice. Only she would not be leaving with her tail between her legs. And not without extracting her promised pound of flesh. She felt shame and more than a little self-disgust. In other circumstances, the younger girl would not have handled her in so dominating a manner. It was hard to be strong in the aftermath of a violent assault, and so easy for the aggressor to press the advantage. But the tables would turn, and, she swore to herself, Laura would soon know how it had felt to be in her position today.

A large bird flew across the sky, just visible through the latticework of tree limbs. She watched it disappear and envied its freedom.

Tears touched Abby's eyes.

Soon, she swore.

Soon I'll be free.

She got to her feet, wobbled for a second, but managed to remain upright. She pushed the hem of her dress down and tried not to be sick as she felt some of the Kincher boy's juice trickle down her thigh. But it was no use. A wave of nausea drove her back to her knees as a horrific possibility struck like a sudden and violent thunderclap: what if the boy's tainted seed took root inside her?

Oh, God . . .

She shook, and fat droplets of sweat beaded on her brow.

It would just fucking figure. The ultimate slap in the face from fate. And yet so perfectly in keeping with the way her life had gone so far. Some twenty men had found their way to satisfaction between her legs. None had used any sort of protection. And yet she'd never become pregnant. Now she hoped she was simply physically incapable of getting knocked up. Because the thought of carrying a Kincher man's child was more than she could bear.

I'd rather die.

The thought so disturbed her she knew there was only one thing to do.

Go to the seer.

Mama Weeks.

Yes.

Now.

Abby hitched in a deep breath, shoved herself upright again, and turned in a slow, woozy circle. She was still disoriented and needed a moment to get her bearings. Then she spotted a familiar, crooked old tree, with big, low branches that hung almost to the ground.

She wiped sweat from her brow and set off toward the east.

Toward the domicile of the ancient and revered Cassie Weeks, known to all in these parts as Mama Weeks.

The fortune teller.

Chapter Eighteen

Some time had passed. He wasn't sure how long. The sun was sinking toward the horizon, its dimming rays staining the sky pretty shades of violet and orange. It was an image he'd like to see on a beach, maybe standing at the water's edge with Megan, his arm draped around her small, almost bony shoulders, the warm tide lapping at their bare, sand-coated feet.

Yeah, the beach would be nice.

Somewhere in Florida, down in the Keys.

Or maybe even Hawaii, spending their honeymoon lolling in the lush tropical paradise. It was a tempting, sweet vision. And a bitter irony. Not so long ago the notion of marriage, specifically to Megan, had frightened him. Had borderline repelled him, to be honest about it. And now, scarcely more than two hours since he'd last contemplated the qualities his eventual wife should possess, none of them embodied by Megan Renee Phillips, he couldn't imagine anything he would like more.

Life could be a real kick in the pants at times.

You spend all your time working hard to steer clear of something, avoiding even the merest mention of the subject, and then something big happens, a tragedy or some other major event. Something that clears away all the bullshit in one big swoop and forces you to face that hidden truth, to deal with it once and for all.

Right then, Pete decided he would propose to Megan if, through some unfathomable miracle, he should ever find himself in her presence again.

The thought galvanized him.

I'm getting the fuck out, one way or another.

He surged to his feet and strode purposefully toward the locked gate of the pen. He grabbed the padlocked latch and rattled it, testing its strength. It barely budged. He looked up and eyed the coils of barbed wire strung across the top of the cage. The chain-link fencing stood maybe a dozen feet high. He was more than fit enough to climb it. That wasn't the issue. The question was what to do once he reached the top. Hell. He would just have to position his body as well as possible and sling himself over the top. His flesh would get shredded by the barbed wire. There was just no way around that. But he thought he could endure the pain. *Hoped* he could endure the pain. For Megan. For both of them, and for the life they might have together.

Pete reached high over his head, curled fingers through chain links. He took a deep breath and tensed his muscles, psyching himself up for what he had to do. Dredging up the mental strength to face the searing pain of the barbs piercing and ripping his flesh.

You can do it, he told himself.

For Megan.

He pictured her smiling face, the cute dimples at the corners of her mouth A shiny shade of lipstick making her lips glisten, inviting a kiss.

It was all he needed.

Pete began to hoist himself up.

"You better not."

The soft voice was devoid of inflection, but something in the warning it carried stopped him long enough to let go of the fence and turn toward the young woman sitting in a rear corner of the cage. It was the first time she'd spoken. The first time she'd even acknowledged him. He'd tried to engage her soon after the departure of Carl and Gil, but she had been unresponsive to the point of near catatonia. He'd given up after the first several conversational gambits, not feeling much like talking himself at that point.

But now that she'd broken the ice, his curiosity was piqued. He walked over to her and squatted in front of her. "Why not?"

She still wouldn't look him in the eye. She kept her arms wrapped around bruised and scraped knees and stared at the ground, rocking in a strange, herky-jerky movement. It was as if there was something inside her she was fighting to contain, something she didn't dare let out, lest it destroy her. And the harder she fought against it, whatever it was, the less she was aware of him.

A full minute passed.

Then another.

"Okay. Don't tell me."

Pete started to rise, but she grabbed him by a wrist and pulled him back down. She stopped rocking and leaned close to his face, her warm, rank breath making his nose curl. He wondered how long it'd been since she'd brushed her teeth. Days? Weeks?

Longer?

Jesus . . .

Her eyes were wide and livid, filled with a terrible knowledge of things Pete was sure he did not want to know about. He trembled in her grip, wishing now she'd kept staring at the ground instead.

Her voice as she spoke was still quiet, but there was no longer anything else soft about it. It was hard and brittle at the same time, vibrating with an unstable, electric intensity. "If you climb, the dogs will bark. They will growl and howl. And if the dogs howl, *they* will come. And if they come, you and I will be punished." And now she smiled, a sick, forced twisting of lips, a terrible perversion of soiled beauty that rivaled Gil's pudgy, dead-eyed leer for the title of most disturbing expression he'd ever seen on a human face. "We will be tortured. Maybe even killed."

Pete swallowed hard. "Jesus . . . fuck . . ."

She let go of his wrist, and he fell backward onto his ass.

She watched him, that sick smile diminished some but still there. "Yes. Jesus has fucked us. This is hell."

Pete wiped moisture from his mouth and scooted backward a few feet. He regarded her warily. Yes, she was a victim, too, and worthy of his pity. But her sanity seemed to have shifted free of its moorings at some point during her ordeal. Her whole manner was that of an utterly deranged person. For all he knew, she might raise the alarm herself if he tried to climb out of here now.

So . . . slight change of plans.

He would wait until she was asleep. Even crazy people had to sleep at some point. He could even feign sleep himself, watch her through half-open eyes until she stretched out and nodded off. It would be better than having to interact with her again in any way. But for now he would allow her to think he'd seen the wisdom in her words.

He forced a nod. "Yeah. Hell. I think you're right."

She licked her lips. "When the sun goes down, you'll fuck me."

"What?"

Her smile shifted subtly, hinted at a twisted eroticism. "When the sun goes down, you'll fuck me."

Pete appraised her again. Cleaned up, she would be very pretty. Perhaps even beautiful. She had a nice figure and a pretty face underneath the grime and the stench. A few showers and a few generous applications of an expensive shampoo would render her dark, matted hair glossy and lush. In another life, another setting, her come-on would have been damn near irresistible.

But here and now?

Like hell I'll fuck you, you goddamn psycho.

But she didn't need to know that yet. It occurred to him he should distract her somehow, steer the conversation in a less-disturbing direction. "I don't even know your name. I'm Pete, by the way."

The woman smiled. "I'm Justine."

"Nice to meet—"

"That's the name you'll be crying out in a little while. Do you like the sound of it?"

"Um . . ."

Justine laughed.

Pete knew he should stop talking now, but a helpless compulsion kept his mouth in motion. "How did you wind up here, Justine? I can tell by your accent you're not from these parts."

Justine's eyes glittered with mad amusement. "You enjoy the sound of my voice?"

Pete didn't bother suppressing the groan that came then.

For fuck's sake, lady.

She laughed again and leaned closer to him, making him cringe. "You're right, Petey Pete." Her voice took on an exaggerated Southern drawl. "I ain't from round these here parts."

Yet more mad laughter ensued.

As did more mad talk.

This time Pete didn't take the bait. He kept his mouth shut and kept one eye on the sun as it continued its slow exit from the warm Southern sky.

CHAPTER NINETEEN

Jessica got off just the one shot before the lawmen on the other side of the roadblock returned fire. The truck's windshield exploded as bullets penetrated. One buzzed by her ear. Jessica screamed and cringed. The .38 fell from her hand and went tumbling into the ditch. The steering wheel slipped from her grip, and the truck veered sharply away from the angled cruisers. The top of her head smacked the truck's roof as its wheels bounced through the ditch. Her feet found the brake pedal and jammed down hard mere moments before the truck's front end struck a tree, bringing her desperate dash to freedom to a sudden, violent halt as the force of the impact propelled her body against the steering wheel. This knocked the breath from her lungs and sent shock waves of pain lashing through her body. She felt as though she had been hit by a freight train.

She pushed herself away from the steering wheel and fell sideways across the seat. Her throat burned as she struggled to pull in a breath. At first she heard only the dying whine of the old truck's engine, but other sounds became audible as the engine gave up the ghost with a final, rattling clunk. Voices. One on a radio, heard through a crackle of static. Another somewhere close by—one of the lawmen urging caution as they drew closer to the truck. And now she heard a crunch of twigs beneath booted feet. A desperate, burning terror stole into her heart. They were so close. Within moments they would have her. She did not want to think about what might happen to her then. Some distant voice inside her urged her to action again, a fading echo of the drive that had brought her this far. The voice told her to drag her battered body through the shattered windshield and flee again into the woods. And Jessica ached to do just that, but the collision with the steering wheel had at least temporarily robbed her of her strength. Get up and crawl through the windshield? Right. Right now she could barely breathe. Even the slightest movement unleashed yet another whipcrack of pain.

A groan of rusted metal made her gasp. She lifted her head and saw a lawman's arm poking through the suddenly open driver's-side door. The barrel of a service revolver was aimed at her belly. Then the cop poked his head in, saw she was no longer a threat, and visibly relaxed. He turned his head and called over his shoulder to the other cops. "Stand down. Bitch is down for the count."

Jessica didn't know where it came from.

The strength.

It was just there.

Strength and a cold, black fury.

Her leg shot out, the sole of her shoe connecting with the lawman's nose as his head turned back toward her. She heard a satisfying crack of bone as his nose splintered. And she saw blood fountain from his nostrils as he cried out and staggered backward, collapsing to the ground. Jessica's eyes went to the truck's floorboard. The lawman had dropped his gun. It was wedged beneath the gas pedal. This time survival instinct overwhelmed pain. She summoned strength again, twisted around on the seat, and dove for the gun. The lawmen were screaming at her, violent exhortations to get the fuck out of the fucking truck and get down on the fucking ground right fucking now. But the men stopped yelling when they saw her moving in the truck. She heard a *pop-pop-pop* as they discharged their weapons. Jessica cringed below the level of the seat, wincing as bullets thunked holes through metal. This was it. She was seconds away from dying. She had the gun, but it was useless to her now, because she couldn't hope to get into a position to return fire, not without instantly being shot down. Her stomach twisted as her flesh anticipated how it would feel to have high-caliber slugs ripping through it.

The whole of her awareness was so concentrated on the prospect of imminent, painful death that she never heard the approach of the other vehicle. But she did hear the subsequent violent rending of metal and shattering glass as it struck the cruisers still blocking the road. The lawmen were screaming again, but it was evident their focus was elsewhere now. Jessica crawled out of the truck and stared down at the lawman she'd kicked in the face. He wasn't breathing and his eyes were turning glassy. It didn't seem possible that she'd killed a man with a single kick to the face. But his body was untouched by stray bullets. She'd killed him, all right. Maybe the blow had driven a bone fragment into his brain. Whatever the case, he was dead.

But the others . . .

Their backs were turned to her now. Another truck, an old one that closely resembled the one she'd stolen, had crashed into the parked cruisers. A man's bloody body lay across the hood. So here was the guy they'd set up the roadblock to catch. He looked like he was already half-dead. One of the lawmen sealed the deal by stepping up to the truck's crumpled hood and putting a bullet through his brain.

Jessica raised the service revolver and fired until it was

empty. The lawman closest to her went down first, taking a bullet square in the middle of his back. The other man spun toward her and got off one shot that went wide. Then a bullet went through his open mouth and sent a rain of blood and brains out the back of his head.

Jessica lowered the gun and walked into the street to survey the carnage.

She thought for a moment, realized she was close to losing count of how many people she'd killed today, and decided it no longer mattered. These weren't people to her anymore. They were just obstacles. If she had to kill a hundred more to get free of this place, she would do it.

But to get free, she needed to get moving again. A cruiser was parked at the side of the road, probably the one driven by the cop who had originally spotted her. It was the only still-operational vehicle in the immediate vicinity. She didn't relish the idea of fleeing in a cop car, but she was out of other options.

She exchanged the empty pistol for a loaded one, prying it from the stiffening fingers of a dead lawman. She took some spare bullets, too, and stood up. Then she took a step toward the intact cruiser and winced, her knees buckling beneath her. With the adrenaline of the moment fading, the pain had come back. She drew in a wheezing breath and continued to hobble toward the cruiser. Each step triggered another jolt of pain. It was worse when she paused to kneel again and retrieve a dropped pump-action shotgun. She felt faint for a moment and almost keeled over. But she got herself upright again and staggered the rest of the way to the car. She slipped behind the wheel and set the guns and bullets on the passenger seat.

Her eyes surveyed the array of unfamiliar cop equipment on the dash. A strained voice squawked through a burst of static over the radio. Keys dangled from the ignition slot. The engine was still running. Jessica put the car in gear and swung out into the road, twisting the steering wheel until she was pointed away from the roadblock. Her fingers curled around the steering wheel as she stared at the empty stretch of road ahead. A road that wouldn't remain empty very much longer. She tapped the gas pedal and the car rolled forward, picked up speed.

She had no idea where she was going.

Her ribs hurt like a son of a bitch. Some of them were cracked, or maybe worse.

She was in perhaps the most conspicuous getaway car in the history of getaway cars.

But she was alive.

Goddammit, she was still alive.

She gritted her teeth and drove.

CHAPTER TWENTY

Megan was still floating somewhere on the edges of sleep when some part of her mind perceived the sound of a key turning in a lock and urged her to consciousness. Her eyes fluttered open and she fuzzily saw the cell door swing inward. Deputy Hal strode into the cell, unsheathing something from his belt as he approached Megan. Alarm bells clanged in Megan's head and she came fully awake, sitting up abruptly on the narrow and uncomfortable cot.

Hal twirled the nightstick in his hand and flashed a dead-eyed, oily smile. "On your feet, cunt."

Megan flinched.

It was the first time a man had ever called her a cunt

to her face. Being called a cunt could never be a pleasant thing, but the epithet itself didn't bother her so much as what it symbolized—the complete lack of respect anyone here had for her.

Hal poked her shoulder with the nightstick, hard enough to hurt. "Hey, bitch. I know you're not deaf. Get on your feet, you stupid cunt." Her pained expression made him grin, and he twirled the nightstick again. "Unless you want me to start breaking bones?"

A sneer twitched at a corner of her mouth. "What good would I be at the Sin Den, then?"

The grin dropped from his face as rage stole into his features. "Fuck you. You should be mine. Goddamn sheriff."

Megan slowly licked her lips, taunting him. "Careful what you say, Hal. It might get back to the man in charge. I bet he wouldn't—"

He snarled and came at her then, grabbing Megan by an arm to roughly jerk her to her feet. He leaned close to her, warming her face with his hot, tobacco-redolent breath as he whispered into her ear. "You asked for this. Remember that."

He dragged her into the middle of the cell and said, "Bend over and grab your ankles."

Her eyes went wide. "No. Why—?"

The nightstick cracked against the back of a knee, making her cry out as she dropped to the floor, banging her knees against the dirty concrete. He grabbed the collar of her shirt and jerked her to her feet again, causing the thin fabric to stretch and tear a little.

Hal brandished the nightstick again. "Your ankles. Don't make me say it again."

Megan whimpered and did as instructed. She was fit and flexible, so it was easy enough to do, but it stretched the muscles in her legs and made the place struck by the demented deputy's nightstick sing with pain. She lifted her head and looked out at the big room outside the holding cell. She heard a voice emanating from an unseen radio, an excited voice that brayed something unintelligible through a burst of static before cutting off. But the room was empty. There was no one to answer the radio call, much less anyone who might rescue her from whatever vile thing the deputy had in mind. Not that anyone in this lunatic asylum of a town would want to help her anyway.

Hal stepped behind her and thrust his crotch against her upraised ass. She winced at the feel of his enormous erection sliding over her denim-covered bottom. This was the second time she'd let him do this. She yearned to fight back. Maybe stomp on his instep while he was distracted and grab the nightstick from him while he yowled in agony. She imagined cracking him over the head with the thing a few times—let him see how much he liked it. It was tempting. But he was big and powerfully built, and she was just a little thing. Stomping on his foot wouldn't accomplish anything good, would maybe only incite him to something worse than molestation. Tears misted her vision as he hooked a hand into the back of her jeans and held her ass tight to his crotch as he writhed against her. He made moaning sounds and started breathing faster, calling her more vile names between short gasps. She wished he would just hurry up and come in his fucking pants, the dumb bastard.

The creak of a door opening on the other side of the room made her look up again. Sheriff DeMars emerged from his office and came striding across the room with a scowl on his florid face. "Deputy, the fuck are you doin'?"

Hal's breath audibly caught in his throat. He let go of her and shuffled backward a few steps. Megan straightened and staggered away from him. She fell against a grime-encrusted concrete wall and stood with her back against it as the sheriff bulled full-steam into the cell, big nostrils flaring as his face went an even darker shade of scarlet. He slammed the base of a hand against the deputy's chest and sent him stumbling backward.

"He hit me with that thing." Megan indicated the nightstick with a nod. It had fallen to the floor and rolled to a stop against a leg of the cot. "Behind the knee. I'll probably have a nasty bruise."

The sheriff wrapped a big hand around the deputy's throat, kept him from falling onto the cot. He leaned close, spittle striking Hal's cheeks with each tersely enunciated word. "Do. Not. Fuck. With. The. Fucking. Merchandise!" His hand tightened around the deputy's throat, making the man's face turn nearly as deep red as his own. "You dumb shit. You know better than to go against my word. Least I thought you did."

Megan watched this with a numb detachment at first. She didn't realize she was going to speak again until after the words were out there. "He said he claimed me fair and square. Said he was gonna keep me for himself no matter what you said."

DeMars's head turned slowly toward her, his scowl deepening. "The hell you say."

Hal tried to speak, the words emerging as a strangled gurgle.

Megan nodded. "The hell I say."

DeMars scowled. "I reckon I believe you." He eyed her up and down and uttered a piggish snort of admiration. "You'd tempt any man, sweet thing." He looked at Hal. "But you know my word's law here, boy, and you damn sure know not to go against it. So I think it's time for an object lesson."

He relinquished his hold on the deputy's neck. Hal

sucked in two big lungfuls of air before trying to speak. "Sheriff . . . I . . . she's . . ."

The sheriff had something in his hand now, something that vaguely resembled an electric razor. Megan guessed it had been attached to his belt. DeMars jabbed it against Hal's belly and pressed a button. There was a sizzle of electricity and Hal's body did a violent little jig before falling in a heap to the floor. Megan gasped, slapped a hand over her mouth, and slid slowly to the floor. Hal was still twitching when the sheriff stooped over him and placed the Taser's prongs against his neck. DeMars said something, but Megan was too horror stricken to hear what he was saying.

Hal was a bastard. An animal. A subhuman, cold-hearted son of a bitch devoid of even the merest scrap of decency or compassion. He deserved to suffer and pay for his transgressions. Earlier in the day she'd entertained violent fantasies of revenge against the men who'd taken Pete. She'd convinced herself she was capable of any level of brutality necessary to get her man back and get gone from this godforsaken place. But as she watched Hal twitch and piss his pants, she was no longer so sure. It was such an awful thing, witnessing this bit of violence done against a human body. How could she ever imagine she might be capable of anything remotely similar?

Still down on one knee, DeMars glanced her way and grinned. "Don't look so down in the dumps, girl. This should make you happy."

Megan shook her head. "No . . ."

Her voice trailed off in a whine.

DeMars smirked and said, "You thought that was bad, darlin'? Well, get a load of this."

Megan's brow furrowed as one of the sheriff's meaty hands grabbed Hal's zipper tab and tugged it down.

Oh, God. What's he doing now?

DeMars pushed down the deputy's underwear, seized the man's largish cock, and pulled it out through the fly of his trousers. The head of Hal's penis was glistening, still wet from leaking seminal fluid. The sheriff gripped it tight and stretched it taut, making it look like a short length of hose. He winked at Megan and extracted something from a pocket with a free hand. "You're too young to remember them old Ginsu commercials. TV ads for these wicked-sharp Jap knives. They'd demonstrate the sharpness of the blades by using them to slice through all kinds of shit." He chuckled, genuine amusement glittering in his pitiless eyes. "Reckon they never thought to try that shit out on a man's wang."

The thing in the sheriff's hand was a large folding knife. It was open now.

Megan shook her head again. "No . . . you can't."

But he could.

He didn't even hesitate, which deepened the horror. Megan couldn't fathom how a human being could do something so awful to another human being so calmly. The blade cut through Hal's stretched-taut shaft with shocking ease, the penis coming away from the balls amidst a gout of bright, leaping blood. Hal came out of his stupor in an instant, screaming as he sat bolt upright and clutched uselessly at the wound. Blood seeped through his shaking fingers and soaked his hands in hardly more than a second. His face was a twisted mask of agony. It hurt to even look at him.

DeMars was laughing again. "Ginsu got nothin' on this bad boy!" He cackled and slapped the severed penis against Hal's twitching, sweat-soaked face. "That's what you get for thinkin' with your dick, dumbass." He showed Megan an expression electrified with demonic delight. "Check that out, honey. That's one bad motherfucker of an object lesson, ain't it?"

Hal shifted toward the sheriff, clawed at him with a bloody hand. The hand slapped his trousers, tracing a big, bloody smear across the fabric.

Sheriff DeMars sneered and slapped the hand away. "You goddamn son of a bitch. Look what ya done to my pants!"

He dropped Hal's dick on the dusty concrete floor and pulled a big gun from his holster, a shiny revolver, and placed the barrel against the dying deputy's sweat-sheened temple.

Hal's lips trembled as he struggled to say something between whimpers.

DeMars spat in his face. "Hush your cryin', sissy boy. You know you're done for."

Fat tears leaked from Hal's eyes, rushed in rivulets down his pale, shaking face.

He whimpered some more, cried out for his mama.

The boom the big revolver made was immense, nearly deafening in the confines of the little cell. The sound was almost as horribly impressive as what the bullet did to Hal's head.

Almost.

Megan was on her feet and moving before she consciously knew she was going to make a run for it. The cell door stood wide open, a temptation impossible to resist in the wake of such close-quarters horror. She found surprising strength in her legs as she shot through the opening and streaked through the big outer room. She passed through the room in a flash, careened down a short hallway, and spied the front entrance. The knowledge that the insane sheriff would be right on her heels drove her forward, gave her an extra kick as she banged through the door and emerged into the fading sunlight. A sense of wild exhilaration burned through the lingering horror. She was out. Free. She didn't slow for even a second, she was so focused on forward motion, that and nothing else, her head down, arms and legs pumping like an Olympian's. That sense of exhilaration flashed through her again. DeMars would never catch her. He was old and fat, and she was young and—

Her foot struck a floodlight embedded in the ground at the far end of the building's small parking lot. She fell fast and hit the ground hard in an awkward tangle of flailing limbs. Urgency brought her to her feet again in seconds, but it was too fast. She felt woozy. She stumbled and tripped again, banged the back of her head on the hard ground. Things went gray for a few moments. When she could see again, DeMars was standing over her. He looked calm as ever, damnably calm, as if he hadn't spared a moment's concern over her possible escape.

"You're a tough little gal, I'll give you that. But fun-and-games time is over." He reached down and grabbed her by an arm, jerked her to her feet. He leaned close. His breath was foul. "You and me are goin' for a ride."

He set off toward the opposite end of the parking lot. She stumbled as he dragged her along behind him, but his iron grip kept her upright. There were some more gray moments. When her head was clear again, she was sitting in the passenger seat of an unmarked Crown Vic. Her hands were cuffed and a seat belt was strapped tight across her waist.

The car was already rolling out of the parking lot. DeMars glanced at her as he turned onto the street. "Sorry that took so long, sugar. Had to clean up the mess and find somebody to mind the store. Had a devil of a time finding anybody. Most of my men seem to be MIA at the moment."

Megan was shocked to hear he'd been gone for a while. She'd been sure only a few moments had passed. The back of her head felt tender from where the ground had thumped it. She hoped she hadn't suffered some sort of brain trauma, because she wasn't likely to see the inside of a doctor's office any time soon.

"Where are you taking me?"

"You forget already?" He flashed another of those oily, shit-eating grins. "You ever pole danced before, girl?"

Megan didn't say anything.

She'd taken a class in pole dancing. It'd been a hip fitness trend for women for a while. She'd been fit and limber to start with, so she'd been good at it. But she'd never done it in front of a crowd of leering, drunken men.

Her gut knotted.

Shit.

The sheriff howled laughter. "Aw, shit. You have pole danced." He brayed laughter again. "I know a natural-born stripper when I lay eyes on one, don't ever let nobody tell you different."

Megan's head spun.

She felt numb and barely even noticed when DeMars covered one of her knees with one of his big hands. The numbness stayed with her until they reached the Sin Den, insulating her from the hopelessness of her situation for a time. The Crown Vic left the town proper and traveled along winding back roads, soon leaving paved roads altogether as it plunged deeper into the darkening wilderness.

Then she saw it through a line of trees.

An array of bright lights—flashing neon and strobe lights. She heard music and laughter. The Crown Vic bounced and shuddered over the rutted dirt path as it came too fast around a corner.

And now here it was.

The Sin Den, in all its decadent glory.

The numbness was gone.

She told the sheriff she would do anything to stay out of that place. She would do anything for him. Do anything to him. DeMars listened to her and rubbed his crotch as she said things that shamed her.

Then he laughed.

They were parked now.

He turned toward her and put a hand on one of her breasts. She didn't bother knocking it away, knowing it would do no good. He squeezed the breast and licked his lips as he stared at it. "Tell you a little something most strangers don't know. There's two Hopkins Bends." It was weird how bland his tone was, given what he was doing. He sounded like a man sharing a bit of local color over a drink at a bar, and not at all like a depraved maniac who was about to sell her into the local sex trade. "There's where you just came from, and that's the public face of Hopkins Bend. Looks like any other little town, almost quaint on the surface. The people who live there are almost what you might call normal. Then there's the hidden Hopkins Bend, where the old families live, out in the woods. They're a strange lot, and you know that's saying something coming from the likes of me. Most of them live like its still the middle of the nineteenth century, backwards as all get-out. Oh, and they're cannibals."

Megan blinked. "What?"

DeMars chuckled. "They eat people. Well, outsiders."

Megan's stomach twisted again. "Jesus . . ."

"Yeah. And this place here? It's run by one of the old families. One of the more enterprising ones. Hell, they're tycoons by local standards. The Prestons."

Megan was shaking. "Will they"—she gulped—"eat me?"

DeMars shrugged. "Probably not."

Megan's shaking intensified. "Oh, God . . ."

"Don't worry, darlin'. Deal I made with Mama Preston

was for five grand. They'll want to get their money's worth out of you. Still, I think you better do your damnedest to impress when they run your sweet little ass out on that stage the first time."

DeMars ran his hand up and down the length of her thigh a few times, but Megan barely noticed—she was shaking too hard.

"Mmm, but you're a nice piece. May have the Prestons deduct a bit from my fee for an hour with you in a VIP room."

He got out of the Crown Vic then and came around to the other side of the car. The door opened. The blare of music and rowdy laughter grew louder as he leaned over her and popped the seat belt loose. She shrank away from him when he reached for her, but it was a futile effort—he hauled her out of the car with ease.

And dragged her quaking and screaming toward what looked to her like the yawning maw of hell itself.

CHAPTER TWENTY-ONE

The squat little shack Mama Weeks called home stood in the center of a small clearing many of the locals said was a haunted place. The old woman's husband went missing some thirty years back, and the gossip at the time was that she'd killed him and buried him right here in this clearing. Whatever the truth was, it had happened before Abby's time, and in the intervening years had become the stuff of local legend. It was said the man's ghost sometimes appeared at night, a shimmering specter that wandered the edges of the clearing, apparently afraid even in death of venturing too near the shack where Cassie Weeks lived.

Abby figured the old woman had really killed her husband. People from the old families didn't just up and leave. And the local law rarely intervened in their affairs, being of the opinion that matters of right and wrong were best left to them to sort out. Jesse Weeks wasn't much missed by anyone, and so no one ever pressed Cassie about it. It was possible his rotting bones were in the ground beneath Abby's feet, where she stood at the edge of the clearing, trying to work up the nerve to go knock on the old woman's door. This didn't bother Abby overly much. She had seen ghosts before and knew they were mostly harmless. Her hesitancy was based on the fear of Mama Weeks seeing too well into her mind. She needed to know whether the Kincher boy's seed had planted an abomination in her belly, but maybe not enough to risk everything else.

The decision was taken out of her hands when the shack's front door creaked open and Mama Weeks shuffled into view. She had silver hair tied back in a bun and wore a frilly ankle-length black dress. She was scrawny and short, no more than an inch over five feet, and stood stooped over in the door's frame. She adjusted the bifocals that sat perched on her hooked nose and leaned forward to peer closely at Abby.

"Stop gawking, Abby Maynard, and come on in. You've been standing there for an age."

Abby kicked at a rock on the ground, didn't move toward the shack. "I don't know, Mama. I wanted to talk to you, but now I'm not so sure."

Mama Weeks stared at her in silence for several moments, frowning over her visitor's reluctance. Then she clucked and shook her head. "Your secrets are safe with me, girl. Now get on in here and talk to me."

She turned her back on Abby and disappeared back inside the shack. Abby stared at the darkness visible through the open door and hesitated only a moment longer. She stood on the cusp of a great change. Making it happen would require enormous courage, maybe more than she could summon. She wanted it to happen so bad. More than anything ever. The desire for it swelled inside her again as she thought about it. She had to make it happen. Anything else was death. And if she couldn't find the gumption to sit down and talk with an old woman, even one as creepy as Mama Weeks, she was doomed already.

Her legs carried her into the clearing without conscious instruction, her whole body thrumming with the urgency and desire she felt in her heart. A dozen long strides, and she arrived at the darkened front door. She paused at the threshold for barely more than the space of a single second and stepped into the darkness.

The little shack's interior wasn't completely dark. A single candle's flame fluttered on a table situated at the approximate center of the room. The place was tiny, barely half the size of the sitting room back home. A queen-size bed jammed into a corner dominated the space. There was a large steamer trunk at the foot of the bed, with piles of junk heaped on top of it. In another corner was a tiny wood-burning stove. There was a cabinet with some plates and other dishes. A small wardrobe stood against another wall. It was hard to imagine how two people could have lived in so small a space without going completely crazy, which maybe explained some things about the old woman's past. But even more disturbing than the cramped conditions were the . . . things . . . hanging from the ceiling by lengths of twine. Charms and wards, she guessed, at least a dozen of them. The one closest to her was a bundle of tiny and brittle animal bones, perhaps those of some largish rodent, wrapped in more twine and sealed in wax. Another looked like the shrunken, dessicated head of a dog, also preserved in wax. Some defensive mechanism in her mind steered her gaze away from others, perhaps sensing these were things any sane person would never want to see. After just a few seconds inside the shack, Abby knew there was yet another reason the local law never bothered with Mama Weeks—they were afraid of her.

Abby just managed to contain a yelp of fright as the woman's bony fingers took her by the elbow and steered her toward the wobbly table. The old woman released her elbow as they reached the table, and shuffled around to the other side. Abby settled onto a wooden chair that felt brittle beneath her skinny ass. Cassie Weeks sat down with an audible creak of old bones and stared across the table at her, a faint smile curling the corners of her thin lips. "I remember when you was just a little girl. Your daddy used to see me about spiritual matters every now and then. Brought you by a time or two. You were a cute little thing, full of vim and vinegar. Even then I knew you'd be different."

Abby's heart thumped faster at the unexpected mention of her father. She blinked moisture from her eyes. "I . . . don't remember that, I'm sorry." Her brow furrowed. "How do you mean, 'different'?"

The breeze shifted outside and a gust of air blew into the shack, making Abby's golden hair fan out around her face and causing the candle's meager flame to dance wildly. The flickering radiance made Cassie's eyes glitter in a way that hinted at madness. Abby knew this had more to do with preconceived notions she had harbored about Mama since childhood than anything connected to current reality, but the vision was no less disturbing for the knowledge.

"How old are you now, Abigail?"

"I'm . . ." Abby stared at the table and watched the little flame dance again as another gust of air came swirling through the doorway. The familiar shame stung her again, and she couldn't bring herself to meet the seer's searching gaze. But she made herself admit the truth in a voice as soft and hollow as a mourner's at a graveside. "I'm twenty."

"And you ain't been with child yet, have ya?"

Abby squeezed her eyes shut as tears rolled down her cheeks. She tried to speak, but the emotion gripping her was too strong. Her face dipped closer to the table as sob after sob racked her body, a body still sore from the violation so recently perpetrated against it. She heard Mama's chair scuff across the wooden floor as the old woman rose with a grunt and moved away from the table for a time. Abby prayed she wasn't coming to comfort her, knowing how awkward any level of physical intimacy would be for a strange old lady who'd shunned such things for so long. She was relieved when she heard chair legs scrape the floor again. She forced her eyes open and saw that the old woman was sitting at the opposite side of the table again.

She frowned.

A crumpled square of aluminum foil lay on the table in front of Mama. On it was a thick lump of some black, tarry substance. Mama packed a pinch of the substance into a tiny pipe and lit it from the candle. She drew on the pipe and in a moment expelled a small cloud of fragrant smoke. She smiled at Abby's puzzled expression. "Hash. Picked up a taste for it after Jesse came back from 'Nam in sixty-seven. The son of a bitch left me with one thing worth a damn, anyway."

"Did you kill him?"

The blurted words startled Abby, emerging through her

lips ahead of any conscious thought given to the matter. Her heart raced and her body tensed, ready to bolt from the creepy shack at the first hint of malice from Mama.

But the old woman's smile never faltered. "Of course I killed him." Mama indicated the clearing outside the shack with a slight incline of her head. "Buried the cocksucker right out there, about where you were standing when I looked out and saw you there."

A chill pricked the hairs at the back of Abby's neck.

I knew it.

"But . . . why did you kill him?"

The old woman drew on the pipe again. Her eyes looked glassier with every hit. But her voice was just as intent as she leaned over the edge of the table and pointed the stem of the pipe at Abby. "I just told you a thing I never told another human being. A big thing, I think you'd agree. And still there are some secrets I'd rather keep. I think maybe you can understand that better than just about anybody in all of Hopkins Bend."

Something in the statement made Abby want to bolt again, but she again made herself stay right there. If Mama sensed her unease, she didn't show it. She just kept smiling and puffing on the pipe while Abby struggled to respond, her eyes shining with drug-besotted amusement.

Then Abby blew out a big breath and found her voice at last. "What do you mean by that?"

Mama set the pipe down and laced her fingers together. "It's said the good Lord made mankind in his own image, and I reckon maybe that's true to a degree, but he damn sure didn't make us all the same. Some—hell, most— human beings are made to tread the tried-and-true path from the day they're hatched till the day they croak. But a goodly few are made another way. For them folk the tried-and-true path is a special kind of torture. It ain't an easy thing being different in this hard old world, Abigail."

Here her voice hardened and her eyes lost some of that glassiness. "But that damn sure don't mean you should let the bastards grind ya down."

Abby gaped in astonishment at the old woman. Mama's face looked younger as its features twisted with surprising passion. It was amazing. People of a less kindly nature would look at Mama and call her crone or hag (although perhaps not to her face). But in this moment she looked youthful and vigorous, her skin smooth and unlined. It was the way she imagined Mama must have looked fifty years earlier. But then she relaxed and settled back into her chair, and the appearance of youth was revealed for the illusion it was, as her features untwisted and the deep wrinkles again became apparent.

Mama smoothed the front of her dress and stared soberly at Abby. "You'll forgive the outburst, I hope?"

Abby relaxed her iron grip on the chair. "Of course, Mama. And . . ." She chewed her bottom lip a moment. She knew what the old woman was saying to her, despite its vague nature. And it spoke to her on a deeper level than she could convey. "I agree with you."

"I'm glad to hear it, Abigail."

"But there's something else I wanted to see you about. Something I need to know." She flinched at the memory of the grunting and sweating Kincher boy thrusting away atop her. And she remembered the powerful release of his seed deep inside her, how he'd just come and come, filling her up. She began to feel sick again as she thought of it. "Something happened to me today. I need to know . . . I need to know if . . ."

Mama's smile brightened. "Abigail, I am truly and deeply sorry this terrible thing happened to you. A woman should never be taken against her will by any man, and that goes doubly for those tainted by the Garner Blight. And so it pleases me to tell you to set your fears aside."

Abby's eyes widened. "You mean . . . ?"

"You are not with child."

Abby beamed at the old woman even as fresh tears leaked from the corners of her eyes. "Thank you. I can't tell you how much that means."

Mama nodded. "I suspect not, but I think I know anyway." Her mouth opened in a wide yawn. "Excuse me, child. I've grown tired. I've enjoyed seein' ya. You did the right thing coming here."

Abby palmed moisture from her cheeks and sniffled. "I think so, too." She pushed the chair back and stood. "I won't keep you any longer. I've got some more thinking to do anyway."

Mama rose from the table and accompanied her to the door. She gripped Abby by the elbow again as they paused for a moment at the threshold. "Remember, you are not bound to live as others say you should. And you can be whatever you want to be."

Abby patted the old woman's hand. "Thank you. Again. For everything."

And then she was gone, striding back across the clearing with a new spring in her step as the little shack's door slammed shut behind her.

She never saw Mama Weeks again.

CHAPTER TWENTY-TWO

The last rays of shimmering orange faded from the horizon as night fell at last on Hopkins Bend. The cruiser's headlights illuminated a winding two-lane stretch of blacktop, the road shrouded on both sides by tall trees that swayed in the quickening wind. The wind made the lower-hanging branches look like grasping tentacles in the encroaching darkness, a perception that did nothing to soothe her live-wire nerves.

Close to half an hour had elapsed since the pileup at the roadblock and the ensuing bloodshed. She'd driven maybe fifteen of those minutes before turning down a paved side street, after realizing it wouldn't be smart to stay on the same damned road under the circumstances. She figured the side street would eventually lead to other streets, maybe even a highway. And then she would be home free. But so far this road was it, and she had a sick feeling it was circling back toward the heart of the town. Frustration made Jessica pull to a stop at the road's shoulder and stare through the windshield as she struggled against the grinding terror taking root within her.

A single word forced its way through clenched teeth: "Fuck!"

She was in a world of shit, but her overriding concern at the moment was the simple reality that she was completely lost. She didn't know Hopkins Bend at all, a situation that wasn't aided any by the total dearth of street signs and lamps. If she could get back to Old Fork Road, she might stand at least some slim chance of slipping away before a net could draw tight around her. But she had no clue how to get from here to there. She didn't even know where *here* was, the name of this goddamn nowhere street, this fucking path to certain doom and damnation.

She slammed the steering wheel with the base of a hand. "Fuck this fucking bullshit!" She screamed, a high, shrill sound that filled the cruiser's interior and made her head hurt. "Goddamn you all, you redneck motherfucking sons of bitches!"

She fell back against the seat, breathing heavily. Her sore ribs were aching again now, a pulsing agony made worse by the manner in which she'd vented her frustrations. She shifted in the seat and winced again. A small part of her felt like giving up then. An oppressive weariness threatened to weigh her down. She felt it in every inch of her body. Her eyes fluttered as she thought about it, and she slid down deeper into the seat. The prospect of surrender became more appealing the closer she drifted to sleep. She couldn't hope to get away with what amounted to mass murder anyway. She should just stay where she was and let the police catch up to her in their own good time. At least on death row she'd have a chance to rest before her inevitable rendezvous with the lethal injection chamber. . . .

A stray thought drifted through her fading consciousness, jolting her back to full wakefulness with a heart-pounding gasp.

"Shit!"

She sat up straight and ground her fists into her eyes. Then she blinked and stared through the windshield again, her thoughts lingering on the stark truth that had brought her back from the edge.

Death row?

That was a laugh. It would never get that far, if whatever remained of the local law had anything to say about it. She would be killed on sight. No jury. No trial. They'd skip all that pansy liberal shit and go straight to the execution phase of things, with maybe some time set aside beforehand for a few rounds of torture and rape. The latter caused that steel to rise inside her again, that hard core of unyielding strength that had seen her through the many battles so far. She felt a piercing shame at having considered surrender for even a moment.

She reached for the gearshift and muttered at the reflection of cold blue eyes visible in the rearview mirror. A killer's eyes. Her own eyes. "Buck up, Jessica Sloan. Daddy didn't raise no quitters."

A wash of blinding white light bathed the cruiser's interior in the same moment she put the vehicle in gear. Her breath caught painfully in her throat and her heart slammed a triple-time beat. *Here they are.* Her right hand shot toward the passenger seat, groping for a gun. Her fingers slid over the stock of the pump-action shotgun even as the grim certainty that she would never be able to bring the weapon to bear in time dealt an almost crippling blow to a psyche still reeling from so many other traumas. But then the cloak of white light slipped away and she heard the whir of a motor passing by. She let go of the shotgun and watched a red blur of taillights plunge deep into the night and disappear around a bend in the winding road. The car was moving fast, had passed through the cone of light projected by the cruiser's headlights, there and gone in a second. But that second was all Jessica needed to identify the vehicle as a seventies junker.

A civilian car.

She stomped on the gas pedal and the cruiser shot

away from the road's shoulder, tires squealing as they hit pavement and caught traction. She kept the accelerator down with one foot and tapped the brake pedal with the other as she cranked the steering wheel and took the cruiser around a sharp bend at high speed. The cruiser went up on two wheels for a wild instant, sending a perverse shiver of exhilaration spiraling through her. The impact of the wheels striking the pavement as they came back down jostled her and caused the pain in her ribs to flare again, but she kept the gas pedal down and leaned over the steering wheel, eyes intent, scanning the way ahead for any glimpse of the speeding sedan's taillights. She licked her lips and felt her breath quicken. Her nostrils flared, and she flexed her fingers around the steering wheel's molded grip. She felt a weird kind of excitement, what she guessed was meant by the old phrase "the thrill of the hunt." But some of that faded as she continued to speed through the deepening night. For a few strained moments, she was sure she'd lost her quarry for good.

Then she saw it.

A seventies sedan. It was stopped at the side of the road some thirty yards ahead. The driver's-side door stood slightly ajar, and the dome light was on. Jessica spied a shadowy single form leaning toward the passenger seat. She tromped on the cruiser's brake pedal and brought the car to a shuddering halt perhaps ten yards to the rear of the sedan. She scanned the cruiser's dashboard and found what she was looking for after a few desperate seconds. The flashing lights atop the cruiser's roof came on, bathing the roadside in strobing shades of red and blue.

She grabbed the dead cop's .38 and took a deep breath.

You can do this.

Sure she could. She thought of all the daring things she'd already done today. The return to Hoke's house after he'd raped her. The abduction. The wild flight into the woods. All the men she'd killed so far. This was nothing. She just had to make the driver of the sedan believe she was a cop long enough to get him out of his car. The number-one obstacle was her civilian outfit. But the jeans and tight black V-neck T-shirt she wore were dark and unremarkable, the T-shirt unadorned by any logo or image. Good enough to get by for those few first crucial moments after she stepped out of the car. Or so she hoped. She set the gun down and pulled her long hair back, twisted it in a quick knot, and looked in the mirror. She squinted and made her face go hard. The reflected expression disturbed her. It made her look tough, maybe even a little mean. Which was not at all how she'd seen herself prior to today. But she wasn't really that person anymore, was she? A slight pang of loss came and went. There would be plenty of time to think about what she had become if she ever managed to make it back home. In the meantime . . .

She grabbed the gun again and got out of the car. The sedan's dome light winked out in the same instant she threw the cruiser's door shut. She hesitated a moment, standing next to the cruiser with the gun pointed toward the ground. And in that moment she was intensely aware of the inherent dangers in police work. The man driving the sedan could be a criminal, might even have a gun of his own. Maybe he'd turned the light out so she wouldn't see him going for a weapon. There were a lot of fucking maybes here, so many ways everything could go wrong. But the hell with it. This was obviously her only chance to ditch the cruiser and put some levels of separation between herself and the murdered cops.

Her fingers flexed around the .38's grip as she took her

first steps toward the sedan. She was close enough now to see that it was a tan Chevy Nova. It was a heap, probably held together by spit and duct tape. She raised the gun slightly, still pointed at the ground but held in front of her, primed to lift and snap like a cobra if necessary.

She reached the Nova and bent at the waist to peer through the open driver's-side window. A young man with short, greasy hair and a day's worth of stubble on his square chin grinned up at her. An unlit cigarette was tucked behind an ear. He looked her up and down and made an appreciate noise. "Damn, darlin'. When did the local law start hiring supermodels?"

Jessica pointed the .38 at the center of his face. "Step out of the car."

The man's grin faltered some, but didn't disappear entirely. "I ain't done nothin' wrong, girl. Why you pointin' that thing at me?"

"Shut up and step out of the car."

The man smirked. "Yeah? Or what? You'll shoot me in the face?"

He laughed.

Jessica thumbed back the .38's hammer. "Yes. I'll shoot you in the fucking face."

The man stopped laughing and the mirth drained from his sparkling eyes. Blue eyes. Greasy hair aside, he was actually pretty hot, at least by Hopkins Bend standards. A strange fantasy coalesced in her head as she stared him down. She saw herself forcing him into the Nova's back seat. Keeping the gun on him as she pulled her pants down and sat on his face. Her lips curled in self-disgust. Could she really be considering perpetrating rape against this man after all she'd been through today?

My God, she thought. *You'd be no better than Hoke.*

Of course she wouldn't do it.

But she kept staring at him, kept thinking things no

woman in her position should be thinking. She imagined her pussy pressed against his red lips, and the arousal rising within her grew to a flame of intense desire. A fresh surge of self-disgust accompanied it. The clock was ticking. She had to get in the Nova and get away from the cruiser and its flashing lights.

The man frowned. "You're not a real cop, are you?"

"No."

There was fear in his eyes now. "Fuck. You stole a cop cruiser. I'm not even gonna ask what happened to the cop. You're gonna kill me, aren't you?"

Jessica bit a corner of her bottom lip, thought a moment. Then said, "Maybe not."

The man's frown gave way to a small, hopeful smile. "It'd sure be cool if you didn't. It's a rotten old world a lot of times, but I sure like being alive."

Jessica realized she liked the sound of his voice. A deep, easygoing drawl with an underlying humor in every syllable. She struggled to keep her face hard. "I bet you do. But it's gonna depend on what you can do for me."

"Like what?"

Jessica allowed the smallest of smiles to shade the edges of her mouth. "Like on how fast this heap of yours is. And on how quick you can get me out of this goddamn redneck shithole town. And maybe even a little on how good you kiss."

The man grinned. He reached for the cigarette behind his ear and wedged it into a corner of his mouth. "Hop in, darlin'. I think you're gonna like the answers to all them crazy questions."

Jessica lowered the gun and hurried around to the other side of the Nova. The man reached across the seat and unlocked the door for her. She slid inside, set the .38 on the dash, and reached for him, seizing handfuls of his shirt and pulling him close. Their lips met and they tasted each other hungrily. Her tongue slid in and out of his mouth. She nipped at his bottom lip, elicited a low growl of lust from the man. Then they broke the clinch and stared at each other, panting heavily.

The man grinned again and shook his head. "Damn. What a crazy night this is turning out to be."

Jessica cupped his crotch and squeezed. "What's your name?"

The man groaned. "Larry. Uh . . . damn, woman. Larry Wolfe."

Jessica licked her lips. "Larry, you don't know the half of it. *Crazy* doesn't begin to cover what I've been through. And I'll tell you all about it after you get me someplace safe."

She let go of his crotch and smiled at the way he shuddered.

This was insane.

She knew it.

And she didn't care. Fate was playing a lot of fucked-up games with her head today. She figured the best way to cope with it was to keep on doing what she'd done so far—just roll with it.

Larry turned in his seat and sat up straight behind the steering wheel. He put the car in gear, and in a moment they were rolling down the road. He glanced at her. "I'll take you to my house. That's where I was headed anyway. It'll be the safest place for now."

Jessica tensed. "No. I told you. I want out of here. Now."

Larry shot her a reassuring smile. "Look, I don't know what you've done or why you're in trouble, but it's obvious it's something pretty heavy. You don't want to be on the road much longer tonight. At my place you'll have a chance to hunker down and let the heat cool off."

Jessica thought about it. "You've got a point."

"Sure I do. And think of the fun we can have with a bit of privacy."

Jessica smiled. "Yeah. Okay. Fuck it. Let's do it. One question, though."

"Yeah?"

"Are you as fucking crazy as everybody else I've run into here? Are you one of the bad guys?" She retrieved the .38 from the dash and held it in her lap. "Because I've killed a lot of people today, Larry. I'd hate to have to add you to the list."

Larry shrugged. "I live on the outskirts of town proper. The real crazies are out in the woods. I know some about the shit that goes on, but that's about it. I don't exactly condone any of it, but it's just the way of things. If you're raised here, you know not to make a stink or talk about the old families and their fucked-up ways in mixed company."

Jessica was silent for several long moments.

Then she sighed.

"Okay."

Larry reached for the dashboard lighter and lit his cigarette. "Cool."

They stayed silent for a while after that.

Jessica stared out the open window on her side, watching the dark blur of trees as the sedan sped down the winding road. She could be making a big mistake by going along with this. Her original thought had been to stuff the guy in the trunk, same as she'd done with Hoke. But this felt right for reasons she couldn't quite put into words. Reasons based on gut instinct and primal lust, which she supposed were as good as any tonight.

She kept one hand on the gun in her lap.

With the other, she reached for Larry's knee. . . .

CHAPTER TWENTY-THREE

It was full night now.

So she wouldn't stop saying it.

"Now it's night. Now you fuck me. Now it's night. Now you fuck me."

On her hands and knees, her round ass wiggling in the air as she moved toward him, looking like a predatory alley cat ready to pounce on prey.

"Now it's night. Now you fuck me. Now it's night. Now you fuck me."

Pete backed up, felt the fence against his back.

Looked down, saw her smiling face staring up at him.

"No."

"Yes."

"Stay away from me."

Her hand on his crotch, squeezing his hardness through the khaki fabric.

Pete moaned.

Reflected moonlight gleamed in her dark eyes, accentuating madness.

She smiled, licked her chapped lips.

Squeezed him again and reached for his zipper tab.

"Stop!"

Pete shoved her hand away—a hand much softer than he'd expected—and moved sideways away from her, into a corner of the cage.

She laughed and came at him again on all fours.

His fingers curled through the chain-link fencing.

"Please stop . . ."

More mad laughter. "I can't wait to feel you inside me. I'm so wet. How do you want to take me first? From behind? On top? You want me to ride you?"

Kneeling at his feet now, soft hand sliding over his crotch again.

Pete whimpered, curled his fingers tighter around the chain-link fencing.

His erection strained the front of his khaki shorts and she gripped it, stroking him through the fabric, the motion soft at first, then harder, twisting his cock and making him cry out.

He cursed his weakness, tried to dampen the arousal by thinking about Megan again, but she seemed far away now, and he stayed hard as the woman manipulated his organ in almost sadistic ways without actually freeing it from its khaki confines. He couldn't understand why this was happening, or why he was so unable to control his physical response to Justine's crude seduction techniques.

She had begun to seem more attractive as the light leeched from the sky, the night obscuring the filth, and the glow of the moon highlighting the lush, sensual curves of her body. And something in her naughty mantra,

. . . *now it's night, now you'll fuck me . . .*

had worked on him in more subtle ways, slithering into the back of his brain and whispering erotic promises of ecstasy to the most primitive parts of his subconscious. And somehow it began to work, revulsion giving way to desire. So now he was on the verge of giving in completely. He could take some solace in knowing he'd fought this. A tiny, almost infinitesimal amount, but solace nonetheless.

Enough to get through this exercise in degradation anyway.

The zipper was down now, the button of his shorts open. She yanked his shorts down and drew him fast into her warm mouth. Pete gasped, arched his back, and screwed his eyes shut. Her head bobbed up and down, her tongue doing things to him Megan didn't know how to do; then her mouth came away from him and he cried out again.

He opened his eyes and looked down at her.

She was on her back now, on the ground, legs spread wide, one hand flexing between her legs, another tweaking the erect nipple of a breast.

She lifted her head to look at him. "Now it's night . . ."

His nostrils flared. ". . . and now I'll fuck you."

He stepped out of his shorts and fell upon her.

The first thrust was among the most glorious things he'd ever felt. Later he might feel only disgust at his weakness. But right now, in this moment, fucking this insane stranger was all he cared about. She growled and wrapped her legs around him. Her nails raked bloody grooves across his muscled back. He took her breasts into his mouth, licked and nipped at the hard nipples. They changed positions twice, and he wound up spurting deep inside her as he banged away at her from behind. But that wasn't the end of it. She shoved him to the ground and sat on his face.

That went on for a while.

When it was over, she dismounted and lay beside him, curling a soft leg around his midsection. Her breath was warm against his ear as she whispered, "Good?"

He shivered and sighed. He swallowed thickly. "Yes. Good."

She walked slender fingers across the sweat-matted hair on his chest. "The Preston boys fuck me sometimes. They're not good. I don't get off at all."

"Uh-huh."

Pete just didn't know what to say to that. It grossed him out to know his captors had also invaded the same warm space he'd just enjoyed. All this aside from the disturbing revelation that her primary complaint regarding their abuse of her was their inability to make her come. Which was a sobering reminder of how very cracked Justine's mind had become during her time in captivity. She'd probably been mentally ill before she was abducted, though he couldn't know that for certain. He didn't know anything about her, really, beyond how very good she'd felt squirming beneath him. Yes, it had been good. He hadn't lied about that at all. Hell, it had been maybe the most intense sexual experience of his young life. He could be honest about that, at least. But he felt like shit for allowing it to happen. He loved Megan, and he had betrayed her.

Justine moved her leg, and her silken thigh slid over his crotch. He felt a fresh stirring of arousal. Pete knew they would be at it again very soon. His guilty conscience would not prevent that. Again, he felt shame for his moral failings. But in these circumstances, locked in a cage and likely facing a very grim future, shame would not override lust. He might never be free again, might not even be alive much longer, but in this moment, right now, a warm human body was pressed against his in the dark.

She placed a finger on his chin, gently turned his face toward hers. "What are you thinking about, Petey Pete?"

"Things."

She giggled. "What things?"

He hesitated at first, not knowing how much of his inner turmoil he should share with her. Some of it involved feelings that should remain private no matter what, but he was also unsure of whether he wanted to talk about anything of substance with Justine. Any amount of real emotional intimacy could lead to some pretty heavy complications down the road. In the end, though, he just couldn't help himself. There were all these thoughts rattling around in his head, a clamor of conflicting voices, and they screamed for release.

"I was thinking about my girlfriend. Her name is Megan." His voice cracked slightly on her name, but he cleared his throat and went on. "I shouldn't have let this happen. I betrayed her."

Justine wasn't smiling now. Her eyes no longer sparkled with off-kilter amusement. "I'm your girlfriend now."

Pete sighed. "No, Justine. You're not. I'm sorry, but that's how it is." He saw her expression harden and scrambled for words that would assuage her feelings. "Don't get me wrong. I'm glad this happened. You made me feel good for a while, and that's no small thing considering what's happened to us. And, hell, I'll probably never see Megan again."

Justine's stony expression didn't change. "I am very stable and normal when I have my medication. I've been without it for a month."

Pete was surprised at how lucid she'd become. "Well . . . I'm sure that's true, but—"

"In the real world, in my real life, men chase after me."

"I believe you, but—"

"I have a good job. And a degree from Wellesley. I'm smart and successful."

Pete squinted, studied her expression closely. He detected no hints of subterfuge or delusion. "Okay. I do believe you. But I don't know what you're trying to say."

Her expression softened a little and she moved her face closer to his. "I'm saying you are not bound to your girlfriend. She is not your wife. And if you get me out of here, there is no good reason why you would not choose me over her."

Her lips were so close now they were almost touching his. Pete desperately wanted to kiss her.

But he made himself say, "We live together. We love each other. Maybe we don't have a legal document proclaiming us man and wife, but we are bound together nonetheless."

"Such a pretty speech."

Pete shook his head. "It's not just a speech. It's—"

"The Prestons ate my fiancé."

Pete blinked slowly. "What?"

Justine shifted her body. Her breasts pressed against his chest, her thigh angled against his crotch. "They stretched him out on a big table and made me watch while they chopped off his arms and legs. He was still alive when they did this."

Pete grimaced. "Jesus . . ."

Justine's expression didn't change as she related the tale, radiating carnality and desire even as she continued with the grisly revelations. Any grief she might feel was locked away somewhere deep inside. "You wouldn't believe the blood. So much of it. Like an ocean of red pumping out of him. Some of their dogs were wandering around in there. They licked my lover's blood off the floor. Jim took so long to die. I wanted him to die by then, of course. Any life he might have after that wouldn't be worth living."

Pete wanted her to stop talking about it, but couldn't bring himself to say so. "That's horrible, Justine. I'm so sorry."

"Why? You didn't do it."

"I know. But—"

"Then they stripped the meat from his bones. Muscles, ligaments, sinew. They cooked the tender parts on the stove. They made me watch that, too."

Pete was starting to feel sick. And frightened. He'd known he'd been taken by crazy people, but even so had not suspected so startling a level of depravity. He imagined heavy blades chopping into his own flesh and felt bile rise in his throat. "Justine . . . please, I'm sorry this happened to you, but could you please—"

"I was forced to eat some of the meat they cooked. I can still taste my lover's seared flesh on my tongue."

Pete swallowed bile again. "Oh, God . . ."

Justine smiled.

Then she began to slide down the length of his body, her tongue tracing a wet trail from the tip of his chin and down his torso to his crotch. His once again erect cock leaped toward her mouth and she swallowed the whole throbbing length of it in one breathtaking gulp. Pete gasped and clutched at the ground. She plied him with mouth and tongue for several moments before disengaging to smile at his pale, shaking face.

"You like that, Petey Pete?"

Pete couldn't say anything. He just groaned again.

Justine laughed.

"I think you understand now why I need you, Pete. I'm going to make you forget all about Megan. You won't be able to help it. Soon you'll be obsessed with me. You'll worship the ground I walk on."

Pete whimpered as she massaged his balls. "I . . . please . . ."

"I'm good at that, you know." She stroked his shaft and licked her lips. "I wrap men around my little finger and make them do whatever I want. You'll be no different." She stopped stroking him. "Now say please again."

Pete let his head settle back against the warm ground. He stared up at the clear night sky and he thought about Megan, nights they'd lain on a blanket on a beach or in a park and stared up at the same sky, whispering sweet promises to each other in the dark.

He closed his eyes.

And he said, "Please."

CHAPTER TWENTY-FOUR

Something poked him.

Hoke groaned in protest and rolled onto his side, still asleep. He was immersed in a lovely dream and wanted no part of anything happening in the waking world. In the dream he'd hooked up with the bitch again, that Jessica, and this time he'd turned things around on her. They were back at his house in Nashville, having escaped somehow from the psychos in Hopkins Bend. And she was so grateful. He was her hero. He'd done some kind of amazing goddamn thing to get them out of the clutches of those fucking backwoods retards and mongoloids. Which made total sense to Hoke, who knew full well how much of a badass he was capable of being. Sure, he'd been knocked around by the Kinchers and generally humiliated by Garner, but it'd always been only a matter of time until he went all Chuck Norris on their sorry mutant asses.

Anyway.

Jessica ...

Yeah, she was all over him, begging him for forgiveness, offering to do whatever he wanted to make up for being such a bitch. But there are some things a man just can't let slide. Like being forced into the trunk of his own car at gunpoint. Or being made to apologize and beg for his life out in the middle of nowhere. Things like that gnawed at a man, made him feel kind of like a bitch. A punk. A fucking pussy. So what he did was, he punched her square in the fucking face. Knocked her right on her pretty round ass. Then picked her up and knocked her down again. At some point fisticuffs gave way to rape, as he tore her clothes off and had her every which way a man could have a woman. All of which was a damn good time, but the best bit was happening as he felt something poke his sleeping body a second time. . . .

He groaned and weakly waved at the thing poking him. "Stop . . ."

The dream grew fuzzy around the edges and threatened to disintegrate, but his subconscious clung to it with desperate tenacity.

In the dream, Jessica was now chained to the Falcon's rear bumper, and he was dragging her down a wide-open two-lane highway at full speed. She'd screamed and cried out for the first hundred yards, but had since fallen silent. He knew he was now dragging a corpse, but that didn't lessen his enjoyment. He glanced frequently at the rearview mirror to watch her broken and battered body bounce and roll, leaving a wide red smear all over a ribbon of clean, freshly laid blacktop. And he rode down that shimmering dream highway with a fat cigar wedged into a corner of his mouth, smirking and cackling like a demented movie villain. Yeah, life was good here in dreamland.

The next poke dug hard into his ribs and jolted him awake. He seized a long pole protruding through slats in the horse-stall gate. The person on the other end of it yelped and let go of it. Hoke pulled the implement close and saw that he was now in possession of an old shovel caked with rust and grime. The handle felt about as sturdy as a blade of grass. He tossed the thing aside with a grunt of disgust and stared into the shifting, formless gloom on the opposite side of the gate. It was too dark to make out details, but he sensed there was more than one person standing outside the stall. He heard it in the subtle variations in breathing patterns, and in the way some patches of darkness seemed deeper and broader than others.

He sneered and spat a wad of phlegm at the gate. "Y'all enjoyin' the fuckin' show?"

Someone giggled.

There was a soft exhalation of deeper laughter.

And a bit of hands-over-mouth unintelligible snickering.

Hoke grabbed the shovel again and got to his feet with a creak of weary bones. Yeah, the thing was flimsier than a whore's lingerie, but he could maybe swat somebody's head with it once, give them a little scare. He hefted the shovel and took a step toward the gate, but stopped cold at the sound of a loud snap in the darkness. A bright light came, bathing the stall's interior in a glare intense enough to make him squint. He shaded his eyes with a hand over his brow and leaned forward to peer through the slats. There were four of them out there. A girl and three boys, one of them holding a Coleman lantern over his head. He knew the one was a gal only because of her enormous knockers. These were porn-star tits. You could float to Africa on them. But her face looked like something he might have puked onto a sidewalk some night after last call in east Nashville. Everything was misshapen. Gigantic, protruding forehead. Mostly bald scalp with a few tufts of limp, dirty hair clinging to it like scrubgrass on a desert plain. Prominent cheekbones that looked as if they had formed wrong in the womb, twisted in ways cheekbones shouldn't twist and grown almost too big for the taut yellow skin stretched over them. The vaguely piggish nose was her most attractive feature. Or least vomit inducing. The boys with her looked as if they'd been puked out of the same diseased womb. They were monsters, all of them.

And they were all staring at him, leering at him, studying him as if he were a specimen in a zoo cage. One of the boys, the tallest and leanest one, was staring at him with sausagelike lips curled and one hand down his pants, the hand going up and down as he groaned.

"You sick little bastards."

The girl covered her mouth and giggled again.

Hoke knew he'd only get one shot with the shovel. Miss Nightmare America and the masturbating beanpole were equally tempting targets. The beanpole's eyes rolled back in his face and a sound like the dying bleat of some big, dumb range animal issued from his wide-open mouth. He arched his back and his engorged rod shot streams of jizz high into the air, the white liquid flashing almost prettily in the lantern's brilliant glare.

Hoke made his decision.

One way or another, he was taking out the scrawny pervert.

He hefted the shovel again and moved toward the gate. The little monsters cringed and moved backward. Hoke derived some small satisfaction from seeing the fear evident in their butt-ugly faces. It lasted until he realized their attention was not on him. They huddled against each other, quaking in terror as something from the far end of the barn approached them. A long shadow rose out of the darkness and fell over them, creating the illusion of a capering figure moving between the horse stalls. This was a shadow composed of sticky darkness, a thing blacker than the heart of the darkest primeval night, and it seemed to swallow the light projected by the lantern as it loomed closer.

Hoke dropped the shovel and backpedaled until his back touched the wall. His heart thumped faster and his knees began to shake. A sick terror began to twist through his innards as he again felt Garner's malevolent presence.

He watched aghast as the oozing blackness engulfed the Kincher children, appearing for a moment to blot them out of existence. The shrill screams that came then belied that impression, and the shadow grew larger, tendrils of blackness writhing in the air surrounding it. The Coleman lantern hit the ground and rolled until it struck the door of another stall. The lantern's powerful beam reached toward the barn's roof, illuminating enough of the narrow space between the rows of stalls to afford Hoke a clear picture of what was happening.

Not that he wanted to see any of it.

God, no.

But his eyes stayed open anyway, impelled by some masochistic impulse of the subconscious to watch. Some sick part of his psyche hungry for fresh nightmare material. And even for a man like Hoke, a rapist, a man with barely any kind of functioning conscience at all, the things he saw then struck him as beyond awful. Things no man should ever see. A thick tendril of darkness wound itself around one of the tall boy's arms, flexed, and ripped the arm from the shoulder. The boy screamed as the limb came loose and blood fountained from the big, ragged wound. The tendril flexed again, and the severed arm went flying through the darkness, landing with a meaty thump inside Hoke's stall.

Hoke screamed.

He covered his eyes, but the same sick, helpless curiosity made him peer between his fingers as the slaughter continued. There were more screams, but these soon petered out, giving way to agonized whimpers and inarticulate pleas for mercy. Hoke heard ripping sounds. More limbs torn from limp, dying bodies, the monster unzipping the flesh of the children. More body parts landed in the stall. The girl's head hit the wall above him and dropped. Hoke shrieked as the ragged stump bounced off the top of his head and tumbled to the ground. He kicked it away and scuttled sideways into a corner. He winced at the wet splat of organs striking the ground around him. A liver or pancreas hit his knee and slid down his thigh, eliciting another high, girlish shriek from his aching lungs. He moved sideways toward the opposite corner, but there was no escape from the rain of gore. A long loop of intestine sailed into the stall, looking for a moment like a lasso slung by a demented demon cowboy, which was actually not far from the twisted fucking truth. The viscus smacked his face and he brushed it away, crying out again but staying where he was, knowing any further attempt to elude being hit was futile. More than that, it was the whole point of the insane exercise—to bathe him in blood and guts, force him down into the putrid depths of utter depravity. Hoke remembered some of the things Garner had told him earlier. Insane things. Vivid glimpses of hell. Nightmare promises from a monster.

And on it went.

Here came a heart.

A lung.

More coiled loops of intestine.

A kidney, a tongue, a hand, an arm, another arm, an eye, a cock, a foot, a shredded stomach, various piles of undefinable glop . . .

Hoke buried his face in his hands and waited for the carnage to end.

It went on.

More vile things hit him, landed near him.

Then it ended with an abrupt atmospheric change. The air in the barn felt lighter, no longer charged with the electric sizzle of demonic energy. Hoke opened his mouth and inhaled deeply, sucking in the clean air, grateful for it even as his mind teetered on the brink of an irreversible descent into catatonia. Somehow he managed to stay away from the edge.

But it was a close thing.

"Open your eyes."

Hoke didn't want to, but there was no denying that stentorian tone.

He moved his hands from his face and lifted his head, saw the slender, dark-outlined form of a man on the other side of the gate.

Garner.

Hoke swallowed hard and piss dribbled from his flaccid cock.

He sniffled. "Why me?"

A grunt. "Right body, right time."

Tears streamed from Hoke's eyes. "What if I help you find someone better? I can get you someone connected in the music industry. Someone with money." Hoke's mind scrambled for ideas. He did know some people. Important people. The important ones were more on the level of acquaintances than actual friends, but he felt certain he could get close enough to them to arrange a private audience with Garner. He'd sell out anyone given the chance. His own mother, even. Anyone to take his place in Garner's scheme. "Come on, brother. Think of what you can do out there with money."

A soft exhalation of almost laughter. "I will not want for money. No, you are to be my vessel. Time is short. Too short to procure an acceptable substitute."

Hoke wiped snot from his nose and flicked it off his hand. "Shit."

He heard the metallic snick of the gate's latch being pulled back. Then the gate moved inward and Garner stepped into the stall. The Coleman lantern dangled from the fingers of Garner's left hand, casting garish illumination over the mess on the ground.

Hoke had to know. "Why'd you kill them that way?"

"Because I could."

Hoke frowned. "Well, shit. That's some cold motherfucking shit, man. You are not right in the head. But hey, what do I care if you slaughter a gaggle of goddamn retards? Aren't their folks gonna be out for blood when they get wind of what you've done?"

Garner's free hand reached into a pocket of his black suit coat and came out with a pack of cigarettes and a lighter. He shook the pack and sucked one of the protruding white sticks into a corner of his mouth. He cupped a hand over the cigarette as he lit it. He inhaled deeply and blew out a cloud of pungent smoke. "Ah." A chuckle. "I do enjoy a good afterglow smoke. Lord Satan granted me dominion over the blighted Kincher clan. They will not retaliate. They will bow and scrape at my feet, as they have done this last century and more."

Hoke eyed Garner's cigarette enviously. "Uh-huh. They're your bitches."

This elicited a deeper rumble of laughter from Garner. "Yes. As are you."

He lifted the lantern over his head and light played over the dramatic angles of his face and elongated chin, glinted off the horns protruding from his hairline.

Hoke shivered.

He made the sign of the cross and said, "Begone, demon."

Garner peered at him curiously. "What was that?"

"Some shit I saw in a movie once. Some *bull*shit, apparently."

"Get up."

There was that undeniable tone of command again. Hoke didn't bother pleading for mercy or disobeying. The bastard was right. He was Garner's bitch, and there wasn't a damn thing he could do about it. Nothing obvious, anyway.

His knees popped as he stood and wiped some of the grue from his face and chest. "Sure you want a vessel with early-onset arthritis?"

Garner turned away from him and walked out of the stall. "Follow me."

Hoke followed the demon into the darkness. "Where are we going?"

Garner's laughter carried a mocking tone this time. "To meet your new mate. Your blushing bride. The woman of your dreams."

"Huh. Is she hot?"

Garner glanced over his shoulder at Hoke. "By *hot* I suppose you mean attractive. And that depends on your own peccadilloes. Tell me, have you ever fucked an octopus?"

A *boom* of satanic laughter.

Hoke gulped.

He prayed for a bolt of lightning to leap from the sky and charbroil him where he stood. He looked up and saw the blinking lights of a jet flying overhead, carrying some lucky assholes far from here, but there were no clouds.

So it was true what his drunk daddy used to tell him.

God just didn't like his sorry ass.

Garner kept on laughing.

CHAPTER TWENTY-FIVE

Megan sat in a metal folding chair in the center of an empty room. The room was small, about the size of the average walk-in closet. There were no windows, and the white walls were unadorned, with the exception of a few pieces of graffiti scratched into the drywall. LINDA LOVES PUSSY. GOD HELP ME. NO WAY OUT. NO SHIT. And so on. The most interesting was a phone number with an area code Megan knew to be in Manhattan. Below the number was a scrawled, messy plea from someone named Sonia begging anyone with mercy in their souls to call her parents.

Megan memorized the number.

She was still handcuffed, but otherwise was unbound. She'd been alone in the room for some five minutes, deposited here while DeMars and one of the Prestons went off somewhere for some last-minute haggling. She got up and walked to the door, tried the knob, and found it locked. No surprise there, but she gave the door a closer inspection. Maybe she could kick it open. But it looked so sturdy. She recalled a video clip she'd seen on YouTube. This guy had been trying to break into some little store well after closing time to steal beer. He kicked the store's door over and over, each kick more frantic than the last, until the final kick. The security footage of his leg snapping was a hard thing to forget.

Megan decided not to kick the door open.

She returned to the chair and sat down.

She was afraid.

Very much so.

But she was also angry.

Rage built inside her with each slowly passing moment. She was a human being. A real, feeling, flesh and blood person. But she was being treated like an animal. Worse than that, like a commodity. Something to be swapped and sold. She could be raped. Beaten. Murdered. Even eaten. And in the eyes of the local law, it was nothing. These things didn't count as crimes, because she wasn't a real person to them. And she knew she was far from the first outsider woman to endure these exercises in degradation.

It was wrong.

More than that, it was evil.

Someone should do something about it, end it once and for all.

Someone.

Somehow.

The door to the room opened, and the muffled thump of a Mötley Crüe song grew louder, became an ear-crunching blare. A man came into the room. Megan looked at his hawklike face and drew in a sharp breath of surprise. It was the same man she'd observed standing next to the van behind the Hopkins Bend General Store. One of the heartless redneck pigs who'd tossed her Pete so carelessly into the van. A face from the beginning of this nightmare, and as such it symbolized everything wrong about this town and its people.

He grinned, flashing rows of rotting, yellowed teeth. "Howdy."

He shut the door. Then he walked up to her and unzipped his pants, pulled out his dick. It was a small one. His exposed crotch stank. The vile man hadn't bathed in days. He chuckled and waved his genitals at her. Megan couldn't imagine anything more repulsive than having to suck the thing. It would be like fellating an animal. But some colder, more pragmatic part of her took abrupt control. She reached toward the man, cupped his sweaty balls in her cuffed hands and leaned toward his limp cock. This was going to be awful, but maybe she could earn some good will by playing the part of the willing, eager new whore.

But the man laughed and swatted her hands away. He pushed his cock and balls back inside his pants and zipped up. "You ain't my type, honey."

Megan licked her lips and arranged her features in an expression of fake lust. "But I'd make it good. Better than you've ever had."

He laughed again. "Wouldn't happen. I guarantee it."

Megan wriggled in the chair, scooted to its edge, leaned forward, and looked up at him. Her shoulders were hunched forward, and her cuffed hands were down between her spread legs. The thrust of her breasts was now very tantalizingly displayed in the skimpy halter top. She dropped her voice to a lower, huskier tone. "Let me prove you wrong."

"Thing is, you ain't black."

Megan frowned. "What?"

"I only like black pussy. I keep a couple of the finest Nubian princesses you ever saw in my own cellar. Wear 'em out day and night. Dick stays hard round the clock at home. Here?" He shrugged, a wry expression on his face. "Not so much. Most other local fellas favor blonde white sluts. Which is why a bitch like you is always a good business acquisition. Reason I took my dick out was to see how you'd react, because that's gonna be happening a lot. Think you can handle it?"

Megan chose not to abandon the wanton slut pose. She

licked her lips again. "I can handle all the dick you can throw at me."

The man tossed his head back and howled laughter.

Megan smiled.

And inwardly she marveled at the words that had come out of her mouth. It was not the sort of thing she would normally say. But this was not a normal situation, which was perhaps the mother of all understatements. The human race had survived through the ages because of its ability to adapt to adverse circumstances. To survive by any means necessary. And in this case that included allowing herself to be subjected, without reluctance, to all the humiliations and transgressions against her body and soul the Sin Den had in store for her. She would submit, and maybe, just maybe, somewhere down the line there would be an opportunity to escape.

The man went to the door and opened it. The blare of the music pounded her ears again. Some other hard-rock song. "Come on, honey. It's time to meet your new boss."

Megan stood and followed him through the door into a long and narrow hallway. The tight space was bathed in a warm red light from ceiling bulbs. Music and faint male laughter emanated from somewhere on the other side of the wall to her right. The walls were painted black and adorned with posters of naked and scantily attired girls in various suggestive poses. Others went beyond suggestive, including one that showed a large-breasted black woman wearing a strap-on dildo. She stood with her long legs spread wide, posing behind the upthrust ass of a slender white woman who was kneeling over the edge of a sofa. Megan supposed the man she was following had picked that one out.

At the end of the hallway, a single door stood open on the left. They were still a good twenty paces or so from the door. The man was staring straight ahead, not looking at her. She glanced over her shoulder and saw they were the only ones in the hallway. Two competing fantasies took almost immediate shape in her head. The first was to turn and run, maybe find some back way out of this place and make a break for the thick surrounding wilderness. The alternate fantasy included murder. She imagined looping her cuffed hands around the man's neck from behind. He was short enough. She could do it. Arms up and then down over his head. Hands and handcuff steel tight around his throat as she rode him down to the floor and strangled the life out of him. The first fantasy was the easiest to dismiss. Sure, maybe she could get outside, but the alarm would be raised in seconds. And say she did get out and into the woods. What then? She imagined a pack of shotgun-toting rednecks and hound dogs chasing her down. Even setting aside the handicap of her cuffed hands, the notion was clearly not feasible on any level. She had no real outdoors survival skills. And the idea of tromping around in strange and dangerous terrain in the dead of night? Forget about it. Now, if she killed Mr. Black Pussy Lover, she might buy herself some time, perhaps even enough to get away and into the woods before the alarm was raised. But ultimately she would find herself in the same position and facing the same set of potential pitfalls and hazards.

So . . . no.

The best approach remained the "go along to get along" scheme. She just hoped there would be a payoff somewhere down the line to make it worth her while.

They reached the end of the hallway and she followed the man through the doorway into a large and brightly lit dressing room. There was a row of primping and makeup application stations along the walls to her left and right. More than a dozen girls in various stages of undress turned to look at her. The women were all very pretty. Some were almost beautiful. Even so, only one or two were even remotely in her class. Megan recognized this as the ruthless side of her personality coming to the forefront again, and she was happy to allow it sway. These girls were her sister prisoners. Slaves. But they were also her competition. She would have to be better than any of them to have any hope of achieving her goals.

And I will be, she thought.

It was interesting to study the expressions of the women as they appraised her. A few clearly evinced empathy and concern. One girl, a short but busty brunette, even had tears in her eyes. Others had carefully blank expressions. A few scowled at her. A tall, stunning blonde wearing only frilly pink panties flipped her off.

The man paused to slap the bare ass of the one black girl in the group. The girl squealed and threw her arms around his neck. "Carl, baby, where you been keeping yourself, honey? You ain't had me out to your place in so long."

Carl grinned. "Could be I'm gonna be looking to cycle in some fresh meat soon, sweet thing." He scratched his chin. "Maybe you should convince me you're the right girl for the job."

The girl made a purring sound deep in her throat and pulled him close. They kissed. It went on for a while. A lot of very enthusiastic tongue-bathing was involved. Megan stood in the center of the room and fidgeted, nervous from the continued silent scrutiny of the other girls. The striking blonde who'd flipped her off approached her. The girl was maybe an inch or two under six feet, much taller than Megan, so it was hard not to feel intimidated. The perfect Nordic cheekbones didn't help matters, adding to the overall impression of a cruel and pitiless ice queen. The girl was smiling, but her eyes projected almost palpable hate.

She leaned down and whispered in Megan's ear. "First chance I get, I'm gonna fuck you up." She nipped at Megan's earlobe, making her flinch. "Smash that pretty face to pieces."

She launched a fist into Megan's midsection. Air exploded from her lungs as the blow nearly lifted her off her feet. Megan stood bent over and gasping for breath. She braced for a follow-up blow, but none came. The tall girl was already back at one of the primping stations, her back turned to Megan as she stared at a mirror and drew a brush through long, lustrous hair.

Megan was upright again by the time Carl broke the clinch with the black girl. He turned to look at her and frowned at her pained expression. "What happened to you?"

"Nothing."

He frowned some more, then shrugged. "Come on, bitch. Business to take care of."

Megan followed him toward a closed door at the far end of the room. She glanced over her shoulder and saw the tall blonde staring at her, a small smile lifting the corners of her pink-painted lips. She hoped her refusal to narc had earned her some goodwill. That was one woman she didn't want for an enemy. Yeah, she'd promised to "fuck her up," but maybe—

Carl opened the door and said, "Stop gawking, bitch, and come on in."

Megan looked at Carl and smiled. "Sorry. Couldn't help it. I love looking at naked women."

Carl chuckled. "Sure you do. But you're playing the game well, I'll give you that." He swept a hand toward the door. "In. Now."

Megan stepped through the door into a roomy office. More posters of naked and near-naked women in slutty poses adorned the walls here. Another door stood open on

the other side of the room, allowing a peek at what was
clearly a bathroom. A row of file cabinets stood against
one wall. Against another were bookshelves stuffed full
with pornographic DVDs. An attractive woman in a blue
silk negligee sat behind a desk. She had been reading a
magazine, but set it aside as they came into the room. Carl
closed the door and nudged Megan toward a chair in front
of the desk. The woman on the other side of the desk had
long, dark hair, so dark it was almost black, and she was as
pretty as any of the girls in the dressing room. But she was
older than any of them by more than a decade.

Carl folded his arms and leaned a shoulder against the
closed door. "Thought DeMars was gonna be here for
this."

The woman smiled and shrugged. "Rich had to leave
in a hurry. Some emergency. Regardless, we were able to
conclude our business satisfactorily. This one belongs to
us now."

"Good, 'cause I got a feeling this one's gonna be
popular with the boys."

The woman opened one of the desk's drawers, reached
inside, and removed something. She flicked a hand in
Carl's direction, and the thing she'd removed from the
drawer sailed across the room. Megan caught a glimpse
of something silver and tiny before Carl snagged it with
an outstretched hand.

"Rich left that. Uncuff her."

Carl stepped in front of Megan and knelt between her
legs. She looked down and saw the little key sliding into
the lock. One little twist and the metal bracelets popped
open. Carl stood up and tossed the handcuffs and key on
the desk. Megan shook her hands and rubbed her wrists,
working the circulation back into them.

The woman kept her gaze on Megan, but addressed
Carl. "You can leave now."

Carl didn't say anything, just left the room and closed the door behind him.

The woman stared at Megan for several long, uncomfortable moments in total silence.

Then she smiled and leaned over the desk. "What's your name, sweetie?"

"Megan."

"You'll need a stage name. Something sexier."

"Okay."

"Stand up."

Megan stood.

The woman's gaze moved up and down the length of her body.

"Turn around."

Megan did a slow spin.

The woman was nodding now. "Nice."

"Thank you."

"Take your clothes off."

Megan stepped out of her shoes, unbuttoned her jeans and began to shimmy out of them. As she did, she heard a low, almost inaudible moan issue from the bathroom. She frowned and glanced that way as she stepped out of the jeans and kicked them aside. The moan came again.

She hooked thumbs in the elastic band of her panties and began to slide them down. "Is someone in there?"

The woman nodded. "Yes."

"Who?"

Megan stepped out of the panties and pulled the halter top off over her head.

"The girl you're about to kill for me."

Megan's fingers froze for a moment on the hook of her bra. She felt dizzy for a second. But only for a second. She unhooked her bra and removed it, let it drop to the floor. "When do I get to kill her?"

"Soon."

"Good."

The woman smiled. "But first . . . dance for me."

Megan returned the smile.

She danced.

And she tried not to think about the girl in the bathroom.

CHAPTER TWENTY-SIX

Something important occurred to Jessica. Maybe it meant something. Maybe it didn't. But she had to know the answer. She didn't like loose ends.

"Why were you stopped?"

Larry arched an eyebrow. "Say what?"

"I saw you go blazing by me, like you were on your way to somewhere important in a big damn hurry." Jessica's thumb caressed the .38's hammer. She felt a strange kind of intimacy with the weapon. An easy familiarity she found comforting. It was a bond forged in blood and noise, in the acrid scent of gunpowder and memories of the still bodies of dead adversaries. She could put this gun to Larry's head, if she had a reason. Put the barrel right up against his temple and squeeze the trigger, watch the bullet blow his head apart. But she really hoped he wouldn't provide a reason. "I took off after you fast as I could, but you should have gotten away. So . . . why did you stop?"

Larry removed the cigarette from his mouth, the third he'd smoked in their brief time together, and said, "I do believe I detect a note of paranoia in that question."

"Maybe. I'd still like an answer."

Larry shrugged and put the cigarette back in his mouth, then removed it again and blew a stream of smoke out the open driver's-side window. "Ain't no big mystery." Yet another drag on the cigarette. A chain smoker. His breath reflected this, but the unpleasant odor had not blunted the sweet taste of his lips. And right then she wanted to kiss him again, this man she was so willing to kill with just the right (or wrong) kind of provocation. How strange.

Strange, but undeniable.

"So spill it."

She clenched her teeth, bit down hard on her lower lip.

Clutched the gun tighter.

Larry appeared to sense the tension seething inside her. He glanced at the gun and shifted uncomfortably in his seat. His cigarette burned down to the filter in the silence. He stubbed it out in the overflowing ashtray and punched in the dash lighter as he shook a fresh smoke from a dwindling pack.

He lit up again and looked at the road as he talked. "I've got this ex. Real crazy broad name of Roxanne. Sometimes she gets liquored up and comes skulking around my place. Really didn't want to deal with her tonight, so I pulled over and called my friend Bill, this guy who lives across the street from me. I asked him to take a peek outside and let me know if the coast was clear."

"And?"

"Bill didn't see her. Didn't see her car, either, which don't necessarily mean anything. She'll sometimes drive it down the road and park out of sight."

"Why don't you get a restraining order?"

Larry snorted laughter. "Local law ain't got the manpower to enforce a thing like that. If they did, they'd be out to my place every other night dragging the bitch, pardon my French, off to fucking jail. And anyway, I'm a big boy. I can take care of myself. Getting a restraining order—hell, that's kind of a sissy thing to do."

Jessica grunted. "Interesting attitude, Larry. Tell me something. Is everyone in Hopkins Bend as big a moron as you?"

Larry's face crumpled, the good, easy humor draining entirely from his features in about two seconds. "You don't need to insult me."

"Where's your phone?"

Larry frowned. "Huh?"

"Your cell phone, Larry. The one you used to call your friend."

"Yeah, you are definitely paranoid."

"You need to show it to me, Larry. Right now."

Larry rolled his eyes and shoved a hand down a hip pocket of his jeans. He extracted a slim black cell phone and held it up for Jessica's inspection. She snatched it from his fingers and flipped it open.

Larry shook his head. "Why, yes, Jessica, you do have my permission to use my phone. In fact—"

"Shut up."

Larry's mouth closed.

The phone's menu was a breeze to navigate, and she found the list of recently dialed numbers within moments. She quickly scrolled through the names and numbers, then flipped the phone shut and shoved it into her own pocket. "This friend you were talking about. Is his name William Murphy?"

Larry eyed her warily. "Well . . . yeah. That's him."

"You haven't called him since yesterday."

"I can explain."

"Don't. How far are we from your place?"

Larry glanced at the gun again and cringed a little

when he met Jessica's fierce gaze. "Look, the shit I told you about Roxanne, it's all true. And I do sometimes call Bill for a scouting report on my way home."

"I don't care. Answer my question."

"I stopped to do a bump of coke. I didn't want to tell you." He indicated the dashboard with a small nod of his head. "Check the glove box."

Jessica opened the glove compartment.

She sucked in a quick, startled breath. It was there, just as he'd said, a small amount of white powder weighing down a corner of a crumpled plastic sandwich bag. She swallowed with great difficulty, the lump in her throat like a ball of smoldering charcoal sliding down her esophagus. She felt dizzy. Sweat collected in her armpits and slid down her sides. She flung the bag back inside the glove box and flipped it shut.

Larry cleared his throat. "You, ah . . . sort of treated my little stash like it was on fire."

Jessica stared at the closed glove box. "I had a small problem with that shit a while back."

"What happened?"

"Rehab."

"Ah, shit. So you don't party at all, huh?"

"I drink."

"Huh." Larry stroked the stubble on his chin and pursed his lips. "Never been to rehab myself. Reckon I'll keep at it until the stuff does me in or I just get too old to party. But the way I understand it, you go to rehab, you're supposed to quit everything."

Jessica looked at him. His earnest expression eased some of her tension. There was genuine human concern there. It was nice to see after facing down so many bad guys. "I live by my own rules and what's right for me. I drink. Sometimes I drink too much. But I don't have a problem with it, not like I did with coke. Trust me."

Larry nodded. "Okay. Good enough."

"I know I'm being bitchy, but I've had kind of a rough day."

"I understand."

A moment of silence.

Jessica watched the trees flash by.

She looked at Larry and his face turned her way, a bemused smile working at the corners of his mouth. "Yeah?"

She touched his knee again. "You're kind of cute for a redneck."

He laughed. "You ain't so bad yourself. Ain't every day I run into a gal kicks more ass than Zoë Bell and looks like a supermodel."

"Supermodel." Jessica snorted. "Right. That's the second time you've used that ridiculous word."

"Yeah, but I ain't kiddin'."

They looked at each other, eyes locking, and a different kind of tension formed between them again. Jessica experienced a dizzying surge of arousal. Her hand tightened around Larry's knee. "Please tell me we're almost—"

Larry grinned. "Hell, we're already there, practically."

He nodded at the road ahead and she saw a glow of electric lights some hundred yards away and coming up fast. Another fifty yards closer and she was able to make out the low-lying outlines of two ranch-style houses facing each other across the road. There were no street lamps out this way, but the smallish lawns were lit by floodlights. The house to the left showed signs of a human presence. Lights were on throughout the house, and a truck was parked in the driveway. The lights were out in the house to the right, and the driveway was empty, obviously marking it as Larry's home, a guess verified in a few moments when he pulled into the driveway and shut the Nova's engine off.

He let out a yelp of surprise as she came at him in a hurry, shoving him back against the seat and straddling his thigh as her wet lips found his mouth and went to work. She probed his mouth with her tongue, her head turning in a blur of constant motion as she attacked him from every angle with her mouth. Kissing him hard and teasing him endlessly with her tongue. She chewed on his lower lip and kissed his neck, making him arch his back and moan.

He was panting when she pulled away. His face was flushed and covered in a sheen of sweat, and his racing pulse beat visibly at his neck. He gaped at her in obvious astonishment as he struggled to catch his breath.

"Like that?"

He nodded and managed a low, hoarse reply. "Yeah . . . oh, God, yeah . . ."

"Of course you did."

She writhed slowly against him, enjoying the way his face contorted. Enjoyed, too, the feel of his strong hands sliding over her body. The sensation was so good it nearly erased the lingering aches that had plagued her since the crash.

"Want some more?"

He nodded. Whimpered.

Such a helpless sound from such a strong man.

She loved it.

She slid away from him, settled back into the passenger seat. "Take me inside, Larry. Now."

Larry didn't have to be told twice. He was out of the car maybe a second later, and she was right behind him. They walked briskly up a path of inlaid stone steps toward the front porch. Jessica watched him from behind, enjoying the interplay of muscles obvious through the fabric of his tight white T-shirt. He looked as if he worked out a lot when he wasn't speeding around in a

goofy Chevy Nova and snorting coke. She was so eager
to wrap herself around his lean and powerful body, she
was almost drooling. A desperate desire for hot, sweaty
sex was a strange thing for a woman in her position to
crave. She recognized and accepted this. Didn't lessen
the desire one bit, though. It even made a crazy kind of
sense to her. She had started the day as the victim of an
assault. Male strength and anger had been used against
her. And now here she was, a few hours later, wanting it
from this man, this stranger, and she was the aggressor,
in a way. But it was about more than that. She'd seen
bloody death up close multiple times. Had felt her heart
slam and almost feel as if it would burst as she narrowly
eluded her own death more than once. She'd heard sex
described as the ultimate affirmation of life, a sentiment
she'd not truly understood before. Now, as she watched
Larry, she thought she understood it perfectly.

God, but I want to fuck this man's brains out.

She thought of the packet of coke in Larry's car and
remembered with shocking vividness how much she
used to enjoy getting fucked all night long while coked
out of her mind. The thought made her lips curl and her
nostrils flare.

Maybe . . .

No.

She shoved the thought out of her mind. Going down
that path again would inevitably lead her back into the
mess she'd left behind years ago. She could not allow it
to happen, not even one little slip. She'd made a promise
to her mother after rehab, and now more than ever, with
her gone, she meant to keep that promise.

Still . . .

No!

Her heart was beating fast, almost too fast, by the time
they reached the porch. Another reminder of the drug

days. She watched Larry climb the steps to the porch and lean toward the yellow glow of the single porch light to sort through his keys. She silently urged him to hurry as she planted a foot on the first step. She needed to be inside and tearing his clothes off. Needed to lose herself in his body and derail the potentially destructive train of thought brought on by the coke memories.

He found the right key and grinned over his shoulder at her. "Got it."

"Hurry."

He opened a screen door and slipped the key in the lock. He chuckled. "Movin' as fast as I can."

He turned the key and twisted the knob.

Jessica climbed another step. . . .

She saw the dark bloom of crimson in the center of his back a fraction of a second before she heard the shot. The sound came again. And again. Larry's body twitched as multiple bullets hit it. He staggered backward, crashed into Jessica, and sent her spinning to the ground. She landed hard and rolled. She wound up on her back, but then heaved herself onto her side. She saw Larry's body sprawled on the ground. He was dead. She saw and understood that right away. But she couldn't comprehend why it had happened. She felt sick and dizzy, her mind swirling with a clash of conflicting, incoherent thoughts. Larry's eyes were open and still, staring straight up at the black sky.

Someone was screaming.

Jessica tore her eyes away from the dead man.

A woman in very short blue-jean cutoffs and a pink halter top stood outlined in the open doorway, a smoking pistol clutched in her right hand. The gears in Jessica's mind spun around like the numbers on a slot machine and landed on a name written in pulsing red block letters across the forefront of her consciousness: ROXANNE.

The crazy ex Larry had talked about on the way here.

He hadn't been lying, after all.

The woman was coming down the porch now.

Coming toward *her.*

She was still screaming, but the sounds coalesced into actual, understandable words now: "YOU FUCKING WHORE! I KNEW THAT SONOFABITCH WAS SCREWING SOME GODDAMN FUCKING WHORE! YOU'RE DEAD, YOU FUCKING CUNT!"

She was standing over Jessica now, red-lacquered fingernails curled around the butt of a .44 Magnum. She aimed the gun at Jessica's face and spoke in a drunken slur. "Say good-bye, bitch. I hope the two of you have fun burning in hell."

Jessica remembered the gun in her own hand.

She raised it and aimed.

Another explosion rang out in the quiet rural night.

CHAPTER TWENTY-SEVEN

The old Maynard cabin looked like a dead thing glimpsed from the outside. A rotting husk. It was strange. Shadows should obscure ugly truth. But the moonlight highlighted the old structure's decrepitude in ways not obvious when viewed beneath the glare of the summer sun. Yes, it looked dead. Frail. Brittle. Looking at it made Abby think of a black-and-white photo she'd once seen of the hull of an old ship washed up on a stretch of lonely beach. The cabin was a standing ruin, a thing left over from an age long past.

Sadness encroached as she neared the cabin's sagging front porch. She had a strong feeling the old ways and the old families were nearing the end of a long road. They had endured against the march of time and progress since before the days of secession and war. But the world outside Hopkins Bend just kept getting bigger, expanding and pushing into areas where before there had only been wildlife and lush wilderness. It didn't take any kind of genius or seer to know the locals couldn't keep the outside world at bay forever. Someday some smart person in law enforcement would begin to put some pieces together, maybe start to pinpoint a general area where so many people had gotten permanently lost on the way to somewhere else. Someone might then dig into the old files on Evan Maynard. And after that, the end would come pretty quick.

As Abby stepped into the cabin's dark interior and paused to light the lantern that hung just inside the door, she wondered why the thought should make her sad. She'd all but washed her hands of Hopkins Bend. She planned to be gone from here forever by this time Saturday. She hated life here. Hated her status as an outcast, which was becoming more entrenched with each passing day. And yet this was the only life she'd ever known, here in this cabin and in the woods she knew well, among these people.

She went into the kitchen and lit another lantern. This one she removed from its hook on the wall and carried with her as she moved through the tight, dark pantry. She opened the door to the cellar and exercised great care as she descended the creaking stairs to the cellar floor. She held the lantern up and looked at Michelle. The woman she'd thought of as "the dinner" until earlier today was asleep, her body hanging slack from the rope securing her to the beam overhead. Her head hung to one side, and her chest softly rose and fell as she breathed in and out.

Abby hung the lantern on a hook and approached Michelle. The woman kept sleeping, apparently undisturbed by either the intrusion of light or Abby's proximity. That, or she was pretending to sleep. Feigning sleep was something most of them did from time to time, even though it never did them any good. Abby felt her breath quicken as she allowed herself a few moments to admire the woman's toned and shapely body. She longed to touch her again. To let her hands go wherever they wanted to go. And do whatever they wanted to do. It was so painfully tempting. . . .

She closed her mouth and held her breath.

Counted to ten.

Let the breath out.

And said, "It's me."

Michelle opened her eyes and looked at Abby. The dark eyes were unreadable in the flickering gloom, but the way they looked at her so steadily made Abby's heart flutter. Michelle made a noise behind the gag, prompting Abby to pull it gently away from her mouth.

"God. Thank you." Michelle breathed heavily. "You have no idea how hard it is too breathe only through your nose all the fucking time."

"Sorry I had to put the gag back. Ma or my sister might've come around whiles I was gone."

"So you did it to keep up appearances."

"That's right."

"Can't you let me down yet?"

Abby shook her head. "Sorry. Ain't time yet."

Michelle frowned. Her eyes shifted from Abby, stared into a dark corner of the cellar. Abby resisted an urge to brush the back of a hand across one of the woman's finely sculpted cheeks. But resistance wasn't easy. There was something about Michelle that made a person ache with the need to touch her. Something beyond the superficial allure of beauty. Perhaps it was a hint of the exotic she found so compelling. A driver's license or passport would identify her as Caucasian, but the vaguely almond shade of her skin suggested a dollop of Latino blood flowing through her veins. The lush lips and big eyes reinforced this suggestion.

Michelle was looking at her again. "Abby?"

"Yeah?"

A corner of the woman's mouth twitched, almost curled into a knowing smirk. "Kiss me."

Abby's cheeks blazed scarlet. "What . . . ? You want me to . . . what?"

Michelle smiled. "I want you to kiss me."

She stretched her neck out, puckered those delectably plump lips.

Abby was trembling. "I—I don't know . . ."

Michelle did smirk this time. "Seemed like you knew what you wanted when you had your hands on me earlier."

Abby's face flushed again. "I'm . . . sorry about that. I had no right."

"It's okay. I liked it."

"You did?"

"Yeah."

Abby wiped sweat from her brow and smiled nervously. "I . . . liked it, too." Her heart was beating so fast, it felt as if it might explode as she made this admission. "You're so pretty."

"You need to kiss me, Abby. Now."

She extended her neck again.

Puckered her lips again.

Abby leaned toward her.

Their mouths met.

The first flick of Michelle's tongue was all it took to make her lose all control. She wrapped her arms around the woman and leaned into the kiss. Michelle hooked a strong leg around Abby's waist and locked their bodies together. Abby felt the thrust of Michelle's erect nipples through the fabric of her dress. The sensation stoked the flame of her arousal to an almost unbearable intensity. She twisted out of the sweaty embrace long enough to pull the dress off over her head. Then she threw herself against Michelle again, desire blinding her to everything, including the way the woman winced as the chains binding her wrists chafed painfully against her flesh. It also obscured the dim creak made by a foot placed carefully on the wooden staircase behind them.

Michelle pried her lips away from Abby's mouth and spoke in a hoarse tone between panting breaths. "Take . . . me down. We'll make love . . . right here."

Abby cupped Michelle's face in her hands and felt sweat against her palms. The slick sheen covering every inch of the woman's body shimmered in the lantern light. To Abby, she looked like a glowing, ethereal goddess. Michelle leaned closer, soft lips brushing her mouth again, breath hot against her tingling flesh. "You can't imagine how good I am."

Abby whimpered deep in her throat.

She struggled for focus. She needed to think past the overwhelming desire consuming her long enough to figure out what to do. It was tempting to say fuck everything else and do what Michelle asked. She imagined herself stretched out on the cellar floor, Michelle doing amazing things to her body with her skilled hands and mouth. That image alone was almost enough to make her fetch the key. But she forced herself to hold on a little longer. To think some more. She'd told Michelle tomorrow evening would be the best time to attempt an escape, but she'd only said that to buy herself some time while she tried to make a final decision about what to do. Her mind had been made up for some time by this point, though.

Okay, she thought. *I'll let her down.*

We'll go tonight.

With Ma and Laura out whoring around—and Laura's brats scattered to God alone knew where—there could be no better time. The cabin above the cellar was empty and might stay that way for hours yet. Abby felt a rising excitement as she saw that the time to make the bold move she'd fantasized about had finally arrived.

"I'll get the key."

Michelle's eyes went wide with surprise. It was clear she hadn't believed Abby would actually do it. "Really?"

Abby cupped the woman's face again. "Really. We're getting the fuck outta here."

Tears formed in Michelle's eyes and rolled slowly down her cheeks. She sniffled. "Thank you."

A voice rang out like an explosion somewhere behind them. "WHAT IN GOD'S NAME IS GOING ON DOWN HERE?"

Abby jumped.

Michelle groaned and said, "Fuck."

Abby unwrapped herself from Michelle's sleek body and turned around to see Laura Maynard standing at the foot of the cellar stairs. Her sister's mouth hung open in astonishment. She stared aghast at Abby, looking at her in the manner of a person in the presence of something truly abominable.

Her sister's voice rang out again: "YOU FUCKING PERVERT!" She moved several steps toward them and thrust a finger toward the cellar stairs. "GET YOUR CLOTHES ON, YOU GODDAMN FREAK, AND GET THE FUCK ON OUT OF MY HOUSE!"

Abby just stared at her.

She imagined her sister hearing the moans and whimpers as she'd come down the stairs. Imagined what she must have thought when she saw them together. When she'd finally understood that something other than the usual abuse of the prisoner was happening. And in that moment, Abby understood just how completely and irretrievably lost her old life was now.

Laura took another step toward her and thrust her outstretched arm back toward the stairs again. "Did you not hear me, you perverted piece of shit? I want you out of my house. Now. God help you if I have to tell you again."

Abby bristled inwardly.

Her house?

As if Ma was dead already.

As if she had already assumed ownership of the Maynard legacy.

Abby lowered her head and charged her sister, her mouth open wide, as a roar of pure fury tore out of her lungs. Laura stood paralyzed in open-mouthed shock for a moment. But only for a moment. She turned and ran for the stairs, hit the bottom step in about a second and ascended the first few steps quickly. Abby let out another yell as she hit the staircase and pounded up the steps after her. Laura glanced over her shoulder as she reached the top of the staircase and screamed at the look of murderous rage on her sister's face. She banged through the door and tried to slam it shut, but Abby rammed her shoulder against the old and brittle wood. The door creaked and splintered, flew to pieces as Abby barreled into the tight space of the pantry. Laura screamed again as she flew through the door to the kitchen and tried the door-shutting tactic again. She undoubtedly meant to lock Abby inside and keep her there until Ma or someone else returned.

But Abby would not be stopped.

She had a destiny to meet.

With Michelle.

Nothing could get in the way of that.

Abby smashed through the door an instant before it could close. Laura screamed again and staggered backward as Abby bulled her way into the kitchen. Her butt met the edge of the dinner table, and she let out a strangled yelp as Abby closed the rest of the distance between. Abby's fist shot forward and slammed into Laura's soft midsection, bending her over at the waist.

Laura wheezed and looked up at her through eyes misty with tears.

Eyes bright with shock and fear.

Abby's fist came down again.

Laura's nose yielded with an audible snap beneath the heavy blow. Blood gushed from her nostrils as she spun away from the table and hit the floor. All coherent thought left Abby's mind then. Abby was gone during that time. In her place was a savage thing made of fury and violence. She straddled Laura and pinned her to the floor. Her fists rained down again and again. Endlessly. A blur of motion as Laura's lips turned to pulp beneath the blows. A few teeth came loose from her gums and her mouth filled with blood. And still the blows kept coming. Abby didn't feel the punishment her fists were absorbing. It was as if she had blocks of steel welded to her wrists.

She had no idea how much time had gone by when she finally stopped hitting her sister. Maybe a minute or two. Maybe ten or fifteen. It hardly mattered by then. Laura was still alive. A blood bubble at a corner of her mouth popped as a weak breath rolled out. But her eyes were glassy and unseeing.

The bitch wasn't going anywhere.

Abby got slowly, shakily to her feet.

She took a look around the kitchen.

There.

The big meat tenderizer.

She grabbed it from a hook on the wall and settled herself atop Laura again. She didn't do anything right away. She watched Laura's eyes. Waited for them to focus and look at her. Waited for her to see what was happening to her.

Laura's vision seemed to clear at last.

She looked at Abby.

"Please . . ."

Abby snarled and raised the heavy steel tenderizer over her head.

Laura shook her head weakly. "No . . . please . . ."

Abby's hand came down.

Steel cracked against skull.

There were more blows.

A lot of them.

When it was over, Abby washed her hands with soap and a jug of water. She felt strangely calm and still didn't feel quite like herself. Maybe that was because she wasn't the same person she'd been just a few minutes ago. She'd undergone yet another change. She knew now what she was capable of doing to get what she wanted.

What she was capable of was anything at all.

I'm getting what I want, she thought.

I really fucking am, and nothing can stop me.

She returned to her sister's limp body and knelt to seize it by the wrists.

Then she began to drag it toward the splintered pantry door and the cellar beyond.

CHAPTER TWENTY-EIGHT

Somewhere around the end of the third or fourth time Justine coerced him to hardness yet again and had her way with him, Pete happened to look at just the right section of darkness beyond the pen and saw that they had an audience. A lean figure stood several feet away, watching them from the shadows. The rear of the house was some thirty yards from the cages, too far away for the back porch light to illuminate the person's face. Pete's first thought was the voyeur was Carl, but no, the dark-outlined figure was too short to be that son of a bitch. This guy had to be the third Preston brother, the one whose name he didn't know. He stretched his neck and squinted his eyes in an effort to make out more detail, and instantly regretted it. He couldn't see the man's hands, but judging by the frantic motion of his right arm, one of them was at his crotch, going up and down like a piston. Pete felt sick. The redneck bastard was jerking off. He wanted to yell at the guy, tell him to stop being such a goddamn pervert, but what was the use? The asshole would just do what he wanted anyway. And he might get mad.

Pete didn't want him mad.

God, no.

Justine's vivid account of her boyfriend's mutilation and murder was always right at the edges of his thoughts, even as she was in the midst of fucking him half-blind, like now. He didn't want to wind up like that. But it seemed inevitable. And every time he thought that, a black hole seemed to open in his heart. Christ, but he didn't want to die, and especially not like that. He was too young. There was still so much to do. So many adventures still to be had. It wasn't fair. And worse, he knew too well how it would go down. He would beg. Plead. He would cry. Promise anything. And they would laugh at him. Taunt him. And then introduce him to a level of pain he'd never imagined could exist.

Justine clamped a hand around his chin and forced him to look at her.

She was on top of him, her body undulating as she rode him. He watched her breasts bounce as his hard-on throbbed inside her. She smiled and her hand went to his throat, closed tight around it, cutting off his air. Pete wheezed. The instinctive panic he'd felt the first several times she'd done this hit him again. But after a few moments, she relaxed her grip and he sucked in hard, filling his lungs with sweet, glorious air. She laughed. She laughed every time she did that. It was scary. But he couldn't bring himself to make her stop. And why should that be a surprise? She'd already proven many times how thoroughly powerless he was against her.

She slapped him and laughed again.

Pete's whole body ached. She'd used and abused him beyond the normal limits of what he thought he could endure. Had he thought this was their third or fourth go-round? It was hard to be sure. The evening had been little more than a blur of sweaty, seemingly endless sex. So he had kind of lost count. This could be the fifth time they'd been at it. Hell, the sixth. Who the fuck knew? It was crazy. He was as horny as the average guy his age. He had a healthy libido. But prior to tonight, he would not have thought it possible to get back in the saddle so many damn times in one night. But the girl had magic fucking fingers. Every time he came, she'd let him rest for a very short while, then go to work on him again. God . . . the things she could do with her fingers, mouth, and tongue. He thought of what Megan was like in bed. Good. Very good.

But nothing like this.

Not even close.

The sting of betrayal he felt every time his thoughts went in this direction was less severe every time. This time it hardly hurt at all. Justine had said she could make men do what she wanted. She could wrap any man around her little finger. Perhaps she hadn't been exaggerating. So what did that mean? That he belonged to her now? He had to be as crazy as she was to even toy with the idea.

Justine slapped him again. "Do you like it when I hit you?"

Pete gulped, looked up into her glittering eyes. "Y-yes."

"You see? You're already mine."

Pete didn't argue. Why bother?

The rhythm of her writhing body slowed to an exquisite grind. Pete moaned and screwed his eyes shut, arched his back toward her.

Then he heard something.

A scrape of metal against metal.

He frowned and thought, *What was—*

Justine yelped as she was ripped away from Pete and thrown to the ground several feet away. Pete lay there panting, his mind a whirl of confusion as he struggled to figure out what was going on. Then he sat up and saw the Preston brother standing in the center of the cage with his back to him. He was fumbling with the fly of his jeans and advancing on Justine, who screeched and scooted backward into a corner. The dogs in the other cages howled and leaped against the chain-link fencing, making it rattle loudly. Pete glanced toward the house and the closed back door, expecting to see it swing open any second as one of the other Prestons came out to investigate the racket. But that didn't happen. The door stayed shut and no other lights came on inside the house.

Pete's attention shifted abruptly to something else.

The gate. It was open.

This was his chance to make a run for it. He had no choice but to give it a shot. He got to his hands and knees, felt his toes curl into the dry ground, his leg muscles tensing like those of a sprinter in the last seconds before the report of the starting gun. Freedom was just six feet away. He could get out of here and find Megan. They could get away from this place and back to the lives these fuckers had tried to steal from them. A voice from the back of his mind screamed at him to go, but he couldn't make himself do it.

Not yet.

He found himself staring at Justine. She was still in the corner, unable to retreat any farther. The Preston brother had his pants down around his ankles and was kicking them off. In another moment or so, he'd drop to his knees and ram himself into her. The man was clearly a prisoner of lust, perhaps had been driven mad with it as he watched Justine do those amazing things with her body. Pete could hardly blame the guy. Watching that would drive any man mad. Mad enough to be careless.

Pete got to his feet and approached the man as stealthily as he could from behind. He was only a few feet away when the man dropped to his knees and leaned toward Justine. Pete let out a roar and launched himself at him, wrapping a muscular forearm around his throat and wrenching him away from her. He rode the man to the ground and shifted his arm so that the crook of his elbow was against the front of the man's throat. The man screamed and thrashed, but Pete locked his arm in place by gripping his upraised wrist with his other hand. From there it was only a matter of keeping his grip in place and steadily increasing the pressure. The man's struggles soon began to abate and finally ceased altogether. Pete kept the pressure on for an additional minute to be sure the guy was really gone. Then he let out a big breath and let go of him. He rolled the man over and stared for a moment at his still features, then sighed.

Then the enormity of what he'd done hit him.

It rocked him, made him feel faint for a moment.

Holy fuck, he thought.

I just killed a man.

He felt a strange twist of grief deep in his guts, but that didn't last long. He remembered where he was and what these redneck fucks had done to him. And then he felt nothing but anger and a rising sense of righteousness.

Fuck this guy, he thought.

Burn in hell, asshole.

Justine was on her feet now.

She came over and spat in the dead man's face. "Pig. You deserved to die."

Pete looked at her. "Truer words have never been spoken. We're getting out of here."

Justine smiled.

Then she threw her arms around him and hugged him so hard he couldn't breathe for a moment, which of course reminded him of what he'd done to the Preston brother. He disengaged himself from her and said, "Yeah, I'm happy, too. But we don't have time to fuck around."

Justine nodded. "Yes. There'll be lots of time for fucking later."

This girl, she had a one-track mind.

Not that he minded.

He found his clothes and hurriedly put them on. Then he clasped hands with Justine and they walked out of the cage, leaving the dead man alone with the howling dogs.

CHAPTER TWENTY-NINE

The place was like goddamn *Green Acres* gone straight to fucking hell. Check that. Gone to hell and turned inside out. And in this Bizarro World version, Eddie Albert was getting ass-raped day and night and smoking crack round the clock just to fucking cope and deal. There were loose chickens clucking and pecking at things on the ground. An old hound dog loped alongside Garner, big pink tongue lolling out of its slobbery mouth. Various young members of the Kincher clan were just hanging out. He saw teenagers lounging sullenly on a rusted-out tractor. They were all ugly as original sin, but this one boy sitting in the tractor's seat made the rest of them look like pinup models. His head was the size of a pumpkin. A big pumpkin. But his face had this sort of mashed-in look, as if a couple of guys had worked him over with Louisville Sluggers. One eye was at least an inch higher than the other, and a thick white pus wept from the other. The boy didn't have a nose, at least not in the usual sense. There were some holes the size of peas in the center of his swollen, diseased-looking features. Hoke guessed the poor bastard breathed through them. The boy's bloated lips twisted and formed the most grotesque smile Hoke had ever seen.

Hoke shivered. "Goddamn. That boy got thumped with the ugly stick so hard the ugly stick done broke. Am I right?"

Garner chuckled. "You admire my work, then?"

"I don't know if *admire* is the right word, but brother, when you set out to put your blight on a bunch of folks, you sure don't fuck around. Got to give you that."

Another chuckle. "You haven't seen anything yet. Wait until you meet Gladys."

"Who the fuck is Gladys?"

"Ah, how soon we forget. Gladys is the Kincher matriarch. She is one hundred and seventy-nine years old."

"Oh, come on."

"Have I lied to you yet?"

"Uh . . . no. Guess you haven't, at that." Hoke frowned. "So . . . Whoa, hold on. How does anyone—and I mean anyone other than demon folk like you—get to be one hundred and seventy-nine motherfucking years old?"

By now they had reached the front porch of a house markedly different from the other ramshackle dwellings he'd seen as the Kinchers steered him through the woods to this place. For one thing, it wasn't a cabin. It was an actual house. Not a new one, granted, but a house nonetheless. Looked like it dated from maybe the middle of the twentieth century, which made it brand spanking new compared to the fucking hovels the other inbred fucks in these parts called home. There was an old-fashioned television antenna on the roof. It was listing to one side and looked ready to fall over. With the advent of digital-only broadcasting, the thing was way obsolete, but it was at least indication of the presence of semimodern technology. Seeing it made him feel a little less like he'd been transported back in time to some hellish version of pioneer days. He was also able to detect the soft glow of electric lights through the gauze of chintzy curtains hanging over the grimy windows.

Garner climbed the two steps to the porch and turned to gaze down at him. "I am not a demon."

"Uh-huh. Then what's with the fucking horns?"

"I am a human-demon hybrid."

"Right. Okay. Wow. Everything makes sense now."

Garner's head tilted to one side in a quizzical expression. "Oh? Good. I'm glad you're catching on."

Hoke rolled his eyes. "That was sarcasm, man. None of this makes sense to me. Not one little bit of it. You say you're gonna use me as your vessel. Take over my body and use it to get around out in the real world where they ain't used to seeing human-demon hybrids every damn day. I get that. Don't like it, but I understand. The concept, I mean. The actual process of making that happen . . . shit, I don't even wanna think about it. But what I totally don't get at all is how a demon could mate with a human and produce a viable offspring. You'd think them damn horns would rip a broad's womb right the fuck up."

A corner of Garner's mouth tilted upward. "It's true. A demon may rut with a human woman, but viable offspring is not possible."

"So what the fuck, man?"

"I was human once upon a time. I told you before, my people had trouble with the Kinchers long ago."

Hoke smirked. "Yeah, way back in the old-timey days. Hey, man. Did you have your very own horse-drawn carriage?"

"I did."

Hoke laughed. "Far the fuck out, man."

"Indeed."

Garner's smile was broader now. He looked genuinely amused. And in an almost benign way, too. Talking to him like this, it was almost like shooting the shit with a buddy over drinks at a bar. You could almost forget the real truth about the dude for a few moments.

Hoke's mind flashed back to the rain of blood and body parts in the horse stall.

Almost forget.

Garner's expression abruptly sobered. "My clan was new to the area. This was a short while after the states war. There was a land dispute. We staked a legitimate, legal claim. Money was paid, and all the right documents filed with the local government. But the Kinchers claimed the land was theirs and vowed to keep it regardless of what some piece of paper said. We tried moving in anyway. One night the Kinchers raided our camp. They took my wife and daughter. They raped and tortured them. My wife died, but my daughter escaped. She came home minus an eye and several fingers. She woke up screaming every night until I put her out of her misery with a dose of arsenic in her tea."

Hoke's face had turned pale. "Damn, bro. No wonder you went medieval on their asses."

One of Garner's blood-red cheeks twitched. More than a century and a half had passed since the atrocity he described had been committed, but the anger was still there, simmering just beneath the surface. "I knew no ordinary form of justice would suffice. I went down to New Orleans and consulted with a witch doctor."

"The real deal, right? Not one of those hokum merchants they got now."

Garner nodded. "As you say, the real deal. He helped me summon a demon. Again, the real deal, straight from one of the inner circles of hell. This demon agreed to help me, at the expense of my soul."

Hoke shook his head. "Goddamn, you are hard-core. Your fucking *soul,* man. Shit."

"Yes."

Garner's dark eyes had a faraway glint for a moment. Hoke supposed he was staring into the distant past. He tried to imagine what it must have been like for the guy, the real Garner, the human. Tried to see himself in his shoes and contemplating that decision. But he just couldn't do it. It wouldn't have happened. He was just too damned selfish. Or maybe it was a combination of selfish and lazy. Sure, he would've exacted some kind of revenge, but it would have been more along the lines of lying in wait for the bastards with a rifle somewhere and ambushing their murdering asses. Something simple like that, and sure as hell nothing as bat-shit insane as going down to N'awlins to find a witch doctor and raise a goddamn demon. Holy shit.

Garner was looking at him again and seemed to sense his thoughts. "I loved my wife and daughter more than I can express to you. More than life itself. Giving up my soul to have the kind of revenge I desired was nothing."

"Okay."

Nothing, my scrawny white ass.

"The deal was sealed in a bath of hellfire. It seared every inch of my flesh and spirit. And when it was done, I was part demon, and my soul was no longer mine. I'll surrender it soon after my eventual descent to Satan's domain."

"Yeah? When's that gonna be?"

"Sooner than I'd like."

"Well, we all gotta go sometime, I guess."

Garner smiled. "It's why I need a mortal vessel. The effects of the hellfire that changed me are beginning to ebb, and when it fades entirely, so will I. However, I can stave off my demise indefinitely by inhabiting a succession of human bodies. Beginning with you."

"Ain't I a lucky motherfucker?"

Garner didn't say anything this time, just kept smiling.

It made Hoke nervous as all get-out, but what could he do?

"Well . . . anyway . . ."

"Are you ready to see Gladys now?"

"I don't know if *ready* is the right word. Ain't like I've got a choice in the matter. And you still haven't told me why we're seeing her."

"Gladys Kincher rode roughshod over the rest of her clan. Wasn't the usual way of things in those days, but the usual way of things has always been somewhat skewed in Hopkins Bend. She gave the orders that doomed my wife and daughter. I wanted her suffering to be exquisitely immense and long lasting. I've used the abilities granted me to prolong her life force. The blight began with her. She had babies that weren't right. They were missing fingers and eyes."

Hoke whistled. "Like your daughter."

"Like my daughter."

"But you didn't stop there. The shit wrong with these fuckers is way beyond missing digits and eyeballs."

"My need for revenge could not have been satisfied with a mere eye for an eye. I wished to ruin their clan forever."

Hoke thought of ol' Pus Eye leering at him from the tractor seat. "Well, all I can say to that is, mission fucking accomplished, bro. I have never laid eyes on a more ruined bunch of motherfuckers in my entire fucking life."

"It gives me great pleasure to hear you say that. It reaffirms my belief that my mission here has reached its proper conclusion. Now that I have ruined them, I must end them. And then I can leave this blighted place once and for all."

"And how are you gonna end them?"

Garner went to the front door and wrapped a hand around the doorknob. "Come. See."

Hoke cast a surreptitious glance at the woods surrounding the Kincher property and gave fleeting consideration to making a run for it. But it was pointless. The goddamn demon—half-demon, what-the-fuck-ever—would haul him back in a heartbeat, and he'd be right back in the same position. Seemed like a lot of fuss and bother to no good end. Why waste his fucking breath?

Yep, I'm a lazy sumbitch.

He heaved a sigh and reluctantly climbed the steps to the porch.

Garner laughed.

There was something insidious and unsettling in the sound. He again considered a run for it. Garner clamped a hand around one of his wrists and held him fast. "You're going nowhere."

Hoke winced as the bones in his wrist creaked. "Okay, okay. Shit, you're gonna twist my fucking hand off. What use would I be as a vessel then?"

More of that demented laughter in lieu of an actual reply.

Garner opened the door and drew Hoke inside after him. He pulled him through a dimly lit foyer and into a living room furnished with pieces that looked as though they'd been salvaged from a pile of Goodwill rejects. An uncomfortable-looking sofa with wooden legs and hideous print upholstery. A rickety green recliner that looked as if it would collapse if anyone weighing more than a buck fifty ever sat in it. A fucking ottoman. Brittle-looking end tables and lamps with holes in the shades. But the decor was the least unsettling aspect of what he saw upon entering the room. The prize for most unsettling went to the array of Kincher freaks who all stood up at their arrival. An about equal number of men and women. Some with big, bulbous heads. A few with more fingers or limbs than anyone really needed. One had a hump so pronounced it forced him to stand stooped over at the waist all the time. Others had faces mashed up and twisted enough to give any sideshow geek the motherfucking heebie-jeebies. But he was almost used to the freakish appearance of the Kinchers by now. This wasn't what bothered him.

It was the fact that they were all naked.

Yeah, that bothered him.

Hoke groaned.

He felt light-headed and began to sway on his feet. "Ah, shit."

Garner strengthened his grip on his wrist and kept him upright. "You see, friend, in order to use you as a vessel, I have to weaken your mind."

Hoke felt pretty weak already.

Hell, he felt like puking.

The Kinchers were coming toward him, moving in close to form a solid circle of deformed flesh around him. He saw things he didn't want to see. One woman had a diseased-looking third breast down around her armpit. One of the men had a thick, enormous schlong that hung nearly to the floor—except that now it was stiffening and rising from the floor.

Oh, God . . .

Hoke was all too aware of his own nudity. He would love nothing more than a barrier of clothes between himself and all these fucking freaks. Scratch that. He'd love nothing more than about ten thousand miles between himself and Garner and these goddamn monstrosities. But he was beginning to understand why Garner had deprived him of his duds. It had been with this very moment in mind all along.

They were closer now.

Closer by the second.

Then their hands were on him, pawing at him.

Garner laughed yet again, relinquished his grip on his wrist, and pushed his way out of the circle. Hoke tried to follow, but the circle closed, and he felt the warm, sweaty press of all that wrong flesh. He whimpered, and tears spilled from his eyes. They grunted and snorted like rutting pigs, made stupid moaning sounds like movie zombies. Their hands roamed over every inch of his flesh. Then he felt their mouths on him, their tongues describing wet, sticky trails of saliva up and down the length of his body. A mouth closed around his cock and began to suck with great enthusiasm. To his horror, Hoke felt it begin to stiffen. He hoped that was a broad sucking him off, then realized it hardly goddamn mattered at this point. He closed his eyes and prayed again for divine deliverance.

Again, it didn't come.

He opened his eyes again when he realized they were in motion. Hoke glanced over his shoulder and saw Garner trailing along behind them, a truly demonic grin stretched wide across his red face.

The half-demon laughed. "I feel rather confident this will break you."

Hoke mewled like a baby. "Why?"

They were in a narrow hallway now, moving toward Hoke had no earthly fucking idea where. Garner casually lit another cigarette with maddening deliberation. "To assume control of your body, to enter your mind, you must be broken. Your consciousness ravaged and destroyed. You have to be driven insane."

The mass of flesh abruptly stopped moving. Hoke twisted his head around and saw that they had reached the end of the hallway.

There was a closed door.

A few of the Kinchers were fumbling with the doorknob.

Hoke's heart beat a mad rhythm against his chest wall. It felt as if it would blow apart at any moment. He wasn't sure what awaited him on the other side of that door, but his gut told him it was worse beyond anything he could imagine.

The door opened.

He saw bright light and filth-enslimed walls.

An ungodly stench rolled out.

The hands on him pushed him forward, shoved him through the circle of flesh into the room, where he got his first look at Gladys Kincher.

Hoke screamed.

Garner's mocking laughter echoed in the hallway.

Hoke screamed again.

The other Kinchers followed him into the room and the door slammed shut.

CHAPTER THIRTY

The girl's wide, terrified eyes stared a desperate plea at her. Muffled whimpers were audible from behind the gag of wadded-up panties and duct tape. She was maybe a shade over five feet tall and probably weighed a hundred pounds in her clothes, which she wasn't wearing at the moment. Her face was pale but lovely, her jawline a delicate, graceful curve of tender white flesh. Longish, straight black hair brushed bony shoulders. She had a slender neck. An Audrey Hepburn neck. Her collarbone defined itself starkly against the pale skin every time she breathed in through her nose. She was a genuinely beautiful young girl, probably no more than nineteen.

"Stick it in her neck."

Megan didn't hesitate.

She slammed the ice pick into the girl's throat and yanked it out. Blood spurted from the hole. A bit of the initial gout splashed Megan's bare chest. The girl's jaw worked pitifully as she struggled to speak through the gag and the blood filling her throat. Her head went up and down and her body bucked as her cuffed hands strained against the shower nozzle overhead. The way her face contorted and her eyes bugged out made Megan think of a fish flopping around on the deck of a boat. Megan watched the girl's blood spill down the front of her body and drip into the tub. She knew she should feel sick, overcome with shame, but she did not.

Not with the cold barrel of that .45 pressed against the back of her head.

She didn't want to be doing this.

But she didn't want to die even more.

Madeline, her new minder, the one wielding the gun, leaned close, placed a hand on her waist. Her voice dropped to a huskier register as she said, "Stick it in her eye."

Some part of her still wanted to go into movie-heroine mode. Do a quick spin about and knock the gun from the cunt's hand with a judo chop. Then jab the bloody ice pick into her throat. Into *her* goddamn eye. Snap off some dark quip as her adversary hit the ground and died like a pig. But she knew it wasn't a real option. She couldn't save the girl. Not now. And any gesture of defiance could result in her own death.

Fuck that noise.

She adjusted her grip on the ice pick and rammed it into the girl's left eye, driving it in hard, angling it upward into the brain. Her stomach did a violent roll, but she gritted her teeth and choked back a tide of nausea as she focused on driving the ice pick farther in. Blood and some other viscous fluid oozed over her hand. The girl's body twitched violently a few times and went still. Megan eased the ice pick out of the bloody socket and dropped it in the tub. She flicked her wrist and thick droplets of blood splattered the body.

Madeline slapped Megan's ass. "Good job, new girl. You may have a real future here."

Megan stepped aside as a bald, burly man moved past her, reached into the shower, and unlocked the cuff attached to the shower nozzle. He then lifted the body up and out of the tub as easily as she'd lift a pillow. Another man unfurled a sheet of plastic on the tile floor, and the burly guy set the limp body on the plastic with surprising gentleness. He then retrieved the bloody ice pick from the shower and shoved it into a back pocket of his jeans. The men rolled the body up and carried it out.

Megan was amazed.

The whole exercise in bloody murder had taken maybe five minutes.

She flinched as Madeline placed the tip of a finger on her left breast and wiped a bit of blood off her still-trembling flesh. The woman put the finger between her lips and sucked the blood into her mouth. She moved the finger in and out, making soft noises as she mimed fellatio. Megan gritted her teeth again, fought back the grimace that wanted to form. She was still in a delicate situation. To understate to the nth fucking degree. It would not do to show disgust at this stage of things.

"I think you're my new favorite, Megan. I really do."

Megan forced a smile. "Thank you."

"I shit you not. I've seen a lot of new girls break in situations like that. Just so you know, I wouldn't have killed you if you hadn't been able to do it. Not after doling out almost five grand of Preston money for your sweet ass."

Megan felt sick.

Madeline's eyes glittered with amusement. "That's right. If you'd decided you couldn't go through with it for moral reasons or some shit like that, you'd still be here anyway. But you looked inside yourself and decided you were perfectly okay with trading another girl's life for a guarantee of your own safety. I like that. With a mentality like that, you'll not only survive at the Sin Den, you'll thrive. You're a cutthroat bitch, just like me."

"Why did you . . . want me to kill that girl?"

Madeline shrugged. "Every once in a while we need to make an example of someone. Sonia tried to escape. She got as far as the parking lot. Which would have been okay if word hadn't gotten out, but all the other girls knew about it, so she had to go."

"What did you say her name was?"

Madeline frowned. "Sonia. Why should that matter to you?"

Megan thought of the name etched into the wall of that little holding room and the accompanying desperate note. She wouldn't be calling the number she'd memorized after all. What could she say? *Hello, this is your daughter's murderer. . . .*

She shook her head. "It doesn't. Not really. I just wanted to know the name of the girl I killed."

Madeline smiled again. "To personalize it—I get it. Makes her a real human being, not just a piece of meat you cut up. And makes it harder to rationalize what you did as anything other than pure murder." She chuckled. "Damn, I like you."

Megan made herself say it: "Thanks. I . . . like you, too."

Madeline laughed. "Oh, I doubt you mean that." She winked. "Yet."

Megan had no idea what that meant. The weird eye

wink or the yet part of her statement. So she made herself smile again and didn't say anything.

Madeline looked her up and down. "You are a mess. Get in the shower and clean yourself off. We'll talk more out in my office."

She left.

Alone at last, Megan started shaking all over. Soft, nervous laughter bubbled out of her. The sound bothered the still-sane part of her psyche, but she was helpless to suppress it. Earlier today she'd been on her way to a big music festival with her boyfriend. A guy she really adored. Life was good. And normal. Now, a scant few hours later, she was looking at a future as a sex slave–stripper. It was like something out of some sleazy grindhouse movie of the seventies. But it was her real life and therefore not funny at all.

So she stopped laughing.

She turned and stepped into the tub, oblivious of the blood pooled around the drain until she stepped in it. She cringed and moved back a step, succeeding only in smearing the blood across a wider section of the tub bottom. She heaved a disgusted sigh and closed the shower curtain. Then she twisted the knobs and stepped into the water spray jetting from the nozzle. The cool water made her gasp as it struck her skin. She fiddled with the knobs again to adjust the temperature. She let the water sluice the blood off her chest and then dipped her head under the spray to get her hair wet. She closed her eyes and stayed there for several moments, enjoying the soothing feel of the rushing water on her flesh.

Then she opened her eyes and saw that there was still a bit of red caked around the drain. But it was slowly breaking up and moving through the dark holes in the metal. She watched what remained of the blood she'd spilled swirl away and felt a sick fascination. It was like watching Sonia herself disappear all over again. She tried to make herself feel the self-disgust she knew should be there, but it was like trying to signal someone on Mars with a ham radio. It was like Madeline had said. She was a cutthroat bitch. She cared only about her own safety, ultimately. That would make her a sociopath, which was not a thing she would ever have believed about herself prior to today. But maybe she was being too hard on herself. Perhaps she was temporarily incapable of being moved or shocked by violence in the wake of what she'd seen that insane sheriff do to one of his deputies.

No.

She couldn't let herself off that easily. Sure, that was a part of it. But Madeline's take on the matter was on the money. Megan found she couldn't deny it at all. Moreover, she would do it again, if put in the same position.

Without hesitation.

The hot water turned lukewarm, and finally she cut it off. She stepped out of the tub, dried off with a towel she pulled from a nearby rack, and wrapped the towel around her body. She braced herself for what was ahead and ventured back into the office.

Madeline was seated behind her desk, reading a copy of *Us Weekly*. She looked up as Megan settled into the chair in front of the desk. She set the magazine on the desk. "You ready to shake your ass for an audience?"

"No."

Madeline laughed. "Too bad. You're going on stage for the first time in about forty-five minutes."

Megan's eyes widened. She sat up straighter in the chair. "But that's crazy! I'm not anywhere near ready. Don't I get some kind of private training first?"

"Sheriff said you pole danced before."

"Yeah, in a private fucking class! With a bunch of other *girls*! This is not the same fucking thing at all. I can't do it. Not yet."

Madeline's face turned hard during this outburst. "You can. You will. And I can tell you this. You won't enjoy your punishment if you refuse."

Megan thought of Sonia.

The ice pick wedged into her eye socket.

Any punishment she received for refusing to dance her first night wasn't likely to be that extreme, but she knew it wouldn't be any barrel of laughs either. There was no point in arguing with Madeline. She would do what was expected of her. Again.

They talked some more and settled on Megan's stage name. Amber Wine. Could have been worse, given some of the possibilities Madeline rattled off. Megan sort of liked it. She would have a light first evening, dancing only to two songs, just enough to break her in. That was something of a relief, anyway. That settled, they adjourned to the dressing room. Most of the girls stared daggers at her again, but at least that tall blonde wasn't around. Madeline led her to a large walk-in wardrobe, where they selected her stage gear—stockings, stiletto heels, garters, G-string, and bustier. The next stop was one of the primping stations in the dressing room, where Madeline watched her dress and instructed her on the proper whorish application of makeup. That done, Megan fluffed her freshly dried hair and looked at herself in the mirror.

She had to admit it—she looked pretty fucking hot.

She looked at the other girls and smirked, letting them know she knew she was sexier than any of them. Some of them looked troubled, as if they believed it themselves. Some of the others shot her angry expressions that hinted at future drama. She guessed they all knew she had killed Sonia. A friend of some of them. Good. At least they would know how far she was willing to go to save her own ass. The only real threat among them was the missing Nordic goddess, but she would worry about her later.

Madeline led her out of the dressing room and down the narrow, dark hallway. The door to the small holding room stood open as they moved past it. Megan glanced in and wished she hadn't. Sonia was in there, her limp body sprawled across the unfurled sheet of plastic. A shirtless, muscular man with a cigarette wedged into a corner of his mouth stood over her. He held a heavy ax propped over one shoulder. The man caught her eye and grinned. Another, heavier-set man saw her and calmly closed the door.

At the far end of the corridor Madeline opened a door on the left and led her into a shorter stretch of narrow hallway. The blaring hard-rock music was louder than ever now. This song was something she didn't recognize, but something about the texture of it told her it was yet another eighties headbanging anthem, which seemed to be about all they played here. They went through another door on the right, and the music grew louder still, reaching near-deafening proportions.

They climbed a short set of steps to a small backstage area. There were three other girls in skimpy lingerie there, all apparently waiting their turn on stage. The tall blonde wasn't here either, which meant she must be performing right now. And judging from the raucous hoots and catcalls audible even through the thundering music, she was a big crowd favorite. Megan wasn't surprised.

Madeline beckoned her to the curtain, where they peered around the edge to watch the show.

Megan gasped.

The eighties anthem ended and a tune of more recent vintage kicked in.

"Crazy Bitch," by Buckcherry.

Megan couldn't imagine a more appropriate soundtrack

to what was happening on stage. A man was tied to a chair at the center of the stage. The man was young, maybe late twenties. He was slim and might have been handsome under better circumstances. But his clothes clung to his body, soaked through with sweat. Sweat plastered longish hair to his scalp. He was shaking and crying, an endless stream of tears rolling down his shiny cheeks. Looking at him punctured the hard shell that had begun to encase Megan's soul. She felt outrage. This man was a victim. A terrified, helpless captive. Just like her. Just like dead Sonia.

And just as with Sonia, there was not a damn thing she could do about it.

The blonde was down to heels, stockings, and G-string. She lay flat on her back in front of the bound man with her legs high in the air. She tweezed her pink nipples to stiffness with her fingers and turned her face to the crowd as she faked an orgasmic expression. Oh hell, maybe it wasn't faked. She sure looked into what she was doing. She flexed her legs, kicking them up and down like a spastic child.

Then she rolled onto her side and reached for something shiny at the front of the stage. Her hand closed around the object and she rolled again, got to her hands and knees. She moved along the front of the stage, slinking like a cat. The men in the seats up front roared to their feet and a rain of green bills fell on the stage. The blonde stayed focused on her act, making no move to scoop up the loose cash as she continued to the far end of the stage, where she shimmied to her feet and struck a dramatic pose with one hand on her hip. She flicked her other wrist and a straight razor popped open.

More roars from the crowd.

Another rain of bills.

The blonde turned away from the ecstatic audience

and sprinted across the stage, slashing at the bound man
with the razor as she passed him. The blade sliced off the
tip of an ear, and the man bucked in his chair, screaming
now as the tears continued to roll down his face. Still in
motion and moving at top speed, the blonde dropped
the blade and leaped into the air. She hit one of the
dance poles high up and spun around it, holding herself
aloft with amazing grace and ease. She turned herself
upside down, held her legs high in the air and spread
them wide as she slid slowly back to the stage, revolving
slowly around the pole all the way down. The men in the
audience were going absolutely wild in a lust-induced
frenzy. Many of them climbed up on their chairs and
screamed through cupped hands. They went even wilder
as she scooped up the razor again and approached the
doomed man from behind.

Megan scanned the faces of the men in the audience.
Some of them dressed like regular guys. They could
almost have fit in with a crowd at a blue-collar bar in
Minneapolis. Neat, combed hair. Blue jeans and stiff,
button-up shirts. But many of the others looked like
rejects from a casting call for a *Deliverance* sequel. Fat and
dirty, clad in decaying overalls and homemade clothes.
She saw a lot of mouths with a lot of missing teeth. There
were jugs of what had to be moonshine on a lot of the
tables. More than one of them had their dicks out and
were playing with them as they watched the decadent
and depraved stage spectacle. Megan tried to see herself
performing in front of these pigs without throwing up.

She wasn't sure she could manage it.

She swallowed hard and thought, *I am so fucked.*

The blonde was standing right behind the bound man
now. She flicked her wrist and popped the blade open
again. With her free hand, she seized a handful of the
man's sweaty hair and yanked his head back, exposing the

tender flesh of his throat. Megan saw his Adam's apple go up and down and felt a flutter in her stomach. But the blonde didn't slash his throat. Instead she forced the blade inside his mouth, wedged the sharp side up against the inside of his cheek, and held the pose as she stared at the audience, allowing several dramatic moments to elapse. During this time, Megan finally realized that another song was playing.

It was yet another Mötley Crüe oldie. She didn't know the name, but could guess. The singer kept yelping about some chick with the "looks that kill."

The blonde yanked her arm back and the blade ripped the man's cheek open. He squealed and thrashed in the chair as blood spilled down his chin and splashed the front of his shirt.

Megan's stomach twisted again.

Madeline leaned close and yelled into her ear in order to be heard over the cacophony of sound. "ISN'T HELGA AMAZING?"

Megan made herself nod.

But what she was thinking was *This is what I have to follow?*

I am fucked.

Fucked hard.

Helga kicked the chair over, and the man tumbled to the stage with it. He lay on his side as Helga stalked the stage, the bloody blade held high as the crowd roared its approval. Yet another flurry of bills rained down around her. When she was finished reveling in the roar of the crowd, Helga strutted back across the stage and stood over the man she'd tortured as part of her act. She planted a foot on the side of his head. A spiked heel dug into his ear canal.

Madeline yelled into her ear again. "WATCH THIS! IT'S AMAZING!"

What else could she do?

Megan watched.

Helga applied her full weight to the man's head, lifting her other leg off the stage to stand on him with one leg. The spiked heel sank deeper into his ear canal. Megan kept expecting the man to try to shake her off, but he didn't move. He was possibly already dead, but that didn't keep the audience from eating it up. Some of the men were up on the tables now, jumping up and down like monkeys. She saw some of them fall and crack their heads on the floor. She hoped the redneck fucks broke their necks, but she knew better than to expect a kind twist of fate at this point. And she was right. They were all on their feet and hooting and hollering again in seconds. It was absolute bedlam out there now. Helga maintained an incredible, perfect balance for many moments before lowering her other leg and planting it on the dead man's neck. She raised her hands over her head and unleashed a roar of triumph.

The music stopped.

Madeline leaned toward her again and said, "You're next."

Megan gulped.

Shit.

Helga stepped off the dead man's head, bowed, then turned and blew kisses to the audience as she headed to the backstage area. Employees of the Sin Den rushed out to collect the piles of scattered bills. It looked like a small fortune. Two husky men in colorful Sin Den T-shirts came out to retrieve the dead man.

Helga blew into the backstage space, shooting a pleased smirk in Megan's direction as she breezed through the room and down the stairs beyond. Had Megan felt intimidated in the woman's presence before? Good Lord, there wasn't a word for what she felt at being close to her this time. She was a fucking force of nature. Despite her inner bravado before, she knew she could never compete against the likes of Helga. The woman was in a league of her own.

The DJ's voice was booming out, announcing and introducing a new dancer at the Sin Den, Amber Wine.

Madeline's hand was at the small of Megan's back, pushing her toward the stage.

Megan's heart raced.

She wasn't ready.

But she had no choice.

Her first song started. Another old hair-metal anthem. Later she would be told it was "Look What the Cat Dragged In," by Poison.

Megan swallowed hard and hit the stage. The crowd roared.

And somehow she found within her the ability to do what was expected of her yet again. It wasn't even that hard. And when it was over, she was stunned by how much she enjoyed the enthusiastic approval of the crowd. It wasn't much different from how she'd often felt during her high-school cheerleading days. She was even called back for an encore. Madeline was impressed.

Megan only wished Helga had been watching.

CHAPTER THIRTY-ONE

Sheriff Rich DeMars was thinking about the word clusterfuck. It was one of many bits of military jargon and slang that had come into common usage over the years. The term referred to an unfortunate convergence of previously unrelated events to form a perfect shit storm of violence and death. And right now his job was to unfuck what looked like the mother of all clusterfucks.

He swigged whiskey from a flask and added it all up in his head again.

Three dead deputies.

Two dead from gunshot wounds, one from some unknown trauma.

Two totaled official Sheriff's Department cruisers.

Another cruiser missing.

A dead suspect from a liquor-store robbery.

Two crashed trucks, both stolen.

He swigged more whiskey as he watched the heavy machinery being used to pull the tangled mess of wrecked vehicles apart. Klieg lights lit up the night. The rural route was blocked off to through traffic for a mile in each direction. Too many civilians had happened across the scene already. He'd paid out an ungodly amount in hush money so far and unfortunately knew he was far from being done with doling out the green. The tidy profit he'd made selling the outsider girl to the Prestons was almost gone. Soon he'd be dipping into city money, which was sure to stir unhappy rumblings from the commissioners, but those old assholes could suck his fucking dick. He would do anything necessary to cover this mess the hell up, regardless of the strain it would put on his relationship with the local power structure. In the end, they would have to admit he'd done what he had to do in the midst of a difficult situation.

Greg Saunders stepped out of his cruiser and came over to where Rich stood leaning against the hood of his own car. "Got a GPS fix on the missing cruiser. It's stationary. Whoever took it must've ditched it. Want me to check it out?"

Rich looked at Saunders. The guy was young. Twenty-three. He was one of just two still-living deputies on the Hopkins Bend Sheriff's Department payroll. Doug Smith, the other guy, was minding the store at HQ. Doug wasn't as green as Saunders, but he had about as much brainpower as the average fence post. In retrospect, offing Hal was looking more and more like an error in judgment. Sure, the cocky bastard got too big for his britches at times, but he had been a good deputy. Would have been a good man to have around right now.

He sighed. "Nah. I'll go have a look myself. You stay here and oversee this operation while I'm gone." He dug into his pocket and pulled out his wallet. He flipped it open and took out a stack of crisp green bills, the last of his take from selling the girl. "Here's a grand. Before they leave, give a hundred each to these men." He waved a hand to indicate the tow-truck operators and the bored-looking paramedics leaning against their meat wagons. "Tell 'em this is just a down payment. They'll get another grand each by tomorrow morning."

Saunders took the money and whistled. "More than ten grand of city money, huh? Wow."

Rich grimaced. "Yeah." He took another slug of

whiskey and screwed the cap back on the flask. "So where's the cruiser?"

Saunders told him.

Rich frowned. "Way out to the eastern edge of town."

Saunders nodded. "Almost to the city limits."

"Shit. I better get a move on."

The one thing he did not want was any whisper of what had happened here today to get out to the state boys. The location of the missing cruiser was close enough to the very edge of his jurisdiction to scare the shit out of him. He dropped the flask in a jacket pocket and got back in his own cruiser without another word to Saunders.

He started the car.

Backed up and turned around.

Then drove away from the scene of the clusterfuck.

Fast.

CHAPTER THIRTY-TWO

The .38 caliber bullet punched a big hole through the center of Roxanne's throat and sent her staggering backward. She was dead weight before her body hit the ground with a hard thump.

Jessica sat up and stared in shock at the dead bodies sprawled across the green lawn. Bathed in the glow of the floodlights, they looked like props from a horror movie. It wasn't fair. Some part of her had really believed the blood and killing was behind her. Which made her feel like a fool. It wouldn't be over until she was far from this place. She looked at Larry's bullet-riddled body and felt a surge of grief. She'd known the man barely a half hour, but she'd experienced what felt like a real connection with him. An instant, electric chemistry she'd known with only a few other men. And now she could never know if there might have been something between them beyond that initial burst of intense desire.

Tears welled in her eyes.

She glanced at Roxanne and felt real hate for the dead woman. She felt like shooting her corpse again just for spite. Pump all the remaining bullets into her skull. Make a fucking bloody mess of her. She almost got up to do just that, but some still-functioning pocket of common sense in her brain stayed the impulse. And after that, she began thinking in a colder, more logical way.

Her first thought was to get in Larry's car and drive away. Just drive and drive until the gas gauge was hovering around that big letter E. Until she'd put a hundred miles and more between herself and this lunatic asylum of a town.

There was just one problem with that.

She couldn't find Larry's keys.

Obviously they had been in his hand when Roxanne started blazing away. And he had let go of them as he died. She checked the porch and the ground around the porch. They weren't there. She searched the ground around Larry's stiffening body and still came up empty. She was feeling pretty frustrated by the time it occurred to her to look *under* Larry. She got on her hands and knees and cringed at the sight of the bloody holes in his chest. Then she gripped him by the shoulder and grunted as she heaved him up onto his side and saw the keys. She snagged them and let go of the dead man in a hurry.

As she got to her feet and staggered across the lawn toward Larry's Chevy Nova, she happened to glance across the street and saw a light turn off close to the front door of the house over there.

Shit.

So someone was awake there. Awake and observing everything that had happened. The light going off was an obvious attempt to hide that. Jessica thought of some things Larry had told her. The man who lived in that house was his friend. He was probably calling the cops right now. And he would tell them there had been a woman with Larry. A woman who shot and killed Roxanne before driving away in the dead man's car. And soon cops would be looking for that Nova. She'd get pulled over. God alone knew what might happen then. Nothing at all fucking good, based on the evidence of everything else she'd endured so far.

She was trapped.

There was one clear course of action available to her, but to make it work she had to get her ass in gear right now. She turned away from the Nova and jogged back across the lawn to Larry's porch. She went inside the house and found a panel of light switches just inside the door. She flipped them all down and the floodlights cut out, drawing a welcome blanket of obscuring black across the lawn.

Then back out of the house and across Larry's lawn at full speed, the .38 held down at her side as she raced across the street. Her feet pounded across the lawn of the other house, and in moments she was standing on a dark porch, free hand wrapped around the doorknob.

She tried it.

Locked. Of course.

She stepped back and aimed the gun at the knob.

She bit her bottom lip and squeezed off one shot. Then another. Then she kicked the splintered door open and stepped into deeper darkness. She reached out with one hand and found a row of light switches. She flipped them up and light flooded a small foyer and adjacent living room. She heard a startled whimper from somewhere in the house. At the end of a foyer was a dark archway leading into another room. To her right was a short staircase leading to a second floor.

Jessica held her breath and listened.

The whimper didn't come again, but she was able to detect the sound of a person breathing rapidly in and out. It was the sound of fear and panic. She could almost smell it radiating from her quarry. She moved slowly toward the dark archway, and the hardwood floor creaked beneath her steps. The whimper came again. Hearing it made Jessica feel like a predator. A killer. Which was apt. She was those things. It was what circumstance had forced her to become.

She reached out and found another row of light switches as she stepped through the archway. She turned on the lights and saw a balding fat man in a bathrobe clutching a portable phone. They were in a small kitchen. The man stood with his back against the stove.

Jessica kept the gun on him and moved closer. "Calling the cops, William?"

The man blinked, startled to hear his name spoken by this gun-wielding stranger. "How do you know my name?"

"Larry told me."

"Larry's dead."

"Yep. What did you tell the cops, William?"

He stretched an arm out, holding the phone with a shaking hand. "Couldn't get through. Number just rings and rings."

Jessica was close enough now to snatch the phone from his trembling fingers. She jabbed the gun against his gut and said, "What's the number?"

He told her.

Jessica punched the number in and held the phone to

her ear. She listened as it rang more than twenty times. She clicked a button to cancel the call and tossed the phone over her shoulder. It landed with a clatter on the linoleum floor.

"Today might be your lucky day, William. I might not have to kill you after all."

His eyes were wet with tears. He sniffled. "Oh, bless you . . . bless you . . ."

"Shut up."

William's mouth snapped shut, biting off yet another *bless you*.

Jessica pushed the .38's barrel harder into his gut. "You swear you were calling the cops? That wasn't some other number you knew would just ring and ring."

His eyes went wide and his mouth dropped open. He sputtered for a moment, temporarily unable to articulate what he was thinking. It was clear to Jessica he'd never considered the idea. His reaction was more convincing than any verbal denial would have been.

"Shut your mouth again, fat man. I know you didn't do that."

William looked relieved.

Jessica stepped away from him and waved the gun at the archway. "Let's go out to the living room and get you situated."

William frowned as he shuffled away from the stove. "What do you mean, 'situated'?"

Jessica aimed the gun at the small of his back. She considered shooting him right then. It would be kinder to kill him when he wasn't expecting it and couldn't see it coming. But she didn't apply pressure to the trigger. She'd killed so many people today. It would be nice to let just one live if she could.

"I'm gonna tie you up so I don't have to kill you. You got a problem with that, William?"

He did not have a problem with that.

In the living room, Jessica shoved a coffee table out of the way and had him lie down on his stomach in the center of the room. Directly opposite a long blue sofa was an entertainment center, housing the usual array of electronic equipment. Television, stereo, DVD player, cable box, and gaming system. She kept an eye on William as she pulled the entertainment center away from the wall and looked at the profusion of dangling wires and cords. She wrapped a hand around several and stepped on the power strip on the floor. They came loose with one savage yank. She shoved the .38 in her waistband as she completed the slightly more complicated task of removing the connecting ends of the wires and cords from the various electronic devices.

She carried the cords over to William and knelt next to him, dropping all but one of the cords on the floor as she yanked his arms up behind his back. She was rougher than she needed to be, eliciting a yelp of pain. It didn't bother her to hurt him. She figured it would keep him intimidated. And an intimidated man was less likely to offer resistance. She wound the cord around his wrists multiple times, looping and winding it in opposing directions again and again. She gave the cord a twist after she was done. It was secure. Perhaps an especially determined man could get free of it after a lot of struggling, but for now it was more than good enough. She grabbed another cord and secured his ankles in similar fashion. She pulled his legs up toward his ass and used the remaining cords to tie his hands and feet together.

When she was done, she stood up and rubbed her hands briskly together. "There. I don't think you're going anywhere for a while, William."

He didn't say anything, just stared up at her bleakly.

She frowned. "Anyone else live here?"

He shook his head. "It's just me. My wife left me last year."

"No chance of her coming by?"

He shook his head again.

"Good enough, I guess." She pursed her lips as she thought. "I should probably gag you anyway."

She went back into the kitchen and searched through the drawers until she found a roll of duct tape. She returned to the living room, and Larry whimpered as he saw what she was holding. "Please don't. I have panic attacks. I won't be able to breathe."

"Well, you'll just have to try your best not to panic, William."

She tore off a strip of silver tape, knelt next to him again, and slapped it over his mouth. She pulled more tape loose and wound another long strip of it around his head for good measure. She tossed the roll of tape aside and stood up.

"Hang tight. I'll be back to check on you in a bit."

She went to the front door, started to pull it open, and pushed it shut again immediately. There was a car parked on the street outside Larry's house. She couldn't make out much in the way of details from here, but something about the shape of it unsettled her. She moved to one of the living-room windows, slipped two fingers between plastic blind slats, and took a longer look. This time she recognized the streamlined shape of a modern Crown Vic right away. She was even able to dimly discern what had to be the shape of a law-enforcement emblem on the side.

Her heart started racing again.

Fuck.

She just couldn't catch a goddamn break. Every time she thought she had things under control. Every time she

believed she was about to finally slip free of this shit stain
of a town. Every goddamn time some new roadblock of
one kind or another got in her way. It was frustrating
enough to make her want to stamp her foot like a spoiled
child. But that wouldn't do her any damn good. She'd
come this far on pure guts and determination alone.
Now was not the time to start unraveling. Besides, in
a way she was still at least one step ahead of the game.
Maybe two.

Yeah.

There was just one cruiser out there.

And she'd spotted them first.

These things alone weren't enough to guarantee things
would break her way yet again, but they were enough to
grant her a little bit of an edge. But she couldn't afford
to hesitate. More cops could show up soon. It could all
come crashing down on her in the blink of an eye. She
had to be primed and ready to act at the very first hint
of real opportunity.

The cruiser's dome light came on.

Jessica held her breath.

Then she saw a big man heave himself out of the other
side of the car. Big was a gargantuan understatement.
The cop was even larger than the trussed-up wimp on
the floor behind her. Yet another little tick on the list
of things in her favor. She could move like the wind,
even with a set of banged-up ribs. Porky there probably
couldn't go more than ten, fifteen yards without getting
winded.

The big cop went up to Larry's Nova and shone a
flashlight beam inside. He walked all the way around the
vehicle, keeping a cautious distance as he meticulously
inspected the interior. It occurred to Jessica to wonder
why he'd stopped at this particular location to inspect
this particular car. It seemed pretty random. Then a bit of

knowledge gleaned from watching too much trashy TV
late at night clicked in her head. Didn't most cop vehicles
these days have on-board surveillance video equipment?

Jessica groaned.

A scenario developed in her head. This cop here had
happened across the abandoned cruiser she'd hijacked.
He played back the videotape and saw everything. Her
getting out of the cruiser. Leveling the gun at Larry.
Driving away with him in the Nova, the camera getting
a clear glimpse of the license plate before it was gone.
Or . . . wait. That equipment wouldn't be on all the time,
would it? Surely it was only turned on whenever a traffic
stop was made. Or . . . shit. Maybe it had been running
from the moment the aborted chase had started. She
wouldn't have thought to look for it or turn it off in the
aftermath of the crash, not when her only concern in the
whole fucking world was getting far away from there.
She didn't know how any of that really worked, but she
did know a few other things right away.

She had to get out there and face down that cop.

Then search his cruiser for damning evidence.

And then maybe go back to the other cruiser to
conduct a similar search.

The cop knelt to look under the Nova, then heaved
himself back to his feet again. He stood there huffing and
puffing for a moment. Then he pulled a handkerchief
from a jacket pocket and mopped sweat from his brow.
After he wadded up the handkerchief and returned it to
the pocket, he turned in a slow semicircle and played the
flashlight beam over the lawn.

Jessica's mind screamed at her.

GO!

She went back to the door and eased it open, flipping
the interior lights out an instant before she slipped
outside. She hurried down the steps and stayed low to

the ground as she hit the lawn and hauled ass toward the street. The moment the cop discovered the bodies was marked by his startled exclamation. By that point Jessica was in the road and only a few long strides away from the cruiser.

The cop started to turn in her direction.

Jessica dropped lower and scuttled toward the cruiser on her hands and knees. She reached the cruiser's fender and stayed crouched there with hands wrapped tight around the butt of the .38.

She heard the cop curse and start back toward the cruiser, muttering all the way. "Holy fucking Christ, what next? Ain't like I ain't got enough to deal with for one night."

Jessica shifted position slightly as he neared the vehicle, her calf muscles tensing as she raised herself a little higher and prepared to pounce.

She heard the thump of his boots on asphalt.

And more muttering: "Don't get paid enough for this fuckin' bullshit."

He was on the direct opposite side of the car now, breathing hard.

Jessica sprang up and brought her weapon to bear.

The cop gaped at her, surprise writ large in his wide eyes and the cartoonishly astonished set of his features. Then he dropped the flashlight and fumbled for the big handgun holstered at his side.

Jessica never flinched.

BANG!

Pause.

BANG!

Two big holes in a big body.

Sheriff Rich DeMars was dead before he hit the ground.

CHAPTER THIRTY-THREE

Abby got her dead sister's body situated in a precarious position at the top of the stairs and gave it a hard shove in the ass with her bare foot. Michelle let out a startled yelp as the corpse came crashing down into the cellar, landing in an awkward heap at the foot of the stairs. Abby descended the stairs and stood with her hands on her hips on the last step as she stared at the body. One of Laura's arms had folded up under her torso at a bad angle, snapping at the elbow. A shard of bone protruded through a rip in the skin. Her neck was broken, too. All of which would've added up to a hell of a lot of bad news for her sweet little sister if the bitch hadn't already been dead. Dead, and with a bashed-up face even a Kincher would have a hard time loving.

She stepped over the body and seized it by the ankles, then huffed and grunted as she dragged it to the darker far end of the cellar. She found a dirty blanket on a shelf and used it to cover the body. The blanket didn't quite cover Laura head to toe. Her bare feet and the top of her ruined head were visible. But Abby was satisfied. No one would think to look for Laura down here for hours, and maybe not even until morning.

The key was on the same shelf the blanket had occupied. So were Michelle's clothes. Abby grabbed the key and the clothes and hurried over to where Michelle impatiently waited. She noted the wary look in the woman's eyes as she approached. It stung a little, but Abby wasn't surprised. Anyone would exhibit a similar expression in the presence of a demonstrably dangerous person. Abby would have to find a way to reassure her yet again, make her see that she was only dangerous when threatened. She had killed her own sister for this woman. Had done it for both of them. Surely she could see and understand that.

Abby knelt and set the folded clothes on the cellar floor. Before standing up again, she took a long look at the ugly blisters on the woman's feet and felt a twinge of shame and remorse. She remembered laughing at Michelle as she lowered her bound feet into the pot of boiling water. Remembered mocking her and slapping her as she screamed and her feet sizzled.

She hesitated a moment longer, unable to tear her eyes away from the terrible sight.

"I forgive you."

Abby blinked, looked up at Michelle's face. "What?"

"For what you did. I forgive you."

Abby's eyes misted, and a sob temporarily rendered speech impossible. The surge of emotion surprised her. She had done similar things to many other outsiders. Worse things. Like the time she'd punctured a man's balls with a screwdriver. Or the time she had pulled a woman's fingernails out with pliers. Things she had thought of as fun at the time. Interesting ways to kill time and amuse herself. And except for that time Ma had gutted that little boy, none of it had ever bothered her much. The outsiders were just human-shaped bags of meat. Dinner and holiday offerings.

Abby sniffled. "How can you forgive me?"

Michelle smiled, an expression that belied the tension evident in her coiled muscles. "Because you're just a product of your environment, Abby. You never knew any better. Hell, you're barely more than a child yourself, which makes you as much a victim as anybody."

Abby squinted at her.

She didn't know about that victim bit. But damned if it didn't speak to some private, achingly hopeful part of her psyche in a powerful way. She wanted to believe what Michelle was saying. Wanted it more than she had ever wanted anything. She didn't want to think she was a bad person at heart.

She blinked tears from her eyes.

"Thank you for saying that. I can't tell you how much—"

Michelle heaved an impatient sigh. "Yeah, yeah, okay. Please hurry."

Abby wiped more moisture from her eyes. "Sorry. I know you're anxious to get loose."

She found a little footstool and used it to step up high enough to unlock the shackles around Michelle's wrists. Michelle dropped heavily to her knees. Abby tossed the shackles and the attached chains to the ground, where they landed with a heavy clunk.

Abby stepped off the stool and stared down at Michelle, who was rubbing her wrists and weeping quietly. Now it was Abby's turn to feel wary. She didn't know how Michelle might act, now that she was free. For a moment she felt like a complete fool. She knew nothing about this woman, other than she liked the way she looked and the way her warm, smooth skin felt beneath her fingers. She could only guess at her private thoughts. Could be she was thinking of ways she might ditch Abby after they were out of this place.

She glanced at the blanket-covered form of her dead sister.

The hell with it. It was too late for second thoughts.

"Get your clothes on. We gotta get movin'."

Michelle fumbled for the clothes with shaking hands. They were the same clothes she'd been wearing the day Jesse Blaylock, the father of three of Laura's children, had dragged her screaming into the cabin. Tight blue-jean cutoffs. A clingy purple V-neck T-shirt. Panties. Some kind of expensive sandals. But her lacy black bra was gone. No telling what had happened to it. As she admired the way Michelle's heavy breasts hung loose in the tight T-shirt, she decided she was glad it had gone missing.

Dressed now, Michelle smiled and extended a hand.

"Friends?"

Abby held her breath, allowed the hand to slide into one of her own. The way their fingers interlocked felt so good. So right. The renewed physical contact melted away most of her trepidation. She imagined the hand gliding over the smooth contours of her body and shivered as her nipples stiffened.

She swallowed and said in a small, soft voice, "Yes. Friends."

Michelle's other hand settled on Abby's waist as she leaned in for a quick, light kiss. "I can't wait to be alone with you later, Abby. I know what a risk you're taking. I'll make it worth your while." She leaned closer still and teased an earlobe with the tip of a tongue, eliciting a low moan from Abby. Then she stepped back and smiled again. "Now get us out of here."

Abby squeezed Michelle's hand and felt her heart beat faster.

This was it.

The very beginning of her new life.

She felt like a child on the eve of her first holiday feast.

She stole another quick kiss from Michelle, then turned and led her to the staircase. The old stairs creaked and trembled beneath their combined weight. Abby felt one of the steps sink noticeably lower than it should. She heard a splintering sound and held her breath, hoping the ancient wood wouldn't give way beneath them. The decrepit condition of the stairs was nothing new. They had been fragile as far back as she could remember. But the process of decay had accelerated in recent times. Ma had been making noises for months about hiring a carpenter to shore them up, but she had never gotten around to it. Abby raised her right leg and set it on the next step up with an extreme degree of caution.

This time the splintering sound gave way to a louder crack.

Michelle sucked in a startled breath. "Abby . . ."

"Just hold on."

She tightened her grip around Michelle's hand.

"Take it easy."

She raised her left leg up.

Set it down.

Pulled Michelle up behind her.

Crrrrrrrrrrrrrrrrrrrrraaaaaaaaaa-CCCK!

Michelle whined. "Oh, Jesus. Oh, shit."

Abby tensed.

Stayed absolutely still for a long moment.

The staircase remained intact.

Abby breathed slowly out. "Next step up. Easy. One step at a time."

She climbed another step up, setting her weight down by slow, careful degrees, holding her breath again as the wood splintered and settled beneath her foot. The slow, painfully tedious process continued until they reached the top. Abby pulled Michelle into the dark pantry and then through into the kitchen.

Michelle clutched at Abby as she tried to stop shaking. "Oh, God, Abby, I didn't think we would make it."

Abby stroked her hair. "But we did. Next poor bastard down them stairs is getting their neck broke, though."

Michelle let go of her hand and moved away from her to take a good look around the kitchen. She opened drawers and sifted through layers of assorted junk.

Abby frowned. "What ya lookin' for?"

"My wallet. My keys."

Abby snorted.

Michelle's brow furrowed as she glanced at her. "What?"

"Ain't gonna find those things. Your car's gone. Done been sold to a local dealer. You'll never see that wallet again, neither."

Michelle slammed a drawer shut. "Shit!"

Abby flinched. "What's the matter?"

Michelle spun toward her and glared. "How the fuck are we supposed to get out of here without money and a ride?"

There was an edge to her voice Abby had never heard before. It was devoid of even a hint of the tenderness of moments ago. And the set of her features was harsher now, lips curled in a sneer, jawline a tight and thrumming high-tension wire. The abrupt and dramatic shift in demeanor made her fear the woman a little.

Michelle stalked toward her and clamped a hand around her shoulder. "Abby? Did you fucking hear me? Please don't tell me letting me out of those fucking shackles was the extent of your escape plan."

Abby's face crumpled. "I'm . . . sorry."

Michelle sighed heavily. "Fuck!"

Abby sniffled. The unexpected aggression affected her in ways she couldn't have foreseen. Her whole body was shaking. It was crazy. She shouldn't be afraid of this woman. If anything, the opposite should still be true. But she was scared, no way to deny it. Michelle was like a whole other person, now that she was no longer a captive. Confident and a thousand times more assertive.

The idea of admitting she had no idea what to do next terrified her.

But then she stopped trembling.

She smiled.

Michelle cocked an eyebrow. "You've thought of something. Spit it out."

"I know a car we can steal. It's real close. And it'll be easy."

Some of the tension eased out of Michelle's features. They loosened, became softer, and a small smile formed. "Yeah? Where?"

Abby swallowed hard, cleared her throat. "Our closest neighbors are the Colliers. They have an old Plymouth. And I can get to the key easy. We can be there in ten minutes."

"The Colliers?"

"Yep."

Michelle squinted and her brow furrowed again. She was trying to think of something. Abby had a feeling she knew what it was, and she was proven right a moment later.

Michelle's eyes widened. "Yeah. You mentioned them before. They're the ones who have Lisa."

"The fat girl. Yeah, they got her."

Michelle's expression hardened again. "That 'fat girl,' as you call her, is my best friend. I've known her since we were babies. So show a little respect, okay?"

Abby's face flushed. Her fingers clutched at her dress as waves of anxiety rippled through her. "I'm s-sorry. I didn't mean—"

Michelle rolled her eyes and shook her head. "Hush, Abby. It doesn't matter. You said you could get to the key. What about Lisa? Could we get to her?"

Abby made herself breathe in and out a few times in an effort to slow the anxious racing of her heart. "I probably could. The Colliers are a bunch of sorry assholes. I maybe could even—"

A frown creased her face.

Michelle had turned away from her in midsentence and was opening cabinets and drawers again. She jerked one drawer so hard it came all the way out of its slot. She dumped the contents on the floor and knelt to sort through them. "Keep talking, Abby. I'm listening."

Abby coughed. "Yeah. Uh . . . anyways, they're all sorta shiftless and lazy. Bunch of sloppy drunks. I know I could get your friend out of there."

"Aha!"

Michelle closed a hand around something and stood up. Abby frowned.

It was an old hunting knife in a sheath. She was pretty sure it had belonged to her father. Michelle unsheathed the big knife and held it close to her face. She ran the ball of a thumb lightly along the sharp, serrated edge. Abby fidgeted and chewed on a thumbnail while Michelle inspected the heavy-duty blade.

Michelle looked at her. "What? You seem bothered."

"That was my daddy's. He's . . . dead."

Michelle blew out a breath and rolled her eyes again. "So fucking what? We may have to defend ourselves at some point. Hey, are there any guns around?"

The question made Abby groan. "Yeah, but . . ."

Michelle's expression was puzzled for a moment. Then her eyes widened. "Don't tell me . . ."

Abby nodded. "Yeah. Couple of hunting rifles. They're in the cellar."

"Might as well be on Neptune."

"Yeah. Something else down there, too. Big jar of cash. Plumb forgot all about it in the excitement."

Michelle scraped the blunt edge of the blade along her chin. "Huh. How much cash?"

Abby shrugged. "Right around fifty thousand dollars."

Michelle's mouth dropped open. She gave her head a hard shake and stalked toward Abby, stopping scant inches from her. "Abby, don't take this the wrong way, but how on earth could a bunch of cracker-ass inbred redneck fucks have fifty grand stashed away?"

Abby gave her an abbreviated rundown on the sordid history of the Maynard family's activities during Prohibition.

Michelle tossed her head back and laughed. Color rose in her cheeks and made them shine in the lantern light. "Oh, Abby . . ."

Abby's brows knit together. Her fingers worried at her dress again. She had a feeling she was being made fun of now. "Why are you laughing at me?"

Some of the mirth faded from Michelle's face as she sobered slightly. "Abby, I'm sorry—you've got some good qualities, but intelligence is not one of them. Did you really imagine you could go around passing eighty-year-old bills without drawing the law's attention?"

"I did wonder about that."

"You wondered about it."

Abby felt a bit of defensive pride kick in. "That's right. I did."

Michelle shook her head. "Oh, hell. It doesn't matter. We'll figure something out. Maybe rob a fucking liquor store on our way out of town for some cash." She paused, pursing her lips. "This town does have liquor stores?"

"One. But I could prob'ly steal some cash from the Colliers."

Michelle laughed again. "Thank God for the fucking Colliers. Come on, girl. Let's blow this dump."

She brushed past Abby and stalked out of the kitchen.

Abby stared after her, hesitating a moment as she watched the woman disappear through the door to the living room. The possibility that she had perhaps made many very large errors in judgment made her guts churn.

Michelle poked her head back through the doorway. "The hell are you waiting for?"

Abby sighed.

Yeah, could be she'd made some mistakes.

But what she'd thought before was still true. She was committed now, for better or worse. Not going through with it was no longer an option. Her sister's broken and battered body provided stark testimony to that truth.

She followed Michelle into the living room and then out of the cabin.

CHAPTER THIRTY-FOUR

The right thing to do seemed obvious to Pete. They should give the Preston house a wide berth and head down the long, dirty driveway to the road beyond. Or maybe seek the cover of the surrounding wilderness, rather than staying out in the open. They could get just beyond the tree line and follow a parallel path to the road. It was the sane, safe way to go. Which probably explained Justine's refusal to go along with it

She gripped him by a wrist and squeezed. Hard. "No."

Pete's face wrinkled in confusion. "Why, for fuck's sake? And by the way, that hurts."

She increased the pressure on his wrist. "No."

Pete twisted his hand free of her grip. It wasn't easy, but he managed it. He shook his hand and massaged an area where her clenching fingers had turned the flesh a bright shade of red. "Okay. You're crazy. We established that a while ago, but I think it bears repeating. You are fucking crazy. So how about this? You go do whatever crazy thing it is crazy people like you do in situations like this, while I head for the road."

Justine shook her head. Long strands of dirty hair fell across her face. "Where I go, you go."

Pete stared at her. He thought of other arguments he might make, but kept his mouth shut. There could be no talking sense to a person like Justine. He knew he should just turn around and start walking. Megan was still out there somewhere. Now was the time to break the weird hold this crazy woman had on him and get back to her.

He brushed the hair from her face and slid a palm across a sweaty cheek.

She smiled. "Megan is your past. Your future is with me."

He just kept staring at her.

This is nuts.

I am losing my mind. Is insanity contagious?

She took his hand from her cheek and kissed his palm, making him shiver. Then she clasped hands with him and started drawing him toward the back of the Preston house. He saw lights on through the windows, but no sign of movement. As they got closer to the house, the penned-up dogs went into a new frenzy of barking and howling. He heard the chain-link fencing rattle as some of them threw their bodies against it. His breath grew short as the fear rose up inside him again, making his heart thump too fast, the way it did at the end of a longer-than-usual run. He choked down a lump in his throat and clenched Justine's hand tighter. They went into a crouch as they reached a window.

Justine looked at him. "Stay down."

She raised her head slightly and peered over the sill.

Pete watched her face, waiting for a reaction, but it remained impassive. He kept expecting her to duck back down, but that didn't happen either.

"What's going on?"

She glanced down at him. "Take a look."

Assuming the coast was clear, Pete raised his head and saw big Gil Preston and his mother sitting in expensive-looking leather recliners. They were watching what looked like some kind of homemade porno movie on a large flat-screen TV. The flickering, unsteady image on the screen showed scrawny Carl Preston giving it to a large-breasted black woman from behind. Another well-endowed black woman lay beneath the other one on a sofa, letting those big tits bounce in her face.

Pete swallowed a yelp and ducked back down. "Jesus!"

Justine looked at him. "What's wrong?"

Pete gaped at her. "What's wrong!? Christ, what's wrong with you? I don't want those fucking psychos to see us."

Justine smirked. "You should take another look."

Pete squinted at her. Even for a crazy person, she seemed remarkably calm, given their proximity to their captors. He supposed it was possible he'd missed something important. He reluctantly raised his head again. This time he saw the profusion of crumpled beer cans on the floor of a den filled with expensive toys. In addition to the flat-screen TV, there was a full bar with rows of gleaming bottles behind it, several sets of bookshelves stuffed full with shiny DVD cases, and a wide array of top-of-the-line electronic equipment. On the TV screen, Carl and the girls had shifted positions. The girl who'd been prone before was now going down on the other one while Carl pounded her from behind, sweat streaming from his sneering, hawklike face. The women were attractive, but as far as Pete was concerned, the involvement of bony,

pasty-white Carl killed any eroticism the images might
have conveyed. He couldn't imagine why the Prestons
would want to watch their relative in a homemade porno.
Then he remembered that they were fucking perverts.
Mystery solved. But it hardly mattered at the moment,
because neither Gil nor Ma Preston were seeing any of
it.

Both were passed out in the recliners.

Stone drunk, with their mouths hanging open and
drool running down their chins. Ma's wrinkled, sun-
weathered face was frozen in an ugly sneer. A beer
can hung loose from the fingers of her left hand. Any
moment now it would slide free and spill all over the
plushly carpeted floor. Well, here was another mystery
solved. No wonder the morons hadn't heard the dogs
losing their little canine minds.

Justine let go of his hand and stood up. "Wait here."

Then she turned and jogged away from him. Pete
turned on his haunches and watched her slim, nude body
streaking toward a large toolshed some fifty yards to the
left. She disappeared inside the shed and didn't come
out for a few minutes, long enough for Pete to begin
to feel antsy. He glanced back at the Prestons and saw
that the beer can had finally slid free of Ma's fingers. A
small quantity of cheap beer glugged out of the opening,
staining the carpet. Both mother and son were still passed
out, and Pete supposed they would stay that way for a
while. There were so many empty cans on the floor, the
place looked like a frat house in the aftermath of a wild
bash.

When he glanced back at the toolshed, Justine had
finally reemerged. He frowned as he watched her jog
back across the yard. She was a little slower this time.
Which made sense. It couldn't be easy for a woman that
small to run fast while holding a chain saw.

She was panting by the time she reached him. "Are you . . . ready?"

Pete's frown deepened as he stood up. "Justine . . . What . . . exactly . . . are you planning to do with that thing?"

A corner of her mouth quirked. "Isn't it obvious, Petey Pete?"

She brushed past him, and Pete turned to see her approach a small set of concrete steps that led to the back door of the house. She climbed the steps and held the medium-sized McCulloch with one hand, while her other closed around the doorknob.

Heart pounding, Pete hurried after her. "You're not going in there!"

She glanced over her shoulder at him. "I am. So are you. Come on."

She twisted the doorknob and pushed the door open. A second later she slipped inside the house and disappeared from view. Pete stared at the empty space and didn't move, gripped by a temporary paralysis as he recognized this moment for what it was—his very last chance to make a break from Justine. He knew that if he followed her through that door, he would be throwing away his last opportunity to run from this place and try to make his way back to his old life and remain the man he'd always been.

It was the logical thing to do.

It was what he *should* do.

He stared at the open door a while longer. He glanced at the dark woods surrounding the property. Then he looked at the open door again.

He shook his head. "Fuck me."

He climbed the steps and entered the house.

CHAPTER THIRTY-FIVE

It was as if he'd walked through a portal straight into some nightmare chamber in hell. The room was big. It had to be, to contain the abomination that lived inside it. The room stank like a sewer. Worse than that. The odor of the rankest New York City sewer was as pleasant as the aromas filling the boudoir of a high-class call girl in comparison, like a bouquet of scented candles, potpourri, and expensive perfume. The stench staggered him, made his knees go weak and his eyes water. There was no way to tell what color the walls had originally been because the paint was underneath so many layers of dried shit and vomit. A glance at the ceiling showed more of the same, only worse. Congealed columns of vomit, shit, and mucus suspended from it like stalactites. And the floor beneath his feet was sticky with the same mix of excretions. The condition of the room was vile enough, but the thing that lived in it was more than monstrous enough to overwhelm the disgust he might have felt at having to walk through that quagmire of filth and shit in his bare feet.

Hoke had occasionally seen news stories of guys so fat they had to be removed from their bedrooms with heavy equipment. Unfortunate fellas who crushed the scales at a thousand pounds or more. Well, those motherfuckers were positively svelte compared to Gladys Kincher. There was no furniture in this hellish space. There wasn't room for it, and Gladys would have no need of it anyway.

She filled the room. It wasn't just that she was fat. She was, but she had also grown well beyond the size of any normal human, even ones considered morbidly obese by normal standards. Perhaps some additional side effect of Garner's demonic influence. The top of her enormous head nearly butted the ceiling. Two of the shiny brown stalactites hung close to her face. Her arms and legs were thick, doughy masses of wattled flesh. The upper arms and thighs were as big around as utility poles. Her obscenely bloated belly and breasts formed a rippling sea of filth-stained blubber. The mottled legs were spread wide, exposing a glistening, hairy vagina. The distended, fleshy folds were almost repulsive enough to put him off pussy forever. Her long hair hung around her face in filthy clumps, obscuring a visage Hoke was certain was several thousand shades shy of angelic.

The giant head tilted down to look at him as the freaks forced Hoke farther into the nightmare room. Her mouth opened and a phlegmy rattle of rancid breath spewed forth. His knees buckled again as her breath rolled over him, but the freaks kept him upright. They were still all around him, doing sickening things to him with their mouths and hands and . . . other things. He let out a whine as he felt something stiff prod against his puckered asshole. Gladys opened her mouth again and another sound emerged. It took Hoke a moment to recognize it as rumbling laughter. He tried to plant his feet beneath him and halt the forward progress, but it was useless. There were too many of them, and he just had no strength left.

Garner was laughing somewhere behind him again. "Say hello to your new lover, Hoke. Gladys hasn't been laid in a *long* time. I'm sure she'll make it special for you."

Hoke shook his head and whined. "No . . . please . . . no . . ."

Garner laughed some more.

The freaks stopped pushing Hoke forward. They were at the juncture between the giant's spread legs now. Bile rose up in Hoke's throat and dribbled in thin brown streams from the corners of his mouth. The woman with the diseased third breast dropped to her knees in front of him and drew his cock into her mouth. Hoke was crying by now. He had never been so horrified or afraid in his life. But somehow the freak's swirling tongue brought him back to hardness. Then she slipped away from him, scuttling between his legs on her hands and knees like a crab. The stiff thing prodding at his butt retreated, too. And in a moment he realized they were all moving away from him. He took a reflexive step back and would have kept on going, but Gladys unclenched the fingers of a massive hand and curled them around his back.

Hoke struggled in her grip, but it was useless.

She spread her legs wider and began to draw him toward her.

Hoke screamed.

His hands flailed at her encircling fingers to no avail. A horrible grinding sound emerged from her throat as she slammed him against her.

And *into* her.

Her fingers began to move rhythmically against his back as she rubbed him enthusiastically against her slimy middle. She groaned and arched her back. His head disappeared beneath a roll of belly fat, and for a moment he couldn't breathe. Hoke was aware of a sensation like firecrackers going off in his head. He knew he'd probably be better off suffocating at this point, but instinct made him struggle for breath. He turned his head to the side and found a pocket of air. His penis sank into her again and again. He had to wonder how pleasurable it could really be for her. His dick was sort of pea sized for the

likes of her. It would do the job for any normal woman—
or so he liked to think—but maybe not for this titanic,
living atrocity.

An answer to this question was supplied shortly after
the thought occurred to him. She pulled him away from
her and held him tight in her fingers while she pried
apart her glistening, plump pussy lips with the fingers
of her other hand. Hoke started shaking his head. She
lifted him off his feet and turned him so that the top
of his head was facing toward her. Hoke kicked his feet
and sucked in a big breath in preparation for a scream.
But the sound died in his throat as she rammed him up
inside her, up to the shoulders. She drew him out and
thrust him back in. Again and again. She moved him up
and down and wriggled him around. She pulled him out
and rubbed his shiny face against her quivering clit. Then
back inside that moist warmth for endless moments.

At some point the thing Garner had hoped for
happened.

Hoke's mind broke.

Permanently.

And by the time Gladys was satiated, Garner had his
vessel.

CHAPTER THIRTY-SIX

Megan sat at one of the primping stations and ignored
the glares some of the other girls frequently shot her way.
She was trying to project an aura of calm confidence,
but in truth she felt like a clueless first-day freshman at
college. She had been told she would be provided an

on-site room to share with another girl. At some point someone would take her there. But for now she'd been left here to wait and wonder what came next. Madeline was back in her office, with the door closed. And no one out here would talk to her yet. She couldn't leave the dressing room to wander about, a fact reinforced by the tall and muscular guard stationed at the door. She felt very alone and scared, and for the first time in a while her thoughts turned back to Pete. She wished Carl would come back so she could ask about him, but she feared any answers he might provide would only break her heart and make her feel even more alone.

The door to Madeline's office came open and Megan's head snapped in that direction.

Madeline poked her head out and said, "Yo, Megan. Get your ass in here."

Megan jumped off the stool and hurried into the office.

Madeline closed the door and smiled. "Have a seat."

Megan settled into the seat opposite the desk while Madeline sat behind it again. Her new boss opened a drawer and pulled out a bottle of whiskey. She screwed the cap off the bottle and poured a little into two shot glasses. She pushed one of the glasses across the desk toward Megan and held the other between slender fingers.

She raised the glass. "A toast."

Megan picked up the glass. "To what?"

"Your success, of course. You wowed them out there tonight, Megan."

Megan knew she had done very well, but chose to be demure about it. She didn't want to seem too cocky yet. Not around her boss, anyway. "I guess I did okay for a first night."

"You did better than that, and you know it."

Megan shrugged and faked a shy smile. "I guess."

"Oh, you know it as well as I do." Madeline gestured with the glass. "Now drink up."

She tossed the whiskey back in a single gulp.

Megan did the same, but struggled not to show a wince as the strong alcohol stung the back of her throat. She summoned another of those shy smiles. "Maybe you're right."

"Of course I am. And I have even more good news for you."

"Oh?"

Madeline poured more whiskey into her glass, but this time she didn't offer Megan any. "One of our regular clients is smitten with you. This guy's a real shark, Megan. A financial heavy hitter from Nashville. It takes a real special girl to impress him. Apparently you're special enough. Not that I'm surprised."

Megan frowned. "From Nashville?"

Madeline knocked back the second shot of whiskey and made a sound of quiet satisfaction. She set the glass down and leaned back in her chair. "Yes. Some outsiders, a privileged few, are aware of the Sin Den and the things that go on here. We're an exotic oasis of decadence and debauchery for these people, and we treat them like royalty when they visit. The man I'm talking about has paid for two hours of your time in a VIP room."

Megan's heart began to thump harder. She cast a longing glance at the bottle of whiskey. "I . . . What happens in a VIP room?"

Madeline stared at her for a long, silent moment.

Then she pushed the whiskey bottle slowly across the desk. Megan grabbed the bottle and splashed brown liquid into the little glass. She knocked it back, and this time the sting wasn't as bad. She filled the glass another time and set the bottle back down.

Madeline kicked back in the plush leather chair and set her feet up on the edge of her desk. The silk negligee rode up high on her thighs, revealing a tattoo of a thorny vine wound around a dagger, on the left thigh. She folded her hands in her lap and said, "You're getting another big test on your first night. It wasn't planned or expected, but it's happening anyway, and you better be prepared. This man and his friends will make use of you any way they like for two hours. You are not allowed to refuse them anything. They can fuck you. They can get rough with you. Within reason, of course. We don't want them marking up the merchandise too much. But you might get slapped around some. And you might be made to do a number of things you'd rather not do. But if you perform to their satisfaction, you could be rewarded handsomely."

Megan threw back her third shot of whiskey and set the glass on the desk. "You mean the Sin Den would be rewarded."

Madeline smiled and spread her hands. "Of course. I won't lie to you. All the money goes to us. You have no use for money now anyway. But a successful session in the VIP room could benefit you in other ways, maybe even gain you privileged treatment. You'd like that, wouldn't you?"

It all sounded pretty horrible. Megan felt herself edging toward panic at the thought of what these men might do to her, but she knew there was no way out of it. The only way to get through it was the same way she'd gotten through everything else. By just letting it happen and doing her best to adapt as she went along.

She let out a slow breath and tried to sound almost bored as she said, "Well, let's get on with it then."

Madeline smiled and reached for the phone on her desk. She put the receiver to her ear and tapped in a four-digit extension. "Hello, Carl? Megan's ready for her date in room four. Come get her whenever you're ready. Okay, see you in a bit."

She set the receiver back in its cradle. "Carl will be here in a minute."

Megan shrugged. "Okay."

Madeline slid a manicured nail up the length of her thigh and leered at Megan. "You're scared shitless, aren't you?"

No point lying about that. "Yeah."

"Relax. I'm pretty sure you'll be okay."

Megan didn't say anything.

Pretty sure?

Fuck.

The door to the office opened, and Carl strutted inside, the black stripper he'd made out with earlier clinging to his arm. "On your feet, new bitch. You've got work to do."

Madeline laughed. "Have fun, baby. Knock 'em dead, okay?"

Megan stood and acknowledged Madeline's comment with a slight nod. Then she followed Carl and the black woman out of the office. Back in the dressing room, Carl laid a wet smack on the woman's plump lips and smacked her on the ass. "Keep that fine ass of yours warm for me, baby. Daddy will be right back."

The stripper put a hand to her mouth and giggled.

Megan felt sickened by the display, but didn't say anything. She followed Carl out of the dressing room and down the narrow hallway. A guard in one of the colorful Sin Den T-shirts trailed along behind them. The big man was bald and sported an immaculately trimmed goatee. A diamond stud sparkled in his left earlobe. He winked when he saw her looking back at him. Megan showed him a flirtatious smile. It couldn't hurt to ingratiate herself with the help.

Carl led them through a door and down a hallway, the same short and narrow passage Madeline had steered her through hardly more than an hour ago. But this time they walked past the door to the backstage area. The thumping music bludgeoned her eardrums again as they arrived at a place where the corridor turned to the right and abruptly ended. An array of large men who all resembled the man trailing behind her stood in a loose group around the entrance to the Sin Den's main room. Carl inserted two fingers in his mouth and unleashed a piercing whistle that was audible even over the Guns N' Roses song blaring from the club's bone-shaking sound system. Some of the men glanced back at them and stood aside to allow them room to pass. A long-haired man with sleeves of tattoos up and down his arms leered at her as she walked by, licking his lips as he eyed the tight bustier and the alluring thrust of her breasts. She examined the faces of the other guards as she strutted by them and liked what she saw. They were all drooling over her. She flipped her teased-out hair and kept her face impassive. She knew she should feel ridiculous for preening for them, but she did not.

Then they were past them and in the main room. There was a girl on stage. A raven-haired slender thing in leather boots with stiletto heels and one of those black Nazi hats with the shiny brims. She was hot and commanded the attention of many of the men in the audience, but a lot of eyes turned Megan's way as she strode into the room. Mouths fell open. Some of the men were no doubt recalling her memorable stage debut and thinking with longing of her trim, athletic body and the amazing display of flexibility and brazen sexuality they'd witnessed.

Megan allowed herself a small, enigmatic smile.

It was weird.

She felt a bit like a celebrity.

She avoided eye contact with any of them as she followed Carl past the tables and booths to the long bar at the far end of the room. She didn't have to look into their eyes to feel their lust. And it was good to seem aloof. It would just make them want her more.

There were a lot of men—and even a few women— at the bar, either sitting on stools or leaning against the gleaming brass rail. Many of them turned to look at her as they walked past, a virtual replay of the reaction her entrance into the main room had earned. Some of what she saw when she looked at the men was surreal. A few of them wore dirty leather dusters and hats. One man stood with his back against the rail and one booted foot propped on a bar stool slat, a glass of brown whiskey clenched between dirt-stained fingers. His duster hung open, and she saw gun belts strapped across his waist, with honest-to-God six-shooters in the holsters. It made her head spin a little. Who in their right mind dressed like that outside of a movie set or costume party?

A woman leaped off a stool and intercepted Carl. "Yo, Carl, how's about a little private time with the eye candy?"

The woman licked her lips and did a slow, head-to-toe (and back again) inspection of Megan's body. She had short, slicked-back black hair and wore a beaten-up black leather jacket. Pegged jeans and steel-toed boots rounded out the charming ensemble.

Carl shook her hand off his shoulder and kept moving. "Sorry, Val. The bitch is bought and paid for tonight."

Val walked along beside him until they reached a staircase at the far end of the bar. "Come on, man. She's got my motor runnin' like you wouldn't believe. I have a thousand bucks cash that's yours if you say yes."

Carl smirked and started up the staircase. "Not this time, Val. Call early tomorrow, maybe."

Val touched Megan's bottom and squeezed as she started up the stairs.

Megan flinched.

Val laughed. "Tomorrow, baby."

The woman turned and strutted back toward the bar. The men were guffawing as she approached. She high-fived some of them. Some of that feeling of pseudocelebrity deserted Megan in that moment. Truth penetrated the defense mechanisms her psyche had erected. She was a piece of meat here. A commodity. A thing to be bought and traded. No. That wasn't quite right. The Sin Den's patrons would never own her. But they could buy her time for a while. Like any common street whore. The line of thought darkened Megan's mood considerably as she followed Carl to the top of the staircase.

They reached a small landing, and Megan stared at a black metal door. Carl punched in a code on a keypad to the right of the door, and it clicked open. He stepped through the opening and disappeared. Megan stood frozen there for a moment. Then she felt the guard's hot breath against her ear and made herself move again. She was scared, but this was tempered by the certainty that whatever awaited her through that door could hardly be any worse than what she had already experienced. Then she cursed that thought, hoping she wasn't jinxing herself.

She held her breath as she stepped through the door, thinking, *Christ, Megan. Things can always get worse. Don't you know that by now?*

They were in another hallway now. A much wider one than before, with red-painted walls and red carpeting on the floor. Soft red light from overhead. Megan heard the metal door snick shut behind her. The perpetual heavy-metal roar of the Sin Den went silent. Completely. There wasn't even the muffled thump she'd heard from the dressing room. It was a relief to her eardrums, but some part of her found the complete absence of external noise disturbing. It was all too easy to imagine a host of sinister reasons for the eerily efficient soundproofing. This part of the club was like a whole other world, a separate place from that swirling maelstrom of raging male hormones and sex on parade. It was calmer here, at least at first blush, but that didn't mean it was any less dangerous. If anything, the privacy made it potentially far more dangerous.

There were four doors on each side of the hallway. Megan followed Carl to the second door on the right. The number 4 was painted in black against the red paint beneath. Carl glanced back at her as he paused to extract a ring of keys from a pocket. "Now you treat our guests right, ya hear? Otherwise I'll have to show you some of the ways I know to hurt a gal without markin' her up too bad."

Megan shrugged. "I'll do whatever they want."

"Damn right."

Carl opened the door and ushered her inside with a sweep of a hand. She purposely brushed his arm with a breast as she walked past him. Maybe he did prefer a different shade of girl meat, but that would give him a little something to think about. By now she was willing to curry favor any way she could. And maybe he—

The line of thought cut off the instant she saw Helga.

Her heart did a hard stutter-thump, and she forgot to breathe for a moment. The leggy blonde goddess sat with her legs crossed on the edge of a chocolate-colored divan in the center of the room. She wore black platform shoes with the usual spike heels. The platforms looked big enough to bludgeon a person to death with. Sheer stockings encased her sleek legs. The only other thing she wore was a pair of lacy black panties. She sat leaning back, with her palms flat against the divan. The perfect jut of her large breasts was emphasized in this position, which Megan realized was the whole point. The woman would be well schooled in how to best show off her assets by now.

Her mouth was moist with freshly applied pink lipstick. The lips tilted slightly upward at the sight of Megan. "Hello, Amber. Nice to see you."

Megan looked at Carl. "What's she doing here?"

Carl laughed. "Didn't Madeline tell you? The guy who paid for you is a real moneybags. He requested both of you bitches. You got a problem with that?"

Helga laughed. "I don't, Carl."

Carl sneered. "Ain't askin' you, bitch."

"It's cool. Seriously." Megan was still rattled by the unexpected appearance of her new rival, but even more troubling was the prospect of what might happen if she showed signs of weakness now. "I'm down for whatever the gentlemen want."

Carl actually cackled then. "Now there's the bitch who said she could handle all the dick we could throw at her." He smirked. "Well, starting real soon we'll get to see just how true that is."

Everyone except Megan laughed.

Carl and the guard left after that. Megan watched the heavy door slide shut and heard the click of a key turning in the lock on the other side. Megan didn't much relish the idea of being locked in a room with a woman who'd promised to hurt her only a short while ago, but there wasn't a thing she could do about it, so she tried her best to ignore Helga's steady, unrelenting stare as she looked the room over. There was a slowly spinning mirror ball hanging from the ceiling. The red walls and carpet matched the hallway decor. In addition to the divan, there were expensive-looking leather sofas against every wall save the one in back, against which was a lavishly stocked bar. A huge plastic tub overflowing with ice sat atop a black coffee table in front of one of the sofas. Several large bottles of champagne were shoved into the ice. Megan approached the table for a closer look and was astonished to see the words *Krug* and *Dom Perignon* on the labels.

Helga laughed. "You should see your face. Let me guess. Mads told you this guy was a big shot, and you thought she was exaggerating. Well, guess what? You were wrong."

Megan couldn't take her eyes off the bottles.

Jesus, she thought. *Those things go for hundreds of bucks a pop.*

Helga was laughing again. "Don't ever be fooled by how nauseatingly white trash the Prestons are, Amber. This place does a lot of serious business with some serious people. I once blew a congressman in the room right across from this one. Ugly old man with a flabby white belly and these disgusting warts on his balls. But I used to see his wrinkly face on CNN all the time."

Megan looked at her. "No shit? You catch anything from him?"

"No shit. And no, I didn't catch anything, by some miracle."

Megan sat on the edge of the closest sofa, and Helga pivoted slightly to look at her. She found she was able to meet the woman's gaze and hold it for the first time since the dressing-room altercation. "So why aren't you beating the shit out of me?"

Helga shrugged. "Oh, I haven't forgotten my promise to you. But this isn't the time or the place for such shenanigans. Besides . . ." She drew her lower lip between her teeth and appeared to think for a moment. Then she smiled. "I came back out to check out your encore. You were fucking hot."

Megan was stunned to find herself blushing. "Um . . . really?"

"Yeah. And I had an idea. Go for it, and maybe I'll forget all about smashing your pretty face in."

Megan's brow furrowed. She wasn't sure she wanted to hear whatever Helga had in mind, but knew she had to at least humor the woman. "Okay. What's your idea?"

"We should be a team."

Megan frowned. "What?"

Helga scooted to the edge of the divan and leaned forward. "Yeah. I've been thinking about working up a new act. It's got to be something really hot, and I think you're just the ticket. You're by far the sexiest fucking thing to show up here since I arrived. We'll play around with a little bit of a lesbian angle. The guys always eat that shit up. Drives them fucking wild. And then we'd maybe team up on more of the same kind of thing you saw me do earlier, only get more creative about it." She smiled. "So what do you think?"

Megan pursed her lips, thought about it.

And she said, "The Torture Twins."

Helga's eyes went wide and she snapped her fingers. "That's it! Fuck yeah! You're brilliant, girl."

Megan smiled and shrugged. "I have my moments."

Helga squealed. "This is going to be great!"

She seemed about to say more, but fell silent as the door opened again.

Megan held her breath and turned to look at the door as the man who'd paid for the use of her body strode confidently into the room. There were two other men with him, but it was clear at a glance who the big swinging dick of this group was. All three men had a certain swagger to them, the kind most successful men exuded without trying. Clad in professionally tailored suits, they looked as if they'd just walked out of a board meeting. There were other hints of wealth. Diamond cuff links. Watches that probably cost more than the monthly rent on her apartment back home. A lot more. All were still relatively young, mid-to-late thirties. Young and virile. All were around six feet tall. Their bodies were muscular and athletic. The physical power was obvious even through the elegant clothes. The three-figure haircuts and manicured nails did nothing to detract from the impression of masculinity in full bloom. But two of them evinced a slight but clear level of deference to their leader, who stood now in the center of the room and stared intently at Megan.

His suit was a very dark shade of blue that was almost black. A tie the same color was knotted with precision over a crisp white shirt. He had a cleft chin and dark, compelling eyes. He had wavy, subtly gelled hair. His prominent cheekbones would stir the envy of any male model. And he oozed charisma. A feeling of immense relief swept through Megan at the sight of him. She still hated the idea of being forced to submit sexually to these strangers, but at least they were clean and attractive.

It could have been a lot worse. The other Sin Den patrons she'd seen were proof of that.

The man pointed at her and jerked a thumb toward the divan. "Up. I don't want you sitting there."

Megan blinked slowly in surprise. "Wh-what?"

One of the other men—the only black man of the group—walked over to where she sat and knelt toward her with his hands on his knees. "HE TOLD YOU TO GET THE FUCK UP, BITCH! YOU HEARD THE MAN. DO IT!"

Megan cringed, shrinking away from the man's barking voice. "O-okay."

She scooted sideways away from him and forced herself to stand. She took a step toward Helga, but pitched forward as the heel of the man's hand slammed into her back and knocked her to the floor. She shrieked as her knees banged the carpet. The heel of a designer shoe sent her the rest of the way to the floor. She lay there and listened to effusive male laughter. Tears welled in her eyes. Something in her gut told her this was going to get much rougher than Madeline had hinted. She held back a sob with a tremendous effort of will. She couldn't allow herself to break. Not yet.

And then the leader spoke, voice quiet but menacing. "Get up. Sit with the other one."

The voice contained an implied promise of pain and suffering if disobeyed. Primitive instinct carried her to her feet again seconds later. She wobbled over to the divan and plopped down next to Helga.

One of the big shot's buddies withdrew a dripping-wet bottle of Krug from the ice bucket and set to work removing the cork. It came free with a loud pop. The man who opened it took several large gulps straight from the bottle. A bit piggish a way to drink for someone so clearly upscale, but Megan supposed she shouldn't be surprised. These were men who'd paid good money to use and abuse them any way they saw fit. All outward appearances to the contrary, they were not classy men.

The leader approached the divan and walked slowly around it, stroking his chin and licking his lips as he appraised the selections he'd made. One of the other men found the room's stereo system while the boss was checking them out. A seventies funk song poured out of the high-end speakers. The black guy sang along for a line or two of the verse before saying, "Hey, Joe. Tell those bitches to make out with each other."

Joe smiled at them. "My friend wants to see you ladies kiss. So do it."

Megan glanced at Helga.

She'd half-suspected something like this would happen

the moment she'd entered the room and seen Helga sitting there. But now that it was actually happening, she was overcome with fear and resentment. She stared at Helga and wondered what the other woman was thinking. She'd been here a while and had probably been through similar scenarios countless times. Maybe she was used to it by now. Megan, however, wasn't sure she could ever get used to this kind of humiliation and degradation.

She felt paralyzed, incapable of obedience or defiance.

Helga put a hand on her thigh and leaned close. She spoke at a volume too low to be heard above the music. "Relax. You might even enjoy this."

Helga kissed her. Megan's lips parted and the other woman's tongue darted into her mouth. Some of the tension deserted her as she closed her eyes and focused on the physical sensations, which weren't at all unpleasant. She was able to forget about the men for a time—even with their hoots and catcalls—and for that she was grateful. She even found she enjoyed the taste of Helga's pink lipstick. Her hand went to one of Helga's breasts, and she felt the nipple stiffen beneath her gliding fingers. She tweezed the nipple between thumb and forefinger, eliciting a low purr from Helga. Megan realized with some amazement that she had become aroused, too. She supposed her excitement was at least in part fueled by the recent violence between them. Which hinted at some previously unexplored capacity for kink within her. She nipped at Helga's bottom lip and was rewarded with another purr.

But the pleasant interlude ended as Joe uttered a simple command: "Stop!"

Sitting on a sofa now, he pointed at Helga and said, "You. Come here."

Helga stood and walked over to him.

He leaned back and looked up at her, his arms spread across the back of the sofa. "Get on your knees."

Helga again did as instructed.

Joe smiled. "I think you know what to do now."

Helga didn't say anything, but she reached for his fly and pulled the zipper down. She then reached into his slacks and pulled his cock out. Even limp it was an impressive size, but it didn't stay limp for long in Helga's hands. She stroked it lightly and it hardened at once, growing to an even more impressive size. Megan couldn't stop staring at his dick. It was porn-star material. This guy was a premium example of the fabled man who has everything. She caught the gleam of a wedding ring on his left hand. Probably he even had a doting wife back home. Megan wondered what wifey would think if she could see her man now.

Helga leaned forward and drew his massive cock into her mouth. Joe groaned and closed his eyes, let his head settle back against the sofa as Helga ministered to him with her expert whore's tongue. Megan stared at the other woman's perfectly round, upraised ass and the smooth, creamy expanse of her tapered back. The black platforms jutted out behind her, hanging off her smallish feet like bricks. Megan heard slurping sounds as the woman's head went up and down in Joe's lap. The sounds were punctuated with little moans from Helga. Megan couldn't decide whether this was evidence of real sexual excitement on Helga's part, or if she was faking it. The latter seemed likely, but the sounds were so convincing it was hard to tell.

The black man came over to Megan and stood in front of her, blocking her view of the action on the sofa. A moisture-laden bottle of Krug dangled from the fingers of his left hand. He used the other to open his own fly and tug his genitals out.

He sneered down at her. "You're not here just to look good, girl. Get to work."

Megan felt a reflexive flutter of revulsion, but knew she had to do what was expected of her. She didn't wish to risk invoking this man's wrath again. She cupped his balls in the palm of one hand and paused a last moment to psych herself up to perform in the manner required.

The music changed.

Something she thought she recognized as being by Isaac Hayes started.

She opened her mouth.

Leaned toward the man's slowly lengthening cock.

And jumped at the sound of the loud, flat crack audible over the music.

Her first thought was it was the third man popping open another bottle of Krug. Then somebody said, "What the fuck!?"

The sound came again, and the chest of the man standing over her exploded in a spray of red. She screamed and scooted out of the way as his body toppled over the divan and rolled to the floor. Megan stared at the dead man in uncomprehending bewilderment for a long moment.

Someone nearby was screaming.

And begging.

That loud, flat crack came again and the begging stopped.

Megan shook her head and the world snapped back into semifocus. She turned away from the dead man on the floor and saw Helga still on her knees in front of Joe. But Joe was dead. There was a hole under his chin and a spray of blood and brain matter on the wall behind him. He didn't look so special now. All that charisma had leaked out of the holes in his head, the one under his chin and the larger exit wound at the crown of his skull. He was just a corpse. A thing.

Death, Megan thought. *The great equalizer.*

Helga clutched a 9 mm pistol in her slender fingers. There was a crazy grin on her face. "Can you believe it? Fucker had it in a shoulder rig. Saw it while I was blowing him. Had him so cross-eyed he didn't know I was going for his piece until it was up under his chin. This guy wasn't a high roller at all. He was a fucking cop. They all were."

Megan blinked in confusion. "But Madeline said—"

"Madeline was duped. This was an undercover thing. Been going on a while, I'll bet: Fucking pigs didn't mind getting their wangs waxed in the line of duty, either."

Megan still felt dazed. She shook her head again. "But . . . what do we do now?"

Helga stood up and came over to her.

She extended a hand and Megan took it.

Helga hauled her upright and said, "What we're doing, girlfriend, is getting the hell out of here."

CHAPTER THIRTY-SEVEN

Jessica kept the gun in front of her and both hands wrapped around the grip, forefinger tensed on the trigger, as she circled the cruiser. She doubted the big cop would be getting back up. Ever. But she wasn't about to let her guard down now. She strained to detect any hint of movement or slight sigh of breath, but the only sound she heard was the soft crunch of her shoes on the pavement.

Then she was on the other side of the car and staring down at the dead man. One glance was all the confirmation she needed. He wasn't just wounded and playing possum. The thing on the ground wasn't a man anymore. It was just a big lump of meat. The body lay half in and half out of the shallow ditch that separated Larry's lawn from the road. Though she was certain the man was dead, she approached the body and kicked it hard in the gut.

Yep, she thought. *That is one dead cop.*

She moved closer and peered at the badge pinned to the front of his jacket. It was more ornate than the ones worn by the deputies. The logical assumption occurred to her then: she had just killed the sheriff of Hopkins Bend. She wondered briefly why the sheriff would be here instead of one of the deputies, but remembered that, duh, she'd killed most of them. Maybe all of them. Hopkins Bend wasn't exactly a bustling metropolis. But surely the state cops would be out here in force soon. This was a pretty serious killing spree she'd embarked upon. Hell, it was maybe even wild enough to warrant the attention of the national media. Some prickling of intuition stirred at the back of her mind, and she stared at the dead sheriff a few moments longer, frowning as her mind worked toward a single inescapable conclusion.

The national media wouldn't be out here any time soon. Or ever.

Nor would the state cops.

Hopkins Bend was a festering, diseased backwater nest of dirty secrets. Things the sheriff and the local power structure would never want to expose to the world. More insights came to her in rapid succession. There would never be a warrant out for her arrest. Not for any of the things she'd done here today, anyway. All she had to do was get the fuck gone and this mess would be behind her forever.

She chewed her lip and frowned again.

Or maybe not.

Yeah, she would never be arrested by the local law. And she'd never openly be fingered as a mass murderer. But they would know about her. Her fingerprints were everywhere. Even if she got rid of the video evidence from the cruisers, she could be identified. Tracked down. She imagined growing complacent as months passed. Saw herself going about her daily life again, until one day a man with a gun slipped into her apartment at night or surprised her in a parking lot. Her guard would be down. It would be easy for them. One round to the head and she'd carry the secrets of Hopkins Bend to the grave forever.

Frustration twisted her features, and she kicked the dead sheriff again. "Fuck!"

She moved away from him and leaned against the cruiser's fender.

"Settle down," she told herself, her voice brittle, on the edge of cracking. "Think, dammit."

Christ, but she'd kill for a cigarette right now. She hadn't smoked in ages, but she knew renewing the old habit of her juvenile years would calm her for at least a few minutes, long enough to get her head clear. She glanced at Larry's Nova. There were cigarettes in there.

And something else, an insidious voice from the murkiest depths of her psyche whispered. *Something better . . .*

She was off the fender and moving again before she was even consciously aware of it. Another voice in her head clamored for attention: *You don't want to do this! This is a mistake! Please don't do this!*

Jessica opened the passenger's-side door and dropped into the bucket seat. The glove box flipped open before she could touch it. She gaped at the small amount of white powder in the plastic bag. It wasn't much, but it would get her focused in a hurry. And that thing with the glove box dropping open had to be a sign. This was meant to happen. Some power she couldn't comprehend wanted it to happen. Sure, on a rational level, she knew a faulty latch was to blame. There was nothing mystical about it. But the rational part of her mind didn't hold much sway right now.

She drew the bag out of the glove box and opened it. Her fingers shook, and the bag almost slipped from her grip. But she forced them to be still and dipped a finger inside, scooping a small amount of coke up with a manicured nail. She lifted the nail to her face and felt her heart surge in anticipation.

This was it.

What some secret part of herself had waited for so patiently for so long—the renewal of a pleasure long denied.

It was wonderful.

And terrible.

Christ, so fucking terrible.

You're stronger than this.

Her hand froze inches from her face and she stared with desperate longing at the little mound of white powder nestled in the scoop of her nail. Moments ticked by. Mere moments. But they felt like slow increments of eternity. She thought about times she'd been strong. Like when she'd first given this poison up. That was strength. It also took strength to get out of bed every day and face the world in the aftermath of your beloved mother's unexpected suicide. A hell of a lot of fucking strength was required for that. Maybe more than the amazing amount of strength and determination she'd displayed again and again throughout the course of this long day.

So certainly she was stronger than this bit of powder.

Jessica sighed.

She flicked the scoop of coke out of her fingernail and leaned out of the car to dump the rest on the ground. Next she dropped the little bag and watched the breeze lift it up and blow it away. She inhaled and exhaled with slow deliberation. Then she got out of the car and breathed deeply of the cool night air. She felt calmer now. And sort of triumphant. But there was still the dilemma of what to do next. Yes, she'd faced down an old demon and won, but her only reward was a few moments of serenity. There'd been no sudden brilliant flashes of inspiration.

Until the cell phone in her pocket chirped.

She pulled it out and looked at the display. The number wasn't one she recognized, but it wouldn't be. This was Larry's phone. She'd taken it from him in the car and had forgotten about it since, in the midst of all the excitement. She stared at the phone until it stopped ringing. Then she flipped it open and punched in a number she did know.

It was answered halfway through the second ring. "Hello?"

Jessica smiled at the sound of the familiar voice. "Daddy. It's me."

Her father's voice softened at once. "Oh, hey, sweetie. What number is this you're calling from?"

Jessica's laughter was humorless. "It's a long story, Daddy. I'm . . . sort of in trouble."

"Trouble?" He sounded alarmed. More than that. Alarmed, but ready to fight. "What sort of trouble? Is it serious?"

More of that humorless laughter. "You could say that."

"Are you in jail?"

"No, Daddy. It's worse than that. A lot worse and a lot more complicated. I've done some things that could send me away forever, if anyone ever found out about them."

Jessica fidgeted during the long pause from the other end. She loved and adored her father. She couldn't bear the thought of him ever thinking ill of her. She knew he was imagining a lot of dreadful possible scenarios. He couldn't know the truth was far worse than anything he could imagine. She clutched the phone tight and waited with dread in her heart to hear what he would say next.

He cleared his throat. "These things you've done . . . Were they justified?"

Jessica's eyes welled with tears. She wiped them away and sniffled. "Daddy . . . I wouldn't be alive if I hadn't done them."

The pause this time was shorter. "Just as I thought. Justified. Tell me everything, Jess." His voice hardened, but still conveyed stunning depths of compassion. "And I do mean everything. Leave nothing out."

Jessica took a steadying breath and then launched into a condensed version of events. "It started when I went to check out this car I saw on craigslist . . ."

It took ten minutes.

As promised, she told him everything.

There was another silence from her father's end after she finished. But this time she wasn't anxious. The silence was contemplative rather than judgmental, and it lasted less than a minute. He cleared his throat again. "I'll make some calls. We'll take care of this. That town's close to where the Dandridge incident occurred."

"The dirty bomb?"

A short pause. Her father grunted. "Yes. That. Belated follow-up operations will be necessary due to new information that's come to light. Don't you worry about any of it. I'll have someone pick you up once the operation's under way."

"Thank you, Daddy. Dad . . ." Her heart was beating hard again. She had no business asking this again at a time like this. But the grief welled up in her again and she just couldn't help it. "Why did Mom do it?"

A sigh from the other end. "Honey, I'd give anything

to know. But I don't." There was another contemplative pause, and Jessica knew he was looking back down through the years of life and marriage with his wife, searching his memory for clues. She knew because she'd done the same thing so many times. She heard a tired intake of breath, and he said, "Some mysteries don't have neat answers. Some never have any answers. That's just a sad goddamned fact of life."

Jessica wiped moisture from her eyes. "I know. I love you, Daddy."

"And I love you, Jess." He coughed and his tone hardened again. "Back to the matter at hand. I do have one job for you. I hate to ask this of you after all you've been through, but it must be done."

Jessica frowned. "What job?"

"The one you spared, Jess. Take care of him. Now."

Jessica drew in a startled breath. She couldn't believe what she was hearing. "What? Daddy, you can't be serious. He's not a threat."

Colonel Sloan's tone stiffened. "Loose ends are not acceptable. You must do it. I'm hanging up now, dear. Do as I've said and lay low until help arrives. Oh, and get that cruiser out of sight."

The line clicked off.

Jessica moved the phone from her ear and stared at it in silent stupefaction for several moments. She flipped it shut and looked at the house across the street. She thought of the man she'd left trussed up there and wanted to weep. She'd killed many people today, but each of them had presented an immediate threat to her life.

This was different.

This would be an execution.

I can't do it, she thought. *I don't care what he says. I just can't.*

Her heart continued to slam as she stared at the

darkened house. Then something cold rose up inside her and wrapped itself around her heart. The jagged rhythm of her heart slowed to a normal pace, and she shoved the phone back into her pocket.

She checked the .38's load.

Two rounds left.

Plenty.

She crossed the street at an unhurried pace and slipped back inside the house. She paused inside the doorway, listening to the man's rapid intake of air through his nose. He sounded congested, as if he was having difficulty breathing through his nose. She stood very still for a moment as she continued to listen to him. Maybe he would die without any extra help from her. She listened and prayed, hoping he would go that way, but the sound went on and on.

At last she sighed and flipped on the lights. The man's head snapped in her direction and he looked at her through eyes shiny with tears and wide with desperation. But they darkened as he recognized her. The shift was about something more than simple fear.

He knows, she thought.

I've come to kill him, and he knows.

She waited to feel the reflexive pang of guilt she'd expected, but there was nothing, not even the slightest twinge. She felt remarkably calm, in fact. She knew it was connected to the conversation with her father. He had a way of making her feel better about anything. He was a problem solver, and he'd helped her solve a number of her bigger problems over the years. Whenever things got too tough, he was there to steer her in the right direction. And it was *always* the right direction. He was never, ever wrong. Which was why she was able to so easily face what she had to do after getting over the initial shock.

She closed the door behind her and moved through

the foyer into the living room, where she squatted next
to the trussed-up man and placed the barrel of the gun
against the back of his head. His muffled pleas gave way
to a desperate whine. Tears flowed in streams down his
flushed face. He blinked rapidly as he looked up at her.

"Close your eyes, William. It'll be easier that way."

For me or for him?

But he just kept staring at her, unable to surrender his
last glimpse of the world.

Jessica kept her finger off the trigger. She wasn't quite
ready yet. She looked William in the eye and said, "I don't
think this makes me a bad person. I've been fighting like
hell to stay alive all day. This wasn't my choice. Being
raped wasn't my choice, either. Yeah, I was raped earlier
today. I've had a full fucking day, man. It's been a losing-
your-faith-in-the-essential-goodness-of-man kind of day
from start to finish. I hope like hell I never see the likes
of it again. Thanks to my daddy, there's a real chance that
can happen. I hate to have to do this, William. Maybe
you're an okay guy, even being from this wicked place.
You were a friend of Larry's, and he seemed like an okay
guy. But it doesn't matter much. You're sort of in the way
of the rest of my life."

She slipped her finger through the trigger guard.

William closed his eyes.

The report of the gun was loud in the enclosed space.

Jessica watched a spreading pool of blood stain the
carpet beneath his head for a moment.

Then she got up and went outside to move the cruiser.
A cool breeze kicked up and mussed her hair. The kiss of
cool air felt good on her skin.

It was a nice night.

CHAPTER THIRTY-EIGHT

They were inside the house now, and Pete could hear voices from the videotape. Carl saying a number of rude and profane things to the women between grunts and thrusts. The women answering with orgasmic moans and shrieks that had to be fake. Right now one was telling him how good he was and saying complimentary things about the size of his penis. The woman had to be a first-rate actress. Pete couldn't imagine how dirty, scrawny, hawk-faced Carl could elicit that kind of reaction from a woman without coercion. And he knew damn well the Prestons were all about coercion.

Pete stood behind Justine in a large dining space with two tables. Immediately adjacent to the dining space was a kitchen, and beyond that was the recessed den where Gil and his mother were passed out in their recliners. One of the tables was a standard-sized round table for meals. The other was something else entirely. It was a long metal rectangle with leather straps mounted on hooks at the corners. The latter had been shoved into a corner to leave more room for the dining table.

Pete kept his voice low as he followed Justine into the kitchen. "Come on, Justine. You're not really planning to, I dunno, *chain saw* these people. Are you?"

Justine didn't answer him. She paused in the kitchen to open drawers and sort through them. Pete fidgeted and glanced past her at the snoring duo in the den. He kept expecting them to wake up at any moment. Justine moved quickly from drawer to drawer. It wasn't just the time she was wasting that bothered Pete. She was making no effort to be quiet. She dumped some things on the floor in the course of her search, including some metal things that rattled on the tiles and made Pete's heart lurch.

"What the hell are you looking for?"

"This."

Her hand came out of a drawer clutching a hunk of black metal he recognized as a large-caliber revolver. Pete knew fuck-all about guns, but he did know this was larger than the average-sized handgun. It looked like one of those big Magnums Clint Eastwood carried around in the Dirty Harry movies. Pete gaped at Justine. She looked like she was posing for a teaser poster for some forthcoming Quentin Tarantino or Rob Zombie movie. Chain saw gripped by the handle in one hand. Big fucking gun in the other. Oh, and she was a wild-looking nude babe with big breasts.

Mondo box office, for sure.

Pete arched an eyebrow. "So . . . what? Are you going to shoot them and then chain saw them? Seems like overkill to me, but then I'm not a crazy psycho person."

Justine smiled and came over to him. "It's not for me."

She pressed the heavy gun into his right hand and forced his reluctant fingers to curl around the handle.

Pete was shaking his head. "No. I'm not shooting them in their sleep."

"Why not?"

"I . . . Well, I don't know. It's not like they don't deserve it. But I've never fired a gun in my life."

"It's simple. This thing has no safety. And it's loaded. Just point and squeeze the trigger. Keep both hands on the handle and be ready for the recoil."

"Fuck. You're really asking me to do this?"

Justine shook her head. "No. I just want you to be ready. A bullet to the head while they're passed out would be letting them off easy. And that's not happening, baby. I'm about to wake our sleeping beauties up. If they give me trouble or it looks like I'm not gonna be able to handle them, just point and shoot."

She turned away from him then and continued on to the den. Pete's heart was in his throat as he followed her through the kitchen and down the three steps to the den. He saw the high-definition image of Carl's sweaty face on the large-screen TV and wanted to throw up. The man's wormy lips were twisted in the ugliest expression of sexual ecstasy Pete had ever seen. And one of the women was saying, "Ooh, baby, that's so good."

Justine walked around the recliners and came to a halt in front of them. She pointed to a spot several feet to her right and indicated with a nod that Pete should stand there. He got himself positioned where she wanted and felt an immense relief at being able to turn his back on the grubby homemade porno.

Justine glanced at him. "Aim the gun at them, Pete."

Pete sighed and raised the gun. He didn't want to do this. Didn't even want to be here. But he was powerless to change anything now. It was the sheer futility of resisting her will that made him do what she wanted. The gun's long, gleaming barrel was now pointed at a spot somewhere between the two dozing bodies. They looked beyond pathetic in this condition. Gil resembled nothing more than a beached whale dressed up in farmer's clothes. And his mother looked like the most hideously wrinkled old hag you might see sitting on a stool at the end of some grimy biker's bar—denim cutoffs and a skimpy halter top covering a bony body adorned with numerous faded tattoos. But his gaze stayed on Gil the longest. His was the face that would haunt his nightmares the most if he survived this night. He only had flashing, brief bits of memory from the rape, but that was more than enough. His fingers tensed around the gun's grip. The hate that swelled within him in that moment was nearly enough to make him just shoot the guy and have it done with. Only the thought of how Justine might react kept him from doing it. She started the chain saw and brought it to a full rev within seconds. The sound made Pete's head hurt and made him want to cover his ears.

The Prestons began to stir almost immediately.

Gil opened one eye and saw Justine standing right in front of him with the chain saw revving. He remained very still for another long moment as his brain worked to decide whether this was something from a drunken dream or reality. The truth soon penetrated the alcoholic haze. The other eye came open and he sat up quick. Pete sucked in a breath and shifted his aim so that the gun's barrel was pointed at the center of the big man's face. Gil's eyes flicked from the chain saw to the gun and back again. At first there was only dumb recognition of what was happening. Then his dark eyes brightened with fear. This was real, and he wasn't getting out of it. He almost looked like he wanted to cry. Seeing this made Pete feel good on a very primal level. He felt his lips curling in an expression that was somewhere halfway between a sneer and a triumphant grin.

And now Ma Preston was starting to come out of her stupor. She shifted in the recliner and yawned, stretching her thin arms high over her head with her eyes still closed. Then her face wrinkled in a frown, and a moment later her eyes fluttered open. She focused on the revving chain saw and her eyes went wide. She let out a scream and jumped out of the recliner. Pete swung the gun in her direction and raised it higher. He squeezed the trigger and fired a shot off over her head. The sound of glass shattering in the kitchen was audible even over the roar of the chain saw. The bullet had smashed into a cabinet. Ma let out another yelp and dropped back into the recliner, cowering now as she stared up at the big gun. Pete's shoulders ached. The recoil was everything Justine had promised. He could hardly believe he'd actually fired the thing.

Justine brought the chain saw down to a low rev and then shut it off. Pete's ears buzzed in the relative silence. He heard nothing at first. Then identifiable sounds seeped back in. The sex noises from the videotape. The rapid, panting breaths of the terrified Prestons. And Justine's mad, mocking laughter.

Gil scowled at her. "How did you assholes get out?"

Justine laughed some more. "You can blame your brother, Gil. Horny bastard got all worked up watching me screw my man and decided he'd help himself to some pussy. Got sloppy and got himself killed in the process."

A sudden wail of grief pealed out of Ma's lungs. "No! Not my Johnny! He can't be dead!"

Justine snickered. "Oh, but he is. My man here choked him to death."

Ma's head snapped toward Pete. Her eyes narrowed to murderous slits, and she rose from the recliner again. "You son of a bitch. I'll kill you."

Pete pointed the gun at her chest. "No. You won't. And sit back down, or I'll be the one doing the killing."

Ma sneered. "Shit. You're just gonna kill us anyways. May as well try and get at ya."

"Take a run at him and he'll shoot your knees out first. Then we'll just hang out and listen to you scream and roll around on the floor for a while. How's that sound, bitch?"

Ma looked at Justine. She was still sneering. "Neither

of you pieces of shit got the balls for that kind of action. Don't make me laugh, ya cunt."

Justine just smiled. "Oh?" She looked at Pete and winked. "Shoot her, baby. Shoulder or kneecap, it's your choice."

Pete just stared at the wrinkled hag. "Um . . . what?"

Ma snorted. "What did I tell ya?"

She came at Pete.

His hands flipped up and he squeezed the trigger. The round clipped her in the shoulder and sent her spinning to the floor, where she landed screaming in a heap of crumpled beer cans.

"Ma!"

Gil heaved himself out of the recliner and Pete swung the gun back toward him. "Stay right there or I put one through your big belly."

Gil stood frozen where he was, belly heaving as anxiety sent a flush of red into his mottled features. He looked at his mother, and his eyes became more expressive than usual. He looked scared and worried. He wanted to help her, but didn't dare move. Ah, a son's love. Such a beautiful thing. The callous turn of his thoughts surprised Pete. He wasn't this kind of person. Or at least he'd never thought he was. But here he was, laughing inwardly at another person's pain. What kind of person was he becoming? These people had wronged him in a big way. He was a victim exacting vengeance. He had every right to laugh as these monsters received their comeuppance.

Didn't he?

He thought so, but a bit of lingering doubt still gnawed at him.

"Here's what happens now." Justine's tone was in stark contrast to his inner voice. The mirth was gone. Her voice was flat, pitiless. "We're going up into the kitchen. Gil, you're walking ahead of me. Slowly. You do as I say every step of the way, or Pete puts some more bullets in your mother. Understand?"

Gil's throat distended as he swallowed with great difficulty, but he at last managed a nod. "Okay. Please don't hurt her no more."

Ma continued to wail and roll about on the floor. She extended a hand toward her son. "Baby, don't go. Don't listen . . . oh, help me, Jesus . . . don't listen . . . to her."

Gil wiped a tear from his eye. "It'll be okay, Ma."

Pete moved a few steps back as the big man walked past her and headed toward the kitchen. He breathed heavily as he trudged up the steps. Justine followed him, glancing back at Pete long enough to say, "Keep an eye on her. I'll call for you in a minute."

Pete nodded.

Justine followed Gil up the stairs.

Pete looked at the wounded woman and felt the first small twinge of pity. Her face was twisted in anguish and pain. She kept clutching at her bloody shoulder and writhing amid the crumpled cans, moaning and sobbing the whole time. He'd never seen anything so pathetic. And he'd made it happen. He heard voices in the kitchen. Or beyond the kitchen. They seemed farther away than that. It was Justine giving orders and Gil protesting. But the actual meaning of the words eluded him as he continued to stare at the wounded, pitiful creature on the floor. Then he heard a scrape of wood across floor tiles. And after that a similar sound. Pete frowned.

What are they doing?

Then he remembered the tables he'd seen in the dining area. He moved a few feet to the left and then had a clear sight line through the kitchen to the dining space. The round dining table had been moved out of the way, and in its place was the rectangular metal table. Justine was giving Gil a wide berth as they argued, standing with her back against the kitchen counter while he stood near the metal table. She was right to be wary of him. He was several times her size and would overpower her easily if he got close enough to her. And the man looked agitated. His face had turned a bright shade of red again. Pete wished he'd paid attention to what they were saying moments ago.

Gil took a lumbering step in Justine's direction. Pete saw her shoulders tense. Gil jabbed a thick forefinger at her. "I ain't doin' it! Matter of fact, I'm thinkin' I'll take that toy out of your hands and put you up there, bitch."

Pete stepped close to Ma Preston and pointed the gun down at her head. He pitched his voice loud enough to divert Gil's attention from Justine. "Do what she says, you redneck sack of shit, or I'll put a bullet through your mother's ugly fucking face."

Gil looked at him. His eyes were thin slits. His jowls quivered and his belly heaved. His meaty fists clenched and unclenched. He looked as if he wanted to tear something apart. Then his expression shifted. His eyes opened wider and his scowl became a leering grin. "You ain't gonna do shit, city boy. Same way you didn't do shit when I shoved my hog up your tight little asshole." He licked his lips and made a grunting sound. "Bet that was because you liked it. Ain't that right, faggot? You loved it when ol' Gil was puttin' to ya. Reckon I'll tear off another piece of that ass after I take my McCulloch back from this skanky whore."

It took Pete a moment to realize his whole body was shaking. His teeth ground together as an ache flared behind his eyes. The gun felt loose in his sweaty palm and he curled his fingers tighter around it. He looked at Gil's leering face a moment longer and felt something break inside him. A fury like nothing he'd ever felt gripped him as a roar tore out of his throat. He knelt and seized a handful of Ma Preston's greasy hair. Then he hauled her screaming to her feet and pushed her ahead of him. The woman stumbled, and her creaky old knees banged against the carpeted floor. Pete again grabbed her hair and hauled her carelessly back to her feet. She howled in agony as he shoved her up the stairs to the kitchen. He kept one hand wound around the length of greasy hair as he steered her through the kitchen and past Justine into the dining space. He yanked her to a stop and put the gun to her temple some six feet away from Gil.

"I don't want to hear any more bullshit from you, Gil. You're a worthless fucking rapist, and you've got no right to run your inbred mouth at your betters. Do what Justine told you to do, right now, or your mother is dead. And before her body hits the floor I'll put every last bullet in this gun through your belly. You think I don't have it in me, Gil?" A vicious grin twisted his face and his eyes blazed. "Try me. Open your mouth one more time and find out."

The leering quality seeped out of Gil's expression. In its place was more of the gratifying fear Pete had glimpsed before. Only now it was a deeper, intensified fear. It was pure terror, and it was a beautiful thing to see. Pete's heart felt as if it were going a million miles per hour. He had never been a violent man. Had only been in a handful of minor scuffles in his youth. Nothing serious. But now he felt ready to do violence. More than that. He *wanted* to do violence. He wanted to cause pain, and a lot of it. And he knew Gil could see that. It was evident in his expression, which had become the hollow and haunted look of a doomed man.

Gil's shoulders sagged.

The fight had gone out of him.

He turned away from them and climbed onto the metal table with weary resignation. Until that moment

Pete had not known the reason for Gil's defiance, but now he understood. The table creaked beneath his bulk, but it was sturdy and did not bend. The big man sprawled flat on his back and stared up at the dirty ceiling. Silent tears leaked from the corners of his eyes. Pete felt no pity. Instead, excitement built within him as Justine set the McCulloch on the floor and approached the table. She stretched his arms and legs to the corners and wrapped the hook-mounted leather straps around his ankles and arms, cinching them off in tight knots.

She retrieved the chain saw from the floor and approached the table.

Ma Preston wailed. "Don't hurt my baby! Please . . . oh, please . . ."

Pete let go of her hair and slammed the butt of the revolver against the crown of her skull. She toppled and her knees loudly smacked the floor tiles. Justine glanced back at him, an implied question conveyed in the set of her eyes.

Pete said, "Hold on. Don't do it yet."

He walked over to the kitchen counter and set the gun down. He pulled a large carving knife from a wooden block and returned to where Ma sat sobbing on the floor. He pushed her face down to the floor and pinned her there with a knee to the small of her back. Then he wound a hand in her hair and pulled her head back.

Gil flailed uselessly against his bonds. *"What are you doing to my mama?"*

Pete's laughter was harsh and ugly. "I'm scalping her, Gil."

He put the sharp side of the blade against her forehead just below the hairline and began to saw. Blood erupted from the gash and spread in a red flood across the white floor. She thrashed beneath him, but was too weak to dislodge him. He was bigger and stronger than she was anyway, but the large amount of alcohol still flowing through her system probably wasn't helping her any. Nor was the blood loss she'd already sustained from the wound to her shoulder. But she still had enough strength to thrash and cry. She was crying and Pete was laughing and Gil was screaming and Justine was giggling like a schoolgirl, and it was all wonderful, wonderful, wonderful. He sawed and sawed, working the blade back and forth across her forehead as he tugged at her hair with his other hand. The skin began to peel away in front, and he worked the blade up inside the widening gash, cutting and sawing as the blood continued to flow. The skin peeled away from the top of her head, and he severed the scalp with a few last vicious slashes of the knife. Then he stood and held the bloody, dripping scalp aloft. He felt like a primitive. Like a caveman. A barbarian on an ancient battlefield. He looked down and saw the bloody dome atop Ma's head and laughed again.

He felt glorious.

Gil stopped screaming and started crying nonstop.

Pete walked over to the table and stared down at Gil's shiny, blubbery face. "I've been thinking you need a makeover, Gil. Your whole look screams 'repressed backwoods cracker.' Well, I'm here to liberate you from that, motherfucker." He pried the ball cap off the man's head and tossed it aside. "We'll start with the hair and move on from there to some anesthesia-free liposuction. How's that sound, Gil?"

He pressed Ma Preston's bloody scalp against the top of Gil's head and worked to fit the dead flesh around the shape of his skull. He straightened the gray hair with his bloody fingers so that it brushed Gil's shoulders. Then he stepped back and clapped his hands in mock approval. "There! Ever so much better. Wouldn't you agree, Justine?"

Justine arched a brow. "And you called me a psycho."

Pete picked up the chain saw. "You mind if I take care of this?"

Justine smiled and shook her head. "Be my guest. I'll have some fun with Ma. She's still with us, believe it or not."

Pete glanced at the scalped woman. She was still on the floor and clearly not about to move, but she was alive. Her eyes were open and staring at him. There was nothing but hate in those eyes. Pete welcomed the hate. Reveled in it. There was nothing she or anyone could do to him now or ever again.

He looked at Justine and said, "Make it last as long as you can."

Justine smiled again. "Of course."

Pete started the chain saw and approached the table. Gil's terrified gaze was glued to the spinning blade. He was saying something, his lips moving rapidly. Pete realized he didn't need to hear it. It was a prayer for forgiveness and mercy. Well, maybe God would have some mercy for this piece of shit.

But he would not.

He lowered the blade and let it bite through the man's overalls and then into his belly. Gil's screams then were audible over the whine of the chain saw as he bucked on the table. All his struggles accomplished was to sink the blade deeper into his body. Blood and slimy bits of viscera spewed from the hole in Gil's belly and sprayed Pete's face and the surrounding walls. The blade chewed and chugged and spat flesh. Pete looked at the man's face and saw features twisted with agony. But he remembered Justine's story of her boyfriend's murder and felt not an ounce of compassion. The dirty deed had probably been committed on this very table.

He pulled the chain-saw blade out of Gil's belly and

shifted his position to aim the whirring blade at the man's crotch. He grinned. "Come on, Gil. You had to see this one coming."

He sniffed the air and smelled something burning as the blade messily castrated Gil Preston. He glanced over his shoulder and saw Justine had something frying in a pan on the stove. He frowned and glanced down at Ma Preston. The frown became a smile. Justine had cut a big strip of flesh from her thigh. The woman was unconscious, but he could see she was still shallowly breathing. Justine used a spatula to flip something over in the pan. He caught a glimpse of tattooed flesh turning brown.

And he laughed again.

Cannibalism. Why not?

It made a twisted kind of perfect sense to eat the cannibals.

He shifted his attention back to Gil and resumed his act of butchery.

It went on for a long time.

CHAPTER THIRTY-NINE

They had been walking in silence through the dark woods for a while. Abby led the way. She knew the woods well and negotiated them with ease even in the scant moonlight filtering through the treetops. Michelle stumbled on several occasions and clutched at Abby's arm to keep from falling, but mostly she kept her distance. Abby guessed it was because she'd spent so much time chained up. Who wouldn't be reluctant to surrender newly regained independence after something like that?

Michelle stumbled yet another time and clutched at her shoulder again. This time she didn't let go right away. "Fuck! Why you people would choose to live out in the fucking wild is a total mystery to me. I get enough exposure to nature watching fucking Animal Planet."

Abby didn't know what Animal Planet was, but didn't say anything lest she come across as even more unworldly than she already seemed. She groped for the other woman's clutching hand, found it, and laced fingers with her. "Here. Just hold on. Don't want ya fallin' and breakin' your neck."

Michelle tensed, but she didn't try to pull away this time. "Yeah, that'd fucking suck after getting out of that dungeon. We almost there yet?"

Abby squeezed her hand. It was nice to be touching her again. "Almost."

They continued in silence a while longer until Michelle said, "Abby?"

"Yes?"

Michelle looked at her. Her eyes twinkled in the moonlight as they moved through a break in the tree cover. She pursed her lips. They looked lush and inviting. Abby remembered how hot and sweet they'd felt on her mouth. She held her breath, hoping Michelle was about to kiss her again.

But she didn't. "That stuff you told me about the holiday. The annual offerings to ward off the Garner Blight. Were your people really planning to . . . cook and . . . eat . . . me?"

Abby's nose wrinkled. She didn't want to talk about this. As far as she was concerned, it was part of her past now, something she was leaving behind forever. But she couldn't just ignore Michelle's question. She looked at her and said, "Yes."

Michelle frowned and stopped in the patch of

moonlight. "And this is something that happens every year?"

Abby stopped with her and turned toward her. "Every summer. Yes."

"And you've participated? You've . . . eaten people? Outsiders?"

Abby looked away from her. "It's the way of things here. We're raised in it. I never knew no better. But now . . ." She looked at Michelle and her eyes were bright with tears. "Now I know it was wrong."

Michelle's expression was blank. "You've seen the light."

Abby swallowed. "Yeah. Somethin' like that. Thanks to you."

Michelle stared at her for a long, silent interval. Then a small smile tilted the corners of her mouth. She squeezed Abby's hand. "I know this is a brave thing you're doing, Abby. I really do." She leaned in quick and kissed Abby lightly on the mouth. "You've been waiting for that, haven't you?"

Abby felt her face flush in the darkness. "Yes."

Abby leaned in for another kiss, but Michelle let go of her hand and pulled away from her. "There'll be time for that later, Abby. How far are we from the Colliers'?"

Abby put a lid on her frustration and took a quick look around to get her bearings. In a moment she smiled and looked at Michelle. "Hell, we're practically there."

She turned away from her and strode quickly out of the patch of moonlight into a deep darkness. Michelle let out a startled cry and hurried after her. Abby smiled at the sound of distress. *That's what you get for teasing me.* Michelle caught up to her and clutched at her arm as they moved through a thicker grouping of trees. This time she didn't let go until they moved out of the darkness to stand at the edge of the clearing where the Colliers' cabin stood.

The Collier place was smaller by half than the main Maynard cabin and was several times more advanced in its decrepitude. The scrubby yard surrounding the cabin was littered with junk. There were tires and rusted pieces of old cars. The Plymouth Abby had told Michelle about was parked alongside the front porch. It looked intact. A small shack stood near the cabin. Once upon a time the shack had functioned as a primitive barn. There was a feeding trough near it, but any livestock once owned by the Colliers was long gone.

Abby nodded at the shack. "She'll be in there. Colliers always keep their holiday catches in that thing."

Michelle's eyes gleamed with surprised delight. "Shit, this'll be easy. They'll never even know we were here. Let's go get her."

"Not yet."

Michelle glared at her. "And why in fuck not?"

"Because we still need the key to that car. For that I'll have to go inside. We'll get your friend after I have the key. Do it beforehand and there's too much chance someone'll happen along before I can get back. And if that happens . . ."

Michelle's expression sobered again. "We'll be fucked."

"Yep."

Michelle groaned. "All right. Whatever. But please try to be quick about it. The notion of being alone out here in the dark spooks the shit out of me."

Abby smiled and turned toward her, brushing her cheek with the back of a hand. "I'll be fast, don't worry. And you'll be fine. Just hang back in the trees until I get back."

Michelle wrapped a hand around Abby's wrist and kissed the back of her hand. "Hold on. Take this." With her other hand she extracted the sheathed hunting knife from her waistband. "You might need it in there."

Abby looked at her father's old knife and shook her head. "Keep it. I ain't gonna need it."

Michelle cocked an eyebrow. "You sure?"

"Yeah. Hell, this'll be the easy part." She kissed Michelle on the mouth again, and this time she was heartened by the way the woman's lips lingered on hers before withdrawing. Abby grinned. "Now get back in them trees."

"Yes, ma'am."

Michelle retreated to the cover of the trees. Abby watched her disappear and then turned back toward the cabin. She started walking. She wasn't afraid. At this point she had nothing to fear from the Colliers. About that much she'd been honest. The thing she wasn't sure about was Michelle's friend. There was a good chance she was in the shack, but it was no sure thing by any means. Last year's holiday was proof enough of that. They'd had nothing to offer, having slaughtered their one catch early during a financial pinch. Human meat kept a family's bellies full as well as any other kind. And Abby knew for a fact Michelle's friend had been their only catch this year. She doubted the Colliers would risk universal scorn from their neighbors by showing up empty-handed to the feast a second year running. But they might.

Some of her doubt began to abate as she neared the cabin, though. There were lights on in the main room, and it was the steady glow of electric light rather than the flickering glow cast by lanterns. So the generator in their basement was running. That had to mean the Collier clan was a bit more prosperous this year. Which was good. It increased the odds of Michelle's friend being alive considerably. There was still a chance they'd butchered her a day early. The day before the holiday—tomorrow—was the traditional preparation day. Some folks jumped the gun so they wouldn't be rushed. But

Abby was hoping they would want to do everything the right way this year after last year's disappointment.

She climbed the creaky steps to the porch and paused at the half-open front door. Low, scratchy music was audible through the opening. That would be the phonograph in the front room. Abby couldn't identify the music, except that it sounded like some crooner from the fifties or sixties. She pushed the door open and stepped inside. Keith Jenkins and Lorelei Collier were stretched out across a grubby old sofa, with Lorelei on top and their limbs entwined. Keith was a brawny but unattractive town boy who frequently came sniffing around old-family females. Abby had fucked him once, mostly out of a lack of anything else to do at the time, but there'd been some pity involved, too. She was thankful to find them still clothed. There were empty beer bottles on the floor in front of the sofa. One lay on its side. They were more than halfway in the bag already. Abby raised a hand and knocked on the open door. "Hello? Sorry to interrupt."

Lorelei's head turned toward her. She smiled. "Hey, Abby. What's up?"

Abby shrugged. "Not much. Was hopin' I could borrow your car. I wanna go to town for some beer."

Lorelei's shoulders went up and down. "Daddy'd throw a fit, but he took off to the Sin Den with your ma. Don't matter to me none. Just bring us back some beer, too. Key's in the usual place."

Abby smiled. "Thanks."

She went into the kitchen and found the key to the Plymouth on a hook. Muffled giggling emanated from the living room. Abby knew they were laughing at her. They all laughed at her these days. But this time it didn't bother her as much. She was about to be done with these people forever. Let them laugh. She returned to the front room and continued quickly to the open door, glancing over her shoulder long enough to say, "I'll be back in no time with that beer."

Keith Jenkins leered at her. "You can suck me off when you get back. I paid for the gas in that old wreck."

Lorelei slapped his chest. "Keith Jenkins!"

Keith cackled. "You can watch. Hell, we'll have a threesome."

Lorelei looked at Abby and waggled her eyebrows. "Shit, sounds good to me. And I've heard talk Abby ain't afraid to eat pussy. She can go down on me after she sucks you off. What do you say, girl? That a fair price for the use of my car?"

Abby paused at the door and blinked slowly at them. There was still some of that mocking quality in their voices, but beneath that she sensed they were serious. And under other circumstances it would have been an irresistible proposition. Lorelei was slender and shapely. She was no Michelle, but she wasn't half-bad. So it wasn't hard to fake enthusiasm. "Hell, I'm up for anything tonight. We'll get drunk and screw all night. Back soon."

She slipped outside before they could reply and pulled the door shut. Michelle came running out of the woods the moment she was outside again. She looked about to say something, but Abby hurried down the steps to the ground and slapped a hand over her mouth. She leaned close and whispered, "Keep your mouth shut. This way."

She grabbed Michelle by an arm and steered her toward the little shack. When they reached the decaying structure, Abby put a shushing finger to her lips and made Michelle stand aside as she slid the wooden latch back and pulled the creaking door open. A sour smell stung her eyes. Abby tensed for a moment, thinking maybe it was a corpse smell. But moonlight filtered in and revealed the form of a very plump, nude woman tied by a length of fraying rope to the joist overhead. The rope creaked as she turned toward them. The woman's eyes widened as she glimpsed Michelle, and she squealed behind the dirty gag in her mouth. Abby experienced a curious mix of relief and disappointment at finding the woman alive. She didn't want to share Michelle with anyone, a feeling intensified by the knowledge that these women already shared such a deep and long-established bond. She was sure theirs wasn't a sexual relationship, but that didn't change how she felt. This Lisa person would command much of Michelle's attention for some time, at least until they were safely beyond Hopkins Bend.

Michelle choked back a sob. "Oh, God, look what they've done to you."

Lisa's torso was covered in bruises and welts. Abby figured the Collier kids had beaten her for the same reason she'd often abused outsiders. Boredom. A broken broom handle lay at Lisa's feet. The rounded end was noticeably darker than the rest. It had probably been inside the woman on more than one occasion. Abby glanced at Michelle's horrified expression and knew she'd drawn the same conclusion. Her bottom lip trembled, and she wiped tears away as she stared at her friend.

Then her face turned stony. "Someone's gonna pay, my sweet friend. I promise you."

Michelle moved deeper into the shack and found a wooden crate. She set it on the ground next to Lisa and climbed atop it. The rotting wood creaked and splintered beneath her weight but didn't break. Abby held her breath as she watched Michelle shift atop the crate and again remove the hunting knife from her waistband. She pulled the knife from the sheath and began to saw at the rope. The rope was old and fraying and gave way to the sharp blade within moments. Lisa dropped to her knees and Michelle hopped off the crate. She knelt next to Lisa and made similar short work of the bonds around her wrists.

Lisa sucked in a deep, wheezing breath and loudly exhaled. Her next several breaths were rapid, almost frantic pants. "Oh, God . . . I can't believe it." She looked at Michelle through tear-laden eyes. "You came for me. It's . . . it's a miracle."

Michelle touched her friend's face. "You can thank her." She nodded at Abby. "She's the reason we're getting out of here alive."

Lisa glanced at Abby and frowned. "Isn't she . . . one of them?"

Michelle looked at Abby. She smiled. "She was. But she's helping us now. You can trust her."

Lisa still looked doubtful, but she nodded slowly. "Okay." Her voice cracked a little. "Can we p-please go?"

"Damn straight we can."

Michelle stood and helped Lisa to her feet. Abby felt her lips curl as she watched the girl's belly jiggle. But she made the expression vanish as the other women turned toward her. "Here." She took a step toward them and pressed the Plymouth's key into Michelle's hand. "You drive. I'll navigate."

Michelle glanced at the key and frowned. "Shouldn't you drive? You're the one knows this place inside and out."

"Yeah, but I ain't so good at drivin'." Her tone became sheepish as she admitted the next bit. "I don't even have a license. Never have. So you drive and I'll give directions. It'll work better that way. You'll see."

"Whatever." Michelle looked at Lisa again. Her brow creased. "Hey, are your clothes in here somewhere?"

Lisa shook her head. "They burned them. Let's not worry about my fucking modesty and just get on out of here."

Abby heard a crunch of footsteps outside. Her heart nearly stopped at the sound. She held a finger up to her lips and retreated hurriedly from the shack's dark interior, pulling the door partway shut behind her. She turned and plastered a smile on her face. Keith Jenkins was coming toward her, a cocky grin twisting his already unlovely features.

"Thought you was on your way into town, girl?"

Abby shrugged. "I am. Just thought I'd take a peek at the Colliers' contribution to this year's feast."

Keith stopped a few feet from her. He laughed. "That fat thing? Colliers ain't too picky, huh? Guess they can't afford to be after last year."

Abby smiled and moved closer. She tugged at the front of his shirt with her fingers and looked up into his eyes. "So what are you up to, boy? Come to check on me?"

Keith put a hand on her ass. "Yeah. Didn't hear the Plymouth start up and thought you might need some help." He pulled her close and she felt his erection pressing against her belly. She slid a hand between them and massaged the swollen crotch of his jeans. "Mmm ... damn, maybe you should forget about that beer and come on inside. I've thought about you a lot since that one time. Always wanted to get with you again."

"That so?" Abby forced a note of playfulness into her voice. "Maybe you should go on inside and get Lorelei warmed up for me. I really wanna go get that beer. We'll have more fun if we can party, too."

Keith laughed. "Hell, Lorelei's already warmed up. Big-time warmed up. She's the one sent me out here, you wanna know the truth. Wants you to come in and do some dirty shit with us."

Abby wanted to scream at him.

Why wouldn't he just go away?

She felt a mounting desperation until an abrupt flash of inspiration hit her. She smiled and tugged at Keith's shirt again. "Okay. I'm pretty fuckin' horny myself. Got all turned on seein' what the Colliers done to that girl. Let's do some stuff to her before we go inside."

Keith grinned. "I like the sound of that. Let's check her out."

He let go of her and walked toward the shack. Abby hurried after him, keeping a nervous eye on the narrow space between the edge of the open door and the shack's dark interior. Abby hoped they'd been listening inside. Hoped Michelle would know what to do. Keith gripped the edge of the door and began to pull it open

She knew he would be frowning now. "Hey . . . What's going—?"

She kicked the back of his left knee as hard as she could and he folded up, toppled into the shack. Michelle pounced on him. The hunting knife plunged into his back up to the hilt. She drew it out and slammed it in again two more times. Lisa knelt next to his twitching body and slammed a brick into the back of his head, something she'd found in the heaped-up stacks of junk in the shack. The brick came down again and again, making a pulpy mess of Keith's skull. It was over in minutes. The man was dead. But Lorelei was still inside. She would begin to wonder about Keith's prolonged absence and come to investigate.

She put a hand on Michelle's trembling shoulder. "It's done. We have to go. Now."

Michelle stood up. Lisa dropped the blood-stained brick and struggled to her feet as well. Abby kept a wary eye on the cabin as they hurried over to the Plymouth. The lights were still on, but she saw no shadows in the windows. Chances were they hadn't been observed. Which was lucky. If they'd been seen, Lorelei would be coming at them with a hunting rifle about now. She tugged open the passenger's-side door and slipped into the shotgun seat. Lisa shoved the seat back—harder than necessary, really—and slithered into the back. Michelle got in on the other side and situated herself behind the high steering wheel before gently pulling the door shut. She glanced at Abby, mouthed a silent prayer, and inserted the key in the ignition. The car started on the first try.

Abby breathed a sigh of relief and pointed across Michelle's lap to a narrow gap in the trees. "That way."

Michelle set the bloody hunting knife on the dashboard and put the car in gear. The Plymouth bounced and shuddered over the uneven ground. Michelle turned the headlights on a moment before steering the car through the narrow gap in the trees. She glanced at Abby. "Where do we go from here?"

"Just follow this trail for about a mile and a half. It'll curve and wind around some, but you won't have to turn anywhere until then."

Michelle nodded, but didn't say anything.

They drove in silence along the dark trail for several minutes, their progress slow due to the way the trail shifted and constricted, narrowing to almost impassable widths at times. The headlights illuminated an eerie forest scene: tightly grouped trees and low branches that looked like groping tendrils emerging from the dark. At one point, the headlights revealed a deer standing in the "road." It bounded back into the woods as they came close. Another time they saw an old man sitting on a stump. He was alone and didn't even look their way as they passed him.

Michelle shivered. "That old dude was creepy."

Lisa leaned over the seat. "This whole fucking place is creepy. Can't we go any faster?"

Abby imagined wrapping her hands around Lisa's thick neck. She knew how the flesh would feel beneath her tightening fingers. Knew how her breath would dwindle to a thin, reedy wheeze, and then just stop. Thinking about it made her smile.

"Here." She looked at Michelle. "See the gap coming up on your right? The trail forks away there. Go another half mile and you'll reach an actual road."

Michelle leaned forward to peer over the steering wheel. "I see it."

She steered the car through the gap, and sure enough they arrived at an actual paved road a short while after. Michelle stared at the road, eyes flicking left and right. "Which way now?"

Abby nodded to the left. "That way. You'll go a couple miles before reaching an intersection. A left turn there would sooner or later take you into Hopkins Bend proper. Turn right and go down a good ways and you'll eventually see signs directing you to the interstate."

Michelle smiled. "Well, shit. We're really getting out of here then. Thank you, Abby."

Abby's cheeks flushed. She hoped Michelle would kiss her now. Let the fat bitch in back stew on that. "Ain't no need to thank me. I'm just glad—"

Michelle lifted the hunting knife off the dashboard and brought it around in a savage, backhanded arc. The blade plunged deep into Abby's stomach. Abby gaped uncomprehendingly at the handle protruding from her flesh for a moment. Michelle's slender fingers flexed around the handle. The pain hit her, and she gasped. A rising whine emanated from her open mouth as she lifted her head to look at Michelle. She felt blood rushing fast from the wound and knew she was dying. She just didn't know why. Couldn't understand how this could be happening. She had trusted Michelle. Had taken great risks on her behalf. Had saved her life and the life of her friend. The depth of betrayal was beyond quantifying.

Michelle held her gaze for a long moment.

Her face was cold. Devoid of pity or compassion.

She gave the knife a hard twist and yanked it out.

Abby screamed.

Michelle adjusted the gearshift and got out of the car to circle around to the passenger's side. The door came open and Abby felt a sigh of cool air against her trembling, sweat-sheened skin. Michelle reached into the car and grabbed her by an arm. Then she hauled Abby out and dumped her on the ground. She rolled onto her back and saw Michelle staring down at her. Warm saliva splashed her face.

Abby's breath hitched.

She clutched at her stomach and whined again.

A sneer tugged at a corner of Michelle's mouth. "I really am grateful, Abby. It took guts to get us out of there. But make no mistake, you're a fucking monster. You tortured me. You burned me." Her voice was quaking now. "You deserve to die alone in the dark. Besides, you were never meant to leave this place. Deep inside, you know that."

Michelle turned away from her then and got back inside the car. Abby was crying by the time she heard the doors thunk shut. They were really leaving her here. They had stabbed her and were leaving her. Her dreams of a different and better life somewhere far from Hopkins Bend were as dead as her body soon would be.

The Plymouth's engine revved.

Then it turned left onto the road, shot forward, and sped away.

Abby stared after the dwindling taillights until they disappeared.

The pain abruptly crescendoed and made her scream again, a sound that seemed to tear apart the night. The sound rose and rose . . . and then just stopped. And the pain started to fade. Abby knew she had only minutes left. If that. She opened her eyes and saw stars through the trees. And something else.

An old man was standing over her.

The same man they'd seen sitting on that stump.

He knelt next to her and grinned.

She managed a question: "Who . . . are you?"

He laughed. "Me? I'm Evan Maynard."

Abby's vision blurred. She shook her head weakly and squinted at the wrinkled face staring down at her. What he said made no sense, but the man did resemble pictures she'd seen of a younger Evan. "But . . . you're . . ."

"Dead?"

A thin trickle of blood leaked from a corner of her mouth. She tried to clear her throat without much success. "Then you're a . . . ghost?"

"You could say that."

Abby coughed and more blood dribbled down the side of her face. "I'm . . . dying."

The apparition stroked its chin. Its grin had faded, displaced by a more solemn expression. "That's right. And that's why you can see me."

Abby's brow creased. "Those girls. They saw you, too."

Evan's grin reappeared. "They did, indeed. And ain't that somethin'?"

Abby's vision blurred again, and the world went away for a while. Couldn't have been long. A few seconds, maybe. Certainly no more than a minute or so. But when her eyes opened again, the ghost of Evan Maynard was gone. And maybe he'd never been there at all. Weren't people said to hallucinate when they were on the brink of death? But Abby didn't believe she'd hallucinated. She was sure the old moonshiner and smuggler had come to visit her. She wasn't sure why. He'd died long before she was born. Maybe it was some lingering sense of family duty. Perhaps he attended to all the Maynards in their last moments. Or maybe she was special somehow. Either way, it would remain a mystery until she too had passed to the other side, which should be any minute now.

Some unidentifiable impulse caused her to roll onto her side. The effort triggered another whiplash of pain, but she gritted her teeth and rolled again, until she was lying facedown in the dirt. The gash in her belly leaked blood on the ground. She placed her palms flat against the ground and let loose a roar of pain as she struggled to her hands and knees. She stayed there a moment as thin threads of blood spilled from each corner of her mouth. Then she roared again and surged to her feet. She wobbled and turned in a slow circle before staggering into the woods. She bounced off trees and swiped at branches with one hand while she held the other over the wound.

Why am I doing this?

It made no sense to her. She knew there was no hope. She should lie down and know a last few moments of peace before the eternal darkness took her. But she kept going, driven ahead by the same mysterious impulse that had caused her to get up and start moving in the first place. She still didn't understand it, but it felt important somehow. Some unconscious part of her believed there was someplace important she had to get to before she died. She walked and walked, she didn't know how long. Seemed forever. This was some amazing reserve of strength she'd tapped, especially considering the ferocious wound inflicted upon her. Her legs felt like rubber, but still she kept forging ahead.

Then the world went fuzzy again.

When things came back into focus, she was down on one knee and on the verge of falling over. But she grabbed at a tree and pulled herself upright, the rough bark of the tree gouging her palm. She leaned against the tree for a brief moment, just long enough to gather the last of her strength. Then she shoved herself away from the tree and continued on through the woods. At last the trees began to thin, and she glimpsed something lit by moonlight.

Mama . . .

She plunged into the clearing and staggered on toward Mama Weeks's tiny cabin. A last weak spark of hope flared in her. The old woman was a seer. A mystic. Some even said she was a witch. Maybe she could heal her. But when she reached the cabin and thumped the base of a fist against the front door, it opened at her touch and swung inward with a loud creak. Abby stumbled into darkness.

"Mama . . ." Her voice was weak, a mere whisper. "Please help . . ."

There was no light inside.

Mama wasn't here.

Abby sobbed and felt despair again.

Why did I come here?

Her thigh bumped against the seer's rickety table and she toppled over, landing painfully on her side on the floor. She rolled onto her back and stared up at the shadow-cloaked ceiling. A dangling charm was just visible through the slant of moonlight coming through the open door. An animal skull adorned with beads. Its lower jawbone dropped open, and the voice of her father said, "Good night, Abby. Time to sleep."

Abby smiled.

"Daddy . . ."

She closed her eyes. This time she didn't open them.

When Cassie Weeks returned to her cabin the next day, she was unsurprised to see Abby Maynard dead on the floor. She had seen . . . *possibilities* during her talk with Abby. A couple of ways things could go. This had been one of them. She wished she'd warned the girl, but had let her go in hopes fate would turn the other way and grant her the happy life somewhere else that she'd desperately desired.

But the poor girl's chance had been dashed.

It had existed, though, at least for a short time. That was

something. And she was at peace now. Mama could feel it. She dragged Abby's body outside, where she dumped it in the hole she'd paid a Kincher boy ten dollars to dig a week ago. She shoveled dirt on top of the body and went back inside.

She sat at the table and smoked hash.

After a time, she laid her head on the table and wept.

CHAPTER FORTY

Getting out of the Sin Den turned out to be a lot easier than Megan had expected. Helga told her Carl would poke his head in at some point to see how his guests were doing, and sure enough he did. The door opened some fifteen minutes after Helga's shooting spree ended, and Carl came waltzing inside in his usual cocky way, a crooked grin etched across his gaunt features. The grin froze when he saw the bullet-riddled bodies splayed on the red-carpeted floor, the corpses' glassy eyes staring up blankly at the spinning mirror ball. By then he was several feet into the room and trapped. Megan saw alarm dawn in his dark eyes the moment before he spun back toward the door.

Helga was blocking the way out.

She shut the door and stood with her back to it, the dead cop's gun aimed at his face. "Hello, Carl. Surprise, surprise."

Carl stared at her a moment.

Then he screamed at the top of his lungs: "MONROE! SHIT'S FUCKED UP! COME HELP ME!"

Megan tensed and stared at the door, expecting it

to burst open any second and send Helga tumbling to the floor. But several moments passed and that didn't happen. Helga's lips curved in a wide smile. "Monroe's not coming, idiot." Helga laughed. "Soundproofed room, remember? Tell me, Carl, how's it feel to be trapped by something of your own design?" Another laugh. "Now that's what I call Karma, baby."

Carl seethed. His arms hung at his sides, fingers clenching and unclenching. The muscles in his neck were sharply defined. "You fucking whore. You just signed your death warrant."

Helga came away from the door and put the barrel of the gun against his chest. "I don't think so, you ugly fuck. But you will definitely be just as dead as these assholes if you don't listen to every word I say and do exactly what I tell you."

Carl's attitude changed the moment he felt the deadly steel pressed against his flesh. His posture changed and his fingers stopped clenching. And he listened in attentive silence as Helga laid things out for him. When she finished talking, he meekly agreed to perform as instructed. Of course he did. His only other choice was death. Megan's excitement had skyrocketed while listening to Helga. She was now sure there was a real chance she would escape the Sin Den, whereas only a short while ago she'd been sure she would spend the rest of her days here. Suddenly galvanized, she slid off the divan and knelt over the corpse of the black cop. She flipped open his suit coat and saw a shoulder rig. She undid the holster's snap and pulled the gun out.

Helga looked over at her and smiled. "Honey, I appreciate your eagerness to help, but how are you planning to conceal that?"

Megan glanced down at the tight bustier and frowned. "Huh. Didn't think of that."

Helga was still smiling. "It's okay. We're only gonna need the one." She jabbed the gun in her hand against Carl, making him stagger back a step. "A 9 mm magazine holds ten bullets. I've only used three. That leaves plenty to kill Carl stone-cold dead if he misbehaves or gives me reason to think he's somehow signaling his lackeys on the way out of this cesspool."

Carl was trembling now. "I—I w-won't do that."

Helga's expression turned solemn. "I know you won't. Because you're not stupid. And you know I mean what I fucking say. So listen to me again. I don't want you mumbling like that or looking scared as we leave. You hear me?"

Carl took a deep breath and nodded. "Yeah. Okay."

Megan set the gun down with some reluctance and stood up.

Helga moved into position next to Carl and leaned against him. She slid the hand holding the gun up under his shirt and glanced over her shoulder at Megan. "Amber, be a dear and get the door for us, okay?"

"My name's not Amber. It's Megan."

Helga laughed. "Girlfriend, do you think my real name is Helga Von Trammpe? That's Trammpe, spelled t-r-a-m-m-p-e, by the way. Madeline came up with that after the first time I trampled a guy on stage."

"So what's your real name?"

Helga smirked. "You know what, I like the stage name better, so let's stick with that. And as for you, I'll keep calling you Amber until we come up with a better moniker for you."

Megan shrugged. "Whatever."

She went to the door and drew in a steadying breath before opening it. Her hand shook slightly as she gripped the knob and turned it. She tensed again as she pulled the door open, but there was no one standing right outside.

She stepped aside and let Helga and Carl walk through the door first. Then she followed them into the hallway and closed the door behind her. She sucked in a startled breath when she saw the big bodyguard who'd accompanied her with Carl on the way to the VIP room.

Helga squealed in fake delight. "Monroe, you sexy thing. Wanna party with us?"

The whole of Monroe's attention was focused on Helga's bare breasts. Too bad for him. He didn't notice when she pulled the gun out from under Carl's shirt. He saw it an instant before she pointed it at his face and squeezed the trigger. Megan grimaced at the sight of the bullet punching through his eye. The sound was loud in the hallway, but no one came to investigate. They paused a few moments longer while Helga had Carl drag the dead man out of the way. Then they resumed their former positions and went through the big metal door and down the stairs into the still-bustling Sin Den. They walked through the bar, acknowledging waves and catcalls with little nods and smiles. Carl was stopped a time or two by associates and spoke convincingly about taking the girls home for a private party. Each time he was asked why he was taking white girls with him, given his preference for darker-skinned beauties, but Carl brushed it off by saying he'd been wanting to mix things up for a while. Then they were out of the bar and heading for the main entrance at the front of the building, where they encountered one last obstacle.

Val was standing outside the door, leaning against a Harley Davidson motorcycle and smoking a cigarette. She looked like a female James Dean in her black leather jacket and slicked-back, shiny hair. "Yo, Carl. That girl." She nodded at Megan. "I'll buy her outright from you. I can lay my hands on twenty grand tomorrow if you'll take a thousand-dollar down payment tonight."

Carl turned slightly to look at her, taking care not to jostle Helga. "Get that twenty grand and she's yours tomorrow. But tonight she's mine, and that ain't open to negotiation."

Val squinted. "Since when do you like vanilla pussy?"

"Since about the time the one you want gave me the best blow job of my goddamn life. You wouldn't believe the things she can do with her mouth."

Val blew out a stream of smoke. "You're killin' me, Carl."

Carl laughed. "Tomorrow, Val. The anticipation will make it even better. Now if you'll excuse me . . ."

He turned away from her and began to walk with Helga into the parking lot. Megan followed at a close distance. She glanced back once and saw Val staring after her. The woman made a V with her fingers and put them to her mouth. Then she stuck her tongue out and wiggled it around. Megan turned away from her and began to walk faster, catching up to Helga and Carl as they reached a late-model black Porsche.

Carl opened the driver's-side door and they got inside, with Carl behind the wheel and Helga in the shotgun seat. Megan slid into the backseat and pulled the door shut behind her. She started feeling anxious again as Carl started the car and backed out of his parking space. She looked out the window and took a look around, expecting to see burly Sin Den employees with guns closing fast on the car, but the only person she saw was Val, still leaning against the motorcycle and staring at them. Then Carl shifted gears, and they began to drive out of the lot. Megan stared through the back window at the Sin Den and the blinking neon sign in the form of a woman in high heels. It was a big building, and the large parking lot was packed. It still seemed surreal that so illicit an operation could be doing such gangbuster business out here in the middle of nowhere. Even more surreal was how she'd entered that place and walked out again all in the same day. She watched it dwindle and disappear as the car left the lot and started down a narrow dirt road.

I'm free, she thought. *I can go back to my life.*

She started to smile, but thought of something that sobered her instantly. She turned around and stared at the back of Carl's head.

"There's one more thing."

Helga glanced back at her. "What are you talking about, girl?"

Megan nodded at Carl. "Earlier today that guy and some other assholes took my boyfriend and threw him into a van. I want to know what happened to him."

Helga's pretty features hardened. She pointed the gun at him again. "Tell her."

Carl looked at the rearview mirror. "He's at my house. Maybe a little worse for the wear, but he should be okay."

Megan looked at Helga. "I want to go get him."

Helga was still looking at Carl. "How hard would it be to get Megan's man out of there? I know you don't live alone."

Carl shrugged. "Shouldn't be a problem. He's in a cage out back. Won't even have to go in the house."

Helga nodded. "Okay. So let's do this. We'll swing by asshole here's house, grab your man, then get out of here and never see this fucking place again."

Megan thought of the suddenly very real possibility that she would be seeing Pete again soon and felt a lightening of spirit that almost made her cry. Some part of her—a big part—had been sure he was dead or lost to her forever. "That sounds wonderful."

Carl fidgeted behind the steering wheel. "What about me? You're plannin' to kill me, I bet."

Helga shook her head. "Play straight with us and don't try to fuck us over, and that won't happen. We'll tie you up or something before we leave."

Carl squinted at her. "You ain't bullshittin' me?"

"Nope."

"Okay then."

Carl seemed to settle down then and faced forward for the rest of the ride out of the woods. In a little while they were on a paved road and zipping along through the lonely rural night. Megan stared through the windows at the dark blur of trees passing by and decided she would spend the rest of her life in the city. The hell with this back-to-nature crap she'd been so keen on before. She'd told that castrated deputy her views on a lot of things would be changing if she somehow survived this. Well, it was true. She was also going to buy a gun and carry it with her wherever she went from now on. Her friends wouldn't know what to think.

They'd been driving maybe fifteen to twenty minutes by the time they arrived at Carl's house. It was a big ranch-style place. There were lights on inside and floodlights on outside. Megan sat up straighter as they drove down the dirt driveway. She looked out a window and saw the blue van Pete had been tossed into earlier. Carl parked beside it and shut the Porsche's engine off.

Helga waved the gun at him. "Okay, out. And no funny shit. Don't think I won't shoot you in the back if you try to run."

"Oh, hell, I know you would."

"Good. Let's go."

They all got out of the car and eased the doors shut. Helga stayed close to Carl and kept the gun at his back as they circled around the house to the back. Megan cringed at the sound of dogs barking and howling. Something had agitated them to the point of absolute frenzy. She remembered what Carl had said about Pete being in a cage out back and wondered if they had locked him in with the dogs. Her fear for Pete's safety came back magnified a thousandfold. She wanted to ask Carl about it, but the dogs were so loud. It occurred to her to wonder why the other people here weren't doing anything to shush them. Her skin prickled with goose bumps and her heart raced as they came around the house and saw the rows of dog pens and cages. The dogs saw them and their frenzy increased. Some of them threw themselves against the chain-link fencing. Then Megan saw that one gate was standing open, and her heart jumped into her throat. There was a body sprawled at the back of the otherwise-empty space. She kicked her heels off and took off running, passing Carl and Helga as she sprinted toward the cage. It had to be the one they'd put Pete in. There were no people in the others. And this guy, even from a distance, you could tell was dead. Megan's eyes filled with tears as she rushed into the cage and stared down at the body.

It wasn't Pete.

Now the tears in her eyes were tears of joy.

The dead man was one of his abductors. He had his pants down around his ankles. That was weird. Pete must have killed him. But where was he now?

She heard a scream followed by a wail of anguish.

Then Carl was next to her, kneeling over the body. "No, no, no, no! Johnny!"

Helga stepped up behind him and put the gun to his head. She squeezed the trigger and an eruption of blood and brains splattered the body on the ground. Carl toppled forward, joining his brother in death. Helga looked at Megan and shrugged. "So I lied to a bad guy. Big deal."

Megan looked at her. "Pete's not here."

They turned away from the dead men to stare at the

house. There were lights on in almost every room, but no sign of activity. Helga stepped out of the big platform heels and clasped hands with Megan. "Come on. We'll find him."

They walked out of the cage and across the lawn to the back of the house. A short set of steps led to a back door. Like the cage, the door was standing open. They climbed the steps and entered the house. Megan's nose wrinkled at the smell of burned meat. Someone had cooked something in here very recently. Then they were through the door and in a dining space, where they came to a dead stop. Megan squeezed Helga's hand hard in an effort to keep from fainting.

Helga squeezed back and leaned against her. "Oh . . . sweet Lord . . ."

Megan shook her head in futile denial. "No. No. What? What? How?"

What was left of the body of a very large man was splayed across the top of a metal table. She belatedly recognized the dead man as the fat man who'd participated in Pete's abduction. There was a chain saw on the floor. It had been used to saw off all of the man's limbs. His belly had been opened, and there was a big, bloody wound at his crotch. There was another body on the floor. A scrawny woman. She had been scalped. Big strips of flesh had been flayed from her thighs and arms. Megan's eyes flicked to ceramic plates set on a round dining table. Her stomach rolled. Someone had butchered this woman and cooked her flesh. And then had . . . *eaten* it.

Pete?

She shook her head fiercely at the thought. No. No way. The Pete she had known could never have done the things someone had done in here. Then a memory surfaced, searing her psyche—*the ice pick in her hand, punching through the slender girl's neck and then into her eye . . .*

She trembled and leaned into Helga. "I think I'm gonna be sick."

"You and me both. I . . . guess your man did this."

"Yeah."

"I wonder where he is."

Megan was shaking even harder now. "I'm not sure I want to know anymore."

Her mind was reeling. Her thoughts and feelings were jumbled and far removed from anything remotely rational. Helga didn't have as much of a personal stake here, but she had to be just as overwhelmed by the grisly scene before her. It was something Megan would think about a lot later when she wondered how they could have been so distracted that they didn't hear the careful approach of footsteps from behind.

Helga let out a pained gasp and squeezed Megan's hand harder.

Megan looked at her. "Helga?"

Helga's mouth was open wide and her head and shoulders were shaking. She looked at Megan and tried to say something. Then she let go of Megan's hand and fell to the floor, where she landed facedown. Megan saw the small red slit in her bare back and frowned. Then she turned slowly around and saw Val standing there with a switchblade knife in her hand. The blade was red with Helga's blood.

Megan shook her head. "No."

Val smiled. "Yes."

She seized Megan by a wrist and dragged her screaming from the house. They went out the front entrance, and Megan saw the big Harley parked near Carl's Porsche. She tried to twist out of Val's grip as she was dragged across the yard, but the woman was too strong. Val stood her against the Harley and slapped her across the face several times, a rap of knuckles following the sting of her palm each time. Then she wrapped a hand around Megan's throat and said, "Listen up. You're gonna get on this bike and ride out of here with me, and you're not gonna put up any more fight. Understand?"

Megan put the back of a hand to her mouth, wiped away blood.

She nodded.

What else could she do?

She was no match for Val and couldn't hope to resist her will. The thought filled her with despair.

Val was talking again. "You're mine now, baby. All mine. I've got a nice cage waiting for you in my cellar. You're gonna spend the rest of your life in there."

Val laughed and slapped her again.

And again.

Megan stood there and took it as tears filled her eyes.

She heard Val's gasp and the shot in seemingly the same instant. She wiped tears from her eyes and saw the woman's body hit the ground. There was a ragged, bloody hole in her chest. Her eyes were blank and unmoving. She had been dead before she hit the ground. Megan frowned.

Then she looked up and turned her head toward the house.

Helga was standing in the open front door, leaning against the frame. The 9 mm was in her hand. She saw Megan and managed a pained smile. Then what was left of her strength ebbed and she dropped to her knees. Megan hurried across the yard and climbed the steps to the porch. She drew Helga into her arms and held her.

She pressed her lips against the limp woman's ear and whispered, "Thank you."

Then she looked to the sky as a new sound began to obscure the howling of the dogs. At first there was nothing, but then she saw them—a closely grouped set of black helicopters moving across the sky. Something about them unsettled her, but she had other things to worry about now. And other things to do.

And no time to waste.

So she got started.

CHAPTER FORTY-ONE

Garner had one last task to attend to before attempting the transference of his consciousness into the vessel, but he put it off a while longer to savor the moment. The time he'd prepared for was finally at hand. Everything was perfect. The work ahead could keep while he allowed himself a last few moments to reflect. The man called Hoke was stretched out on the sofa in the living room of the house once occupied by a family called the Prathers. Garner had killed them fifty years earlier and claimed the property for himself. He wasn't bothered by the similarity between this act and what had been done to his family so long ago. The distant past no longer concerned him. Human notions of right and wrong had become alien to him. Besides, his family had been well avenged. It was time to move on.

Indeed.

He turned away from Hoke and smiled at the handful of Kinchers cowering near an archway. One of them was a big man in overalls. He had a double-barreled shotgun propped over one shoulder. And he had a grotesquely deformed nose that somewhat resembled an elephant's trunk. The man's pupils dilated as Garner stared at him. He was shaking. Garner laughed. The man lifted the shotgun off his shoulder and wedged it under his chin. There was an explosion, and the front of his head blew apart, spraying blood and bone fragments on the ceiling. The big body toppled backward through the archway and landed with a heavy thud in the hallway beyond.

Garner laughed again.

The others were crying now. But there was no shock evident in their twisted features. Many of them had suspected this day would come. One of the younger Kinchers fell to his knees and clasped his hands in front of him. He bowed his head and began to mumble a prayer.

Garner's nostrils flared as he focused his will. The air in the room became charged as he began to gather what remained of the supernatural energy available to him. He could feel it crackling under his skin like electricity flowing through his veins. He flexed his fingers and snarled as he felt the power there. The texture of his flesh changed, and he knew they weren't really seeing him now, except as a black blur, a shifting distortion of air and energy.

Then that blur came at them, and they screamed.

Garner slaughtered them.

He ripped arms from sockets and flung them across the room. He twisted heads off shoulders and crushed them like ripe melons in his powerful hands. He opened soft bellies and pulled out organs and dripping viscera. Some of this he ate to feed the energy buzzing inside him. Then it was done. Seven Kinchers torn to pieces in a matter of moments. Blood was everywhere. But it wasn't enough. It wouldn't be enough until they were all dead. He went outside and found more of them. Adults and children. They weren't trying to hide. They knew it was useless. Some screamed and cried as he waded into them, but others closed their eyes and accepted their fates with surprising stoicism. Garner killed them all. He ripped skin from a child's face and broke its back over a knee. He tore a pregnant woman's stomach open and pulled the tiny fetus from her womb. He ate it in a single gulp before crushing the woman's head. He opened a fat man's protruding belly and devoured diseased innards. When he was done with the ones in the yard, he went into the barn and found more cowering in stalls and behind bales of hay. He spared none of them, and when he was finished, every last member of the Kincher clan was dead and in pieces.

Except one.

Garner went back into the house and down the hall to the room where he'd kept Gladys for so many years. She squealed at the sight of him and reached for one of the windows, smashing the glass out with her oversize fingers. Shards of glass lacerated her skin, and blood poured in thick streams down her flabby arms.

Garner smiled. "No way out. Not for the likes of you."

He gathered his will again and sent it in a devastating burst toward her heart. It blew apart and she was dead in an instant. Killing her so fast was a kind of mercy, although mercy was not his motivation. He had only a small amount of energy left to him, and he would require every bit of that for the transference spell. He stripped the sustaining magic from the big corpse, and it began to instantly decay, turning black and shriveling to a much smaller size before crumbling to ash.

Garner walked out of the room and back down the hallway to the living room. He found a chair and set it next to the sofa. Then he sat down and stared at the vessel. The man was physically fit and relatively young. He was also handsome, an asset that should serve him well in the coming years, at least until he was ready to move on to another vessel. The body was clean now, having been washed by the Kinchers after Gladys had sated herself with him. They had fetched his clothes from the barn and dressed him.

He was ready.

The time had come.

Garner clasped hands with the unconscious man and drew in the last bit of demonic will he was able to tap as he began to recite the simple incantation taught to him by that New Orleans witch doctor in the nineteenth century. As he uttered the last line, his body became rigid and everything went black. It was as if he simply ceased to exist for an indefinable time. There was nothing. He was nothing. Then he was sucking in air as consciousness returned. He opened his eyes and stared from the sofa at the vacated body sitting on the chair. The demonic energy gone, it began a rapid decay process similar to what he had seen happen to Gladys. So strange a thing to see one's own body dissolve to a heap of ash. Strange, but gratifying. It was a symbol of transition. The thing he'd devoted his existence to was finished, a part of the past. And now it was time to move into the future. He sat up and stared at his hands, flexing his fingers. And here was another strange thing. The enormous power he'd been able to draw upon in the hellfire-enhanced old body was gone. And it would never be available to him again. But that was okay. It had nearly been burned out anyway. He didn't miss it. He was human again. And that was better. He wasn't a freak anymore. He could go back into the larger world and lead a life that was almost normal. Which was all he wanted. He didn't crave power or aim to subject another group of unfortunates. He just wanted to live and experience all the simple human pleasures he'd missed for so long. And with careful planning and a succession of vessels, he would be able to do just that practically forever.

He got up and walked out of the house with a broad smile on his face.

He walked through the yard and into the woods, not sure where he was going but content to allow instinct to steer him. Soon he would be able to look into the dormant consciousness of the man whose body he'd stolen and know everything he'd known. And feel everything he'd ever felt. But that would take time. He was, however, able to glimpse a visual record of the man's recent memories, and that was enough to know he was going the right way. He continued through the woods with hands shoved lazily into the pockets of his khaki shorts, whistling a pleasant melody he did not know, a sign of an already growing ability to read the consciousness he'd deposed. Soon he came to a clearing and saw a car. The clearing was actually the dead end of a dirt road. The car was old. A red convertible with the top down. The trunk was standing open. He experienced a mild shock of recognition and knew the car had belonged to his vessel. Seeing it made him smile again. Garner had never driven a car, but he felt confident he would be able to tap enough of Hoke's knowledge to make a competent effort. This machine would carry him to . . . Nashville. Yes. To Nashville. And to his new life there.

He approached the car and reached for the handle on the driver's-side door. His fingers were curling under it when he heard a voice calling out to him.

"Hoke. Hey, Hoke!"

Garner turned his head and saw a woman coming down the road. Quite an attractive woman, actually. Blonde and slender with a pretty face. He felt his groin stir. And what a marvelous sensation it was. He was so happy to be human again. He couldn't wait to experience all the things denied to him during his twilight existence as a demon hybrid. Sex was high on his list of things to savor again. This

woman would be a good first partner. He stared at her
shapely body and knew he would have her, one way or
another. He would take her by force if necessary.

Jessica.

The name came to him unbidden.

So Hoke had known her.

A friend, perhaps?

But as she got closer a tingle of fear went through his
body. He wasn't sure why. She surely did not look like
a threat. He tried to peer deeper into Hoke's memories
for some insight into this reaction. There was an image.
Jessica on a floor, looking up at him as he thrust into her.
This was curious. Why should Hoke fear a lover?

She was very close now.

A dozen yards away.

Closer.

She was raising her arm.

There was something in her hand.

It was pointed at his face.

Garner couldn't understand this. Frustration gripped
him as he struggled to tap Hoke's memories again. She
was so close. The gun was in his face now. He was shaking.
This couldn't be happening. It wasn't what he'd planned
at all. He opened his mouth to say something. Perhaps he
could ward her off somehow. Surely there was some kind
of misunderstanding.

"Hey, sugar. Let's talk this over. You don't wanna—"

Jessica stared at the body on the ground and felt only a
tired relief. The sense of righteous justice she might have
felt earlier in the day wasn't there. Maybe she'd feel some
of that later when she had time to reflect, but right now
there was only a numb gratitude that the man whose
heinous act had set her down this nightmare path was
gone.

"Finally."

She spat on him. Saliva splashed the hole in his forehead.

"Rot in hell, you fucking rapist piece of shit."

Someone coughed behind her.

She turned and saw one of the men her father had sent. He was a slim man dressed in black and wearing a lot of army gear. There were more men behind him. They had probably come running when they heard the shot.

She smiled. "I told you guys you could go. I'll be okay."

A corner of the lead man's mouth twitched. "I'm reluctant to let you out of my sight until you're safely beyond the perimeter of our operations here." He glanced at the body, and his mouth twitched again. "Someone you know?"

"He raped me this morning."

The man nodded. "No one will ever know what happened to him. You don't have to worry."

Jessica reached into a pocket and dug out the key that had been there all day. She moved to the rear of the Falcon and flipped the heavy trunk lid shut. Then she faced the squad leader again and flashed the key at him. "Okay, I'm gonna go, guys. Thank you for your concern and for everything you've done for me tonight. I appreciate it. But now I need to get gone from here, and I won't be needing an escort." She smiled sweetly. "Okay?"

The squad leader sighed. "Your father wouldn't like it."

"And I love my daddy, but he doesn't get to make all the decisions. And definitely not this one. Good-bye, guys."

She didn't wait for him to protest again. She moved away from the trunk and stepped over Hoke's body. Then she was in the car again and seated behind that big red

steering wheel for the first time since that morning. She
slid the key into the ignition slot and turned it, enjoying
the way the big V-8 engine roared to life. She pumped
the gas pedal a few times and smiled again. She loved that
loud rev. She reached for the gearshift behind the wheel
and wrenched it over to D. Then she let the Falcon roll
forward several feet before cranking the wheel to turn in
a big, looping circle to get herself facing the road again.

She waved to the soldiers and blew them a kiss as she
drove past them.

The poor guys.

They had a long night ahead of them. By morning the
news would be trumpeting the exposure of a homegrown
terror cell in Hopkins Bend. The very same group, it
would be said, who successfully detonated the small dirty
bomb in nearby Dandridge. A lot of people were going
to die in Hopkins Bend before sunrise in the name of
keeping the country safe. The media and some segments
of the public would be dubious, but Jessica knew it didn't
matter. It was like her daddy said. They were gullible
sheep. And in the end they would swallow the lies their
government told them. Business as usual.

Jessica sped down Old Fork Road and after some trial
and error found her way back to the interstate. She hit
the blacktop at seventy MPH and kept the pedal down
until she was going almost ninety. The wind whipped her
hair about as the engine roared. She turned the radio on
and found that gospel station again. She kept one hand
high on the big steering wheel and scrunched down a
little in her seat, getting comfortable.

She drank it all in.

The roar of the engine.

The hiss of tires beneath her.

The cool air on her face.

The night.

The beautiful, clear night.

The endless miles of wide-open highway ahead of her.

She'd never felt freer.

Epilogue: Survivors

Part I: The Torture Twins

The excitement of the crowd was a palpable thing even in the relative quiet after the house lights went down. The murmur of whispered conversations rose as the moment lingered. The anticipation built. Then came the first note of music. A sinister industrial beat. Someone in the audience whistled and cheered. Then there were more cheers. People began to clap.

The emcee's amplified voice filled the room: "Ladies and gentlemen, the Velvet Coffin is proud to present . . . THE TORTURE TWINS!"

Cheers and whistles gave way to screams of delight.

A spotlight hit the center of the stage, illuminating a man bound to a chair. He squirmed and flinched at the light. A dark form in high heels strutted onto the stage, and the emcee's voice boomed out again. "PLEASE WELCOME, ALL THE WAY FROM STOCKHOLM, THE SWEDISH MISTRESS OF PAIN, HELGA VON TRAMMPE!"

A big segment of the crowd shot to their feet as Helga moved into the circle of light and seized a handful of the bound man's hair. She wore her trademark six-inch stiletto heels, a tight leather bustier, black stockings, and an SS-style hat with a shiny brim. Gripped in her right hand was a cat-o'-nine-tails. She wedged it under the man's chin and grinned at the audience.

The music thundered.

The audience went crazy again as another form ventured onto the stage. Another dark figure in high heels. The emcee's booming voice only barely managed to exceed the volume produced by the frenzied crowd this time: "AND NOW HELGA'S EXQUISITE PARTNER IN PAIN, ALL THE WAY FROM THE FROZEN NORTH, VIVIAN ICE!"

Megan stepped into the circle of light and moved to the front of the stage, where she struck a dramatic pose and leveled a fearsome gaze at the audience. The excitement was still there, more palpable than ever, but the crowd became almost quiet again as she stared at them. The look she gave them exuded a mix of sexiness and malevolence that intimidated everyone present. Her reputation proceeded her. She and Helga were cult figures on the underground club scene by now. There were numerous fan Web sites devoted to them, but the official one that had just gone online required a paid membership and allowed unlimited access to explicit videos. They were making money hand over fist, enough that they technically didn't even need to do the club circuit anymore. But Megan wouldn't have it. She enjoyed the thrill of performing live too much. She wouldn't have envisioned anything like this kind of life for herself a year ago, but she wouldn't have it any other way now.

The music reached a crescendo and abruptly stopped.

Megan glared at the audience a moment longer.

Then she turned her back on them and strutted slowly over to the bound man. She turned and sat on his lap, then leaned back against him. Helga leaned over her and slid a hand down the front of her bare torso.

The crowd began to go nuts again.

Megan suppressed a smile.

Helga had been right about so many things.

They had adjoining suites at the Cleveland Hyatt. They returned there after the performance. Megan took a shower and afterward put on a robe and went out to the balcony to stare at the city lights. From here it looked like any other city. She and Helga had visited so many. And had conquered them all.

She went back into her room and opened the connecting door to Helga's suite. The gorgeous blonde goddess wore a black silk negligee. She sat at a table, leaning over the keyboard of her laptop. She glanced up and smiled as Megan came into the room. "Great show tonight, huh?"

Megan went over to the minibar and poured herself a glass of expensive wine. She returned from the table and sat down across from Helga. "It was good. I still wish there was a way to simulate that head-standing thing you did at the Sin Den."

Helga frowned. "I do that every night."

Megan shook her head. "No, no. The other thing. The heel sinking into the ear."

Helga laughed. "I don't think there's a way to do that without killing a dude. We're popular, but I don't think we're popular enough to get away with on-stage murder." Her eyes widened. "Oh! Speaking of the Sin Den . . ."

Megan arched an eyebrow. "Yes?"

"I got an e-mail from Madeline tonight. She's reopened the Sin Den in Nashville. It's all aboveboard now. She's even got a few of the same girls with her. Anyway, she's invited us to come do our show there. What do you think?"

Megan thought about Madeline. And she thought about how an ice pick felt in your hand when plunged into living flesh. A thing Madeline had made her do. But it was all a matter of perspective and circumstance, wasn't it? Madeline had not come to the Sin Den willingly in the beginning either, but she had nonetheless somehow carved out a grim but enduring existence at the top of the food chain there. Megan didn't care for what it said about her as a human being, but in her most secret thoughts there lived a belief that she would have become just like Madeline had she been forced to spend years imprisoned in that place. It was a thing she could be honest about with herself, if not with anyone else. Only Madeline would understand. And perhaps Helga.

She sipped wine and thought some more.

Then she smiled.

"Tell her we'll do it."

Helga grinned. "Awesome."

She leaned over the keyboard and started typing rapidly. Then she clicked a button and said, "Done!"

She stood up and peeled off her negligee. "I'm gonna hop in the shower. Make me a drink while I'm gone?"

Megan smiled. "Double martini?"

"Of course."

Helga turned and walked away from her. As it always did when she got a look at Helga's bare back, Megan's gaze went to the scar left by the knife wound. It had healed nicely, but the livid white line would always be there. Helga did not try to hide it. And why would she? It added to her mystique. But every glimpse of it brought back vivid memories of that long night of madness. The hard things she'd endured. The awful things she had been forced to do. All of it culminating with the stunning revelations about Pete. Sure, there was no concrete proof he had done the things she suspected, but she knew the truth of it in her heart. Like her, he had suffered unspeakable things. She had been changed by those things in ways that were a mix of good and bad. She would bear the psychological scars the rest of her life. The experience clearly had changed Pete, as well, but in his case it had broken him. Wherever he was now, he was no longer the man he'd once been. No longer the man she'd once loved.

He was a killer.

A savage.

But maybe she was being too hard on him. He'd only killed his captors and had not bothered with the two black women kept in cages in the basement of that house. She'd freed those women, and they'd helped her get Helga into Carl's Porsche, and they'd stayed with her until they reached a hospital in a neighboring town. They made it out of Hopkins Bend a heartbeat or two ahead of the army clampdown. That was something she still didn't understand. The things that came out in the media afterward baffled her. The ludicrous claims made by the government bore no clear relation to the very real horrors she'd witnessed in that godforsaken town. But she knew better than to come forward with her own version of events. The feds would disappear her in a heartbeat. And hell, maybe there really had been some kind of redneck, homegrown terror cell in Hopkins Bend. Who could say for sure?

Megan finished off the wine and went back to the bar. She fixed two double martinis and carried them back to the table. She sipped her martini and patiently waited for Helga to return. She had a new idea she was eager to run past her partner.

A way to almost mainstream the Torture Twins act. She knew it could work. They were doing very well now, but soon they could be genuinely rich.

She thought about it some more, and her smile broadened.

She was so happy she'd finally found her real niche in life.

Part II: The Happy Couple

There were few things more lovely than the ocean at night. And few things more soothing than the gentle lap of the tide rolling in and back out again. From his prone position on the Corona beach towel, Pete stared up at a moon swathed in clouds. Moonlight reflected prettily on the ocean water below, a shimmering overlay of white radiance that filled him with a quiet awe. He wished he could capture this moment perfectly in his mind and be able to recall every sweet aspect of it whenever he wanted. But memories always faded, even the sweetest ones. He sometimes still thought of Megan and tried to connect with the feelings he'd once had for her. They had been happy. It seemed they had been happy.

He certainly remembered having fun with her.

But had they really been in love?

He didn't know anymore.

But it didn't matter, because he was without question 100 percent in love with the one woman he could imagine being with until the end of his days. He sat up and stared at Justine. She stood up to her ankles in tidewater down at the edge of the ocean. He watched her kneel and use a little plastic shovel to scoop something into a bucket. More seashells probably. He admired the soft, feminine swells of her nude form and felt a tingle of arousal. They had this stretch of private beach all to themselves and had already made love in the sand a couple times. Pete felt sure she would be up for another round. She always was.

She stood and turned away from the ocean, then walked up the beach to where he sat. She plopped down on the beach towel next to him and set the bucket between them. Pete peered inside and saw sand and a few curved shapes that had to be shells.

He smiled. "Find anything good?"

She leaned closer and touched his face with a soft palm. "I found you."

"And that's a good thing?"

Her smile became shier. "Yes, silly." She hugged her knees to her chest and looked out at the ocean. "It's beautiful here, isn't it?"

Pete nodded. "Sure is."

They were on a beach on Tybee Island, a barrier island off the coast of Georgia. It had been Justine's idea to come here. She'd vacationed with her family more than once in Tybee as a child, and the last time, her clan had stayed in the big beach house behind them. The house had several immaculate rooms and enough amenities to please Donald Trump. Pete was looking forward to another dip in the balcony hot tub later in the evening, especially now that there was more of a nip in the air down here on the beach.

He shivered and grinned at Justine. "What do you say? Time to get back inside?"

She hugged herself again and her teeth chattered. "Y-yes please."

He stood and offered a hand to help her to her feet. She let him help her up, and they walked hand in hand up the beach to the house beyond the dune barrier. They entered the property through a gate and skirted a swimming pool deck en route to a flight of white stairs that carried them up to the third floor. They entered a large and well-appointed living room through a set of balcony doors.

Pete grinned and waved as they came back inside. "Hey, gang. Happy to see us again?"

The other occupants of the house stared at them, but remained silent. Pete chuckled and closed the door behind him. He walked over to a portly middle-aged man tied to a chair and knelt in front of him. "Hello, Frank. We've had a lovely evening on the beach and would like to thank you again for your hospitality."

Justine giggled.

She did several ballerina-like spins around the room.

In one of her hands was a screwdriver. She stopped spinning at one point and slammed it through the back of a bound woman's age-spotted hand. Frank roared behind the layers of duct tape wrapped around his mouth and head. The other bound people made similar sounds of outrage and terror. There were four of them altogether. Four left. There had been nine at the start of the evening. The other five were dead now. Parts of their bodies adorned various end tables and shelves, providing a macabre counterpoint to the quaint knickknacks and old books.

Pete picked up the knife he'd left in Frank's lap earlier and smiled. "I think it's time for that other ear to come off." Frank rocked in the chair again and Pete laughed. "Oh, stop being a baby. Besides, it'll make you symmetrical again."

This elicited another giggle from Justine.

She came over to him and dropped down beside him, draping an arm over his shoulders. "Can I do it this time? *Please?*"

Pete handed her the knife. "As you wish."

She got up and moved into position behind the man. Pete watched her go to work on him and again experienced that by-now-familiar sense of contentment he felt every time he observed the delight evident on Justine's face when she did something like this. He had long ago lost count of how many people they had killed together. He knew it was more than thirty and maybe as many as forty. This escapade tonight would be by far the most they had done at one time. But no matter how often they did these things, it never got old. That same electric thrill and amazing sense of power was still there every time.

He watched Justine chew on the man's bloody ear and felt his stomach growl.

It was about time to cook again.

But first . . .

He stood and drew Justine into his arms. They kissed deeply, with a passion he'd never experienced with anyone else. Not even Megan had come close to making him feel this way. Eventually he eased her down to the floor and they made love as their captive audience watched and awaited their turns to die.

PART III: THE ASSASSIN

Fort Campbell, Kentucky

A woman sat alone in a spare room with no windows and a single table with four chairs. She wore a crisply pressed uniform and kept her hands folded primly on the table as she waited for someone to come in and tell her why she had been summoned here the night before she was set to be deployed to Afghanistan. She had been in the room alone almost a half hour. Waiting was something you got used to in the army, or you did if you hoped to survive the experience with your sanity intact. She was a patient woman now. This had not always been the case.

At last the door opened, and two men walked into the room. One was a midranking officer in uniform, and the other was a tall but otherwise nondescript man in a black suit. The woman stood and saluted the officer. The officer returned the salute and said, "At ease, Private Sloan."

The officer closed the door and gestured at the table. "Please be seated, Private."

Jessica sat at the table again and folded her hands in the same prim fashion. She kept her expression blank as the men pulled out chairs and sat across from her. Something odd was happening here, but she didn't have the first inkling what it might be. The guy in the black suit wasn't army, but he wasn't civilian either. He didn't exactly exude menace, but something in his posture and the cast of his eyes told her he was a dangerous man. Well, that made at least two dangerous people in the room.

The officer cleared his throat. "Private, this gentleman is Mr. Mitchell. He is here to make a proposition. You are not obligated to accept, but you should listen."

He stood and pushed the chair back under the table.

Jessica started to rise again, but the officer had already turned away from her and was opening the door. Then he was gone, with the door shut firmly behind him.

Jessica frowned.

Well . . . that was fucking strange.

She sat down again and stared at the man on the other side of the table. His smile was perfunctory and didn't reach his eyes. He set a leather briefcase on the table and opened it. He extracted a manila folder and shut the briefcase. He set the folder on the table in front of him and folded his hands over it. Jessica squinted at a label on the folder and saw her name and rank printed there.

Jessica looked him in the eye. "You're not army."

Another of those perfunctory smiles. "No."

"So what are you? I know you're something. Some kind of spook, right?"

The man's smile glowed with a touch more wattage for a moment before he quite deliberately dialed it back down. "Astute. I am not army, but we share the same employer and a number of the same goals."

"Goals?"

"To defeat and eliminate the enemies of this country."

"I see."

The man opened the folder and began to flip through the file's contents. Jessica waited as he skimmed several typed pages. Then he closed the folder and folded his hands on the table again. "Miss Sloan . . . May I call you Jessica?"

"Um . . . sure. Why not?"

The man tapped the closed folder with an index finger. "Jessica, I work for an organization with no official association with the U.S. military or government. The lack of official sanction is for the usual plausible-deniability reasons. We are, however, funded by many pieces of craftily conceived government legislation. Do you understand what I'm saying?"

Jessica nodded slowly. "I . . . think so."

She thought, *Black ops.*

The man's expression remained unreadable as he studied her. "Yes. Yes, I think you do." He tapped the folder again. "I've read a meticulously detailed account of your actions on the night of June eleventh last year. This account was supplied by your father."

Jessica didn't know what to say, so she stayed quiet. Her father loved her more than anything else. She did not question that, not even for a second. He wouldn't have supplied this information to this man and his organization without a damn good reason.

The man cleared his throat before continuing. "Jessica, we want to offer you a job."

Jessica blinked slowly. "What?"

"There will, of course, be an extensive training program before you become a field operative. In school you demonstrated an impressive facility for languages. We'd like to exploit that as well, and also further your education in that area. This skill will serve you well in the future."

Jessica thought of her impending deployment to Afghanistan. The army wasn't in the habit of letting new recruits out of such things.

The man's smile this time was deeper and more genuine than before. "You're thinking about your deployment orders. This will not be a concern if you accept our offer."

Jessica looked away from him. She stared at the closed door and tried to think.

This was all so strange.

And yet . . .

She looked at him again. "This job . . . What is it?"

The man's smile faded. "Acquisition and liquidation of select targets."

Jessica was silent for a beat.

She stared into his eyes.

His cold, hard eyes.

She said, "An assassin. That's what you're asking me to be."

"That isn't the terminology we use, but . . . yes. I understand you'll need time to consider our offer. I'll be back to see you again in—"

"I don't need to think about it."

The man's head tilted and he squinted at her. This wasn't an easy man to surprise, Jessica felt sure, but she had done it. "Oh? Then your answer is . . ."

"I'll do it."

His smile returned. "Excellent." He reached across the table and she slid a hand into his. "I think you'll be a truly outstanding asset to our organization."

She thanked him, and they talked some more.

Some more details were ironed out.

Her deployment would be delayed, and he would be in touch again at a later, to-be-determined date. That night she lay awake in her bunk bed in the barracks and stared at the ceiling as she thought about her future.

There were strange days ahead.

Dangerous days.

There would be death and violence galore.

She smiled in the dark.

She was looking forward to it.

☐ **YES!**

Sign me up for the Leisure Horror Book Club and send
my FREE BOOKS! If I choose to stay in the club, I will
pay only $8.50* each month, a savings of $7.48!

NAME: _____

ADDRESS: _____

TELEPHONE: _____

EMAIL: _____

☐ I want to pay by credit card.

☐ *VISA*   ☐ *MasterCard*   ☐ *DISCOVER*

ACCOUNT #: _____

EXPIRATION DATE: _____

SIGNATURE: _____

Mail this page along with $2.00 shipping and handling to:
Leisure Horror Book Club
PO Box 6640
Wayne, PA 19087
Or fax (must include credit card information) to:
610-995-9274
You can also sign up online at **www.dorchesterpub.com**.
*Plus $2.00 for shipping. Offer open to residents of the U.S. and Canada only.
Canadian residents please call 1-800-481-9191 for pricing information.
If under 18, a parent or guardian must sign. Terms, prices and conditions subject to
change. Subscription subject to acceptance. Dorchester Publishing reserves the right
to reject any order or cancel any subscription.